"Lauren Royal knows how to make history come alive."
—*New York Times* bestselling author Patricia Gaffney

Lost in Temptation

"After brilliantly evoking the splendor of Restoration England in her six previous books, Royal brings her flair for mixing richly detailed historical settings with sinfully sexy romance to the Regency world in the beguiling start to a new trilogy featuring the Chase sisters."
—*Booklist*

"A deeply satisfying and original read."
—Historical Romance Writers

"This deliciously humorous, tender, touching romance, with a dash of recipes from the era that you can try, is a delight for the heart, soul, and stomach. Royal takes history out of the doldrums and gives the era brightness and color that draw readers straight into the story."
—*Romantic Times*

"Wonderful . . . likable lead protagonists . . . Fans will enjoy Alexandra's chase after the man she loves."
—The Best Reviews

"A delightfully captivating tale. Rich period details, interesting characters, sensual romance, and a story that will not disappoint. I encourage everyone to read this worthwhile and passionate novel!"   —Romance Junkies

Praise for Lauren Royal's Flower trilogy

Rose

"Bringing her Ashcroft sisters trilogy to a delightful close, Royal vividly details the seductively glamorous court of Charles II."
—*Booklist*

"A rip-roaring tale."
—Romance Reviews Today

continued . . .

Emerald

"A passionate tale that brings late seventeenth-century England vividly alive . . . fast-paced and filled with action from the very first page to the climax."
—*Midwest Book Review*

"With strong characters and an action-filled plot, *Emerald* is a Royal flush."   —*Affaire de Coeur*

"An entertaining read. When the two [protagonists] come together, they make for a fun-loving, sensual couple."   —*The Romance Reader*

"Warm and wonderful . . . the story is one that will enthrall. Exhilarating."   —Heart Rate Reviews

"Brimming with action, adventure [and] love. Ms. Royal brings Restoration England to life right before the reader's eyes. I highly recommend *Emerald*."
—Romance Reviews Today

Amethyst

"An accomplished debut."   —Patricia Gaffney

"All of these characters are so well drawn and developed. . . . A promising debut."
—*The Romance Reader*

TEMPTING
JULIANA

Lauren Royal

A SIGNET ECLIPSE BOOK

SIGNET ECLIPSE
Published by New American Library, a division of
Penguin Group (USA) Inc., 375 Hudson Street,
New York, New York 10014, USA
Penguin Group (Canada), 90 Eglinton Avenue East, Suite 700, Toronto,
Ontario M4P 2Y3, Canada (a division of Pearson Penguin Canada Inc.)
Penguin Books Ltd., 80 Strand, London WC2R 0RL, England
Penguin Ireland, 25 St. Stephen's Green, Dublin 2,
Ireland (a division of Penguin Books Ltd.)
Penguin Group (Australia), 250 Camberwell Road, Camberwell, Victoria 3124,
Australia (a division of Pearson Australia Group Pty. Ltd.)
Penguin Books India Pvt. Ltd., 11 Community Centre, Panchsheel Park,
New Delhi - 110 017, India
Penguin Group (NZ), cnr Airborne and Rosedale Roads, Albany,
Auckland 1310, New Zealand (a division of Pearson New Zealand Ltd.)
Penguin Books (South Africa) (Pty.) Ltd., 24 Sturdee Avenue,
Rosebank, Johannesburg 2196, South Africa

Penguin Books Ltd., Registered Offices:
80 Strand, London WC2R 0RL, England

First published by Signet Eclipse, an imprint of New American Library,
a division of Penguin Group (USA) Inc.

First Printing, November 2006
10 9 8 7 6 5 4 3 2 1

*For my best friends and fellow writers,
Glynnis Campbell and Sarah McKerrigan,
because they hate stories that include dancing at balls,
so I couldn't resist dedicating this one to them.*

*Thanks for your friendship—
it means more than I can say.*

Acknowledgments

I wish to thank:

My critique partner, Terri Castoro, for coming through for me (yet again); my fabulous editor, Laura Cifelli, for being so understanding when life intervened to delay this book (and for her wonderful ideas to improve it); Katarina Grant, curatorial assistant at the Foundling Museum in London, for invaluable research into the history of donations to the Foundling Hospital; Brent Royal-Gordon, for designing and maintaining my ever-growing Web site (and also for great brainstorming); Nancy and Charles Williams, for many (many!) fabulous book signings at Highland festivals (I hope you enjoy your retirement!); Jack, Brent, Blake, and Devonie, for suffering weeks of fast food (almost uncomplainingly) while I finished this book; my official First Readers—Ken and Dawn Royal, Herb and Joan Royal, Taire Martyn, and Karen Nesbitt—for feedback on early drafts; my awesome Street Team (*way* too many names to list, but you can see them all on the Street Team page on my Web site) for their enthusiasm and support . . . and, as ever, all my readers, who are constantly sending me letters that bring smiles to my days and send me back to my computer to write more.

Thank you, everyone!

Chapter One

Lady Juliana Chase's family often accused her of looking for trouble. Of sticking her nose where it didn't belong. Of exaggerating—if not outright imagining—other people's problems and sorrows and miseries.

But she would swear she'd never seen anything so sad in her life.

Upstairs in the Foundling Hospital's picture gallery, she stared through the window down into the courtyard. There, arranged in six neat, regimented lines, a hundred or more young girls performed calisthenics, resignation written on their faces. In all her twenty-two years, Juliana couldn't remember ever feeling that grim.

"William Hogarth was a genius."

Sighing, she turned from the window to see her younger sister scrutinizing the art on the gallery's pale green walls. "I thought you preferred the Dutch masters."

"I do," Corinna said. "But look at the characters in this painting."

The work was titled *The March of the Guards to Finchley*, and the people depicted were, indeed, characters. Humor, rowdiness, and disorder abounded. "The drummer looks quite amused," Juliana said, swiveling back to look out the window.

The painting seemed a complete contrast to the figures outside.

Miss Emily Neville, Juliana's eight-year-old next-door neighbor, stood gazing through the glass beside her. "The girls do not appear to be ill. So why are they in hospital?"

"*Hospital* is an old word that originally meant 'guesthouse,'" Miss Strickland, the battle-axe of a woman assigned to shepherd visitors through the orphanage, explained in her no-nonsense way. "This is a charitable institution for children whose mothers couldn't keep them."

"My mother died." Still staring outdoors, Emily absentmindedly raised a hand to stroke a slim, olive green snake that rested upon her shoulders. "May I play with them?"

Ranging in age from about five to perhaps fourteen, the children all had identical haircuts and wore aprons of stiff, unbleached linen over brown serge dresses. Juliana smoothed her palms over her own soft yellow skirts. "I'm afraid your snake might scare them."

"The girls are not playing. They are exercising. Outdoor exercise is advocated for maximum health." Miss Strickland crossed her arms across her ample bosom. "And you couldn't play with them in any case, young lady, with or without that horrid creature."

"Herman is not horrid," Emily said, slipping her hand into Juliana's. "He is naught but a common grass snake. Can you not tell by the black bars along his sides and the yellow collar behind his head? He is absolutely harmless, I assure you."

Juliana hid a smile. My, such a vocabulary for a girl of eight. Emily certainly was articulate.

But carrying a snake around was just not done.

Emily was Juliana's latest project, and Juliana was sure—positively sure—that with a bit of patience she could turn her into a perfect little lady. A few more outings with Herman ought to convince the child that the creature wasn't welcome in public.

She squeezed Emily's hand and turned back to Miss Strickland. "Do the girls *ever* play?"

"Of course they do," Miss Strickland said. "For an hour every Sunday." As though suddenly remembering her duty—principally to encourage donations—she spread her lips in a smile that appeared rather forced. "Are you ladies enjoying your visit to the gallery?"

"Very much." Corinna moved to view the next painting. "George Lambert," she breathed. An artist herself, she'd suggested this day's outing to the Foundling Hospital's gallery. "What a lovely scene."

Mr. Lambert's picture *was* lovely, but Juliana couldn't peruse the painted people for long. Not when there were real people—disadvantaged children—to consider.

"What do the foundlings do all day?" she asked. "If they don't play?"

Miss Strickland squared her shoulders and began reciting by rote. "They rise at six and prepare for the day, the older girls dressing the younger children, the boys pumping water and such. At half past seven they breakfast, and at half past eight they begin school. At one o'clock they dine and return to school from two until dusk." She paused for a much-needed breath. "After supper, those not employed about the buildings are instructed in singing the Foundling hymns and anthems, and in their catechism. At eight they go to bed."

What a life. Thinking about her own days and nights filled with parties and shopping and dancing, Juliana swallowed a lump in her throat. Still, the children looked healthy, warmly clothed, and well fed—which was more than could be said for much of London's youth, she supposed. "Is there anything I can do to help?" she asked.

"Certainly, my lady. We are always pleased to accept monetary donations."

Juliana knew that was one of the purposes of the gallery. Popular artists donated paintings and sculpture, a scheme that not only gave the artists a chance to cement their social positions through well-publicized acts of charity, but also ensured that their work would be seen by those most wealthy and aristocratic—exactly the sort of people who might commission works of art for themselves and be persuaded to become patrons of the Hospital.

It was a most satisfactory arrangement for all concerned. But unfortunately Juliana hadn't the option to become a patroness at present. While it was true that her late father had provided a substantial dowry, and she wasn't in any way deprived—quite the opposite, in fact—as an unmarried woman she had no money of her own, other than a small allowance granted by her brother, Griffin. "I cannot donate significant funds," she said apologetically.

Miss Strickland aimed a rather disbelieving look down her knife-edged nose, pointedly skimming her gaze over Juliana's fashionable dress.

"I cannot," Juliana repeated. "But I should like to do something." She could ask Griffin to donate, of course—and she would. But she wanted to do something herself. "Perhaps I could make clothing for the children." Surely her allowance would cover the fabric.

"The children have no need of clothing. They wear uniforms, as you've seen."

Juliana had seen the boys eating luncheon in their dining room, all wearing white linen shirts with military-style suits made of the same brown serge as the girls' dresses. "But someone has to *make* the uniforms."

"The girls make and repair them during their sewing lessons."

"Then perhaps I can make treats," she suggested. "The ladies in my family are rather renowned for our sweets."

"The children are all fed a plain, wholesome diet. Sweets are not allowed except on very special occasions. However, food does account for a large proportion of the Hospital's budget, so your monetary donation would be much appreciated." Before Juliana could repeat that she had no money to give, Miss Strickland continued. "This is a reception day. Perhaps seeing some infants might change your mind."

Though Juliana knew nothing could change her mind, she loved babies and could scarcely wait to have one of her own. "We should very much like to see the infants," she said, drawing Emily toward the door.

"I'm not finished looking," Corinna said, finally moving to view the next painting.

The battle-axe cast her a speculative glance. "Well, then, the horrid snake can stay with you."

"Herman is not horrid!" Emily said, pulling her fingers from Juliana's. "If Herman stays, I shall stay." She marched over to take Corinna's hand instead. "There's an infant right here in this picture."

Corinna nodded her dark head. "It's Andrea Casali's *Adoration of the Magi.*"

Juliana would never understand how anyone could stare at a single painting for so long. But then, she'd never been as interested in things as she'd been in people. "What is a reception day?" she asked, following the battle-axe from the room.

Miss Strickland led her down a corridor. "On the second Saturday of every month, mothers are invited to bring their babies for possible admission."

"Possible?"

"They must meet specific criteria. An acceptable candidate must be under twelve months of age, the mother's first child, and healthy, so as not to risk infecting other children. In addition, although only illegitimate offspring are admitted, the mother must establish her good character. A secondary purpose of the Hospital, you see, is the restoration of the mother to work and a life of virtue. Some children are the result of rape, but most petitions come from women who claim to have been seduced with promises of marriage and then deserted when they became pregnant. In such cases, many mothers can avoid disgrace and find employment only if they do not have to care for their children."

"A sad truth," Juliana said, her heart hurting at the thought of women being forced to give up their babies.

Miss Strickland opened a door. "The Committee Room," she whispered.

And Juliana's hurting heart broke clear in two.

Inside the elegant chamber, a queue of young mothers clutched their infants tightly, the expressions on their faces a mixture of anguish and hope. Their simple cloaks and aprons were a poignant contrast to the silk gowns of a few fashionable lady patronesses who had come to observe the spectacle.

And what a spectacle it was.

As Juliana watched, a young woman was invited to the front, where a well-dressed man held out a cloth bag. Shifting her whimpering baby, the woman reached a trembling hand into the bag and pulled out a little red ball. She swallowed hard and, gripping the ball in her white-knuckled fist, stepped off to join a small group of mothers and babies huddled at one side.

Abandoning the battle-axe, Juliana walked over to join the other spectators. "What does the ball mean?" she asked in a whisper.

A tall, middle-aged woman answered in kindly tones, "The system is called balloting. These mothers have already been screened and deemed acceptable. But the Governors can accept only ten infants at a time, and there are many more qualified mothers wishing placement for their children. Balloting is the fairest method of allocating places."

As she finished her explanation, another young woman drew a ball—a black one—and dropped it to the floor, sudden tears spilling down her cheeks as she ran from the room, taking her baby with her.

"Black is bad?" Juliana asked.

"Mothers who draw black balls are immediately turned out of the Hospital. A white ball means the baby will be examined and admitted if it is healthy. Mothers who draw red balls are invited to wait to see whether any babies are refused admittance, in which case they are given a second chance to enter the lottery."

An agonizing lottery. Juliana watched as two more mothers drew black balls and one lucky woman nabbed a white one. "How many mothers are hoping for placement today?"

"About a hundred, which is typical."

And only ten would see their babies provided for. The fortunate woman with the white ball was ushered toward a corner, where a doctor waited to evaluate her child— a girl, if Juliana could judge by the scrap of ribbon crookedly tied in the baby's sparse, downy hair. During the short examination, a dozen more mothers drew balls—nine chose black, one red, and two jubilant women got white. When the first baby was declared healthy, the mothers waiting with red balls visibly drooped, gripping their infants more tightly. The lucky mother—if one could call her that—was given a num-bered document that certified the Hospital's acceptance of her baby, and a lead tag with a corresponding number was threaded on a necklace and placed around the child's neck.

A tightness squeezed Juliana's chest as she watched the tearful parting, the mother kissing her baby girl over and over before regretfully surrendering her to a Hospi-tal employee. "Is she given that paper so she can reclaim her child?"

"Partly. The babies are baptized with Hospital names—the child is never told the identity of the mother, and the mother won't know her child's new name. But if at a later date she can convince the Gover-nors of her reformed character and improved circum-stances, the paper and matching necklace number will prove they restore the right child to her."

"But you said 'partly,'" Juliana prompted.

The woman sighed. "Truthfully, that seldom happens. She is more likely to use the paper for her own defense; if she is accused of having disposed of her baby by mur-der, the certificate might save her from the gallows."

"Dear heavens." None of the mothers looked like criminals—they were just women in tragic circumstances. "I saw no infants in either the girls' building or the boys'. Have the babies lodgings of their own?"

"The babies aren't kept at the Hospital. They'll be baptized with their new names at Sunday services tomor-row and then placed with wet nurses in the countryside on Monday. The nurses receive a monthly wage and keep the children until they are five years or there-abouts, at which time they return to live here."

Juliana watched as the infant was carried off. "Does anyone make sure the babies are treated well?"

"Oh, yes. Inspectors visit regularly. They're responsi-ble for the nurse's pay and the child's medical fees, and for purchasing clothes for the infants—"

"Purchasing clothes?"

"Baby clothes. Babies are sent to their new 'mothers' with frocks and caps and clouts and coats and blankets—"

"Do the girls not make these in their sewing lessons?"

"The baby clothes aren't uniforms—"

"Then I can provide them, then!"

"Pardon?"

"I can make them. I can make baby clothes and donate them to the Hospital."

The kindly woman blinked at her. "I don't know about that. I don't believe anyone donates anything besides money."

Juliana watched another mother draw a red ball and, trembling, take her baby to join the small group of hopefuls. She imagined having to wish someone else's child proved ill so her own child could have a chance for a decent life. Or at least she tried to imagine it. The very thought was heartrending.

She turned back to the lady patroness beside her. "The fact that the Hospital hasn't accepted nonmonetary donations in the past doesn't mean it cannot do so in future." Maybe providing baby clothing would free enough funds for the Governors to accept another child or two. She wouldn't allow them to refuse her. "There's a first time for everything, isn't there?"

Chapter Two

SPICE CAKES

Take three scoops of Flower and put into it a
Spoon of ale-barm, crushed cloves, mace, and a
goode deal of cinnamon. To a halfe Pound of
sweet Butter add a goode deal of Sugar and mixe
together. Stir in three Eggs and work until good
and stiff, then add a little cold Rosewater and
knead well. Knead again, pull it all in Pieces and
bake your Cakes in a warm oven.

*I've heard tell that should you eat one of these
before a gathering where you are likely to meet
available men, their spiciness will clear your head
and allow you to choose wisely. This did not, however, work when I baked them for my daughter.*

In any case, they are delicious.
—Amethyst Chase, Countess of Greystone, 1690

"How many baby clothes do you need to make?"

"A lot." In her bedroom at the Chase town house in
Berkeley Square early that evening, Juliana set down
her little pot of lip pomade and picked up the list the
Governors had given her. "Three frocks, three caps,
three nightshirts, one mantle, one coat, one petticoat,
two blankets, and ten clouts. And that's *per* child. There
will be ten babies."

Emily bit into one of the spice cakes she and Juliana

had baked after returning from the Foundling Hospital. "So you need to make thirty frocks?"

"Yes." The girl was articulate *and* good with arithmetic. "And thirty caps, thirty nightshirts, ten mantles, ten coats, ten petticoats, twenty blankets, and a *hundred* clouts. All within a month, before the next reception day."

Juliana set the list on her dressing table. Upside down, so it would stop taunting her. Whatever had she got herself into? She'd been thrilled when the Governors accepted her offer to provide clothing for the next intake of infants—until she'd realized just how *many* clothes she'd need.

She wasn't worried about the cost of the materials, because she was certain she could cajole Griffin into paying for whatever her allowance wouldn't cover. But the mere thought of making so many items was daunting. "You'll help me, won't you?"

Emily frowned. "I'm not very good with a needle."

"You can hem blankets and sew clouts. That's not very difficult, and it will be good practice." Reaching over the girl's snake, Juliana wiped a few spice cake crumbs off her mouth. "I'm going to invite my sisters to help, too. We'll have a sewing party. It will be fun to work together." She dipped a finger into the lip pomade. "But I think you'll need to leave Herman home."

"I told you, he's not dangerous."

"His danger, or lack thereof," she told the child, watching her in the dressing table's mirror as she slicked pomade on her lips, "is not the point. Little ladies do not carry snakes."

Emily's delicate chin went into the air. "I do." She adjusted the long, olive green reptile where it was wound around her neck, the better to eat another spice cake. "What are these cakes supposed to do again?"

"Help me choose a husband wisely."

"All the gentlemen will want you. You look beautiful tonight, Lady Juliana. Of course, you always look beautiful," she added with a wistful sigh.

Juliana lifted a pot of rouge. "You'll look beautiful when you're my age." It was true. Other than her unfortunate attachment to the reptile, the child was a model of femininity. She always wore pink. Emily's blond hair and large, luminous gray eyes held much promise, and she was tall for her age. Since Juliana was slightly built, the girl would be as tall as her in no time.

"I'm certain you'll be wildly popular," she assured the child, "if only you'll get rid of the snake."

"Mama and I found baby Herman in our garden," Emily told Juliana for probably the hundredth time. "She said we could keep him and watch him grow."

Emily's mother had been dead some four years. Having lost her own mother three years prior—although, thankfully, at age nineteen, not age four—Juliana felt for the young girl.

"Your mother would understand," she told her gently. "Surely she didn't intend to keep Herman long. I'd wager she hadn't an inkling that little baby snake would grow to be five feet long, and I'm certain she didn't make a habit of carrying him around. Why, I'd warrant she's looking down on you right now, waiting for you to grow up and stop toting that horror-inducing creature everywhere."

"Herman is not a creature. He's a *pet*."

"A cuddly kitten is a pet. A rambunctious dog is a pet. A snake is not—"

"Are you ready yet?" Corinna arrived in the doorway and frowned. "A Lady of Distinction doesn't hold with wearing rouge."

Juliana's gaze flicked involuntarily to a book on her night table, *The Mirror of the Graces* by A Lady of Distinction. Their brother had given them both copies, hoping that learning deportment would help them find husbands more quickly.

"A Lady of Distinction is a twit." To emphasize her point, Juliana brushed more color on her cheeks before rising. "Yes, I am ready. Have a spice cake while I deliver Emily home."

Corinna took one. "Aunt Frances is already waiting in the carriage. You know she abhors being late to balls."

"Aunt Frances abhors being late to anyth[ing.]" Frances liked everything just so. But she [was a] dearing lady nonetheless, and it was quite [kind of her] to act as their sponsor and chaperone for the [

Juliana didn't grumble. She took Emily by the hand and led her downstairs, Corinna following in their wake.

It was raining—seemingly an everyday occurrence this summer—but a quick walk next door brought Emily safely to the house she usually shared with only her father and a gaggle of aging servants. Emily had two older brothers, products of two earlier marriages, but one was married and the other was away at Cambridge most of the year.

Their gaunt butler, a man who must have been eighty if he were a day, swung the door open as they arrived.

Emily stepped inside. "When shall I see you again, Lady Juliana?"

Who could deny that adorable, pleading face, even if it *was* framed by a snake? "Monday," she promised the girl. Rain pattered onto her parasol and puddled at her feet. "I'm sure your father is looking forward to being with you tomorrow, but on Monday the two of us shall visit the shops and choose fabric for the baby clothes."

"Will Lady Corinna not wish to come, too?"

"I believe she will prefer to paint." Corinna always preferred to paint; she was happiest when filling her days with color, oils, and turpentine. "I shall see you Monday," Juliana promised softly and headed through the drizzle to the carriage.

Inside, Corinna waited with Aunt Frances, their matching deep-blue eyes impatient. The women's eyes, however, were their only similarity. Aunt Frances's peered from behind round spectacles in a face surrounded by clouds of soft gray hair—prematurely gray hair, considering she was still in her forties. Corinna's hair was a swing of wavy brown, her face as fresh as only a twenty-one-year-old woman's could be. She had no need of cosmetics.

Juliana, on the other hand, figured she needed all the help she could get. Due to circumstances beyond her control—namely, several successive deaths in the family, which had kept her in mourning for several years—this was her *first* Season. At twenty-two! And the Season was more than halfway over already, yet she'd failed to find a man to catch her interest.

Not that her brother hadn't been trying his damnedest to locate one.

He was waiting at the ball when they arrived, looking over the crop of men. Unfortunately, this far into the Season, Juliana had already met almost everyone there was to meet. The *ton* comprised all the people who mattered in society, but that was a limited social group, after all. Yet he'd managed to line up candidates for her first three dances and was keeping an eye out for more.

Griffin was leaving no stone unturned in his quest to marry her off. Though she had no objection to marrying—or dancing, for that matter—she wasn't sure she appreciated her brother's interference. But she knew his heart was in the right place, and she did like to dance, so she dutifully danced with the three men, smiling and chatting pleasantly, even though none of them was even remotely what she was looking for.

Lord Henderson was too tall. Lord Barkely was too dark. And Mr. Farringdon was kind but a mite dim, not to mention he had a most unfortunate, distracting tic. She could hardly take her eyes off his twitching cheek.

The spice cakes were not going to help her choose wisely, she thought with a sigh, if no acceptable men bothered to attend this ball.

Chapter Three

James Trevor, the Earl of Stafford, hadn't been to a ball in years. And he hadn't particularly wanted to come to this one. However, being a man who liked to look for the good in things, he'd decided to regard tonight as an opportunity to renew a few acquaintances. Griffin Chase, the Marquess of Cainewood, was one of them.

But his old chum didn't look very happy.

"Whom are you glaring at, Cainewood?"

"My sister." Cainewood's frown deepened. "She's not dancing."

James's gaze followed the marquess's across the ballroom, landing on what looked like a dainty sprite. He lifted his quizzing glass and squinted through it. "That wheaten-haired little thing?"

"Wearing yellow? Yes, that would be Juliana, wasting precious time."

"She's conversing with another woman—"

"Another sister. But Juliana is *supposed* to be meeting men. I despair of ever finding her a husband."

"Ah." Dropping the quizzing glass, James let it dangle on its long silver chain and focused on Cainewood, who'd been a boon companion in their days at Oxford. He hadn't seen the man in years, and he'd never met his family, but in an odd way he still felt he knew him.

He couldn't help but smile at his old friend's consternation.

"Juliana is twenty-two," Cainewood added as though that explained everything.

"That doesn't sound particularly old." James himself was twenty-nine.

"I'll have to marry Corinna off after her." Cainewood gestured toward his other sister, a pretty girl with long, wavy brown hair. "I'd hoped to get them both settled this Season, but Juliana is not cooperating. Unfortunately, I believe she's already met everyone here, except . . ." His green gaze narrowed on James. "Perhaps you."

"Me?"

"Yes, you," Cainewood said with the easy smile that had won him so many women in their university years. "Will you at least suffer an introduction to Juliana? You're an earl now, are you not? An earl needing a wife."

An earl needing a wife—the same exact words James's mother had used to describe him earlier this evening as she'd all but dragged him from the carriage into this house.

But although James had inherited the title almost three years ago now, he still had a hard time thinking of himself as an earl, let alone *an earl needing a wife*.

A second son raised in a close family, James had never thought he'd become the Earl of Stafford. That had been his older brother's future, not his. Following university, James's father had bought him a commission in the army. He hadn't ever minded being an officer. It was expected. He wasn't drawn toward the clergy, and many of his friends—Cainewood included—had embraced the military life. After less than two years, though, James had been wounded and sent home.

Thinking back to those days now, he shifted and flexed his left knee, which always ached in the sort of cold, wet weather London had seen this summer. On days like this he still walked with a slight limp, but he was profoundly grateful the army surgeons had managed to save his leg rather than amputating it. So grateful that, needing another profession after his recovery, he'd become a physician. He hadn't been long out of medical school before he'd realized he'd found his true calling. In the years following his return to England, James had been a man completely happy with his choice of work and his life, especially after he fell in love and married.

Then everything had fallen apart.

His brother had died first, leaving James reeling with the realization that he'd someday be the earl. He didn't *want* to be an earl—he *liked* being a physician. He liked helping people, and he liked feeling that he made a difference. Every day was unique and challenging, and there were always successes to balance the disappointments. Managing an earldom seemed such a tedious, thankless task in comparison.

Then, while he was still coping with the loss of his brother, his father's heart had stopped, and suddenly James *was* the earl, like it or not.

The first months after that had passed in a dark, painful blur, but his young wife had helped him through those days and weeks, until one morning James had awakened and realized he was happy. Perhaps a bit guiltily happy—he still mourned his brother and father, after all—but happy nonetheless. He'd found he quite liked sitting in the House of Lords—it was another chance to make a difference—and managing the earldom wasn't as thankless a task as he'd believed. And, in addition, his wife had convinced him that he could be a physician as well as an earl, regardless of the narrow views of society, and help more people than ever, now that he had no need of the income. Utilizing the vast fortune left to him, James had opened a facility in London where children whose families were too poor to pay for doctors could get smallpox vaccinations, an endeavor dear to his heart. Life had been good again. And he and his wife were expecting a baby, their first child.

What man wouldn't have been happy?

Then his wife had died in childbirth, and their baby, born too early, had died along with her. All the physicians, James included, hadn't made a bit of a difference. And James had wondered if he'd ever be happy again.

Now, two years later, he was still wondering. But his

mother was pressuring him to remarry and sire some heirs, and although he didn't expect to find happiness or love again, he figured he might as well at least consider making *her* happy. She was a good, caring mother, after all, and perhaps a wife, even one not loved, would ease some of the loneliness he'd suffered these two years past. So he'd allowed himself to be dragged to this ball. And now he forced himself to smile and answer Cainewood.

"Yes, I am an earl. And I'd be pleased to meet your sister."

Cainewood wasted no time marching him across the room and introducing him to both of his sisters. As James bowed over Juliana's hand, he caught himself staring into dancing eyes that were full of life. He'd thought he'd be immune to Cainewood's sister, so he found himself surprised. Or perhaps *shocked* would be a better word.

And it felt wrong somehow.

But Cainewood's sister was a pretty thing, and he couldn't seem to wrench his gaze from those eyes. Green eyes. No, blue. He couldn't decide. They seemed to change as he watched.

"Will you honor me with a dance?" he asked, bemused.

"It would be my pleasure," she assured him.

He hadn't danced since his wife died. He wondered if he remembered how. But there was a waltz playing, and Juliana fairly melted into his arms.

He remembered.

"What color are your eyes?" he asked.

She laughed, a joyful, tinkling sound. "Hazel. Why?"

"I couldn't tell. They looked green at first, but now they look blue."

"Well, they're hazel," Juliana repeated, wishing he would stop staring at them. It seemed almost as though he could see right through them, as though he could see into her head. As though he could glimpse her very soul. And that was an unnerving thought, no matter that she had nothing to hide.

She glanced away, her gaze landing on her married sister. Alexandra had come to town for the Season while her new husband claimed his seat in the House of Lords.

How happy they looked dancing together, Alexandra's dark eyes locked on Tristan's steady gray gaze. Their road to romance had been a rocky one, but they'd been fated to be together from the first—and Juliana had known that, of course.

If only she could find such a love for herself.

Still feeling Lord Stafford's gaze on her, she shifted in his arms and met his eyes, mentally daring him to look away. He didn't. His eyes were a warm brown, and she had to look up to see them. Way up.

She could get a crick in her neck dancing with such a man.

"I haven't seen you at any other balls," she commented. "You must take your duty to Parliament seriously."

The corners of those warm eyes crinkled when he smiled. "That and my profession."

"Your profession?"

"I'm a physician."

"I thought you were an earl," she said.

One of his dark brows went up. "Can I not be both?"

"Of course you can," she said quickly, although she'd never heard of an earl-physician. "What do you do, exactly? Have you many patients?"

"Some, although I'm not taking on any new ones. Most of my time is spent at my facility, the New Hope Institute."

"New Hope," she mused. "I've heard of that. Something to do with smallpox?"

"I provide vaccinations, yes. To anyone willing to receive one, regardless of the ability to pay."

"That sounds like very important work," she allowed. He was a most unusual man. And an excellent dancer. Having noticed a slight limp as he'd initially approached her, she wouldn't have thought he'd dance so gracefully.

However, much as she enjoyed dancing, finding a man who excelled at it wasn't her priority. After all, it was not as though she had a shortage of dance invitations—she danced her feet off at every ball, with or without Griffin in attendance. She had no problem attracting men; the problem was finding one she considered husband material. And Lord Stafford had many short-comings.

When the music came to an end, he led her by the hand off the dance floor. "It was a pleasure, my lady."

His voice was warm like his eyes, low and smooth as rich chocolate. The very sound of it seemed to weaken her knees. "Thank you," she said. The musicians struck up a country dance, and as he was still holding her hand, she half expected him to lead her straight back to the dance floor. Instead, he raised her fingers toward his mouth. Then, rather than pucker his lips in the customary salute in the air above her hand, he lowered them to actually touch her glove.

Scandalous. She could have sworn she felt the kiss through the white silk. A tingly sensation.

"Thank you," she repeated more faintly.

"Thank *you*," he echoed with a smile.

A smile that looked as dazed as she felt.

No sooner had he turned to leave than Griffin descended, snapping her back to reality. "Well?" he asked.

She watched Lord Stafford walk away, shoulders broad beneath his tailcoat. Loose, tousled curls grazed his black velvet collar. Many fashionable men achieved a similar look with pomade and curl papers, but his hair looked *naturally* tousled. Like he was too busy to bother to control it.

"He's too dark," she said.

"Pardon?"

"You know I prefer golden-haired men. And he's entirely too tall—I felt like a child dancing with him."

Griffin looked down on her, both literally and figuratively. "Face it, Juliana—you're short."

As though she hadn't noticed most of the world towered over her. "He works," she said. "He has a *profession*."

"And this makes him unacceptable as a husband?"

"Should I marry him, he wouldn't have any time for me." She wanted a grand love, like Alexandra and Tristan's; she wanted a husband who loved her to distraction. She wanted endless hours spent in passion with the man she decided to marry. And for heaven's sake, *this* man couldn't even find a few minutes to comb his hair properly. "I'm sorry, but he just won't do."

The fact that Lord Stafford's work was important was hardly a mitigating factor—and the fact that her heart had stuttered when he'd so impertinently kissed her hand had no bearing whatsoever.

Griffin released a long-suffering sigh. "I shall keep looking."

"You do that," she said, patting his arm and silently wishing him luck. The spice cakes had clearly been a waste. Poor Griffin. "In the meantime, I must speak with Alexandra."

She scanned the ballroom in search of her older sister and finally found her talking to Aunt Frances.

"Who was that you were dancing with?" Alexandra asked as she approached.

"Lord Stafford."

"He's very handsome."

"His hair is too dark." At Alexandra's blank look, Juliana shrugged. "Can you come to the Berkeley Square house next Wednesday afternoon?"

"I expect so. Why?"

"I need help making clothes for the Foundling Hospital babies."

"Your newest project, I take it?" Alexandra's brown eyes sparkled with mischief. "What have you got yourself into this time?"

If only she knew. "Corinna wanted to see the Hospital's art gallery, but oh, the poor foundlings were heartbreaking. And their mothers." Just thinking back on the balloting, Juliana wanted to cry. "I *must* do something to help them."

"Of course you must," Aunt Frances said. "With you, it's always something."

That much was true; Juliana couldn't deny it. "And what does that make me?" she wondered. "Impulsive? Melodramatic? Judgmental, overwrought, overemotional?" She stopped there, knowing she was all of those and more. Honestly, she could go on and on.

Which was why she wanted to hug Alexandra when she said, "No. That makes you compassionate, giving, hopeful. Kind and unselfish and vulnerable." Her perfect, responsible, married sister gifted her with a quiet smile. "It makes you lovable, Juliana. That's what it makes you the most."

She *did* hug her sister then, and her aunt, too, her heart not broken now but aching with warmth and affection instead. Yet all the while she was wondering: *If I'm so lovable, why can't I find a husband to love?*

Chapter Four

"This pink is pretty," Emily said Monday at Grafton House, a draper's shop in New Bond Street.

"It is," Juliana agreed, watching a snooty woman give the girl and her ever-present snake a wide berth. "But silk isn't sturdy enough for babies. And pink won't do— the Governors want white, so all the clothes will suit both girls and boys." She fingered a length of thick white wool.

Emily cocked her golden head. "Will the babies not be overly warm in frocks made of that?"

"I am considering this for the blankets. We'll buy linsey for the frocks."

"I'll look for linsey, then," Emily said and walked away.

Juliana nodded absently, deciding the wool would do fine. She was about to ask the price when she heard a little shriek, followed by a familiar voice. "Gracious me, Miss Neville! Are you *still* carrying that varmint everywhere?"

Juliana turned, surprised to see another Berkeley Square neighbor, Lady Amanda Wolverston.

Young Emily looked much more affronted than surprised, however. "Herman is not a varmint," she protested, returning to slip her hand into Juliana's. "He's a pet."

"Not a very proper one," Lady Amanda said.

Although she agreed, Juliana squeezed Emily's hand. Amanda could sometimes be a bit *too* proper. Still, since she and Amanda had grown up as neighbors, Juliana considered her a friend.

"I'm so glad you've come to town," she told her with a smile. "I've invited my sisters to a little sewing party on Wednesday afternoon, to make some clothing for the Foundling Hospital babies. I do hope you'll join us." Her tall blond friend was slouching—a habitual posture for her. But she seemed to be slouching even more than normal, and she looked uncommonly pale. Juliana blinked and peered up at her wan face. "Where have you been hiding all Season?"

"In the countryside. My father is *still* excavating the Roman ruins he found on the estate." Amanda gestured toward a chair in a corner of the shop, where her aunt sat primly. "Aunt Mabel accompanied me, though she didn't want to come to town this year at all."

A slight, pinch-faced woman in a baggy gown, the poor lady was as pink-cheeked as Amanda was pale. She seemed to be wheezing a little. "You know she's always suffered from asthma," Juliana said sympathetically, vaguely musing that Amanda must have inherited her fashion sense—or rather, lack thereof—from her aunt. "The London air doesn't agree with her. However did you convince her to come?"

"Father convinced her. Or rather, he ordered her." Amanda's gaze slid to Emily and back, wordlessly telling Juliana she had something to confide.

Dying to hear the news, Juliana squeezed the little girl's hand again. "Could you do me an important favor, sweetheart, and see if you can find that linsey?"

"All right," Emily said, happily wandering off.

"Well?" Juliana asked when Emily was out of earshot.

Amanda's voice dropped to a whisper. "Father has arranged my marriage. He sent me and Aunt Mabel to put together a trousseau, which is why I'm here at Grafton Hou—"

"He's arranged your marriage?" Juliana interrupted. "To whom?"

Amanda closed her blue-gray eyes for a moment,

releasing a slow breath before she reopened them. "Lord Malmsey," she said despondently.

"Lord *Malmsey*?"

The man was shorter than Amanda, quiet, mild-mannered, and meek. But the predominant image in Juliana's mind was that of a creased forehead beneath a receding hairline.

"The man must be forty, at least!"

"Forty-five," Amanda corrected. Almost twice her age. She was a year older than Juliana, which made her all of twenty-three. "I met with him last evening—not that either of us had much to say to each other. We're to be married four weeks from Saturday, in a private ceremony by special license."

The same day as the next Foundling Hospital intake, when Juliana had to have all the baby clothes ready. Amanda looked to be in the dismals, which was no wonder. "Can you not refuse to wed him?"

She shook her head. "Father has made it clear that if I fail to go through with this wedding, he will disinherit me—which would leave me slim chances of ever wedding at all."

It was on the tip of Juliana's tongue to argue the point, but she wasn't one to lie—not outright, anyway—and Amanda was only stating the truth. In five Seasons, no one else had offered for her, and without her substantial inheritance, it was unlikely any man ever would.

"I am miserable," Amanda added unnecessarily.

One thing Juliana was sure of: Griffin would never expect her to wed other than where her heart led her. For that, she supposed she should be grateful. "Have you told your father how you feel?"

"Countless times. My protests fall on deaf ears. Nothing I can say will make him breach a contract. His honor, apparently, is more important to him than my happiness."

Lord Wolverston had always been rather emotionless and uncaring, but this went beyond that. It was downright cruel. "There is nothing at all honorable about putting his reputation before his own daughter. He should want to see you in love."

"He believes that when it comes to marriage, there are much more important matters to consider."

Juliana couldn't disagree more—concerning her own marriage, at least. Her parents had wed for practical reasons, and her mother had never known true happiness. She did realize that much of society had other priorities for evaluating matches, but for her, love came first.

Amanda slouched even more. "He's pleased beyond belief to have an offer for my hand at all, let alone one from a baron. I suppose he's right when he says I'm lucky Lord Malmsey is willing to marry me."

"Amanda!"

"I'm a confirmed wallflower, Juliana."

Amanda *did* look rather plain, but Juliana had always assumed that was because her mother had died giving birth to her. Much like little Emily, she'd grown up without anyone to offer guidance. Her Aunt Mabel was certainly no help. Amanda wore dowdy clothes in all the wrong colors, her brows were too heavy, her blond hair was pulled back into an excruciatingly tight braided bun, and she never met anyone's eyes—not even Juliana's now. Her blue-gray gaze was focused in the vicinity of her unfashionably shod feet.

In short, Amanda was a project just waiting to be tackled.

"Who else knows about your engagement?" Juliana asked.

"We arrived only yesterday. You're the first one I've told."

"Excellent." Lord Malmsey wasn't the type to spread news, either. Although the man was a fixture at society gatherings, Juliana couldn't recall more than a dozen words ever leaving his mouth. "Don't tell anyone. I shall save you from this dismal fate."

The older girl glanced up. "How? Do you truly believe it possible?"

"Without a doubt." Juliana had never been one to disregard anyone in need. "Let me think on the matter."

"Look here, Lady Juliana!" Emily returned, holding forth Herman coiled upon an armful of white fabric.

"Perfect, sweetheart." Juliana smiled, hoping the clerk

wouldn't faint when she asked for a length to be cut. Or maybe hoping the clerk *would* faint, because that might convince the girl, once and for all, that toting a snake about was not a good idea. She looked back to Amanda. "You'll come to the sewing party Wednesday, will you not? One o'clock. By the time you arrive, I am certain to have a solution."

Chapter Five

"Where is Amanda?" Juliana said Wednesday afternoon in the drawing room.

Rain pattered outside the windows. "You've asked that more times than Emily's pricked herself," Alexandra observed as she patiently knotted a thread.

Alexandra could afford to be patient, Juliana thought, stitching a tiny frock more frantically than patiently. She wasn't the one who'd promised to deliver twenty dozen articles of baby clothing in one short month. "Amanda said she'd be here."

"No, she didn't," Emily pointed out, rearranging Herman on her shoulders. Unfortunately, the clerk at Grafton House hadn't fainted. She'd only glared, which had done nothing toward convincing Emily to part with the dratted snake. "You invited her, but she never actually said she would come."

"Perhaps not in so many words. But she'll come." Amanda *had* to come. Juliana had devised a plan. An excellent plan, which she couldn't wait to explain—

"Ouch!" Emily exclaimed for the fifth time, sticking her pricked finger in her mouth. She really *wasn't* very good with a needle. "This blanket is turning out dreadful."

Juliana leaned over to inspect the girl's handiwork. "It isn't that bad." The hem was rather uneven, but it wasn't *dreadful.* Babies, after all, weren't prone to criticize. "The blanket will keep an infant warm no matter what it looks like."

"But I want it to look *good.*"

"With more practice, it will." Corinna stopped sewing long enough to gesture toward an easel set up by the large picture window. Even in the dim rainy-day light, the scene on the canvas—a man pushing a laughing lady on a swing by a reflective lake—conveyed movement, vibrancy, a sense of life. "My first painting didn't look like that."

Alexandra smiled, still patiently working her own needle into the little cap she was making. "If I recall correctly, your first painting was a willow tree that looked more like a haystack."

"We're none of us expert seamstresses, Miss Emily." Aunt Frances squinted at her own handiwork through her spectacles. "We've only ever done samplers and embroidery. After a few more practice blankets—"

"This isn't practice," Juliana interrupted. "Every single item will be used." If she was lucky, today's efforts would produce five or six finished garments. And she needed two hundred and forty! Although it was a bit early to panic, she realized already, less than an hour into her first sewing party, that she was going to have to host many more of them. "Where is Amanda?"

Just then the knocker sounded in the foyer.

"That must be Amanda," she said, the frock falling to the floor as she jumped up and rushed from the room.

Though their butler, Adamson, was almost as short as Juliana, he always managed to look dignified nonetheless. "Good afternoon, Lady Amanda," he intoned as he opened the door.

"Good afternoon, Adamson," Amanda replied formally.

"Where on earth have you been?" Juliana asked, very informally indeed.

"Playing chess with Aunt Mabel. I couldn't leave in the middle of such an exciting game."

"Exciting?" Juliana could think of little less exciting than chess. She preferred games that were light and relaxing, not so cerebral. Even sewing was more fun. "Come into the library."

Amanda peeked through the open door across the way. "Isn't everyone in the drawing room?"

"Yes. That's the point." Juliana took her in the opposite direction, closing the door behind them and ushering her friend toward two leather wingback chairs. "We must keep your engagement a secret. I've a plan to break it."

Amanda sat and clasped her hands in her lap, suddenly looking nervous. "What is the plan?"

Picturing her sisters with their ears to the door—after all, she'd often done so along with them—Juliana lowered her voice. "We shall arrange to get you compromised by—and therefore betrothed to—a man closer to your age than Lord Malmsey. Your father will be forced to agree once the public has seen you and this other man in a compromising position."

"A compromising position?" Amanda's sudden laugh was shrill enough to make Juliana wince. "Gracious me, I've never even been kissed!"

"I haven't been kissed, either," Juliana said. "Not that men haven't tried." To the contrary, men tried all the time. But she always managed to duck them, because as much as she wanted to experience her first kiss, she wished for it to be with someone she cared for, at least a little.

"Well, no one's tried with me," Amanda said dourly. "And it will take more than a kiss to force my father's hand. There's not a chance a young, eligible man is going to compromise me. Not willingly, anyway."

"I didn't mean *un*willingly." Juliana would never be party to such a devious plot, and furthermore, such a thing wouldn't be necessary. When she was finished with Amanda, men would be falling over themselves trying to compromise her. "Not to worry, my dear." She leaned closer to pat her hand. "Are you free tomorrow and the day after?"

"To be compromised?"

"To be fitted for a few ball gowns. You'll require a new wardrobe, among other things. We'll need to visit a seamstress as well as comb all the shops."

Amanda appeared both dubious and hopeful, if such an expression were possible. "My father did give me leave to assemble a trousseau."

"Excellent." There was little Juliana enjoyed more than transforming an ugly duckling into a lovely swan. "We have a lot of work to do before Lady Hammersmithe's ball on Saturday."

"I cannot attend Lady Hammersmithe's ball."

"Of course you can. I shall summon Madame Bellefleur to trim your hair—"

"My hair has never been cut." Amanda's hands went protectively to her head. "And I cannot attend—"

"Ouuuccch!" The howl was so piercing, it shot from the drawing room, across the foyer, and through the library's closed door.

"That's Emily!" Juliana exclaimed, bolting from her chair. Lifting her skirts, she dashed out the door. "Emily!" she shouted, running through the foyer and bursting into the drawing room. "Emily, what's happened?"

And there she stopped, a sudden sickness in her middle, a disturbing lightness in her head.

Emily was *bleeding.*

"It *hurts*," the girl wailed, bent over her hand. Tiny red spots dotted her pink skirts. Although clearly the injury wasn't serious—they were *tiny* spots, not a stream—Juliana knew she should hurry to help. To comfort. To make everything all better.

But she couldn't. Because the sight of those red spots seemed to make it hard to breathe.

Everyone *else* was helping. Well, maybe not helping, precisely, but at least they weren't riveted in place. In the scant seconds Juliana stood there—because that's all the time it was, really—her sisters and Aunt Frances leapt up and surrounded Emily, making all sorts of clucking, compassionate noises.

At least that hid the sight of Emily's wound. But all that sympathy seemed to do little but make the girl sob harder. "M-my needle s-slipped. It—it didn't just poke me this time, it ripped—"

"Gracious me," Amanda said in a rather disgusted tone, pushing past Juliana and into the little cluster of females. "It's just a little blood. For goodness' sake. Someone take the snake." While Corinna moved to do so, Amanda reached for some linsey and tore off a strip, then drew Emily to her feet. "Let's clean it up and bandage it, shall we?" she said, leading her from the room.

Juliana walked to her chair, her knees feeling shaky. Which was ridiculous, and she knew it. As Corinna seemed to delight in pointing out to her, it was absurd for any female past puberty to find the sight of blood distressing. But her own monthlies never bothered her. A woman's periodic blood was natural; other bleeding was not.

Thankfully, Corinna hadn't seemed to notice her abysmal lack of action, and neither had anyone else.

"Emily will be fine." Corinna held Herman at arm's length, looking almost as ridiculous as Juliana felt. "Why didn't you bring Amanda straight in here?"

"I wanted to talk to her regarding Lady Hammersmithe's ball on Saturday. Talk her into attending, I mean."

"Why wouldn't she?" Alexandra asked.

Juliana shrugged—casually, she hoped. "She's rather shy around eligible gentlemen. I've offered to help her with a new wardrobe, which I'm hoping will boost her confidence."

"That's kind of you," Alexandra said.

Corinna looked suspicious. Or maybe just wary of the snake. "Whyever did you feel the need to talk privately? We could have helped you convince her—"

"Here she is, all repaired," Amanda announced, walking back in with Emily.

Emily sported a neat little linsey bandage wrapped around her finger. When she reached for Herman, Corinna didn't hesitate to hand him over. Juliana's sister still looked wary, though. Or suspicious.

Drat.

"Shall we get back to work?" Juliana asked cheerfully.

Emily shook her head. "I'm not sewing anymore."

"You can start cutting the clouts," Juliana suggested, handing her a bundle of cotton fabric, a pair of scissors, and a simple pattern. She hoped that when the cut rectangles were folded and sewn, they would turn out the right size to cover a baby's bottom. Refusing to even *think* about doing that a hundred times, she gave Emily's half-finished blanket to Amanda. "Here. This is almost done."

It wasn't, of course, and Amanda proved to be no handier with a needle than the rest of them. Not only was Juliana going to have to host more sewing parties, she was also going to have to invite more women— hopefully including some who had sewn more than samplers. "I hope you'll all help me recruit more ladies at Almack's tonight."

"I'm not attending," Alexandra said, a sparkle in her brandy-brown eyes. "Since Parliament isn't sitting, Tristan wants to stay home, just the two of us."

It wouldn't be *just* the two of them, of course—a marquess had a bevy of household help. But still, Juliana envied her sister's settled life. Since Almack's was foremost a matrimonial bazaar, Alexandra could afford to skip going and spend a relaxing evening at home instead. At the rate Juliana *wasn't* finding a husband, she wondered if she'd ever have that luxury for herself.

Corinna looked up from the petticoat she was stitching. Suspiciously. "Amanda, you'll be attending Almack's, will you not?"

"No," Amanda said. Juliana held her breath, half expecting her to blurt out that she had no need to attend given that she was already engaged. To her great relief, Amanda added instead, "Aunt Mabel isn't feeling up to chaperoning me these days."

"Is it the asthma again?" Aunt Frances sighed. "Poor Lady Mabel. I shall have to pay her a call."

"She'd appreciate that very much," Amanda said, hemming the blanket almost as crookedly as Emily.

If anything, Corinna looked even more suspicious. "But Juliana said you're going to Lady Hammersmithe's ball."

"As I tried to explain to her, I don't expect Aunt Mabel will be well enough by Saturday, either. The London air—"

"Aunt Frances can chaperone you along with us," Juliana said.

Amanda's needle slowed, not that she'd been plying

it with masterful speed in the first place. "No one will ask me to dance, anyway."

"Oh, yes, they will." Alexandra smiled down at her handiwork. "Juliana will teach you *the look*."

Now Amanda's needle stopped. "What look?"

"Allow me to demonstrate." Juliana looked up from her little frock. "First you choose a man you wish to entice—"

"Entice?"

"Enticement is the objective of *the look*. Trust me, should you do it properly, men are guaranteed to fall at your feet."

"Are they?"

"Positively," Alexandra declared, making Juliana speculate on her sister's life with her new husband.

Jealously speculate.

Amanda looked from one sister to the other. "I'm listening."

"Excellent. First you choose a man and command his gaze." Juliana focused on Amanda, making her eyes blatantly sensuous.

The older girl swallowed hard. "And then?"

"Glance down, bowing your head a little to display your lashes against your cheeks. Then sweep your eyelids up, gaze at the man full on again, and slowly—very slowly—curve your lips in a seductive smile."

Amanda's forehead wrinkled. "Show me again."

"Watch closely." Taking her time, Juliana silently repeated the demonstration.

Corinna snickered, but both Amanda and Emily sighed. "Can I learn, too?" Emily asked.

"It's never too early to begin practicing. Amanda, give it a try."

Amanda stared hard at Juliana, closed her eyes, popped them open, and stretched her mouth into a wide grin.

It was Juliana's turn to sigh. She had her work cut out for her.

Chapter Six

"I really must be on my way, Aunt Aurelia." James forced his lips to curve in a smile. "You're healthy as the day you were born."

"Are you certain?" A tad plump, but elegant for all of that, Aurelia reclined on her peach-draped bed. Her entire house was decorated in peach. In fact, sometimes when James was here—which seemed to be way too often lately—he fancied he was *in* a peach. "My heart was paining me so," she continued. "I tell you I could barely breathe. Won't you check it one more time with that ingenious new instrument of yours?"

"If you insist." Suppressing a sigh, he opened his black leather bag and drew out the ingenious instrument, which really wasn't ingenious at all. It was simply a foot-long cylinder of wood. One end had a hole to place against the ear, and the inside was hollowed out in the shape of a cone. The thing was so *un*ingenious, in fact, that James was tempted to kick himself for not thinking of something like it years ago. Instead, just this past March, a young French physician named Laennec had invented the instrument and christened it the stethoscope, derived from the Greek words for "I see" and "the chest."

James leaned close and placed the wider end of the

instrument over his aunt's heart. Her scent wafted to him, a unique combination of camphor and gardenias, the latter applied a little too liberally. On second thought, he silently thanked Laennec for his brilliance. Without the stethoscope, he'd have to press his ear to Aunt Aurelia's potent, pillowy chest.

Her heartbeat sounded strong through the tube, the thump-*thump* clear and distinct. "Regular as Grandmother's clock," he assured her.

"You're certain?" She shook her coiffed gray head disbelievingly. "And my lungs?"

"Sit up, if you will." He braced a hand on the headboard and applied the stethoscope to her corseted back. "Breathe in," he said as patiently as he could. "Out. In. Perfect. You're healthy as a newborn babe." He dropped the instrument back in his bag and fastened the clasp. "Now I really must leave, Auntie."

She climbed from her bed and accompanied him downstairs. "You're expected in Parliament?"

"Not today. It's Wednesday." The House of Lords sat on Mondays, Tuesdays, Thursdays, and Fridays. "But I was expected at the Institute hours ago. Only one other doctor volunteered for the early shift today."

"I do appreciate your visit." She squeezed his hand, making his heart squeeze as well. Aunt Aurelia was a dear, even if she was a hypochondriac. In the foyer, she glanced at Grandmother's tall-case clock. "Such a shame that Bedelia hasn't returned. She'll surely want to see you, too. She had a horrid case of the putrid sore throat this morning."

Bedelia, his mother's other sister, shared the house with Aurelia. Two childless widows whose lives centered on their imaginary physical ailments.

"Tell Aunt Bedelia to gargle with salted water. I am certain that will cure her."

"Do you expect so?" Aurelia's blue eyes looked dubious.

"Absolutely." James doubted Bedelia's throat was putrid; if her throat hurt her at all, it was likely due to nothing more serious than incessant chattering. "I'll see you again soon," he added, escaping to his carriage before Aurelia could ask him to clarify what he meant by *soon*. If she had her way, *soon* would be tomorrow—if not an hour from now.

On the way to New Hope Institute, he scribbled more notes for the speech he planned to deliver in Parliament, recommending compulsory smallpox vaccinations for infants. So immersed was he in his work, his carriage drew up to the door of the Institute before he noticed all the people queued in a line that stretched down the street.

Way down the street.

They might be London's poor, but they were good people, trying to do their best for their children. Mothers shivered in the cold, damp air, their faces set in resigned, unhappy lines. Babies cried. Small children whined, and restless older children taunted one another. Rather than wait, people were giving up and leaving, walking away from the Institute.

For the second time within a month.

Without waiting for the steps to be lowered, James bounded from the carriage and dashed through the drizzle into the building. In the reception area, more babies wailed on impatient mothers' laps. Two boys playing tag raced around the room, bumping into the knees of those seated. Slipping off his tailcoat, James looked to the counter for help.

No one was behind it. He untied his cravat as he pushed through the door into the back.

His private office was tiny—not much more than a desk and chair, since he preferred to do paperwork in his study at home. He tossed his coat and cravat onto the chair, then poked his head into the first of three treatment rooms, finding it empty although the next patient should be waiting there. The second room held one harried-looking physician along with a mother and her teary-eyed three-year-old.

Unfastening the top button of his shirt, James frowned. The vaccination procedure went more smoothly with a cooperative patient, and candy—a real treat for a poor child—usually proved a good distraction. "Where are the sugar sticks?" he asked.

Dr. Hanley shrugged, setting aside the ivory lancet

he'd used to inoculate the little girl. "I haven't a clue where . . . what is that new assistant's name?"

"Miss Chumford."

"Ah, yes." He tied a fresh bandage around the girl's arm. "I haven't a clue where Miss Chumford keeps the sugar sticks. I cannot seem to locate anything on those shelves. I consider myself lucky to have found a supply of the vaccine."

"Where *is* Miss Chumford?"

"In the next room. Crying her eyes out. And I don't expect a sugar stick will help." Dr. Hanley stood the sniffling child on her feet. "There you go, sweetheart. If you want a sugar stick, follow Lord Stafford."

"Dr. Trevor," James reminded him. He preferred not to be called "Lord" at the Institute—it intimidated the patients. As did his aristocratic clothing, which was why he always shed the more formal items. "I shall send in the next patient," he added as he ushered the girl toward the reception area. "Did Dr. Hanley tell you what to expect?" he asked her mother.

Clearly awed to be in a peer's presence, the woman answered shyly. "Yes, my lord. A big blister but no pox."

"That is correct. It may take some weeks for the blister to heal, and it will leave a scar. But your daughter will be spared from the smallpox."

"Thank you," she breathed, lifting the little girl and holding her close. "If I could pay you, I would."

Noting the telltale pox scars on her face, he knew her words came from the heart. He usually encouraged parents to be vaccinated along with their children, but that had obviously been unnecessary in her case.

"Thank *you*," he returned, "for doing your part. We're not in need of your money. But please tell your friends and neighbors about New Hope Institute. With your help, we can annihilate this dreadful scourge once and for all."

James would be happy with no less. It was his belief that if only everyone everywhere were vaccinated, smallpox could be wiped off the globe. It was a daunting task, he knew, but he was determined to do his part in London.

Unfortunately, London was not particularly cooperative. The poor were sadly skeptical and uninformed, and some churchmen preached that vaccination interfered with the will of God, believing smallpox was sent to chasten the population. In addition, the Institute could handle only a certain number of people per day. But James paid men to canvass the poorer parishes and talk people into bringing their children, which made it all the more frustrating when those who agreed were forced to stand out in the cold and rain.

He found a box of sugar sticks and sent the girl and her mother on their way, then settled the next patients in the two vacant treatment rooms. Once he ascertained that Dr. Hanley had a quantity of vaccine, sugar sticks, and other necessary supplies, he knocked on the door to the third room. "Miss Chumford?"

A prolonged sniffle was the only answer.

"Miss Chumford, may I come in?"

"It's your Institute," the young woman pointed out in a tiny voice.

Yes, it was. He opened the door. Then almost closed it at the sight of Miss Chumford's red, splotchy face.

There were few things he avoided more than a woman's tears. Emotional tears, in any case. As a doctor, he'd learned to endure tears caused by pain, but the other sort was another matter altogether.

With a sigh, he stepped into the room. "There's a queue outside, and if it grows any longer it's likely to reach all the way to Surrey."

"I'm sorry," she whimpered.

"Whatever could be amiss?"

Both of her hands pressed to her middle, she raised flooded eyes to meet his. A lone tear trickled down her cheek. She said nothing.

He shifted uncomfortably, torn between heartrending sympathy and heart-hardening annoyance. He had the Institute to run. People in need. He'd employed her to keep the physicians well supplied and make sure the patients were seen as quickly and efficiently as possible. A simple job, really, and necessary to the smooth operation of the facility. And she was the second assistant within a month to . . .

He looked back to her hands, which were rubbing her middle now. "You're with child, aren't you?" he suddenly realized, even though her belly looked flat.

After all, that was the reason his last assistant had left.

She nodded miserably, with the longest, most pathetic sniffle yet.

"And you're not wed, of course," he surmised less than brilliantly. After all, she was *Miss* Chumford.

This time she nodded and words tumbled out of her mouth. "Papa will k-kill me, or at least throw me out of the house. Harry, my . . . the f-father of my child, cannot afford a home of his own. We shall have to live with his p-parents, and his mother hates me, and his father—"

"Your Harry is willing to marry you?" James interrupted. "To take responsibility for his offspring?"

She nodded again, still blubbering. "H-Harry is a good man, m-my lord, and a hard worker. B-but—"

"Wait here, Miss Chumford." He could take no more of her tears. There were plenty of things to be miserable about that couldn't be fixed. Fixing this would be a simple enough matter.

He had a small safe in his private office, from which he withdrew fifty pounds. A pittance to him, but enough to cover a small family's rent and food for two years or more. It would provide Miss Chumford and her baby's father with a start, and should Harry be as good a man and hardworking as she claimed, he and his new wife and child would weather this disaster quite well.

After Miss Chumford left—tearfully blubbering her thanks—James sighed and lettered a HELP WANTED sign, propped it in the Institute's front window, and settled down behind the counter for what he knew from experience was likely to be many hours spent interviewing candidates.

Well, at least his mother wouldn't be able to drag him to Almack's tonight.

Chapter Seven

TRIFLE

> Take yokes of four egges and a pinte of thicke
> Creame, and season it with Sugar and Ginger and
> Rosewater, so stirre it as you would then have it
> and make it warme on a chafing dishe and coales,
> and after put it into a Silver piece or a Bowle, and
> so serve it to the board.
>
> *Extra-strong Rosewater will put Roses into
> your cheeks.*
>
> —Lady Jewel Chase, 1687

Over the next two days, Juliana helped Amanda order
an entire new wardrobe. They shopped for cosmetics,
hats, shoes, hosiery, and other assorted fripperies. They
practiced posture and walking, devised new alluring
smiles, and perfected *the look*. Juliana taught Amanda
how to apply the cosmetics so skillfully that no one
would notice she was wearing any. She plucked Amanda's heavy brows, hardening her heart to the older girl's
squeals of pain and protest—after all, all but the luckiest
of women suffered for their beauty.

With each hour, Amanda's confidence grew, as did
Juliana's certainty that her plan was going to work.

Finally, Saturday dawned.

Juliana dragged Corinna out of bed early—at noon—
to help her make trifle before Amanda arrived to dress

for Lady Hammersmithe's ball. Unfortunately, Corinna was hopeless in the kitchen on the best of days. And considering she'd stayed up until seven o'clock in the morning to finish a painting, this day was not her best.

"My arm hurts," she complained. "And I'm tired."

"Just keep beating those eggs until they're creamy, please." Juliana added two more handfuls of rose petals to the water she had boiled. She was determined to make sure Amanda's cheeks would be nice and rosy. "I cannot understand why you won't go to bed at a reasonable hour."

"I am not a reasonable person—I'm an artist," Corinna reminded her. "*I* cannot understand why you won't ask a kitchen maid to beat these eggs."

Juliana consulted their family's heirloom cookbook, an ancient volume to which each lady in the family had traditionally added a recipe every Christmas since the seventeenth century. Many of the sweets were thought to be magic charms. She poured the rosewater into a pot of cream and sprinkled it with a bit of ginger. "How many times must I tell you that the Chase family recipes must be made by Chase family members if they're to work?"

Corinna rolled her eyes. "You and your traditions. I cannot countenance why you and Alexandra believe such nonsense."

"It hurts no one to try. Besides, the trifle will be delicious—you'll have some, won't you? If you and I and Amanda all have rosy cheeks tonight, perhaps we will all find husbands."

"A rouge pot would be a more efficient method of obtaining rosy cheeks, regardless of A Lady of Distinction's opinions on the matter." Corinna started grating sugar into the eggs. "Although I suppose poor Amanda can use all the help she can get."

"I've worked wonders with her," Juliana said, giving her mixture a vigorous stir. "Wait until you see. Her gown will be exquisite, her complexion flawless. I've summoned a hairdresser—"

"Just don't make Amanda so beautiful she steals your own suitors."

"That's an unkind thought." Juliana snatched the

sugar loaf from her sister before she could add too much as usual; Corinna's sweet tooth was legendary even among the sweets-loving Chases, and she had no concept of the proper amount of any ingredient. "I've no suitors I wish to marry anyway," she added with a sigh.

"You're trying too hard," Corinna said. "Just relax and enjoy all the attention."

But how could she relax? Next year she'd be twenty-three. Twenty-three and unmarried. At what age did one become a spinster, and how did one know when one reached it? Had Aunt Frances simply awakened one morning and decided to put on a spinster's cap?

"There, it's creamy." Corinna banged the bowl onto the big wooden table and rubbed her arm. "Am I finished? Assuming I can still hold a brush, I'd like to varnish my painting."

"Varnish away," Juliana said and watched her sister leave the kitchen. Even without the security of a happy marriage like Alexandra's, Corinna seemed content with her life. She wished she could say the same for herself.

The trifle was chilled in its silver bowl by the time Amanda arrived with two footmen carrying boxes. The French hairdresser was waiting, and less than an hour later, Amanda's once knee-length hair reached only the middle of her back. She watched in Juliana's dressing table mirror as her golden tresses fluttered to the floor, her face white as linsey, her eyes wide and apprehensive.

Juliana scooped trifle into a cup, thinking it might distract her friend. "Eat this. It will make your cheeks rosy."

"What is it?" Emily asked, adjusting Herman on her shoulder. "May I have some?"

"It's trifle, and yes, you may."

The girl cocked her blond head. "Our cook's trifle has cake and fruit."

"This is a very old recipe."

"Our cook is probably older," she said, then spooned the sweet into her mouth and smiled. "It's good. Your hair looks pretty, Lady Amanda."

Amanda drew a sharp breath. "Do you truly think so, Miss Neville?"

"Absolutely," Juliana answered for the girl. "Shorter hair is the thing. I cannot imagine why you hid those gorgeous curls in that plait." Juliana had always despaired of her own stick-straight hair, but at least she knew better than to scrape it all back into a braid so tight it looked plastered to her head.

Amanda grimaced at another snip.

"Hold your head still, if you will." Madame Bellefleur clipped off a final inch. "*Parfait.*"

"It's trifle," Emily corrected. "Not a parfait."

"In French," Juliana told her, "*parfait* means 'perfect.' That length will be so much lighter and easier to put up."

Madame smiled and nodded. "Now, some shorter tendrils around the face, *oui*?"

"Brilliant." Juliana resumed unpacking the boxes, admiring all the dresses they'd ordered. The seamstress had sent only one of the ball gowns, but promised the rest would be ready next week. "Your hair will be stunning," she assured Amanda.

Amanda responded with a rather maniacal laugh.

Juliana winced. "You must practice a new laugh. An alluring laugh, like tinkling bells."

"Like this?" Amanda attempted a girlish giggle.

Even Herman recoiled.

By the time they'd perfected the new laugh, Madame Bellefleur had experimented with different hairstyles, ultimately choosing one in which Amanda's blond mane was loosely gathered, twisted up, and pinned, with the remaining curls arranged artistically on top of her head. The hairdresser left, and Juliana swept the ball gown off her bed.

Amanda looked from the lavender silk dress, to Emily and Herman, and back to Juliana. "I would prefer not to disrobe in front of a snake," she said stiffly.

"So that's why you refused to strip to your chemise in order to be measured." Juliana laughed, remembering how the seamstress, Mrs. Huntley, also hadn't been very keen on working with Herman in attendance. She called her maid and asked her to walk Emily and the creature home. But after Juliana and Amanda were alone, it turned out Amanda didn't want to undress in front of *her*, either.

"Turn around," the older girl instructed.

"It's just me."

"Turn around."

Sighing, Juliana did so, hoping this didn't mean Amanda would be loath to bare a little skin in front of the man she chose to compromise her. Much rustling followed, evidence of Amanda's struggles dealing with garments that weren't meant to be donned without help. "Gracious me!" she finally exclaimed, sounding anything but gracious. "I cannot wear this."

Juliana spun around to find her friend staring down at her chest in dismay. "Of course you can. You look beautiful." She could hardly wait to see society's reaction to the new Amanda. "Turn around and let me button you up in back. Once you see the dress properly fastened, you're going to love it."

Unfortunately, turning around brought Amanda face-to-face with the looking glass. Her hands flew up to cover her cleavage. "This is entirely too low," she complained. "I'll have to wear a different gown."

"You have no other suitable gowns. Besides this, Mrs. Huntley sent only a few day dresses. The rest of your order won't be ready until next week."

Frowning, Amanda yanked up on the bodice. "I am certain the example Mrs. Huntley showed me had a much more modest neckline."

Of course it had, else Amanda would never have approved it. But that was before Juliana gave Mrs. Huntley her instructions, which, thankfully, the seamstress had followed to the letter. Although Juliana had always considered her friend a bit chubby, Amanda had a surprisingly lovely shape once she was rid of her baggy clothes. And Juliana intended to show that off, the better to snag a young husband. "It is not too low," she said, reaching around to tug the bodice back down.

"It is so." Amanda pulled it higher.

Watching her friend in the mirror, Juliana could only laugh. "Look at yourself!"

Amanda's neckline was indeed very near her neck—which meant the ribbon sash that was supposed to ride beneath her breasts was perched absurdly on top of them. Her mouth quirked, then spread into a reluctant smile, followed by a nervous titter.

"Tinkling bells," Juliana reminded her, and Amanda responded with her new, practiced laugh.

"Much better." Juliana reached once more to pull the bodice into place, dragging it a bit too low in the process. When an unusual fleur-de-lis-shaped birthmark was revealed on Amanda's left breast, a delighted smile curved Juliana's lips. "Quite seductive," she murmured, raising a brow.

"Pardon?" Amanda looked down, then tugged the lace-trimmed bodice up to cover it. "You weren't supposed to see that."

"Whyever not? It's a delicate, pretty thing. I'm sure a man would find it enticing."

"Enticing?" Clearly scandalized, Amanda blushed. "It's *private*."

Tying the sash, Juliana sighed, wondering again if—in spite of her newfound beauty—Amanda might be rather too reserved to attract men. But at least the blush brought out the roses in her cheeks.

She gave her more trifle, just in case. And brushed on a little extra rouge, as Corinna had suggested. As she applied the rest of her friend's cosmetics—as artfully as her sister painted—she drilled Amanda over and over. "Let me see your smiles one more time. And you must practice *the look* again before we leave."

All this preparation was *not* going to be for nothing.

Chapter Eight

"There he is," Amanda said dourly as they stepped into Lady Hammersmithe's ballroom.

"There is who?" Juliana asked.

"Lord Malmsey." A frown marred Amanda's newly flawless complexion. Apparently questioning Juliana's plan, she turned to her surrogate chaperone. "Should I dance with him, Lady Frances?"

Unaware that Amanda was engaged to him, Aunt Frances patted her hand. "I expect someone younger would suit you better, my dear. But if you've already been introduced, of course you should dance with him if he asks."

Juliana doubted Lord Malmsey would ask—although if she could judge by the man's pained expression, he was attempting to screw up his courage. Figuring ten seconds in his arms would cure Amanda's second thoughts, she laid a gentle hand on her friend's back. "You definitely should dance with him," she declared, subtly steering her protégé toward her ill-chosen fiancé. "It would be the polite thing, after all. And after that, we'll see about having Aunt Frances introduce you to some more-promising men."

Lord Malmsey's eyes widened as they approached, and Juliana saw him swallow hard. Taking pity on the poor man, she smiled when they drew near. "Lady

Amanda was just telling me she hoped you'd ask her to dance."

"Very well," he said. Amanda said nothing. The strains of a waltz rose into the air, and the two of them walked off.

Or rather, they shuffled off. Frances joined Juliana and watched them face each other and begin dancing. "They don't seem a proper match."

"No, they don't," Juliana agreed. She'd never seen a more awkward couple. Due to Amanda's height, she and Lord Malmsey danced eye to eye. But beneath his high, creased forehead, Lord Malmsey's gaze looked shy and hooded, flicking only briefly toward his fiancée. Amanda looked utterly despondent.

On the other side of the ballroom, Juliana spotted Lord Neville ambling out of the refreshment room. "Wait here," she told Frances. "I see Emily's father, and he rarely stays long at any ball." Since the man had two heirs and no plans to take a fourth wife, he spent his evenings with various mistresses or gambling at his club. "I simply *must* speak to him about that snake before he leaves. It will take but a moment, and then as soon as Amanda is finished dancing, we'll find some men who are more suitable."

What a lucky thing Aunt Frances had her head perpetually in the clouds. Amanda's own aunt would have been unlikely to cooperate with undermining her father's plans, Juliana thought as she made a beeline for Viscount Neville.

"Lord Neville, if I may speak with you for a moment?"

"Ah, yes, my dear, of course." Emily's father was blond and gray-eyed like his daughter, tall and a bit hefty—not fat, but a big man. As he seemed to overindulge in everything, Juliana wasn't surprised to see a plate in his hand, filled with a variety of morsels from the refreshment room. He took a hearty bite of a biscuit. "What can I do to help you?"

"It's about Emily—"

"Ah, yes. I do appreciate the interest you've taken in my girl."

"She's a delight." Juliana smiled as he swallowed the

biscuit and followed it with a grape. "But I'm wondering if I can prevail on you to discourage her from taking Herman out in public. It's not the thing for a young lady to carry a snake."

"Ah, yes," he repeated. "But my Emily is very attached to Herman. She and her mother found him in the garden the very day before my wife died." He plucked three more grapes off the bunch and popped them into his mouth.

"I'm aware of that, sir. But earlier this week when we visited the shops, a patron at Grafton House fainted dead away at the sight of Emily's snake." While that wasn't quite true, it *could* have been true. A number of customers at Grafton House had been horrified, not to mention the poor seamstress, Mrs. Huntley. "If only you'd heard the shrieks of dismay, Lord Neville. It was not the sort of scene a young lady should inspire."

Apparently the viscount found that more amusing than distressing, because he laughed.

And then he stopped.

In fact, not only had he stopped laughing, it looked as though he'd stopped breathing as well. The plate dropped from his hands, shattering on the parquet floor as he clutched at his throat and chest. His mouth was open, but he seemed unable to speak. His skin was turning blue.

"Dear heavens!" Juliana exclaimed loudly enough to have the people nearby looking over. "Lord Neville, are you all right?"

Clearly he wasn't.

"Help!" she yelled, moving to thump him on the back, the way everyone seemed to do when someone swallowed the wrong way and went into a coughing fit. But he couldn't even seem to cough. His eyes bugged out in his blue face, panicked.

Just then, Griffin ran up with his friend Lord Stafford in tow. "A chair," Lord Stafford instructed. "Now."

Griffin rushed to do his bidding. In the meantime, Lord Stafford very quickly—and rather calmly, under the circumstances—untied the viscount's cravat and loosened the buttons at his throat. All the while, he murmured soothing words in the same smooth, chocolatey voice that had weakened Juliana's knees when they danced together last week.

But Lord Neville did not look soothed. In fact, Juliana feared he might die right there on the spot. Lord Stafford didn't seem to think so, though. Decidedly *un*-panicked, he continued to murmur calmly while he waited for Griffin to bring him the chair.

She couldn't imagine why Lord Stafford wanted a chair, but when it appeared a moment later, he plunked it down in front of the viscount and shoved the man's big body to lean over the back. Quickly, again and again. After several thrusts, an intact red grape shot out of Lord Neville's mouth and landed at Juliana's feet.

The viscount took several gasping, gulping breaths while Lord Stafford moved the chair around and helped the man lower himself onto it. Lord Neville slumped there, the color returning to his face while he breathed deeply, as though the simple act of drawing air was the most satisfying thing he'd ever done.

Juliana released a long sigh of relief, in concert with several other people who had become riveted by the emergency.

"You saved his life," she told Lord Stafford, impressed. After all, she was a woman intent on helping others, and Lord Stafford clearly did the same. But rather than acknowledge her compliment, he only shrugged and crouched down by Lord Neville, asking to have a look in his throat.

Supposing now was not the time to press Lord Neville about his daughter's snake, Juliana turned to see how Amanda was faring on the dance floor. But apparently the waltz had ended sometime during the excitement. A quadrille was playing instead, and Amanda was nowhere to be seen.

"I told you Lord Stafford was a good man," Griffin said beside her.

She glanced at the man, who was now examining the back of Lord Neville's throat through a silver quizzing glass attached to a chain around his neck. His dark, tousled curls flopped over his forehead.

"He saved the viscount's life," Griffin added.

"That's his job," she snapped. Lord Stafford's quick,

impressive actions didn't mitigate his shortcomings. He was *not* what she was looking for in a husband. "Where in heaven's name is Amanda?"

"Right there," Griffin said, gesturing toward a cluster of men across the room.

If Amanda hadn't been tall enough that Juliana could glimpse the blond curls piled on her head, she would never have believed it. And to think she had fretted earlier concerning Amanda's ability to attract suitors. Her worries had proved to be groundless.

The trifle was clearly working.

By all appearances, Amanda hadn't needed Aunt Frances to make any introductions. She was completely surrounded by men. Old men, young men, and men in between. Even Lord Malmsey was there. He stood at the edge of the clutch of admirers, looking somewhat disconcerted to find his betrothed suddenly commanding so much attention.

Juliana made her way over and wormed her way into the crowd. She touched Amanda on the arm, and when Amanda glanced down, she whispered, "The look." Obviously flustered by her new popularity, Amanda appeared nonplussed for a moment, but quickly smiled one of the smiles Juliana had made her practice over and over, then chose a man and flirted through her newly darkened lashes.

"Would you honor me with a dance?" he asked immediately.

"With pleasure, my lord," Amanda said, just as Juliana had taught her. As she went off on the man's arm, she glanced back to meet Juliana's gaze, her own eyes filled with wonder. "They're falling at my feet," she mouthed silently.

Of course they were. Hadn't Juliana told her that would happen?

It looked as though they'd be able to find a man willing to compromise Amanda, after all. Now all Juliana had to do was find the *right* man—a man who would make her friend happy.

At least a dozen men were showing keen interest in Amanda. The fact that Juliana herself had rejected each and every one of them had no bearing whatsoever. She and Amanda were very different women, with very different requirements in a husband. And half of the dozen men met Amanda's foremost requirement—that is, they were young men, or significantly younger than Lord Malmsey, at least.

One of them ought to do just fine.

Without Amanda at the center of it, the group slowly dispersed. But Lord Malmsey still stood there, gazing toward the dance floor dejectedly. Although Juliana didn't know him well, he'd always seemed a kindly man. If he wasn't precisely handsome, at least he was pleasant-looking, even now, with his mouth set in a straight line. But his pale green eyes seemed haunted.

Quite suddenly, Juliana realized there was a flaw in her perfect plan. In seeing to Amanda's happiness, she was making Lord Malmsey *un*happy. And that would never do.

"What are you plotting now, Juliana?"

She looked over to see Corinna and Alexandra. "Nothing," she told them both.

"I recognize that look on your face," Alexandra said.

Juliana never had been able to fool her older sister. "Oh, very well," she admitted. "I am trying to find a match for Lord Malmsey."

Looking startled, Corinna glanced to the melancholy man and back. "Holy Hannah, what put that thought into your head?"

Juliana had no answer for that—at least no answer that wouldn't reveal her friend's predicament.

"Something is going on." Corinna narrowed her eyes. "Something to do with Amanda."

Juliana sighed. She should have known Corinna would weasel the truth out of her one way or another. "Can you keep a secret?"

"Of course we can," Alexandra said, looking a little hurt. "Have we broken a confidence ever?"

Well, no, neither of them had. Not to Juliana's knowledge, anyway. She leaned in closer and lowered her voice. "Amanda's father has betrothed her to Lord Malmsey."

"I knew it!" Corinna exclaimed at the same time Alexandra said, "That's dreadful."

"Quite. Amanda is understandably upset, but Lord Wolverston will hear nothing of it. He has told her that if she refuses to go through with the wedding, he will disinherit her."

Corinna gasped. "Then no one else will *ever* offer for her." Of the three of them, she always *had* been the most blunt.

"Precisely," Juliana said. "Which is why I am engaged in helping Amanda entice a younger man, in the hopes that he will offer for her before it is too late." While that wasn't the complete plan, it was close enough. She wasn't about to admit that they'd also have to persuade the man to publicly compromise her friend in order to force Lord Wolverston's hand. "But I cannot find love for Amanda at Lord Malmsey's expense. That would be terribly unfair."

"Juliana always wants to see *everyone* happy," Alexandra reminded their sister.

"In all his many years," Corinna pointed out, "Lord Malmsey has never proposed to anyone before Amanda. He's too shy to approach another woman."

"Then a shy spinster will be a perfect match." Juliana's gaze wandered the ballroom. Miss Hartshorn was too old; Lady Sarah Ballister was too young; Miss Ashton was entirely too outgoing. She scanned past her chaperone, then back. "Aunt Frances," she said, nodding to herself with more than a little satisfaction.

"Aunt Frances?" Corinna's brilliant blue eyes widened. "You're thinking to match *Aunt Frances* with Lord Malmsey?"

Alexandra frowned toward their aunt, no doubt considering her spectacles and unstylish gray hair. "I've never seen Aunt Frances show romantic interest in a man."

"That's only because no man has ever shown an interest in her," Juliana said. "And that will all change when she receives Lord Malmsey's love letter."

"What love letter?" Alexandra and Corinna asked in unison.

Juliana shook her head. "The one I'm going to write, of course."

Her sisters simply had no imagination.

She suddenly spotted one of their cousins, looking lost. "Rachael!" she called with a wave, starting toward her.

Corinna grabbed her arm. "Are you plotting something else?"

"Of course not," Juliana said, although she hoped to get her brother to dance with her cousin. Rachael and Griffin belonged together, but Rachael had seemed a bit down lately and hadn't attended many events, which had hampered Juliana's efforts to match them. "I just want to invite Rachael, Claire, and Elizabeth to my next sewing party."

Chapter Nine

Wary of Juliana's grin, Griffin watched her heading his way with their gorgeous cousin.

"Griffin," she said, stopping in front of him. "Rachael would love to dance with you."

Rachael's sky blue eyes narrowed, making Griffin suspect she found Juliana's statement as preposterous as he did. An awkward moment passed while he shifted uncomfortably. "I would be honored, Lady Rachael," he said at last, "if you would join me for the next dance."

"Splendid." Juliana smiled as a waltz began. "Please excuse me," she said, waving them toward the dance floor. "I must speak with Alexandra."

"She was just speaking with Alexandra," Rachael informed him as they started waltzing. "Do you always allow your sisters to run roughshod over you?"

Griffin refused to take offense at her question. For one thing, she felt entirely too good in his arms—which was completely inappropriate—and for another, the remark was made with good humor. "Only Juliana," he told her lightly.

"Like hell," she said. Rachael could curse like a sailor, but he considered that part of her charm. "Alexandra and Corinna know how to play you equally as well."

Since he couldn't really argue, he twirled her and changed the subject. "You've been hiding this Season."

The good humor vanished, replaced by a melancholy air. Even the chestnut tendrils around her face seemed to droop. "I haven't felt much like mingling."

She didn't have to say why. Griffin knew—although his sisters didn't—that Rachael had been dealt a blow several months earlier when she'd learned the man she'd called "Papa" since birth hadn't actually been her father.

"It doesn't signify," he said quietly.

"It signifies to me. I feel like my life has been a lie."

"Has something changed at home? Is Noah treating you differently? Or Claire or Elizabeth?"

"No. Not at all. But I feel as though they should."

"You still all shared a mother. They're still your brother and sisters."

She sighed, obviously shaken. "I know." Her eyes grew suspiciously moist, making him fear that her chin—her adorable, dented chin—might begin to wobble next.

And Griffin found himself wanting to help her.

The entire affair was none of his business. God knew he already had enough on his plate between running a marquessate and marrying off his sisters. But Rachael was young and beautiful. She should be enjoying herself, searching for a husband, falling in love. She was his cousin—in name, if not by blood—and he wanted to see her happy.

The haunted look in her cerulean eyes caused a tightness in his chest.

"Do you want me to help you find your father?" he asked.

"No," she said unequivocally. "He's dead." The music ended, and she drew away from him and dipped into a curtsy. "Thank you, Lord Cainewood," she said, not meeting his eyes. Before he could protest that, whether her father was dead or not, learning his identity might afford her some peace, she walked away.

Her curtsy had been way too formal, given their shared childhood. But Griffin decided it was for the best. He shouldn't have offered to help her anyway—he always found himself clenching his teeth when she was around. The last thing he needed was a woman like Rachael complicating his life.

As he made his way from the dance floor, the Duke

of Castleton walked up. "When are you going to sell me Velocity?"

Grateful for the distraction, Griffin laughed. "Never. When are you going to give up asking?"

"Never." Although Castleton gave a determined nod, not a hair on his carefully coiffed blond head moved. "I heard he made a good showing at Ascot."

"A pity you missed the meet," Griffin said, remembering Juliana preferred fair men. "You've a fine stable, Castleton."

"It would be finer with Velocity."

"Velocity—as I've told you at least a dozen times—is not for sale." Considering the subject closed, Griffin gestured across the room. "I say, would you care to meet my sister Juliana?"

Everyone who was anyone was at Lady Hammersmithe's ball. Including Cornelia Trevor, the Countess of Stafford—James's mother—and her older sisters, Aurelia and Bedelia.

In the refreshment room, James handed them all glasses of champagne. "How is your throat, Aunt Bedelia?"

"Better. But my chest has been paining me." She put a narrow hand to her flat bosom—Bedelia was as skinny as a rail. "Perhaps you should stop by Monday morning and have a listen to my heart with your new stethoscope."

James sipped champagne, doing his best to appear concerned. "Perhaps I will do that."

"Certainly you will," his mother said, but she softened that with a smile that reached her brown eyes. Besides sharing James's eyes, she had the same dark hair, and he thought, not for the first time, that she was still very attractive for a woman of her years. Aurelia might be a mite plump, and Bedelia a bit too thin, but Cornelia was perfectly in between. "Have you enjoyed the dancing this evening?" she asked him.

"Am I supposed to?" he responded dryly. "I thought marriage was the object, not enjoyment."

"Grandchildren are the object," Aurelia put in. "And grandnephews and grandnieces."

He'd thought as much. But he couldn't imagine marrying any of the women he'd danced with tonight, let alone siring offspring with any of them. Try as he might—and he *was* trying, for his mother's sake if not his own—he feared he couldn't imagine marrying at all. Because he'd had love and marriage once, now one without the other—marriage without the love—just seemed plain . . . impossible.

And loving a woman besides Anne was unthinkable. Just considering it felt disrespectful, as though he would be desecrating Anne's memory.

Not that she'd have objected, mind you. Anne had been generous and giving. She'd not have wanted him to be unhappy or lonely all his life. If he'd asked her permission—which he hadn't, of course—she would certainly have said he could fall in love with someone else after she was gone.

But that wasn't going to happen. Whenever he'd danced with a lady tonight, Anne's serious, loyal face had seemed to shimmer before his eyes.

"I only want you to be happy," his mother said.

"I know." He knew, too, that she understood how he felt. Or at least she should. She'd also loved and lost a spouse. "Why aren't *you* dancing, Mother?"

"Me?"

Perhaps if he turned the tables, she might realize she was pushing too hard. That he wasn't yet ready. "Yes, you."

Aurelia and Bedelia tittered. Maybe it was the champagne, but he thought not.

"What?" he said, turning to confront them. "Father has been gone longer than Anne. And your husbands have been gone even longer. All three of you should be dancing."

The sisters exchanged startled glances. "We're too old," Aurelia said for all of them.

"Nonsense." Aurelia and Bedelia were well into their sixties, but his mother was only fifty-six. He put down his champagne, then took their three glasses and set them down, too. "You're not going to find new husbands while standing around the refreshment table. Come along."

Grabbing his mother's hand, he drew her toward the ballroom, trusting her sisters to follow. After all, the three of them stuck together as tightly as a bandage to a wound.

His profession required prescribing medicine . . . perhaps it was time they got a taste of their own.

Chapter Ten

While Amanda was off dancing with her fourth or fifth potential suitor, and Juliana was inviting—well, perhaps begging—Rachael's two sisters to attend her little sewing party tomorrow, Griffin brought a strange man to meet her.

Not that he was actually *strange*, mind you. But he was definitely a stranger. Which Juliana found intriguing, because, honestly, she'd thought she had met every eligible man who'd bothered to come to town this Season.

"My sister," Griffin said by way of introduction. "Lady Juliana."

The man was handsome, fair-haired, and not too tall. Juliana smiled and curtsied.

"Juliana, I would be pleased for you to meet David Harcourt, the Duke of Castleton."

A duke! Handsome, fair-haired, not too tall, *and* wealthy and well connected. Juliana's heart fluttered with excitement as the duke bowed over her hand. "Would you honor me with a dance, Lady Juliana?"

"It would be my pleasure," she said and let him lead her onto the floor.

The duke's dress and bearing were both impeccable, and he proved to be a fine dancer. "Where have you been all Season?" she asked.

"Abroad, seeing to some of my interests now that the war with France has come to an end."

"Ah." Though he wasn't holding her very closely, she could smell his costly eau de cologne. "All your many interests keep you busy, then?"

"Not usually." He had calm, pale blue eyes. "It's been years since I've been overseas. I much prefer to stay here in town and fill my life with amusements."

No profession, nothing to keep him from spending lots of time with her. His blond hair was neatly groomed—unlike tousled Lord Stafford, he obviously had time to tend to it. He was sounding better and better. Perfect, as a matter of fact.

"I adore being amused," she told him and gave him *the look*.

Unfortunately, he did not fall at her feet. In fact, he appeared rather discomfited. "It was cold on the Continent," he said, as though she hadn't just tried to attract him.

So he was proper and reserved. She supposed she could deal with that. "As cold as it's been here?"

"Not quite. And certainly not as rainy."

"It *snowed* this month. In June!"

"Amazing, isn't it?"

"Yes, amazing."

Not exactly scintillating conversation, but then, they didn't know each other yet. There would be plenty of time later to speak of deeper things, Juliana told herself.

When the dance ended, the duke quite properly delivered her back to her brother.

"Well?" Griffin asked after the man had bowed and walked away. "I suppose you want me to keep looking?"

"To the contrary," she said. "I expect it's very likely that no more introductions will be necessary. How old is the duke? Do you know?" He didn't *look* terribly ancient, but most of the dukes she knew were in their dotage.

"You're not dismissing him out of hand?" Griffin looked vastly surprised—and pleased, not to mention relieved. "I believe he is thirty-two."

While she'd prefer a man in his twenties—she was searching for love, not early widowhood—thirty-two was not so very old. The man appeared more ideal by the moment.

A deep voice interrupted her musings. "Good evening, Lady Juliana."

She glanced over to see Lord Stafford. "Good evening," she returned.

"Cainewood," he said, addressing Griffin, "you wouldn't happen to know any aging widowers, would you?"

"Looking for more patients, Stafford? Old ones, with many ailments?"

"No." He gestured toward three mature women standing in a tight cluster. "I'm looking for dance partners for my mother and her sisters, Lady Avonleigh and Lady Balmforth."

"Dance partners?" Juliana asked, her interest piqued. "Or possible suitors?"

"My sister fancies herself a matchmaker," Griffin explained.

"I do not," she retorted. "I simply try to help people, make them happy."

"A noble endeavor," Lord Stafford assured her. "However, I am not looking for husbands for my mother and aunts. Dance partners will do."

Lord Malmsey came to mind, but although he was too old for Amanda, he was too young for Lord Stafford's mother. And besides, she'd already decided he belonged with Aunt Frances.

"May I borrow your quizzing glass?" she asked.

Instead of taking it off, Lord Stafford handed it to her with the long chain still around his neck. She leaned closer to raise it to her left eye. He smelled not of costly eau de cologne but something closer to soap.

Very male soap.

A quick scan of the room through the quizzing glass revealed a few likely dance partners for his relations, and she wasted no time corralling them and introducing them to the three women. Not five minutes later, she stood hip to hip with Lord Stafford, the two of them watching his mother and aunts perform a quadrille.

Or at least they would have been hip to hip had he not been so overly tall.

"That," Lord Stafford said, looking a little stunned, "was impressive."

Juliana shrugged, much the same as he had when she'd remarked that he'd saved Lord Neville's life. "I am good at what I do."

"You certainly are." The musicians finished the quadrille and struck up a lilting waltz. "May I have this dance?" he suddenly asked.

Although she would rather have danced again with the duke, it wouldn't be seemly to refuse. "It would be my pleasure."

When he took her hand, a peculiar flutter erupted in her middle. That had nothing to do with him, of course. It was just because everything was going so well. She'd found the duke, and Amanda had her pick of young suitors, and Lord Malmsey was going to fall head over heels for Aunt Frances. She might even be able to match Lord Stafford's mother and aunts with eligible widowers this Season, no matter that he only wanted them to dance. All of her projects were beginning to work.

No, that flutter had nothing to do with Lord Stafford. She had no interest in him whatsoever. In fact, he might well be the ideal man for Amanda. He was a doctor, after all, and Amanda wasn't sickened by blood. She would make him a good wife. And Amanda was tall, so the two of them would look excellent together.

And perhaps she, Juliana, would be a duchess! She could already picture herself walking down the aisle with the duke.

She glanced up to find Lord Stafford staring at her again, like he had last week when they'd danced. And again she found that unnerving. He seemed a very intense sort of man.

She racked her brain for something to say that would get him talking instead of staring. "I missed you at Almack's last Wednesday."

His chocolate eyes widened. "You missed me?"

She hadn't meant it like that. "You weren't there. Do you not like Almack's?"

James abhorred the very idea of the place—it was a veritable marriage mart, the men in attendance little more than targets for young girls and their scheming mamas—but he wouldn't say that to Juliana. "My mother obtained a voucher for me," he said instead, which was nothing less than the truth, "but there was trouble at the Institute that night, so I was unable to attend."

That was nothing less than the truth as well, although another truth was that he'd have found a different excuse to back out had that one not presented itself.

"How unfortunate," she said. "I hope the trouble wasn't too dreadful."

"A shortage of staff. I had to fill in myself, as well as interview new candidates."

"What sort of staff were you looking for? Did you find anyone?"

Given her inclination toward helping people, he wouldn't be surprised should she offer to find someone for him. "A young woman to act as an assistant. To keep the physicians well supplied and make sure the patients are seen as quickly and efficiently as possible. And yes, I found someone. I wouldn't be here tonight if I hadn't."

Her blue-green eyes narrowed. "You would work on a Saturday evening?"

"Smallpox doesn't know the day of the week; we must immunize as many as possible. And working people cannot visit during normal working hours. When I'm in town, New Hope is open from ten o'clock in the morning until ten o'clock at night, every day except Sunday."

Most shops kept the same hours, so he wondered why she looked so disapproving. And he wished she didn't. Because, truthfully, the more he saw of her, the more he liked her. She was so full of good intentions and the liveliness that had been missing from his life.

He realized, quite suddenly, that Anne's face wasn't shimmering before his eyes. In fact, he hadn't thought about Anne at all while dancing with Juliana. Not for the barest moment. Although Juliana couldn't be more different from Anne—his wife had been a very serious young lady—he could almost imagine marrying her.

Almost. But not quite. Because he'd have to fall in love with her first, and that wasn't going to happen.

Even should he someday feel ready to fall in love—

even should he someday manage to get over the notion that it would be too much of a betrayal—love would never happen with Juliana. She wasn't right for him, no matter how appealing he found her. Although she might be "good at what she did," what she did was entirely too frivolous for a man of his demeanor.

But she felt rather good in his arms. In the light from the chandeliers overhead, her hair gleamed, an intriguing mix of pale gold and light brown and every shade in between. And those blue-green-hazel eyes—he couldn't stop himself from staring at them, trying to figure out what color they were.

When the dance came to an end, he wasn't sure whether he was sorry or relieved.

"I have someone I'd like you to meet," she said.

He didn't want to meet anyone. He wanted to go home to Stafford House. Without his mother. Maybe she'd sleep at her sisters' town house tonight, the three of them giggling like young girls discussing their latest conquests. A man could hope.

No, she'd come home as always, probably vexed with him for making her dance with a man not her husband. That had been the whole idea, hadn't it? To make her realize grieving spouses didn't belong on the marriage mart?

"You don't mind, do you?" Juliana's enthusiastic voice snapped him back to attention. "Lady Amanda is really quite lovely."

Oh, yes, she wanted him to meet someone. Lady Amanda. Right. "I don't mind at all," he lied. "Where is this lovely lady?"

She shot him an unreadable glance before heading across the ballroom. "Follow me, Lord Stafford."

"James."

"Pardon?"

He watched her shapely, swaying bottom as he followed her. "My given name is James."

She slowed down until he caught up. "We scarcely know each other, Lord Stafford."

True. But he'd been thinking of her as Juliana practically since the moment they'd met. Not Lady Juliana, just Juliana.

Odd, that.

"We've danced together twice," he pointed out.

"That hardly makes us intimates."

Intimates. The word caused a vision to swim through his head. A very inappropriate vision, even though he'd already decided she was entirely too frivolous. "Just call me James," he snapped.

"Very well." She huffed out an impatient sigh and came to a stop before a clutch of men. "Come along," she said and pushed in.

A blond woman was in the center. A lovely blond woman. A lovely blond woman who caused no visions to swim through his head.

Juliana smiled. "Lord Stafford—James—this is Lady Amanda Wolverston. Amanda, Lord Stafford."

"Lady Amanda," he said with a proper bow. He wasn't tempted to call her just Amanda. Or even think of her as just Amanda. She was Lady Amanda through and through.

But Juliana was just Juliana.

This entire evening was proving most disconcerting.

"Lord Stafford," Lady Amanda returned formally. "I'm delighted to meet you."

She was lovely and delighted. Being a gentleman, he had to do the polite thing. "May I have the honor of the next dance?"

Lady Amanda smiled a lovely smile, though it looked a tad forced. "With pleasure, my lord," she said, not sounding as delighted as she claimed.

Juliana shot them both a grin.

At least someone was happy.

Lady Amanda was a fine dancer. But she didn't feel particularly good in his arms. Although she wasn't nearly as animated as Juliana, she chatted amiably enough, and she *was* quite lovely, but when the dance ended he wasn't sorry; he was only relieved.

Another man claimed her immediately. James's mother sidled near, breathless. "What a lovely girl."

"Yes. Did you enjoy your dance?" he asked, expecting to hear she hadn't. Expecting to hear she wasn't ready to think of men other than her departed husband. Expecting to hear her apologize for encouraging him to court women when he clearly wasn't ready, either.

"They were delightful," she said instead.

"They?"

"The dances. All three of them. And all three men. Aurelia and Bedelia thought one dance quite enough, so I danced with their men, too." She took both his hands in hers. "Thank you, my dear. I'll admit I thought the very idea was daft, but it's high time I resumed a social life, and I appreciate your little push."

He groaned. Silently, of course.

"I'm going to spend the night with Aurelia and Bedelia," she added, looking happier than he'd seen her in ages. "Good evening, dear. I'll see you tomorrow."

He certainly wanted her to be happy, he thought as she walked off, and he'd been wishing for a night home alone. So why did her news make him grit his teeth?

"Well, Stafford, you've certainly danced with your share of the ladies."

He turned to see Cainewood. "I'm finished," he said, relieved to be out from under Cornelia's watchful eye. But he wasn't ready to go home yet—suddenly *home alone* sounded lonely. "Can I interest you in a game of chess?"

"Chess? Haven't touched a board since I left the army." Cainewood sipped some of the concoction in his half-empty glass. "Sure. For how much?"

"You want to wager?"

"Afraid you're going to lose?" Grinning, he sipped again. "Ten guineas."

"Deal." The stake was steep—certainly much more than they'd ever bet in their schooldays—but James grinned in return. "Follow me," he said, leading his friend toward the card room.

He wasn't going to lose. Cainewood was looking a bit foxed.

"You're looking a little foxed, Cainewood."

Griffin looked up from the chessboard where he and Stafford were playing, to find Castleton standing over them. "I'm quite sober, I assure you," he told him, fascinated to hear a slur in his own voice. But just a bit of a slur, because he was just a bit foxed. Which was perfectly understandable, since he'd had much to celebrate this evening.

Juliana had finally—*finally*—found a man she wanted. This man right here.

He took a sip of the Regent's Punch in his glass, an inspired mix of six different spirits. "What do you think of my sister, Castleton?"

The duke shrugged. "She's a little lively."

"Yes, isn't that nice? Nothing like a lively young lady." Griffin blinked his eyes. Castleton looked a bit blurred. And a bit stiff. He wondered what his sister saw in the man. Castleton was a keen judge of horseflesh—a fine recommendation, to Griffin's mind—but surely Juliana cared little about that. She sat a mount well and certainly enjoyed riding up and down Rotten Row in Hyde Park, the fashionable place to see and be seen, but she'd never been a particularly horsey sort of girl.

Griffin supposed, however, that a lady might think Castleton handsome in a pale, pasty sort of way. And, oh, yes, he was a duke. There was that.

Hell, why did it matter why Juliana wanted him? The fact that she did was good enough.

"It's your turn," Stafford said.

"So it is." Griffin focused on the board—or at least tried to focus. He was losing, but what the hell. Life was too good at the moment to worry overmuch about a chess game or a few guineas. Pondering his strategy, he took another sip to celebrate. He'd never cared much for punch until tonight, but it was astonishingly good stuff.

He moved a rook and looked back up at Castleton. "I suppose you've come over to ask for permission to call on my sister?"

"Actually, I didn't. I was just sitting over there playing cards and noticed you looked foxed."

Castleton sounded a bit pompous and disapproving. The prig. Why again did Juliana like him? Oh, yes, he was a duke. And her reason didn't matter. Griffin wanted his sister to be happy—he wanted all of his sisters to be happy. If Juliana had her heart set on Castleton, he would do whatever it would take to see her marry the prig.

"Did you know," he said, noticing that slur again in a detached, amused sort of way, "that Velocity is part of Juliana's dowry?"

The horse wasn't, of course. Until now.

"You don't say," Castleton mused, suddenly looking much more lively himself. "I hadn't heard that."

Chapter Eleven

SHREWSBURY CAKES

> Beat half a pound of Butter to a fine cream, and put in the same weight of Flour, one Egg, a measure of grated loaf Sugar, and small spoons of Nutmeg and Cinnamon. Mix them into a paste, roll them thin, and cut them with a small glass or little tins, prick them, lay them on sheets of tin, and bake them in a slow oven. Serve spread with raspberry Jam if you wish.

> *Should you wish to convince someone of something, these cakes will do the trick.*
> —Helena Chase, Countess of Greystone, 1784

Despite having convinced her cousins to attend her party, Juliana had no more ladies sewing than last week. Corinna, while present today in the drawing room, was "involved" with her latest painting and refused to pick up a needle. Aunt Frances was at Amanda's house, visiting with Lady Mabel. And Sunday was the one day of the week Emily's father made sure to spend time with her.

Luckily, Rachael's mother had been artistic and had taught her girls to sew. Since they were sewing much faster—not to mention better—than last week's crew, Juliana was able to avoid panicking. And since Aunt Frances and Emily were missing, she took advantage of their absence to explain Amanda's situation to her cousins.

After hearing of Amanda's woes, Rachael sighed. But then her smile made Juliana hopeful she was becoming a little cheerier. "Well, you certainly were last night's Incomparable, Lady Amanda." Her needle flew in and out of the miniature coat she was making. "Were you enthralled by any particular gentleman?"

"Lord Stafford," Juliana answered for Amanda. "He is absolutely perfect."

"I'm not certain." Seated on the drawing room sofa between Rachael's younger sisters, Claire and Elizabeth, Amanda stitched as slowly and clumsily as ever. Juliana doubted she'd ever progress beyond blankets. Perhaps *this* blanket. "Lord Stafford *is* handsome," Amanda said.

"He's gorgeous," Corinna corrected from where she was painting by the picture window.

"Quite," Juliana agreed, reaching toward the platter of Shrewsbury cakes. She might not personally prefer James's dark looks, she thought as she spread raspberry jam on one of the sweets, but she couldn't argue with her sister's assessment.

"But I'm not struck by love," Amanda said, her stitches getting even shakier.

Fearing her friend might stab herself and bleed, Juliana pulled the needle from her hand and put the cake into it instead. "It might take a while," she said gently.

"Not everyone marries for love," Claire pointed out, her unusual amethyst gaze fastened on her expert handiwork.

Elizabeth reached for a spool of white thread. "Your parents didn't marry for love, did they, Juliana?"

"No," Juliana said. "And that was a big mistake."

"Not this again." Corinna frowned at her painting. "Our family was perfectly happy."

"Not Mama. She loved Father desperately, and he never returned her feelings." As Juliana had grown older and more aware, she'd found her mother's unrequited love painful to watch. "Although he gave her children, he never found any other use for her. Never spent time with her, never truly made her part of his life."

She wouldn't let that happen to her. Until she found

a man she loved—a man she knew loved her madly in return—she was determined to remain unwed.

"Mama's life wasn't that tragic," Corinna argued. "Amanda cannot afford to wait to fall deeply in love."

Claire nodded. "Her wedding is quickly approaching."

Perhaps they were right. Unfortunately, Amanda hadn't enough time to get to know Lord Stafford well. Juliana patted her friend's hand. "You might have to find someone you like a lot and marry him, then be struck by love later."

Amanda took a bite of cake and swallowed convulsively. "Grow into love, you mean?"

"Exactly." Juliana spread jam on another cake. "Lord Stafford is not only handsome, he's young and well-off."

"What are you looking for in a man?" Alexandra asked Amanda. "Besides appearance and status, that is. Looks fade, after all. Shared values and interests are much more important."

"Very true," Elizabeth said. They all deferred to Alexandra as the expert among them on marriage.

Amanda seemed to mull over that question a minute. "I would like a man who is interested in Roman antiquities."

Juliana looked up from the cake, startled. "Since when are you interested in Roman antiquities?"

"Since my father found the ruins on our property."

"Three years?"

"More or less. It's a fascinating subject."

"Hmm," Juliana said. While she suspected Amanda's interest had begun as a hopeless attempt to gain her father's favor, she supposed it might have transformed into a sincere fascination. After all, the girl had to find *something* to amuse herself during all those months and years stuck in the countryside.

However, she sincerely doubted James shared an interest in Roman antiquities. When would he have time to pursue it? The man couldn't even find a few minutes to comb his hair. "What else are you looking for in a husband?" she asked.

Amanda pondered the question a moment more. "I would like for him to play chess. If I'm to live away from Aunt Mabel, I'd like someone with whom to play chess."

Juliana doubted James had time for chess, either. Which was why she was surprised to hear Rachael say, "Lord Stafford definitely plays chess."

"However do you know that?" she asked.

Having finished sewing the coat, Rachael knotted the thread. "When Griffin came out of the card room last night, I overheard him saying he'd lost thirty guineas to Lord Stafford playing chess."

"Thirty guineas!" Although Juliana enjoyed a hand of cards now and then and certainly understood the appeal of a bet, she wasn't sure she approved of wagering significant sums. Surely that sort of money could be better spent elsewhere—donated to the Foundling Hospital, for instance. "I had no idea Griffin gambled such high stakes."

"I don't expect he usually does," Rachael said, looking amused. "He seemed a bit foxed, which isn't usual for him, either. In any case"—she smiled at Amanda—"Lord Stafford does enjoy chess."

Juliana jumped on that positive attribute. "See, there is more to him than appearance and status."

"He's also a physician," Claire reminded her.

"That, too. Which means he's intelligent and he cares for people."

"He limps," Amanda pointed out.

"Only slightly. And does it signify?"

"Indeed, it shouldn't." Corinna looked up from her easel. "He sounds like a paragon. Why don't *you* marry him, Juliana?"

"Don't be a goose. I'm being courted by a duke."

How quickly her dismal prospects had changed. Was it only yesterday she'd despaired of finding a husband? Not only had the duke danced with her *twice* at Lady Hammersmithe's ball—making brows rise and tongues wag—but toward the end of the evening he'd very kindly asked if he might pay her a call tomorrow afternoon.

She'd accepted, of course. She wasn't an idiot. There wasn't a man in London more perfect than the duke. Maybe she wasn't in love yet, but she was certain she would be soon.

"By the end of the Season, I may be the Duchess of Castleton."

Amanda's mouth dropped open. "You'd marry the Duke of Castleton?"

"Wouldn't you?"

"No!" She looked horrified at the mere idea. "Everyone knows he's a by-blow."

Everyone but Juliana, evidently. During all those Seasons she'd missed while in mourning, it seemed she'd also missed some fascinating gossip. "What do you mean?"

"It's an open secret," Rachael explained. "The previous duke was away for a year, looking after his interests on the Continent, when his wife conceived a child here in London. To this day, no one knows who sired the child. It really doesn't signify, though, since the last duke arrived home before the current duke was born and acknowledged him as his son."

"It signifies to me," Amanda disagreed. "Marriage to a known by-blow would taint my family."

"How?" Juliana asked. "He's a duke, for heaven's sake. His parentage hasn't affected his standing in society. He's accepted in the best circles."

"I'd never be certain of my children's true heritage. For all we know, the duke could have been fathered by a footman!"

"I cannot see why that makes a difference," Rachael said, "considering the last duke claimed him for a son."

"I'd never trust him to be true to me."

"Why would he be unfaithful?" Juliana wondered. "I imagine the last thing he'd want would be to subject his own children to the shame he's had to live with."

Amanda raised one of her newly plucked brows. "You know what they say: like father, like son."

"They also say the sins of the father shouldn't be visited on the child." Juliana felt sorry the man had been forced to grow up under this cloud. "The circumstances weren't any fault of his. He was a victim, not to blame. You're being entirely too judgmental."

But facts were facts, and the fact was that straitlaced Amanda would never consent to marry the duke. Of course, that didn't matter, since Juliana wanted him for herself. Amanda belonged with Lord Stafford.

Juliana handed her a second Shrewsbury cake, hoping

it would help convince her that James was the right man for her. That was why she'd risen at dawn this morning to bake them, after all—they were supposed to help convince people. "Did you meet any man you liked better than Lord Stafford?"

"No," Amanda said. "But there are many more men to meet."

"Not this Season. They seem to be staying home." Juliana smeared jam on a cake for herself. "I wonder if it's because of all the cold and wet."

"Now *you're* being a goose." Corinna swirled her brush in green paint. "I'm having a marvelous time this Season—there are plenty of eligible men."

Of course she was having a marvelous time. It was her first Season, and Griffin wasn't pressuring her to marry. Not yet, anyway. Juliana was supposed to wed first. "Don't tell me you've fallen in love."

"I'm not in any hurry." Corinna dabbed at her canvas, creating a grassy field out of nothing.

Juliana would never figure out how she did that. Feeling edgy, she rose and wandered closer to scrutinize the bucolic scene. A man and a woman walked hand in hand over rolling hills. Corinna never used to paint people—only landscapes and still lifes. But this past year she'd been adding people to her paintings more and more often. And not just any people. Lovers.

Maybe she *was* falling in love. "Are you sure?" Juliana asked.

"I don't have time to fall in love right now." Corinna added a dab of white to the green paint on her palette. "My art is more important. Next year, I plan to submit to the Royal Academy."

Juliana nearly choked on her cake. "No women have been elected to the Royal Academy for years."

"Forty-eight years, to be exact. Not since 1768." Corinna mixed the colors together, creating a lighter shade of green. "But I'm not expecting to be elected immediately. My first step is to submit several paintings for next year's Summer Exhibition, in the hopes that one will be selected."

It was a preposterous plan, but apparently the Shrewsbury cakes were somewhat effective, because Juliana was half convinced it might work. However, the cakes didn't seem to be affecting Amanda's view of James, and Juliana wasn't about to see her own project fail.

Although she knew she should resume sewing, she stepped to the window and gazed out at the unceasing rain. The trouble was, assuming the Shrewsbury cakes didn't work magic, there was only so much she could do herself. James would have to do the rest.

Obviously his good looks weren't enough to do the trick. Maybe she should coach him in the ways of wooing. After all, he was a man consumed by his avocation—with all the time he spent doctoring, perhaps he hadn't had the opportunity to acquire the sort of aristocratic polish necessary to win a lady like Amanda.

Of course, getting him to agree to such training could prove a delicate matter, since, in her experience, the male of the species was often reluctant to admit to any deficiency. But she would bring along some of the Shrewsbury cakes and hope they would help convince him.

She turned from the window, returning to her chair and the third of thirty frocks. New Hope Institute was closed on Sundays, but she would pay James a visit tomorrow.

Chapter Twelve

"What do you think of this dress, dear?" Sitting across from James at the breakfast table Monday morning, Cornelia held up her copy of *La Belle Assemblée*, open to one of the hand-colored fashion plates. "Shall I order something like it for the next ball?"

"It's lovely, Mother." Given that she hadn't shown any interest in clothes since his father died, James knew he should be pleased to see her enjoying life again. But instead he was rather annoyed that his plot to convince her to stop pressuring him had failed so miserably.

"I had a wonderful time dancing," she said for at least the dozenth time since the ball. The only respite he'd received from her happiness was the few hours she'd spent overnight with her sisters. She'd enjoyed that, too, to hear her tell of it. Aurelia and Bedelia's peach-ridden town house was near Oxford Street with all its shops. A perfect distance from his own mansion in St. James's Place—close enough for an easy visit but far enough that he didn't see his aunts every time he stepped out the door.

He folded the *Morning Chronicle* and set it carefully by his plate. "I have an idea, Mother."

"Hmm?" She flipped a page of her magazine.

"Why don't you move back in with your sisters? You could help them redecorate and get rid of some of that peach. I'm sure you'd enjoy that more than living here with me."

Cornelia hadn't always lived with him. When he'd returned to England following his years in the army and at medical school in Edinburgh, he'd established his own household. After his father's death, when James inherited Stafford House and the country estate that went along with his title, his mother had moved in with her widowed sisters, wishing not to intrude on his life with his wife. But then Anne died two years ago, and Cornelia came running back home to "help" him.

And there she'd stayed. For too long. He loved her dearly, but a man was entitled to some privacy and autonomy. He'd truly appreciated her "help" while he'd needed it, but he had long since recovered some semblance of a life, even if he didn't feel ready to fall in love and remarry.

"Don't be foolish, James. Should my sisters ever decide to redecorate, I can help them from here. Who would run this household if I abandoned you? Stafford House is one of the largest homes in London."

One thing he wasn't lacking was money. "I have a staff. And I can hire more people should I need to."

"That's not the same as having family oversee matters." She flipped another page, tilting her head to peruse the dress pictured. "I won't even think about moving out until you have a wife."

Yet another reason to marry. But he'd have to fall in love first, and that wasn't going to happen.

"Very well, then," he said. It was senseless to pursue this any longer. That would only cause hard feelings, and the last thing he wanted was to hurt his mother. "I must be off." He pushed back from the table and rose. "I wish you a pleasant day."

She looked up. "I trust you haven't forgotten that Bedelia is expecting you this morning?"

Damnation. He had. His mind had been on other things. Especially a hazel-eyed sprite he had no business thinking about.

Most annoying.

"I haven't time, I'm afraid." He shrugged into the tailcoat a footman held out. "Only one doctor volunteered today, so I must fill the other spot," he said, buttoning the coat. "I'm expected at the Institute by ten."

"The people can wait a little longer for their vaccinations. Bedelia has been suffering with chest pains."

"Bedelia is fine, Mother."

"I'm sure you're right." She paused for a sip of her tea. "But what if she isn't?"

"This doesn't look like a nice neighborhood," Aunt Frances said with a worried frown.

Reaching over the basket of Shrewsbury cakes on her lap, Juliana pulled the carriage's curtains closed. "It's perfectly safe, I assure you."

"Herman doesn't like the dark," Emily said, reopening them.

"Herman should have stayed home," Juliana told her. Aunt Frances was peering out the window again, looking even more nervous, so she reached into her reticule for something to distract her. "Here, Auntie. I forgot to give you this letter. It arrived in the morning mail."

Emily stroked Herman's olive green scales, for all the world like he was a real pet. "I never get letters."

"I never get letters, either." Eyes wide behind her spectacles, Aunt Frances broke the seal and held the paper up to the light. As she scanned the single page, she sucked in a breath. "Goodness gracious!"

Juliana stifled a smile. "What does it say, Auntie?"

Frances's cheeks were suddenly so rosy, she looked like she'd eaten an entire bowl of trifle. "It's a poem."

"A poem? Does it rhyme?"

Frances nodded violently.

"Who is it from?"

"I'm not at all certain. He didn't sign his name."

"How do you know it's a 'he,' then?" Emily asked. "It might be from a girl."

The older woman raised a hand to pat her modestly covered bosom. "He signed it"—her voice dropped conspiratorially—"*Your Secret Admirer.*"

"Oh, Aunt Frances! That's so romantic!" Juliana sneaked a glance out the window, wondering how much longer she could distract her. "Whoever he is, he must have been at Lady Hammersmithe's ball Saturday night and seen you in that beautiful brown dress."

Frances looked doubtful. "I've worn that dress dozens of times."

"Well, then, we must order you new ones, don't you think? Before next Saturday's ball."

Though she hadn't bought a new dress all Season—or for that matter, all decade—Frances nodded. "I suppose we must."

Juliana toyed with the handle of her basket, finding it harder and harder not to grin. To her vast relief, the carriage drew to a stop before a small, neat building with a sign that said NEW HOPE INSTITUTE.

The neighborhood hadn't improved, but her aunt no longer seemed to care. When a footman lowered the steps, she practically floated down to the street. Carrying the basket, Juliana climbed out after her, and Emily and Herman followed.

The door to the Institute opened, and a woman came out and down the steps, holding two children by the hand. The three of them were clothed rather poorly, but Aunt Frances didn't seem to notice. "What color dresses shall we order?" she asked Juliana.

"Pastels will look best with your golden-brown hair."

On the Institute's steps, Emily turned and frowned. "Her hair isn't brown."

Juliana smiled. "It will be after I summon Madame Bellefleur to dye it."

They all went inside. The reception area was noisy but looked very new and clean, especially compared to the people waiting there on the chairs. "A snake!" a boy exclaimed, and several children ran over to cluster around Emily and Herman.

A young woman with an air of authority walked out from behind a counter. She was dressed a little better than the patients, which wasn't saying much. "Twenty-three!" she called.

A mother stood up with a baby and followed her through a door into the back.

When the young woman returned to the counter and began adding some rather scary-looking supplies to the jumble already on the shelves, Juliana went over to her. She handed Juliana a worn square of paper with a big black "36" written on it. "You're number thirty-six," she said very slowly and clearly, as though Juliana couldn't read it for herself. "Please be seated. I will call you when it's your turn."

Juliana put the paper in her basket. "I wish to have a word with Lord Stafford, if I may."

"Lord Stafford?" The woman blinked. "Oh, you mean Dr. Trevor. He isn't here, milady."

Drat! Juliana hadn't even considered the possibility. "Do you know when he's expected?"

"I'm sorry, milady, but I don't. Only one doctor volunteered for today, so he should be here to vaccinate the other half of the patients. But his note said only that he'd be delayed—"

Just then the door opened, and in walked James, his coat and cravat draped over one arm. Even though he was scandalously undressed, Juliana couldn't have been more delighted. "Lord Stafford!" she exclaimed. "I'm so glad to see you!"

He looked shocked—and maybe pleased. "I'm glad to see you, too."

She hadn't meant it like that. "I thought you'd be here, but you weren't."

"I was examining my Aunt Bedelia. She's been suffering with imaginary chest pains."

"The poor, sweet lady." She paused, just realizing what he'd said. "Imaginary?"

"Aunt Bedelia is the healthiest woman I know. Except possibly Aunt Aurelia." Unfastening the top button of his shirt, he cleared his throat. "What can I do for you this fine afternoon?"

Frances suddenly turned to her. "I was wondering that myself. Why *are* we here, Juliana?"

The woman could be oblivious at times, but Juliana had found she could use that to her advantage. "Aunt Frances, have you met Lord Stafford?"

James offered Frances a bow. "Good afternoon, Lady Frances."

"Good afternoon, my lord." She looked at him sharply. "Did I see you at Lady Hammersmithe's ball?"

"I had the pleasure of attending, yes."

Frances's gaze grew more focused. At first Juliana assumed she was staring at the little V of exposed skin where James's shirt was unbuttoned, which Juliana found rather fascinating herself. Other than her brothers'—and they hardly counted—she'd never seen any part of a man's chest. Of course, her dress left much more of her own chest bare, but that was different. She had to force her eyes away from that intriguing bit of golden skin.

But then she realized Frances wasn't specifically looking at that little V, and, in fact, her blue eyes had turned speculative behind their lenses. Dear heavens, her aunt must be wondering if James was her secret admirer! How oblivious could the woman get? She'd have to write another love letter from Lord Malmsey and sign his name to it this time—before Aunt Frances set her hopes on someone much younger and better-looking.

A little gasp from James interrupted her thoughts. "Is that a *snake* in my reception room?"

Across the room, the children were still gathered around Herman, enthralled, while Emily, in her glory, proudly lectured them on his care and allowed them turns to touch.

Juliana smiled. "That's Viscount Neville's daughter, Miss Emily, and—"

"Get it out of here."

"No need to worry." The light in here was odd; James was looking rather pale. "It's perfectly harmless, Lord Stafford."

"James," he corrected distractedly. "And I want it out. It's frightening the children."

It was doing no such thing, but Juliana wasn't about to argue. She had much more important matters to discuss with him. "Aunt Frances, would you please take Emily and Herman outside?"

Frances was still gazing speculatively at James. "It's dreadfully cold out there," she said without taking her eyes off him.

"You can wait inside the carriage. I won't be long, I promise."

"The neighborhood—"

"The coachman and three footmen are there for your protection." Juliana took her aunt's arm and started easing her toward Emily. "You'll be safe. I'll be out in five minutes."

Her gaze no longer focused on James, Frances consulted the little watch pinned to her dress. "You'd better not take any more time. The Duke of Castleton is calling at half past two."

Following a short negotiation, Juliana finally shut the door behind Aunt Frances, Emily, Herman, and several children who refused to stay inside when there was a snake outside to admire. "Now, if I could just have a few moments of your time, Lord Stafford—"

"James," he interrupted.

"James." She looked around. "Is there someplace private we could speak?"

Wondering what she wanted of him, James led her to an empty treatment room. He also wondered why the thought of Castleton calling on her was so annoying. It must be because Castleton was so very wrong for her. The duke was a prig; she was much too lively for such a stuffy fellow. Not to mention the prig wanted her only because she came with a celebrated racehorse.

The treatment room held only a chair and a table with the necessary implements, but Juliana glanced around as though she found it interesting. She was wearing a dress with a very tiny bodice.

Well, in truth, it wasn't any tinier than the bodices other young ladies of her class wore—high-waisted dresses with low necklines were in fashion, after all—but he wasn't used to seeing women in fashionable dresses at the Institute. The women who came to the Institute generally wore very frumpy clothes. He wouldn't have noticed her tiny bodice at a ball, but here at the Institute it made him suddenly—uncomfortably—aware that he was alone in a room with an eligible young lady.

An eligible young lady he found entirely too attractive.

He left the door open.

"That child doesn't sound happy," she said, referring to the sobbing girl in the next room.

"Dr. Hanley will give her a sugar stick."

Sure enough, the sobbing stopped. Juliana smiled. "I love sweets." She handed him the small basket she was carrying. "I brought you these."

He lifted the number "36" on top and peered underneath. Appetizing scents of cinnamon and raspberry wafted out.

"They're Shrewsbury cakes," she said. "Chase ladies always bring sweets when we pay calls."

"People don't generally 'call' at the Institute."

"It's not in a very nice neighborhood," she allowed. "Why is that?"

"Those who live in nice neighborhoods are vaccinated by their own doctors. The patients we serve cannot afford to take a hackney coach to Mayfair."

"Oh," she said, looking abashed. "That does make perfect sense."

He offered her an amiable smile. "Have you been vaccinated?"

She glanced warily toward the instruments. "Actually, I was variolated as a small child, before Dr. Jenner invented vaccination."

Variolation was an older procedure, a method of taking pus from the pocks of someone suffering from smallpox and inoculating healthy people with it. James was both surprised and impressed that she knew the difference. Perhaps she wasn't quite as frivolous as he'd thought. "Where did you learn about Edward Jenner?"

"I do read newspapers and magazines, and not just to see the latest fashions. It was quite brilliant of him to figure out that giving people cowpox could keep them from getting smallpox." She glanced toward the instruments again. "I don't need a vaccination, do I?"

"Not if you were variolated. Smallpox variolation grants lifelong immunity. You're lucky you lived through it, though." Variolation usually caused only a mild case of smallpox, but about two patients in a hundred developed a severe case and died. Because those odds were much better than when one caught smallpox naturally—which carried a thirty percent risk of death—many well-informed upper-class parents did have their children variolated throughout most of the eighteenth century. But vaccination with cowpox was much safer.

Juliana looked relieved. "Were you variolated as a child?"

"No, but I was vaccinated while in the army. My commanding officer didn't want his men dying of smallpox." He set the basket on the table. "Can you enlighten me as to the nature of this unexpected call?"

"Try a Shrewsbury cake." She waited while he chose one and took a bite. "I was wondering what you thought of Lady Amanda."

He hadn't thought of Lady Amanda even once since Saturday's ball. "She's lovely," he said tactfully.

Juliana beamed. "I'm so glad you think so."

She was much more interesting than Lady Amanda. "That was delicious," he said, polishing off her cake.

"Have another." She reached into the basket and put one into his hand. "Do you expect you might wish to marry Lady Amanda?"

He nearly choked but managed to cover it with a cough. "I've only danced with her once," he pointed out.

"Quite true," she admitted. "I expect you'll want to court her for a while before making such a decision."

He didn't want to court her at all. But it wouldn't be very seemly to say that out loud, so instead he said, "Yes, one doesn't come to such a decision lightly."

The *yes* was a mistake. Juliana's lips curved in a delighted smile. "I'm so happy to hear that. I've been wondering, though . . . since you spend so much time here at the Institute, have you much practice at wooing ladies?"

"Practice?" What man needed practice at such a thing?

"I just thought that since you've been too busy to court many women, it might help if I give you a few lessons."

Lessons? "What sort of lessons?"

"Have another Shrewsbury cake, will you?" She shoved the basket toward him. "The lessons wouldn't be very strenuous, I assure you. I'm thinking you could simply accompany me on a few occasions, such as to the theater. I could show you the proper seats to purchase and what sort of refreshments to fetch for Lady Amanda during the intermission. And if we went riding in Hyde

Park, I could point out the popular places and you could practice being gallant."

James didn't know whether to be insulted or amused, but either way he was going to refuse her offer. Certainly he didn't need lessons in gallantry and wooing women.

He hadn't taken a third cake, so she selected one for him. "The lessons won't require too many outings," she added soothingly. "After all, if plans with you fill my calendar, I won't be available for the duke to pay court to me."

The cake halfway to his mouth, he froze. She thought she was offering him a favor, but actually, the opposite was true. If he played along, he'd be saving her from wasting her time with Castleton. She and the duke were extremely ill-suited. Nothing between the two of them could possibly work out.

So therefore, by agreeing to her "lessons," *he'd* be doing *her* a favor.

He did like helping people. It was very gallant.

"Fine," he said. "When shall our first outing be?"

She actually clapped her hands. "How about tomorrow? Are you needed here at the Institute?"

"I have two doctors scheduled from ten o'clock to four, and another two from four o'clock to ten."

"Excellent. We can visit the shops and select a few gifts for Lady Amanda."

Shops? He hated visiting shops. "I thought we were going to the theater."

"I have plans for tomorrow evening, so our lesson will have to be earlier. Shall we say after luncheon, at one o'clock?" She smiled sympathetically. "Worry not, James. We'll be done in plenty of time for Parliament. Choosing a few appropriate gifts shouldn't take very long at all."

Chapter Thirteen

Before the duke left on Monday afternoon, he'd asked if he might pay Juliana another call on Tuesday. Two calls in two days! Since she already had plans with James at one o'clock, she'd suggested noon.

Which is how it happened that, on Tuesday, as the duke was leaving and James was arriving, they crossed paths.

"Castleton," James said.

"Stafford," the duke returned. And with a stiff little bow, he left.

As the butler closed the door behind him, Juliana turned to James. "Do you not like the duke?"

He shrugged. "I do not know him very well. But he seems a bit stuffy."

She was about to disagree when Aunt Frances came down the stairs, her footfalls so light she seemed almost to be skipping. A piece of paper fluttered in one of her hands. "Juliana! You'll never *believe* what arrived in the morning mail!"

"What is it, Auntie?"

"Another love letter from my secret admirer. Only"— as she reached the foyer, she paused for dramatic effect—"his name is no longer a secret."

"Who is he?" Juliana crossed her fingers behind her back. "Is he anyone I know?"

"Oh, yes," Frances said. "It's Lord—" She cut off, finally noticing James.

Oblivious as always, Juliana thought.

Her aunt clutched the letter to her bosom, two rosy spots appearing on her cheeks. "Good afternoon, Lord Stafford."

"Good afternoon, Lady Frances."

"Who is your admirer, Auntie? Lord Stafford will keep your secret."

James nodded. "My lips are sealed."

Frances hesitated a moment more, but it was obvious she was dying to tell. She leaned closer to Juliana. "It's Lord Malmsey," she whispered, her lips curving in a thrilled smile that made her look ten years younger.

"Aunt Frances, how wonderful!"

"Isn't it, though?" Clearly Frances didn't mind Lord Malmsey's age or appearance. In fact, judging by her expression, one would think she'd been pining after the man for years. "I'm so glad you made plans to visit the shops this afternoon. I must order a few new dresses, and at least one must be ready by Saturday. Lord Malmsey indicated in his letter that he will be attending Lady Partridge's ball."

James cleared his throat.

"Yes?" Juliana asked.

"I thought we were going to quickly choose a gift?"

"Several gifts," she corrected. "You'll want an assortment so that you can give one to Lady Amanda every few days over the next two weeks."

"Several?" He didn't look happy. "What happens after two weeks?"

"We'll cross that bridge when we come to it." He'd indicated he needed a while to court Amanda before proposing marriage, but a fortnight would have to do. With Amanda's wedding approaching, they simply hadn't any more time. Juliana had high hopes he'd win Amanda's affections by then, and vice versa, because the three of them needed time to plot Amanda's public compromise before she was married to Lord Malmsey.

He still didn't look happy, though, and Juliana liked the people around her to be happy. "You won't mind if Aunt Frances orders a few dresses, will you? It shouldn't take long, and she'll be coming along in any case, to chaperone." Regardless of the fact that this outing with James wasn't romantic in any sense, it wouldn't do for the two of them to gad about town together unescorted.

Before James formulated an answer, a knock came at the door. The butler opened it. On the other side stood a footman in Neville livery with young Emily. And Herman, of course.

The pink parasol Emily was twirling clashed horribly with the olive green reptile. "Is it time to leave, Lady Juliana?"

James took a step back. "Don't tell me *she's* coming, too."

"I'm giving her lessons as well," Juliana explained. "In being more ladylike. An outing like this can be very instructional."

In the gray light of the rainy day, he looked pale. "Surely she won't be bringing that snake."

Emily stopped twirling. "If Herman doesn't go, I don't go."

"That's fine by me," James said.

He seemed unhappy again, so Juliana laid a hand on his arm. "James, do you not like children?"

He glanced down at her hand, and she snatched it away, appalled at herself. Her hand was gloved, and his arm was sleeved, but it still wasn't proper to be touching him.

And the look on his face was worrisome. Although she and Amanda had never discussed children, she was sure Amanda wanted some. Every woman did.

"Of course I like children," he said. "I vaccinate children every day at the Institute."

"Of course," she echoed, relieved. She should have realized that. "Amanda is good with children," she told him, remembering how well Amanda had handled Emily that day she'd bled. Motioning for him to follow, she stepped farther away from the little girl. "I know you're worried that some patrons of the shops might be upset by Emily's snake," she said quietly. "But that's the whole idea, don't you see? She needs to learn that it's not ladylike to carry a snake, and the only way that will happen is by demonstration. Once she's convinced that

Herman upsets people, she'll realize she should leave him at home."

"I see," he said tightly.

They headed outside to where James's carriage was waiting. It was splendid—all polished rosewood and rich green velvet—and the pair of matched bays drawing it looked to be prime horseflesh. Juliana meant to sit beside Aunt Frances, but somehow she ended up beside James instead. Aunt Frances sat opposite James, with Emily catercorner from him. When he squished himself into the corner, as far away from Juliana as possible, she supposed that was to make sure he wouldn't touch her inadvertently.

But then he kept touching her anyway.

During the drive to Pall Mall, he touched her three times on the arm, in the bare area between where her short puffed sleeve ended and her short white glove began. The touches were all accidental and innocent, of course, but the little jolt she felt every time was . . . well, not bothersome exactly, but disquieting. Or exciting in an odd sort of way.

Of course, she wasn't used to being touched by men. All those deaths in the family had kept her and Corinna from socializing for so long, she was certain she was the oldest unkissed woman in all of England.

Except for Amanda. And maybe Aunt Frances.

In any case, she had to assume she'd feel this way if she were touched by any man. Most especially if she were touched by the duke. In fact, she was certain the duke's touches would be even *more* exciting because, after all, he was the ideal man for her. But despite two social calls in two days, the duke hadn't touched her since they'd danced at the ball last Saturday night. And that had been over her clothes while they were both wearing gloves, which was quite different.

He hadn't touched her bare skin. He hadn't even kissed her gloved hand. He respected her too much to do any such thing.

He was as proper and reserved as Amanda, but certainly he wasn't stuffy.

Aunt Frances was so anxious to order her dresses, Juliana decided they should do that first. Mrs. Huntley sighed when she saw Emily and her snake again, but after all, Juliana and Amanda had ordered a *lot* of dresses, and no shopkeeper with half a brain would turn away that sort of business. So she pressed her thin lips together and pulled out her measuring tape.

"Sit over there, Emily," Juliana instructed, waving her toward where two chairs sat against a wall. "And James, you sit beside her. When you visit the shops with a lady, you must wait patiently until she is finished."

"I'll wait outside," he said.

"You shouldn't do that if you wish to please Lady Amanda. A man should appear interested in a lady's purchases."

"I'll keep that in mind," he said, heading toward the door.

"It's raining out there," she reminded him.

"I won't melt."

True to his word, James didn't melt. It took so long to order Aunt Frances's dresses that it had stopped raining by the time the ladies joined him outside. And he certainly didn't look melted—in fact, he looked a little stiff.

Well, even if it wasn't raining, it still was quite cold.

"Where to now?" he asked dourly.

"I believe you should send Lady Amanda some flowers." Juliana indicated a florist's shop across the street, and they all started toward it.

"What sort?" he asked, sounding resigned.

"Red roses," Emily suggested beside him. "My mother loved red roses."

"Red roses it is, then." He crossed to Juliana's other side and took her left arm. When she glanced up at him, startled, he said, "A gentleman should escort a lady across the street."

"Excellent," she said, pleased with his progress. "That is very gallant. But I don't think red roses would be appropriate. They symbolize love, and it's a little too soon for that. You wouldn't want to appear too forward. Pink or yellow would be perfect."

James's arm felt tense beneath hers, and she was aware of their contact all the way into the shop. She guessed Amanda would find that awareness very plea-

surable, which would help James persuade her to
marry him.

When they entered, a woman shrieked and ran past
them out the door. Three other patrons left directly,
muttering to one another.

The florist was a tall, thin man with a long, narrow
nose and eyes that looked hard as he glared at Emily.
"Take that snake outside, young lady."

Emily stroked Herman. "Snakes don't eat flowers, Mr.
Flower-Man. Only frogs and mice."

Aunt Frances took Emily outside, and James ordered
an arrangement of two dozen pink roses. Quickly.

Back outdoors, the people walking along Pall Mall
were giving Emily and Herman a wide berth, and there
was a lot of "Well!" and "I never!" to be heard.

"She should have left that snake at home," James
said.

"She will next time, I'm sure." Juliana offered him
her left arm again, thinking some more practice in escorting ladies might be appropriate.

"Where are we going now?" Emily asked beside him.

He crossed to Juliana's other side and took her right
arm instead.

Juliana thought he seemed a little impatient. "Harding, Howell, and Company," she decided. Down the
street just a bit, Harding, Howell & Company was a big
department store that took up all the floors of an old
mansion that used to be called Schomberg House. Perhaps James would be happier if they could find the rest
of Amanda's presents all in one place. "You don't enjoy
shops very much, do you?" she asked as they started
walking toward it.

"I'm a man," he said.

She'd noticed. She'd walked arm in arm with women
before, but it had never felt like this. The tingly sensation rather stole one's breath. Amanda was going to
love it.

Aunt Frances and Emily walked in front of them, the
two of them getting more and more ahead. People were
crossing the street to avoid them. "We should catch up
to them," Juliana said.

James didn't change his pace. "I believe a gentleman

should walk leisurely with a lady, to accommodate her shorter stride."

"That is considerate," she allowed. "You really are quite an apt pupil, James."

Amanda was going to fall in love with him for certain.

"I'm famished," Emily announced the moment they stepped through Harding, Howell & Company's grand mahogany double doors. "May we visit Mr. Cosway's Breakfast Room?"

"It's not breakfast time," James said, "and, in fact, it's past luncheon."

Juliana laughed. "Mr. Cosway's Breakfast Room serves refreshments all day long." Located on the floor above, the restaurant offered wines, teas, coffee, and sweetmeats. "Have you never been here before, James?"

"I'm a man," he said.

The department store *was* patronized mostly by women. Juliana hadn't ever noticed that before, but she did now. Especially because a good number of the women were emitting little squeals and hiding behind the delicate pieces of furniture that were for sale.

Emily started up the wide staircase with Herman and Aunt Frances. When Juliana went to follow them, James held her back. "She really should leave that snake at home," he said once Emily was far enough ahead of them to be out of earshot.

Juliana was getting a bit tired of hearing that. "Are you hungry?" she asked.

"I'm a man," he said, and she laughed.

He really *was* quite a man.

Upstairs, Mr. Cosway's Breakfast Room had a glorious view over St. James's Park to Westminster and the Surrey hills beyond. Aunt Frances and Emily were already seated across from each other at a table for four. Juliana slid into the chair beside Aunt Frances, but James just stood there, more frozen than the ice cream in the restaurant's glass display case.

And that's when Juliana realized he didn't want to sit beside Emily. Or walk beside Emily. Or have anything to do with Emily at all—at least not while she was holding a snake.

Though it wasn't very kind or ladylike, Juliana couldn't help herself. A little smile quirked on her lips. A tiny giggle escaped. And finally—inevitably—she burst out laughing.

Chapter Fourteen

"You-you-you're afraid of Emily's snake," Juliana chortled. "Don't tell me you're not."

James felt heat creep up his neck and into his face. He'd never seen a woman quite so consumed by hilarity. It was humiliating.

Every diner in Mr. Cosway's Breakfast Room was staring at them, and he wasn't sure whether that was because of Emily's snake or Juliana's laughter. Either way, it was humiliating, possibly the most humiliating moment of his life.

Juliana thought him laughable.

But he couldn't deny her accusation. "Deathly afraid," he confirmed with as much dignity as he could muster. "I was bitten by an adder at the age of seven."

"Oh, my," Juliana said. Her peals of laughter dwindled to giggles as she apparently tried to control herself. "That must have been dreadful."

"Very. It was quite painful, and my ankle swelled up horridly, and I was consumed by fever." He had also cast up his accounts several times, but he wouldn't say so in the presence of ladies. "I should never want to experience that again," he added, eyeing the damned snake with contempt.

"But Herman isn't an adder," Emily said, stroking the terrorizing creature with gentle fingers. "He's a harmless grass snake. He doesn't have any poison, and he doesn't bite."

James knew that. He was well aware that adders were the only venomous snakes in England, and Herman was quite obviously not an adder. Herman was longer and more slender than an adder and had different markings on his back. James knew his fear was irrational.

But irrational as it was—and he was cognizant of the fact that, in the twenty-two years since he'd been bitten, his fear had expanded beyond all proportion to the incident—he couldn't bring himself to get close to Herman or any other snake.

Even now, though he was standing a good six feet away, the sight of Herman made his pulse feel thready and his guts clench. If he got any closer, he feared he might cast up his accounts right here in Harding, Howell & Company's froufrou little restaurant.

Juliana was no longer laughing. Instead, she was watching him very closely, so closely he was half convinced she could see right into him, see his churning stomach and his racing heart. See just how pathetic a man he was, a man too pathetic to conquer his fear of a simple grass snake.

Still watching him, she suddenly pushed back from the table. "I've just realized I'm not hungry."

"But I am," Emily said.

Juliana turned to her with a bright smile. "You can stay here with Aunt Frances while Lord Stafford and I find a few gifts for Lady Amanda."

Lady Frances began rising. "You and Lord Stafford cannot go off alone."

"Of course we can." Juliana eased her aunt back onto the chair. "We're in a public place, surrounded by dozens of people. We'll be back in a few minutes." And with that, before Lady Frances could voice another protest, Juliana placed her arm in James's and headed out of Mr. Cosway's Breakfast Room.

James wasn't certain, but he thought Juliana might have just saved him from complete humiliation. In any case, she'd definitely saved him from losing his luncheon. His stomach was feeling better already, and his pulse had gone back to normal.

"Thank you," he said as they headed down the staircase. "You must think me an utter coward."

"Don't be silly. We all have our fears."

He doubted that. "What is yours, then?"

"Blood," she said without hesitation. "I would make a terrible doctor. And unlike you, I don't even have a reason for my fear. No traumatizing bloody events in my childhood."

She laughed, but this time it was at herself, not him. Which made all the difference.

Which made him like her even more.

"Lady Amanda is not afraid of blood," she informed him. "I should think you'd be pleased to know that, since I expect it's an important attribute for a physician's wife."

"I don't think that really matters," he told her. An affinity for blood was not on his list of wifely requirements. Not that he was looking for a wife, anyway. He tightened his grip on Juliana's arm, smiling to himself when she leaned closer to him. Even though it was cold and rainy outside, she seemed to smell of sunshine and flowers.

"I think Lady Amanda would like a fan," she said, guiding him past the glazed mahogany partition that separated the fur and fan departments.

He didn't want to buy Lady Amanda a fan, but he didn't want to disappoint Juliana, either. And he especially didn't want her to give up on their "lessons," because then she'd have more time to spend with stuffy Castleton, who was entirely the wrong man for her. So he bought a fan.

"I think Lady Amanda would like gloves," she said next. And although he didn't want to buy gloves for Lady Amanda—although he didn't want to buy *anything* for Lady Amanda—he dutifully paid for the lacy pair she picked out.

She thought Lady Amanda would like perfume, so they stopped by the perfumery department. She thought Lady Amanda would like candy, so they visited the confectioners. In no time at all, he was burdened with bags and boxes.

He'd always hated shopping—and he knew very well

he'd had a horrible attitude from the beginning—but all in all, Emily and her snake aside, this day wasn't turning out nearly as bad as he'd anticipated. He rather enjoyed being gallant and saving Juliana from stuffy Castleton.

Seeing that man at her house earlier had made him grit his teeth.

They were buying some fancy writing paper when Lady Frances and Emily sought them out. "Lady Juliana," Emily said, "you are taking *forever*."

Looking startled, Juliana turned from the stationery counter. And the next thing she did was immediately move to put herself between Emily and James. He could have kissed her for that.

Not that he'd actually kiss her, of course—that would be highly improper.

But he wanted to . . . and *that* was frightening as hell.

More frightening than Emily's snake.

He wasn't ready for this. He didn't think he'd ever be ready. He might be getting used to the idea of remarrying someday, but only to make his mother happy. And because he needed an heir.

Certainly *not* because he was in love.

Juliana looked between him and Herman. "Goodness, Emily," she said, "you're right. We *have* taken forever. In fact, we've taken so long that Lord Stafford is going to be late for Parliament. We'll have to take a hackney coach home so he can go there straightaway."

James might have been a coward, but he wasn't a fool. He knew she'd said that to save him from riding with Herman in his carriage.

He could have kissed her for that, too.

Chapter Fifteen

ALMOND MACAROONS

Beat Whites of Eggs with salt until stiff, then add Almonds ground fine, Sugar and a bit of ground Rice. Put in little mounds and make flat on Paper, then add an Almond in each middle before baking in your oven.

When I wish to see my husband amorous, I feed him these macaroons. They've never failed me yet.
—Katherine Chase, Countess of Greystone, 1763

Juliana placed little mounds of dough on a paper-lined baking tin, spacing them carefully while she hid a yawn. She'd been up since dawn. After spending the morning with Emily—who *still* refused to relinquish Herman—now she was making almond macaroons with Amanda.

According to Chase family legend, the macaroons were supposed to make a man amorous. Juliana planned to give some to James and tell him to eat them tomorrow, hoping they would induce him to act warmly toward Amanda at Lady Partridge's ball tomorrow night. Since she wasn't certain whether the macaroons needed to be made by the woman seeking attention—her grandmother, who'd penned the recipe, hadn't been clear—she'd decided to ask for Amanda's help just in case.

"Put an almond in the center of each macaroon," she said through another yawn.

"That's the third time you've yawned," Amanda observed, plopping the nuts on top rather haphazardly. "Are you sleepy?"

Juliana's fourth yawn seemed to echo off the basement kitchen's walls. "This week has been exhausting."

She'd been very busy since Monday's visit to the Institute and Tuesday's jaunt to the shops. Not only had she hosted another sewing party and spent every free minute stitching, but the duke had called on her every single day and danced with her twice at Almack's Wednesday evening. He said the nicest things to her. His attentiveness was encouraging, and she was certain it was only a matter of time before he asked for her hand. A perfect gentleman, he remained careful not to touch her, demonstrating the respect due a lady.

James, on the other hand, touched her so often she was beginning to think the incidents might not all be accidental.

On Wednesday afternoon, when she and James had taken advantage of a few glorious dry hours to go riding in Hyde Park, he'd found excuses to help her on and off her horse on six different occasions—to buy refreshments from a stand, to look at some flowers, to take a stroll by the Serpentine—and his hands had seemed to rest on her waist longer and longer each time.

James had missed attending Almack's again Wednesday night—apparently he'd had another problem at the Institute—but Thursday evening, when they'd attended the theater, he'd set his chair so close to hers in the box that his thigh was against her skirts during much of the performance. In the intermission, he'd brought her a syllabub and then claimed twice that she had white cream on her face and wiped it off with his thumb.

"Did I tell you I received another gift from Lord Stafford?" Amanda flattened a macaroon and stuck a piece of almond in it. "Three gifts in one week!"

"Use the whole almonds, Amanda. You want the macaroons to look pretty, don't you?" Juliana picked out the broken nut and replaced it with a perfect one, thinking Amanda was almost as hopeless at cooking as Corinna.

It was a good thing that as an earl's wife she'd never be expected to set foot in the kitchen. "What did he send you this time?" she asked.

"The most elegant lace gloves. I'm not sure Aunt Mabel would approve of something so personal. Fortunately she was napping when the package arrived. I suggested maybe she should return to the countryside, since Lady Frances is doing such a fine job as chaperone."

Juliana supposed Aunt Frances was a fine chaperone, if one considered *oblivious* to be synonymous with *fine*. "I'm glad Lady Mabel doesn't mind Aunt Frances filling in for her." Not least because it would be impossible to carry out their plan with the dear lady watching over Amanda. "Still, I hope she isn't feeling poorly enough to leave London. I enjoyed her company at Wednesday's sewing party."

"She surely enjoyed attending, too. It was much less strenuous than going on outings. Why, she hardly even wheezed."

And she'd proved a much better seamstress than her niece, completing four blankets in two hours. Unfortunately, even with Lady Mabel's help, Juliana had so far collected only thirty-three of the two hundred forty items she needed. And she had only three weeks left—the same three weeks Amanda had to find a new fiancé before she was forced to marry Lord Malmsey. "You're planning to keep the gloves, then?"

"I wouldn't dream of returning them. The workmanship is utterly stunning. The pink roses were beautiful, too. And I adore the painted fan," Amanda added as she placed another almond off center. "Lord Stafford has exquisite taste, don't you think? Especially for a man."

Juliana was glad she'd taken it upon herself to have each of James's gifts delivered rather than trusting him to remember. Tomorrow evening, she would make sure Amanda wore the gloves and carried the fan, which should please him. She could scarcely wait until the ball, when he'd dance again with Amanda and ask for permission to court her. She was certain Amanda would agree.

Everything was going perfectly.

Hearing the tall-case clock chime upstairs, she hurried

to place the last almonds. She had only half an hour to ready herself before James arrived for today's excursion to the Egyptian Hall. "Thank you for your help," she told Amanda as she shoved the pans into the oven. "I'll have a footman deliver half the macaroons to your house as soon as they're finished."

Not usually one to show affection, Amanda wrapped Juliana in a loose, awkward embrace. "Thank *you*," she said. "I had no idea that macaroons make one's eyes sparkle, but I appreciate your telling me and letting me help bake them."

"You're very welcome," Juliana murmured, feeling a bit guilty about misleading her. But only a bit. Honestly, she'd had no choice. Amanda was entirely too proper and reserved to bake macaroons with the intention of making a man amorous.

After Amanda took her leave, Juliana went upstairs to change her dress and put on a little rouge and lip salve. She was on her way back down when she heard the knocker bang. As she arrived in the foyer, expecting to see James, Adamson opened the door to reveal a deliveryman holding an enormous arrangement of red roses.

"Holy Hannah!" Paintbrush in hand, Corinna came in from the drawing room. "There must be five dozen!"

Aunt Frances came in from the library. "Goodness gracious, I can smell them from here. And just look at that gorgeous silver vase!"

"Do you expect they're from the duke?" Corinna asked.

"They must be," Juliana breathed, setting the gloves she was carrying on the marble-topped hall table. *Red* roses. The duke must be even more enamored than she'd hoped.

The heady scent was almost overwhelming. After tipping the deliveryman, the butler put the arrangement on the table. She plucked the card from it with shaking hands.

"A small token in comparison to the great love I hold in my heart," she read aloud, her pulse pounding harder with each precious word. "And it's signed—"

Her mouth gaped open, mute.

"Who signed it?" Corinna demanded. "Are the flowers not from the duke?"

Juliana closed her mouth and held the card out to Aunt Frances. "They're from Lord Malmsey. They're for you."

Frances's hand flew up to cover her heart. She looked like she might swoon for a moment, but in the end she just said, "For me?" in a squeaky little voice.

"For you," Juliana repeated, thrilled at this evidence her project was working. And thrilled for Frances, too, of course. Seeing her aunt sway on her feet, she eased her onto the striped satin chair that sat by the table. "Are you all right, Auntie?"

Her hand still splayed on her bosom, Frances blew out a breath. "Heavens, child, I've never been better." Her eyes looked misty behind their lenses. "But I do feel just a bit faint."

A kitchen maid came up from the basement and handed Juliana a small basket covered with a lace doily. "Your macaroons, my lady. A dozen, as you requested."

"Thank you," Juliana said and set the basket beside the flowers.

"May I speak with you a moment?" Without waiting for her to answer, Corinna took her by the arm. "In the drawing room."

They left Frances staring at her roses.

"Do you not think," Corinna said once they were behind closed doors, "that this is going a little too far?"

"What?" Juliana asked, feeling bewildered.

"Sending Aunt Frances flowers and claiming they're from Lord Malmsey. Really, Juliana, what do you think is going to happen tomorrow at the ball when she thanks him for them and he tells her he didn't send them to her?"

"He *did* send them to her," Juliana said.

"He didn't."

"Well, who did, then? Because *I* didn't. I had nothing to do with those flowers."

Corinna eyed her skeptically, rather as if she were a very bad painting. "He's engaged to marry Amanda. Why would he send flowers to Aunt Frances? What would make him think she'd be receptive to receiving them?"

"The love letters he received from her."

"*What* love letters?"

"The ones I sent," Juliana said, exasperated that she would have to explain such an obvious thing. "It wouldn't do to have Aunt Frances be the only one getting mail. A true love must be two-sided."

She'd never written so many sappy letters in her life. In a week of incessant activity, Aunt Frances's romance had proved to be her most exhausting project. Besides writing all the letters, she'd had to take Frances shopping for shoes, bonnets, and accessories to match all of her new dresses; buy cosmetics and practice applying them; and hire a dancing master to teach Frances all the new steps. And Frances's hair—oh, her hair! Madame Bellefleur had had to visit not once, but twice—the first time to dye Frances's hair with henna and walnuts, and the second to trim it and tinker with various styles.

But it was all worth it. Aunt Frances was going to look beautiful tomorrow night. And Lord Malmsey was already in love with her.

He'd sent *red* roses.

"You sent fake letters to both of them?" Corinna pointed the paintbrush she was still holding at her. "What do you think will happen when they compare notes?"

"They won't," Juliana said confidently. "Neither of them will be willing to question their good fortune." The knocker sounded again. "Excuse me. That will be James."

She went back to the foyer, but it wasn't James at the door. It was another deliveryman with flowers. White roses, and there were only a dozen, but they were in a beautiful crystal vase.

"What does the card say?" Corinna asked behind her.

Not assuming anything this time, Juliana pulled it from the arrangement. "The Duke of Castleton," she read with some relief.

And happiness, of course.

"That's it? No message?"

"The flowers say it all, do they not?" She gestured grandly toward the arrangement, which, in truth, looked rather paltry next to the extravagant one Lord Malmsey had sent. But the duke was not an extravagant man. He was restrained and refined and everything that was good and proper. "I don't *need* a written message," she said. "I know perfectly well how he feels."

"How who feels?" James asked, walking in the still-open door.

"The Duke of Castleton," Corinna informed him. "He sent flowers to Juliana."

"Did he?" He scanned the foyer, blinking as his gaze landed on the hall table. "That is a *lot* of roses. *Red* roses."

His tone implied he found something objectionable about the roses, although Juliana wasn't sure whether it was the amount of them or their color. Or both. And why would he care, anyway?

Frances's hand was still over her heart. "They're mine," she said, sounding awed.

Corinna nodded. "The *other* arrangement is from the duke."

"White," James said with a raised brow. He turned to Juliana. "He must think you very pure."

What on earth did he mean by that? She *was* pure. Not that that was entirely by choice. The only man she had an interest in respected her too much to touch her.

Which was more than she could say for James.

She swept the little basket off the table and thrust it at him. "Here," she said rather ungraciously. "I baked macaroons for you."

"Why?" he asked, looking nonplussed.

She hadn't anticipated that question. She didn't want him to think she'd made them as a gift, because he might take that the wrong way. But she couldn't very well tell him she hoped they'd make him amorous toward Amanda.

Or that they'd make his eyes sparkle.

"I thought you'd want to eat them tomorrow. They're reputed to give a man stamina."

That brow went up again. "Stamina of what sort?"

How many sorts were there? "Extra strength and endurance."

"I see." His lips quirked, as though he were trying not to laugh. "But pray tell, why should I need extra endurance tomorrow?"

"For the dancing," she said. "At the ball. You're not accustomed to hours on your feet."

"Ah," he said. Just *ah*. But something about the way he said it told her he was well aware she was making all of this up as she went along. "In all my years in medicine," he drawled, "I've never heard macaroons prescribed to improve stamina. I shall have to pass this wisdom along to my colleagues."

He wouldn't, of course; she was sure of it. He'd be laughed out of the Royal College of Physicians. "You do that," she said, snatching up her parasol and turning to Frances. "Are you ready to leave, Auntie?"

Chapter Sixteen

As James's carriage crawled toward the Egyptian Hall through the miserable London traffic, he smiled to himself. Juliana couldn't fool him. Although she claimed these outings were meant only to give him practice so he could court Lady Amanda, she enjoyed his company. She liked him, whether she was willing to say so out loud or not.

The proof? She'd baked him macaroons.

Feeling much more pleased about that than he probably should, he lifted the froufrou doily and pulled one out.

"No!" Juliana cried. "You're supposed to save them for tomorrow."

"There are plenty of them," he said, popping the little macaroon into his mouth. It was so light and toothsome it all but melted on his tongue. He'd never heard of a lady of the *ton* making sweets—or anything else that required entering a kitchen—but given Juliana's talents, he found her unusual hobby charming. "These are delicious," he told her and pulled out another.

"Please don't eat them," she pleaded, sounding concerned.

Quite concerned. Certainly much more concerned than the occasion warranted. They were only macaroons, after all. Since he hadn't believed for a moment that she really thought they lent a man stamina, why should it possibly matter whether he ate them today or tomorrow?

He reached for a third.

"I'd prefer you save them," she said firmly, taking the basket right out of his hands. She set it on the seat beside her, scooting closer to him in order to do so.

Not that he minded *that*. To the contrary. But as he finished the third macaroon, he glanced across to Lady Frances, thinking she might object to her charge sitting practically in his lap. Fortunately, Lady Frances seemed to be off in another world. Behind her spectacles, her blue gaze looked dazed.

Once again, although it was a rainy, gray day, Juliana smelled like sunshine. And flowers. So good and sweet it took everything he had not to sneak his arm around her shoulders and pull her even closer. Which he would never do. At least not with Juliana's chaperone watching, even if her eyes were unfocused.

Maybe Lady Frances would fall asleep. It seemed unlikely, but a man could hope.

For he *did* want to pull Juliana closer. Ever since that day in Harding, Howell & Company when he'd realized he wanted to kiss her, he'd thought of little else. Although the very idea had seemed appalling at first, it didn't any longer, because in the interim—during the hours he'd spent riding with her and accompanying her to the theater—he'd come to realize something else: He was no longer going on these outings to prevent her from wasting her time with Castleton.

Not that he wanted her to spend time with Castleton. Seeing the flowers the man had sent her had made him grit his teeth, because he knew for a fact that the prig was only courting her for a damned horse. He wished he'd told Juliana as much in the beginning, but news like that could deal a serious blow to a woman's self-regard, and he hadn't wanted to hurt her. He wanted even less to hurt her now. But the man was not only a prig—he was an ass.

Yet the fact remained that James was no longer going on these outings to save her from the ass—or at least not *only* to save her from the ass. He also just plain liked being with her. She was bright and enthusiastic, and she cared about other people. She'd cared about *him* when he'd feared a stupid snake. And, all right, she was attractive. Very attractive. Excessively, utterly attractive. Any man with eyes in his head would be hard put to argue with that. Especially considering she always seemed to wear dresses with tiny bodices.

All of which added up to a simple truth: He desired Juliana Chase.

It had been a long time since James had felt desire. It made him feel more alive, like something in him that had lain dormant for two years was starting to wake up. And the way he saw it, there was little he could do about it.

He didn't love Juliana—he didn't *want* to love her or anyone else. But love and desire were two very different and distinct emotions. And simply desiring another woman was not a betrayal of Anne. He was a man, after all, and everyone knew a man had little control over his desires. Surely he could kiss Juliana even though he wasn't in love.

Was all of that rationalization? Possibly, he acknowledged with a yawn. But he couldn't bring himself to care. Juliana had baked him macaroons, and that meant he was one step closer to kissing her.

Life wasn't too bad right at the moment.

She followed his yawn with one of her own and tried to cover it with a hand. "I saw that," he said.

"I'm not bored, I promise."

"I didn't think so," he assured her. "It's a medical fact that yawns are contagious."

She smiled, making him smile, too. He appreciated a woman who appreciated his admittedly weak attempts at humor.

"Are you as short on sleep as I?" she asked.

"I'm afraid I am. I was up half the night finishing the speech I plan to deliver this evening in the House of Lords."

"A speech?" She looked impressed, which he found much more encouraging than he probably ought. "What does it concern?"

"A bill I've put forth to publicly fund smallpox vaccinations and make them compulsory for infants."

"Compulsory?" Her blue-green-hazel eyes widened. "That's a rather radical idea, don't you think?"

"Not at all. England is terribly behind the times. Vaccinations were made compulsory in Bavaria in 1807, Denmark in 1810, Norway in 1811, Bohemia and Russia in 1812, and now this year in Sweden." He hoped he had all those dates right; he'd had to memorize them for the speech. "If we're to wipe this scourge off the face of the earth, everyone must cooperate."

She seemed to mull that over for a minute. "This is very important to you, isn't it?"

"Yes, it's very important."

"Why is that?"

"Must there be a reason? Can it not just be for the good of humanity?"

"I think not," she said. "Not when you're so vehement about the subject."

He mentally added *perceptive* to the list of her qualities. "My brother died of smallpox."

"Oh," she said quietly. "I'm sorry."

"There was nothing I could do to help him. Nothing I could do but watch him die. It's a terrible, horrible disease. Have you ever seen someone suffering with it?"

She shook her head. "No, I don't think so. At least not in the final stages."

"I hope you never will. The pain is excruciating, and the pocks—well, never mind." He wouldn't sicken her by describing the way they'd proliferated on Philip's body until he'd looked like little more than one huge, oozing pustule. "Suffice it to say that I'm hoping someday no one will ever suffer with it again. And I wish to do my part to make that happen."

Her gaze was full of admiration. "You're a good man, James."

Although the tone of her voice made his heart swell, he shrugged. "This is a unique circumstance. Vaccination has given us an opportunity we've never had before—a chance to destroy something that has afflicted mankind for centuries. We'd be fools not to take advantage of it."

"I hope you can convince Parliament, then," she said and reached to take his hand.

She'd actually reached to take his hand. She was holding it. He was afraid to react, for fear she might notice and snatch hers away. Keeping himself still, he shifted his gaze toward her chaperone, but Lady Frances was humming softly under her breath and staring out the window.

He looked down at their joined hands. Juliana wasn't wearing gloves. Prior to flouncing out to the carriage, she'd grabbed her umbrella but left a pair of white gloves sitting on the marble-topped table. Lady Frances hadn't noticed in her current, bemused state, and James hadn't thought to remind Juliana to take them, either.

Or maybe he hadn't wanted to.

Her hand felt small in his, her palm smooth and warm. He couldn't remember ever being so aware of anyone touching him before. It was a wonder she didn't seem to be feeling it, too.

"I see now," she said. "Your brother's death is why you became a physician. I've been wondering what would compel an earl to take up doctoring," she added, squeezing his fingers with kindly understanding.

He tried not to squeeze back, lest she realize she was touching him. "That's sound reasoning, but not the way it happened. Philip was my older brother—he was supposed to be the earl. I became a physician before his death, not after, because, as a second son, I needed a profession. I was at his bedside as his physician when he died."

"You don't blame yourself for his death, do you?" Concerned sympathy flooded her eyes. "Just because you're a doctor—"

"Good God, no." Even in his darkest days, he hadn't tortured himself with *that*. "Variola major—the more severe form of smallpox—defies treatment. There is really little a physician can do but keep the patient as comfortable as possible and hope for the best." Oh, there were things physicians *tried*, but they generally involved bleeding, emetics, and purgatives—treatments James feared weakened a patient rather than strengthening him. He'd done everything he'd thought could conceivably help his brother; he was totally at peace on that score. "I don't blame myself at all. But I *would* blame myself if I allowed more people to contract smallpox without trying to do anything to stop it."

"I understand." Her eyes looked blue now, a blue softened by compassion. "I'm truly sorry you lost your brother to such a devastating disease."

"You must have lost a brother, too," he realized suddenly. "Else Griffin wouldn't be the marquess. He wasn't meant to be, was he? After Oxford, he joined the military, same as I did."

"Our brother Charles died of consumption," she said. "A year after our mother succumbed to it first."

They called consumption a "gentle death," but James knew better. Its victims might fade away rather slowly and gracefully, but watching a loved one die was never easy. And Juliana had suffered through that twice.

"Consumption seems to descend upon certain families," he told her. "Probably because it's not easily transmitted like smallpox, but after weeks and months in the same home—"

"I thought it wasn't contagious." She looked shocked. "We all cared for my mother and brother with no concern of risking our own health. The doctors told us consumption is caused by the patient's own constitution and runs in families only because relations are so often alike."

"That may be the prevailing wisdom, but I don't believe it. And I'm not alone. More than two thousand years ago, Hippocrates himself warned doctors to be wary of contracting it from patients. And early in the last century, Benjamin Marten wrote a paper theorizing that consumption is caused by 'wonderfully minute living creatures' that can pass from one person to another, although rarely without extended periods of contact." His explanation didn't seem to be making her rest any easier, so he tried a different approach. "I don't expect you need to worry about catching it now if you haven't already. Nor should your sisters or Griffin. Whatever 'minute creatures' might have been in your home are long gone, I'm certain, and you needn't fret that you were all born with constitutions that will cause you to develop it, either."

"So Charles caught it from our mother, but none of the rest of us did." She drew and released a breath. "I've been wondering if we might all succumb eventually. Is it wicked of me to be relieved that we won't?"

"It's natural to be relieved," he said. "And I could be wrong. Most physicians wouldn't agree with me."

"I think you're right," she said. "I think you're a man who thinks for himself, who looks for his own answers instead of blindly accepting what others claim. We need your sort of men—and women. You're the people who discover things that make the world better for all of us."

If she was wicked to be relieved, he must be even more wicked to want to kiss her because she believed in him. He'd faced a lot of censure over the years from colleagues who scoffed at his refusal to bleed patients and his unorthodox insistence that cleanliness helped prevent infection. Not that he was the only physician to believe such things—it had been almost sixty-five years since Sir John Pringle, a former Surgeon General of the Army, had coined the word *antiseptic*. But he certainly went against the norm.

"Thank you," he said, squeezing her hand.

A mistake. Looking startled, she pulled it away. "So." She cleared her throat. "Tomorrow evening at the ball . . . just how are you planning to ask Lady Amanda if you might court her?"

The quick change of subject made him feel as though his brain had just fallen off a cliff. How did women manage to do that? How had Juliana gone from holding his hand to assuming he was still planning to court Lady Amanda?

He wasn't. He'd decided he'd rather court Juliana— or rather, tempt her into letting him kiss her.

But he didn't quite know how to answer her question, because she hadn't asked him *if* he was planning to court Lady Amanda. She'd asked him *how* he was planning to ask for permission.

She must have taken his silence to mean he couldn't figure out how, because when he didn't immediately respond, she added, "Perhaps I can help you devise some particularly gallant method."

"Like what? Shall I ride into the ball on a charger, dressed in armor?"

"Really, now, James, be serious."

He *was* serious. He was serious about wanting to kiss Juliana. And touch her. And do all sorts of other things with her that would make Lady Frances faint dead away if she ever managed to come out of her fog enough to notice.

"James?" Juliana asked. "Why are you looking at me like that?"

Another question he couldn't answer. He could hardly tell her the truth—that he was looking at her while imagining scenarios that would ruin her reputation beyond repair.

Lucky for him, the carriage rolled to a halt in front of the Egyptian Hall.

Chapter Seventeen

The exterior of the museum at Number Twenty-two Piccadilly bore a vague resemblance to an Egyptian temple. A very vague resemblance. In fact, it would look rather Palladian, Juliana thought, were it not for the ankhs along the cornice and the two full-length statues that flanked a window above the entrance.

"Are those sculptures supposed to be Egyptian?" Frances asked.

"An Egyptian god and goddess." James gestured toward the figures. "That's Isis on the left, and her brother and husband, Osiris, on the right."

Juliana wondered how he came to know such things. "They look like American Indians with headcloths," she said.

He laughed. "I suppose they do. Shall we have a look inside?"

He gave the doorman three shillings for their admission, took a guidebook and handed it to Juliana, and ushered her and Aunt Frances into the museum.

"So many people," Frances said, looking dazed as they jostled their way down a corridor.

"They've all come to see Napoleon's carriage," Juliana told her. "And," she added, reading off the cover of the guidebook, " 'the Collection of Fifteen Thousand

Natural and Foreign Curiosities, Antiques, and Productions of the Fine Arts.' "

"I'm feeling faint," Frances said.

"You don't have to look at all of them, Auntie. Listen to this." Pausing in the first of the exhibition rooms, Juliana quoted from the introduction. " 'The museum's owner, William Bullock, formed his collection during seventeen years of arduous research at a cost of thirty thousand pounds.' "

"Thirty thousand pounds," James said in wonder. "Just think how many vaccinations all that money could have provided."

Or how many foundlings it could have fed, Juliana thought. But there were other good uses for money. "Widening the horizons of the man in the street is also a worthy cause. Do you not agree, Aunt Frances?" She glanced around. "Aunt Frances?"

"There she is." James pointed toward an exhibit of stuffed African animals. "On that bench, by the rail."

Juliana wove through the crowd to sit beside her, beneath the raised trunk of a massive gray elephant. "Are you unwell, Auntie?"

"I'm fine, child. I thought I'd sit here a while and rest." Frances patted her chest with a happy sigh, and Juliana knew she was thinking about Lord Malmsey and his red roses. "You young people go ahead and start looking. I'll join you in a few minutes."

"We cannot just leave you here," Juliana said.

"Of course we can," James disagreed. "You wouldn't want to risk your aunt's health by taxing her, would you?"

"She doesn't look unhealthy to me. Her cheeks are rosier than ever I've seen them."

"Fever," James said succinctly.

Concerned, Juliana turned to feel her aunt's forehead. "She's not hot."

"Impending fever, then. She needs to rest as a preventative measure." When Juliana failed to rise, he reached for her hand and pulled her from the bench. "Will you argue with a physician?"

"Go on," Aunt Frances put in, waving her gloved hand in encouragement.

Juliana suddenly realized her own hand was bare, and James's felt very strong and warm.

"Come along." He tugged on her hand. "Your aunt will be fine. I believe Captain Cook's artifacts are in the next room."

She pulled her fingers free. Holding her hand in the carriage was one thing—and no doubt the result of those macaroons—but she shouldn't allow him to do so in public. "We haven't seen the things in this room yet."

"A bevy of stuffed animals," he said dismissively. Besides the African display in the center, the walls were lined from floor to ceiling with creatures in glass cases, stacked one on top of another. "What is so interesting about that?"

"There are hundreds of different species."

"You're too short to see most of them," he said. Then, apparently deciding the discussion was over, he draped an arm about her shoulders and began drawing her from the room.

Shocked, she darted a glance to her aunt, but Frances was staring into space, a vague smile curving her lips. Daydreaming, no doubt. She certainly wouldn't be smiling if she'd seen James's arm around her.

Unless, on second thought, seeing James's arm around her had made Frances begin fantasizing about Lord Malmsey holding her in the same fashion. Because Juliana had to admit that being tucked up against a man like this was a pleasurable sensation.

She wondered if Amanda would like it. Probably not, she decided. James was acting a bit more amorous than she'd had in mind. She'd had no idea the macaroons would prove to be so potent.

The next chamber's walls were covered with historical arms and armor. Still attached to her, James walked slowly, admiring the collection as though nothing were out of the ordinary.

"James," she said quietly.

"Hmm?"

"You have your arm about my shoulders."

"I know. I'm practicing for wooing Lady Amanda."

Oh, dear, just as she'd feared. She'd known she

shouldn't have let him eat those macaroons. "I don't think Lady Amanda would want you to do this."

"Why not? It feels good, doesn't it?"

She couldn't argue with that, so she didn't.

"We fit perfectly," he added, studying a curved sword.

They *did* fit perfectly. She'd thought him too tall, but he was just the right height for her to fit perfectly under his arm. Not, of course, that that made it at all proper. And in any case, he wouldn't fit perfectly with Amanda, since Amanda was much taller.

"Um, James?"

"Hmm?"

"People are going to see us and assume you're courting me instead of Amanda."

"We aren't acquainted with anyone here," he said easily, "so they're not going to assume anything." He looked up higher, to peruse a battered shield. "Fascinating, isn't it?"

Unsure whether he was referring to the armor or to the fact that no one would make assumptions, she tried to wriggle away without looking conspicuous. "I cannot really see it. I'm too short. Perhaps we should go see Napoleon's carriage instead."

"Use my quizzing glass," he offered, handing it to her with a smile.

She really had no choice but to take it. Like at the ball, he'd left the long chain around his neck, so she had to lean yet closer to raise the glass to her eye. Dear heavens, he smelled good. She couldn't seem to focus on the shield.

He moved behind her, which was a relief. But then his fingers brushed her neck, and a little shiver ran through her. She blinked through the lens at an ancient, pitted rifle. "What are you doing, James?"

"Just pinning up a strand of your hair that's fallen down."

Her hair was so straight it sometimes slid right out of its pins. But she'd never had a man fix it before. Studying the rusty edge of a cutlass, she wondered if she should stop him.

"I'd do the same thing for Lady Amanda," he said,

apparently reading her mind. "It's very gallant, don't you think? I'm getting some excellent practice."

She switched to examine an old flintlock. "Are you finished yet?"

"Not quite."

That deep, chocolatey voice was making it hard to pay attention, especially since it seemed to be coming from right behind her ear. "You're standing a bit close to me, James."

"You're holding my quizzing glass," he pointed out.

And whose idea had that been? "Do you expect Captain Cook used this pistol?"

"What pistol?" he asked, his hands leaving her hair to rest lightly on her shoulders.

She could feel his breath, warm on the back of her neck. "This pistol I'm looking at on the wall."

"That's part of Bullock's collection." His voice sounded even closer. "Captain Cook's artifacts are in a case to your right."

She turned her head to the right, and his lips met her nape.

Heavens, they felt hot and soft. She almost groaned when the brief contact ended.

"You shouldn't do that," she whispered, scandalized—although, to be honest, she was mostly scandalized because it had felt so good. "I understand that you wish to practice, but you are taking things too far."

"What things?" James asked.

She dropped the quizzing glass and whirled to face him. "You kissed my neck."

"In public? I think not." His expression was one of studied innocence. "You have an active imagination, Juliana."

She'd been told that before, but she hadn't imagined *this*. "You'd better not do that to Lady Amanda," she warned. "She wouldn't like it."

"I wouldn't think of kissing Lady Amanda. She's rather stuffy, isn't she? Rather like Castleton."

"The duke is not stuffy!"

He shrugged and motioned toward a glass case with a few people standing before it. "Did you want to see Captain Cook's artifacts?"

"Yes," she said and made her way over. She'd wanted for months to see Captain Cook's artifacts, ever since the *Morning Post* had printed an article about their arrival at the Egyptian Hall. But they weren't nearly as interesting as she'd expected. As she stood before the glass case, her gaze wandering over yellowed shark's teeth and ugly specimens of cloth made from bark, she wondered how it would feel should the duke kiss her neck like James had.

Perhaps she ought to give the duke a few macaroons so she could find out.

"Do you expect those old bones are really from the grave of an ancient Hawaiian chief?" she asked.

"If Captain Cook said so, I'm sure they are."

She wondered if Amanda would find all of this more interesting. Probably, considering she was fascinated with crusty objects from ancient ruins. "Are there any Roman antiquities in this museum?"

"I've not noticed any yet, but there might be." James slipped an arm around her waist. "Would you like to have a look around and see?"

"Not particularly." Remembering that he'd known the identities of the Egyptian statues outside, she asked, "Would you recognize Roman antiquities?"

"Most certainly," he said dryly. "Both my grandfather and my father were obsessed with the things."

"Really? Lady Amanda is, too." What an amazing coincidence. "Do you find Roman antiquities fascinating?"

"I wouldn't put it so strongly," he said, drawing her closer against his side. "Mildly interesting, perhaps."

Perfect. Amanda had said she wanted a man who was interested in Roman antiquities. Her friend was going to love coming here with him—as long as he didn't eat so many macaroons first. "Shall we go see Napoleon's carriage now?" she suggested, sidestepping away.

He sidestepped with her. "Absolutely, if that's what you wish."

As they headed to the next room, he kept his arm firmly around her. Endeavoring to ignore that, she opened the guidebook and read from it. "The Emperor's carriage was captured at Waterloo and later purchased from the Prince Regent for twenty-five hundred pounds," she reported. "And it's bulletproof."

"A wise precaution on Napoleon's part." He halted in the archway. "Good God, would you look at all those people?" The carriage was completely surrounded. "Perhaps it would be better to return another time."

She wouldn't be returning with him—his next visit here would be with Amanda. They would look at Roman antiquities. "I want to see the carriage now," she said, picturing his arm around Amanda's waist instead of hers and wondering why that vision was so unsettling. Probably because Amanda wouldn't approve, she decided as she broke away from him and he followed her to the front of the crowd.

"Pardon me," he kept saying in a tone that sounded half exasperated, half apologetic. "Excuse me. Pardon." Short as she was, she was very good at burrowing her way through a pack of people, but apparently he wasn't.

Up close, the vehicle was beautiful, painted a rich, dark blue and ornamented in gold. She looked up and back at James, who had come to a stop behind her. "Even the wheels are gold," she said.

James examined it over her head. "It's such a crush in here," he complained.

"The newspaper reported that ten thousand a day are visiting just to see this carriage."

"There seem to be twenty thousand today." He bumped into her from behind, then placed his hands on her waist to steady her. "My apologies," he murmured by her ear. "These people have no manners."

Although nobody seemed to be jostling, she let him keep his hands there, just in case. "There's a blanket inside, embroidered with the initials *NB*. Do you expect Napoleon actually slept in here?"

"He'd have been smart to, considering it's bulletproof." He wrapped his arms further around her, overlapping them under her breasts. "There's a desk inside, too."

It was built in below the front window, with many compartments for maps and telescopes. "Very clever," she murmured, leaning back into him so no one would nudge her. His body was warm. His scent swamped her again, making her curiously dizzy. She felt very cozy and safe.

"Do you think Lady Amanda would like this?" he whispered.

"The clever desk?"

"No, me. Holding her like this."

"Oh, yes," she breathed, followed by a horrified, "No!"

What had she been thinking? She could feel his quizzing glass against her spine, which she was certain Amanda would find quite uncomfortable. "Lady Amanda wouldn't like this at all," she said, twisting out of his embrace. "You're right. It's entirely too crowded here today." She pushed through the crowd and began retracing their steps back to Frances. "I believe we should fetch my aunt and leave. You cannot be late to Parliament if you're giving a speech tonight."

Frances was still sitting where they'd left her, gazing happily into space. "Come along, Auntie," Juliana said. It took a few minutes for the coachman to bring James's carriage around—a few minutes during which she marveled that her macaroons had had such an astounding effect. No sooner had they climbed into the carriage than she burrowed into the basket to count how many macaroons were left.

"What are you doing?" James asked.

"I forgot to keep some for myself." She pulled a handkerchief out of her reticule. "I'm sure Aunt Frances will want some."

"I don't need any macaroons, child." Her aunt patted her newly golden-brown hair. "A lady should keep a trim figure."

Frances had never had a care for her figure before. "Corinna will want some, then," Juliana said, piling them onto her handkerchief. She couldn't leave all the macaroons for James. She needed some for the duke, and besides, the mere thought of James eating nine macaroons made her cringe. Nine! If three had made him so amorous, nine would likely bring on behavior Amanda would never forgive.

James took the basket and peeked inside. "One? You cannot leave me with just one."

Maybe he was right. She *did* want him to act warmly toward Amanda tomorrow night—just not as warmly as in the museum. "Two, then." She put one back in the basket and folded the handkerchief around the remaining seven. "But don't eat them until right before the ball tomorrow," she instructed as she slipped the bundle into her reticule. "You're going to need extra stamina, so you mustn't forget."

Chapter Eighteen

"I cannot see," Frances complained. "I should never have let you talk me into taking off my spectacles."

"But you look beautiful, Auntie." Juliana patted her on the arm. "Just wait until Lord Malmsey gazes into your big blue eyes. You won't be sorry then." Having just arrived at Lady Partridge's ball, she looked around for the man in question, smiling when she spotted him across the room. "There he is."

"Where?" Frances glanced around wildly. "I cannot see him."

"Right there, Auntie. Leaning on the mantel." Since it was quite cold for June, Lady Partridge had ordered the fireplaces lit on both ends of her impressive ballroom. "Come along. I'll take you to him."

Frances drew a deep breath and smoothed her soft peach dress down her sides, eyeing her lower-than-usual décolletage—although it wasn't very low compared to what most of the ladies were wearing tonight. "Do I look all right?"

"You look perfect," Juliana assured her, taking her arm as they started across the room. It was true. Frances looked much younger in the fashionable dress with her hair dyed and styled, and Juliana's skillful hand with the cosmetics had completed her transformation. She seemed to be trembling, but there was nothing Juliana could do to help that.

Standing in the glow of the fire, Lord Malmsey also looked nervous. Well, he should be. Not only was he falling in love for the first time in his life, but he was doing so while betrothed to another lady—and while Juliana knew that would soon cease to be a problem, he didn't.

It was unfortunate a gentleman couldn't call off a wedding, because that would solve everything. He'd be free to marry Aunt Frances, and Amanda's father would have no grounds to disinherit her, leaving *her* free to find another suitor without so much pressure. But it just wasn't done. Although a woman could back out of an engagement—assuming she was willing to be labeled a jilt—a gentleman had no honorable way to withdraw an offer of marriage.

As Lord Malmsey noticed them approaching, a tentative smile spread on his face. While it didn't quite transform him—it didn't, after all, smooth his creased forehead or improve his unfortunate receding hairline—he did seem more attractive than Juliana remembered. Perhaps it was his stylish suit, which was obviously brand-new, or perhaps it was because what was left of his hair had been neatly trimmed. Or perhaps it was a glow that came from simply knowing someone of the opposite sex actually cared about him.

Love could change a person.

When they reached him, his anxious gaze met her aunt's. "Good evening, Lady Frances," he said shyly.

A youthful blush suddenly tinted Frances's cheeks, making her even more alluring. "Good evening, Lord Malmsey."

"Please," he said, gazing into her big blue eyes, "call me Theodore."

Juliana had never heard the man's given name—in fact, she felt somewhat surprised to hear he even had one. But Aunt Frances stopped shaking, and her lips curved in a timid smile. "Call me Frances, then, please."

Lord Malmsey held out his arm. "Would you honor me with a dance . . . Frances?"

"My goodness, I'd love nothing more," she gushed,

which sounded nothing like the formal words of acceptance she'd practiced with Juliana. But it sounded better, more genuine, and made Lord Malmsey grin in response. Shooting Juliana a disbelieving—and myopic—glance, Frances took his arm and sailed off with him.

Juliana sighed as she watched them drift toward the dance floor. Love was so inspiring.

"Did the macaroons work? Are my eyes sparkling?"

She turned to find Amanda standing beside her, wearing the dress Juliana had chosen because its gray-blue hue intensified the color of her eyes. Alas, those eyes weren't noticeably sparkling, but Juliana wouldn't tell her so. "You look lovely," she said instead. Amanda did look lovely, actually, whether her eyes sparkled or not. Juliana's hard work with her had definitely paid off. "Are you carrying your new fan?"

Amanda held it up. "And I'm wearing the gloves, like you told me to."

"Excellent. Have you seen James—I mean, Lord Stafford—yet?"

"No. I don't think he's arrived." Amanda's not-sparkling eyes looked apprehensive. "His gifts are wonderful, but what if I still don't like him particularly?"

"You will." How could anyone not like James? He was warm, intelligent, kind, and caring, and even though he didn't have time to go out much in society, Amanda shouldn't care a fig about that. It wasn't as though she was a social butterfly herself.

If anything, Juliana was more concerned about James liking Amanda, mostly because he seemed much more affectionate than Amanda. But soon he would discover they had interests in common—chess and antiquities— and hopefully the macaroons would work to make Amanda warmer than usual. Or at least more receptive to *his* warmth.

Amanda frowned toward the dance floor. "Is Lord Malmsey waltzing with your aunt?"

"Yes. Isn't it wonderful?"

"He's engaged to *me*," she said.

It was Juliana's turn to frown. "You're planning to break that engagement, are you not? Under the circumstances, I should think you'd be happy to see him show-

ing interest in another woman. It's not your goal to
devastate him, is it? Besides, *you've* spent the last week
dancing with other men."

In fact, two other men were approaching now. As Rachael had said, Amanda looked to be this Season's
Incomparable—at least until her novelty wore off.

"Smile, Amanda," Juliana instructed through a fixed
smile of her own. "You're not engaged to Lord Stafford
yet, so you might need one of these gentlemen."

Before she turned her new, practiced smile on the
potential suitors, Amanda had the good grace to look
chagrined. Which was a good thing, because given her
earlier attitude, Juliana had been tempted to call the
whole plan off. Except then Lord Malmsey would have
to marry Amanda, which would hardly be fair to either
him or Aunt Frances.

Having multiple projects was proving to be complicated.

As Amanda went off to dance with the luckier of the
two men, Juliana sensed a presence behind her and
turned to see the Duke of Castleton. "Lady Juliana," he
said, his tone cultured and reserved as always, "may I
beg the honor of your company for a dance?"

"By all means, your grace." She loved calling him
"your grace" and thinking that someday—maybe someday soon—other people would say that to *her*. She took
the duke's arm and headed toward the dance floor. "A
waltz," she said happily, shooting him a smile. "Now
you'll have an excuse to touch me."

She'd uttered the words in a flirtatious manner, but
although she was a very accomplished flirt, the duke
didn't seem to take her hint. "You're looking beautiful
tonight, my dear," he said, and then he held her at a
respectable distance throughout the entirety of the
dance, and he didn't touch her anywhere that wasn't
strictly necessary.

None of that meant he wasn't enamored. He'd sent
her flowers, after all. And he'd called her "my dear."
But all the same, Juliana had enjoyed the affection she'd
received from James, and she wished the duke would
loosen up a bit and show a little physical affection, too.
Even a smidgen would be encouraging.

Luckily, she'd transferred the handkerchief-wrapped macaroons into the pretty yellow reticule that matched her dress. As they came off the dance floor, she slid the beaded purse off her wrist and opened it.

"Thank you for the waltz, my dear," the duke said very formally.

"It was my pleasure." She pulled out the bundle and handed it to him. "I baked macaroons for you."

He looked startled. "In the kitchen?" he asked, as though there were somewhere else—someplace more acceptable—a proper lady of the *ton* might bake.

"Yes, in the kitchen. Chase ladies are known for making all sorts of sweets." Since he wasn't moving to do so, she unwrapped the macaroons for him. "Won't you try one?"

Looking discomfited, he selected an especially small one and surreptitiously slipped it into his mouth, chewing and swallowing thoroughly before stating his opinion. "They are absolutely delicious," he said. "I can see why the Chase ladies are known for their sweets." He held forth the handkerchief with the rest of them.

She didn't take it. "I'm so glad they meet with your approval. I hope you will enjoy *all* of them." Seven macaroons might seem a bit much, considering three had made James overly affectionate, but she suspected it could take at least that many to ease a manner as reserved as the duke's. "Thank you for the dance," she added, with a very proper curtsy. Then she took her leave, before he could try to hand them to her again.

Men didn't carry reticules—and the duke was entirely too fastidious to put a bundle of macaroons in his pocket.

He'd have no choice but to eat them.

Chapter Nineteen

The weather was always a popular topic of conversation, but it seemed even more so this year. In fact, James reflected as he stood in a circle of men at Lady Partridge's ball, it seemed that lately people talked of little else.

"The sunspots are responsible for the cold," Lord Cravenhurst was saying. "Clearly there is something amiss with the universe."

Lord Davenport inclined his head sagely. "Nine groups of sunspots have been counted, plus several single ones scattered from the eastern to the western side of the sun. I fear they portend the end of the world. The sun is cooling off."

"I think not." James found himself half-amused by these absurd theories, but his other half was rather disturbed to think the country was being run by the crackpots expounding them. "Sunspots are hardly new. Galileo noted them more than two hundred years ago. If you'll but examine the temperature records, you'll find Britain has seen both uncommonly cold and uncommonly warm summers since then, and such periods have nothing to do with sunspots."

Lord Hawkridge nodded. "Stafford is right."

James gave the man a subtle nod in return, glad to have another non-crackpot in the discussion. He knew

Hawkridge from his Oxford days, although not terribly well—the man had been a much closer friend of Griffin's. A newcomer to Parliament and a fellow Whig, Hawkridge had impressed James so far on the floor. He seemed a true gentleman, with a clear head and a keen sense of honor.

"I agree with Hawkridge and Stafford," Lord Haversham announced. "Sunspots are not responsible for the cold. The moon is to blame."

Hawkridge rolled his eyes at James before asking, "And how is that?"

Apparently not scientifically minded, Haversham shrugged. "It's common knowledge that the cycles of the moon affect everything."

"Nonsense." Everyone turned to Lord Occlestone, a man who sadly—or fittingly, depending on one's estimation of the fellow—resembled nothing so much as a pink-faced porker. "It's not the moon *or* sunspots," he declared loudly, spewing sputum on everyone else in the process. "It's the fault of those upstart Americans."

James wiped his face. "How the devil can you blame this on the Americans?" Occlestone had been another classmate at Oxford—one James hadn't liked then and liked even less now. A staunch Tory, generally against any progress or reform, Occlestone was doing everything he could to block James's bill to make smallpox vaccinations government-funded and mandatory for infants.

"North America is suffering even colder weather than ours," Hawkridge said. "Their newspapers have been predicting famine in the coming months due to crop failure."

"That's not only a concern in North America," Davenport put in. "I've seen reports of famine in Switzerland as well."

"Famine or not," Occlestone said, plainly disinterested in something so unlikely to affect him personally, "we can lay the blame at the feet of an American. Benjamin Franklin, to be precise."

"At the feet of Benjamin Franklin?" Incredulous, James blinked. "I expect Mr. Franklin's feet are decomposed by now. He's been dead more than twenty-five years."

The others laughed, but Occlestone's porcine eyes narrowed. "Dead or not, he invented the lightning rod, did he not? I'll have you know that the interior of the earth is hot due to electrical fluids circulating about beneath the surface. That heat is usually discharged into the air around us, but because of Franklin's lightning rods—which are now being installed all over not only his country but ours as well—the earth's process of releasing heat into the atmosphere has been interrupted."

"That's not how I've heard it explained," Cravenhurst said. "Quite the opposite, in fact. Since lightning is heat, the lightning rods have taken the heat from the air. Hence we shall never again see summer."

Davenport rubbed his balding pate. "Either way, Franklin would be responsible. But I still blame the sunspots."

James decided that, Hawkridge excepted, they all had more hair than sense—even shiny-headed Davenport. Still, it wouldn't do to call them idiots to their faces.

"Like all of you," he said carefully, "I've given this much thought. And that, coupled with keen observation, has led me to dismiss these predictions of doom. There's been a haze overhead the last months. I believe that haze is temporarily blocking the sun."

Occlestone crossed his arms. "A haze?"

"Yes, a haze. Or a fog, if you will, or perhaps it is some sort of dust, since it appears to be dry. The rays of the sun seem to have little effect toward dissipating it, as they easily do to a moist fog arising from the water. Since the sun does not seem to be penetrating this haze, it logically follows that its rays are not reaching the earth and warming it as usual."

"And to what do you attribute this haze?" Occlestone demanded.

"That I couldn't tell you. I'm a physician, not a meteorologist. But I see no reason to jump to the conclusion that the condition will continue indefinitely."

"Do you expect there's a haze above America as well? I think not." Occlestone's pinkish face was turning rather purple. "I was forced to listen to your damned two-hour speech in Parliament, Stafford, but I don't have to listen to you here." And with that, he walked

off, muttering so loudly James suspected he was audible
halfway across the ballroom.

"Good evening, Tristan," James heard a familiar feminine voice say behind him.

He turned to see Juliana, dressed in such a cheerful
bright yellow she seemed to make up for all the missing
sunshine. But he didn't like hearing her address Hawkridge by his given name, and he liked even less seeing
her smile when the man walked closer, raised her hand,
and pressed a kiss to the back of it. "You're looking
lovely tonight, Juliana."

James didn't hear what they said next. He was too
busy telling himself he had no business caring who
courted Juliana, and she was entitled to have genuine
suitors, and at least Hawkridge wasn't a prig and an
ass. The next thing he knew, Hawkridge was gone—and
Juliana was looking at him with a puzzled expression on
her face.

"Are you all right, James?"

He blinked. "Of course. Why shouldn't I be?"

"You just looked . . . odd."

He shrugged. "Hawkridge is a fine fellow, isn't he?"

"Yes. It's a shame he was shunned by society for so
long. I'm so glad Alexandra managed to clear his name."

"Alexandra?"

"My older sister. His wife."

"Oh." Whatever scandal had afflicted Hawkridge, it
must have happened while James was preoccupied by
grief. Feeling an absurd rush of relief, it was all he could
do to hold back a grin. Hawkridge wasn't Juliana's
suitor—he was her *brother-in-law*. "I didn't realize he
was married to your sister."

"I forgot you've met only Corinna. I shall have to
introduce you to Alexandra." She caught sight of someone and frowned. "That man doesn't like you much,
does he?"

Awestruck once again at her lightning-fast change of
subject, James followed her gaze. "Occlestone?" He
hadn't realized she'd overheard their conversation. "He
doesn't like any of the bills I propose in Parliament. But
I don't like him much, either, so we're even."

"Two hours," she said, looking impressed. "How was

your speech received? Other than by Lord Occlestone, I mean."

He sighed. "I don't think the House of Lords is prepared to expend more money fighting smallpox. They awarded two grants to fund Edward Jenner's research—in 1802 and again in 1806—and they consider that enough. In addition, there are those who feel that making immunization obligatory would be a problem in itself. A matter of civil liberty. They believe imposing vaccinations is not acceptable in a country with a tradition of freedom."

"They have a point," she said thoughtfully.

He nodded. "When it comes to weighing personal freedom against the greater good, I admit to some ambivalence." Very little in this world was black and white. "But I do wish there was more support for public funding of the effort to eradicate the disease."

"Has your bill come to a vote?"

"Not yet, but I fear I know the outcome already." His two-hour speech had been followed by four hours of debate—mostly not in his favor. "I shall try again next year. Perhaps for funding alone, given the resistance to making vaccination compulsory."

"You're a reasonable man, James."

He shrugged. "Merely pragmatic. No matter how strongly I feel about conquering smallpox, I'm coming to believe there is nothing I can say that will override others' desire to protect individual rights. And I'm not even sure their position isn't legitimate."

"But will money alone help? You're already paying for other people's vaccinations."

"Only here in London. After all, my income, though not insubstantial, is limited. But government funds would go toward more than doctors and supplies—they would also pay for education. If everyone learned the importance of immunization and therefore decided to have their children vaccinated, the end result would be the same as if it were required." Thinking this was quite a serious discussion for a young lady at a social event, he smiled and changed the subject. "Are you enjoying Lady Partridge's ball?"

"Of course. I didn't see you arrive."

"That's because you were dancing with Castleton." The ass had looked as stuffy as ever, even with Juliana in his arms, which had cheered James tremendously. "Can I convince you to dance with me instead?"

"You're here to dance with Amanda," she reminded him. "Did you eat the macaroons before you came?"

"Absolutely. I assure you, I shall have enough stamina to dance with you both."

"Very well," she said with a laugh. "We can talk about your strategy as we dance."

James didn't want to talk about strategy. But he did want to get his hands on Juliana, with the intention of making more progress toward eventually kissing her, so he mumbled something that sounded like consent and drew her toward the dance floor.

Chapter Twenty

"So," Juliana said to James as they waltzed, "have you decided how you're going to ask Amanda's permission to court her?"

He pulled her closer. "I thought I'd start with 'May I have this dance?' and take it from there."

"That doesn't sound particularly gallant."

"I think it will work," he said dismissively. "After all, I bought her several gifts." He pulled her closer still, until their bodies were almost touching, which had the odd effect of making her tingle. "Have I sent her all of the gifts yet, or just some?"

"Only the fan and the gloves so far," she said, feeling breathless as his hand smoothed slowly down her back. "And the flowers, of course. You'll send the rest next week."

"You'll see to that, I presume," he said dryly as he slid his hand back up. "All those gifts are very gallant, are they not?"

"That's why I suggested them."

"Well, then," he said, skimming his fingers down again and making her pulse race a little faster, "should that not be enough? They do say that actions speak louder than words."

His actions were speaking volumes. He shouldn't be rubbing her back in the middle of a crowded dance floor, but she expected the macaroons were to blame for such forward behavior—and she had to admit it felt very nice. If he did the same to Amanda, that, coupled with the gifts, could very well be enough to make her want to marry him.

As the waltz came to an end, she was pleased to notice her older sister conversing with Amanda. "There's Alexandra now," she said, maneuvering so that James would lead her off the dance floor in their direction. "Let me introduce you."

James told Alexandra he'd been delighted to learn Lord Hawkridge had wed—in fact, he seemed more happy about that than was warranted—and Alexandra was glad to meet the man who was discussed so avidly at Juliana's sewing parties, although she didn't say so, of course. After the introductions were complete, it was a simple matter to suggest that James and Amanda dance. Unfortunately, the musicians struck up a country tune, not a waltz, but the two of them headed off, looking very good together. They were both tall, and James's dark handsomeness contrasted with Amanda's pale beauty. Anyone would agree they made a perfect couple.

Juliana turned and spotted James's mother gazing happily toward her son, clearly pleased to see him with the lovely Amanda. Lady Stafford looked different tonight—or younger, maybe—wearing a very fashionable dress of deep rose with almond trim. Juliana recalled seeing something similar in the latest issue of *La Belle Assemblée*. Remembering that James wanted his mother to dance, she looked around for an eligible gentleman and found one nearby.

"Lord Cavanaugh," she said, smiling when he shifted to face her. A dapper widower in his mid-fifties with a patrician nose and silver hair, he was ideal for Lady Stafford. "Are you enjoying the evening?"

He grinned down at her, looking surprised to have a lady so much younger engage him in conversation. "Very much, Lady Juliana. And you?"

"Very much as well." She started edging toward James's mother. "Have you been dancing much tonight?"

"Not yet," he said, interpreting her question as an

invitation, just as she'd intended. "But I'd be honored to—"

"Excellent," she said, walking him right up to Lady Stafford. "Good evening, Lady Stafford."

James's mother turned, the smile still on her face. "Good evening, Lady Juliana."

"Your dress is beautiful. Is it new?"

Her brown eyes, so like her son's, sparkled much more than Amanda's. She reached to touch Juliana's arm. "Why, thank you, and yes, it is."

"I believe you know Lord Cavanaugh?" Juliana smiled in the man's direction. "He would love to dance with you. I hope you enjoy yourselves," she added and sailed off.

Corinna stepped into her path. "Very smooth, Juliana."

Since she was so happy with the way everything was going, she ignored her sister's sarcastic tone. "Thank you."

"Has it ever occurred to you that some people might not appreciate your meddling?"

"I'm not meddling. I'm helping." She gestured toward the dance floor, where Lady Stafford was performing a quadrille with Lord Cavanaugh. "They're both smiling."

"They're being polite."

"They're happy. He's a wealthy widower; she's a lonely widow. Why shouldn't they be happy to dance together?"

"Maybe because you pushed them into it?"

"Some people need a little pushing." She eyed her sister, thinking she looked a bit lonely. "Shall I find a dance partner for you?"

"Holy Hannah," Corinna said and walked off.

Juliana looked back to the dance floor. No matter what her sister said, it was obvious Lord Cavanaugh and James's mother were thoroughly enjoying their dance. And Lord Malmsey and Aunt Frances were dancing again, their eyes locked on each other in a way that made Juliana sigh with envy. If only the duke would look at her like that. Well, maybe he would now, having eaten the macaroons.

She was looking around for him when Amanda walked up. "I talked to Lord Malmsey."

"About what?" Juliana gasped, picturing her giving him a piece of her mind about dancing with Frances.

But Amanda surprised her. "About our betrothal. You were right—I had no call to disapprove of him showing interest in another woman. I told him that I understand his change of heart, and feel the same, and I'm going to find a way out of the marriage that will leave him with his honor intact."

Juliana slumped in relief. "You've decided to marry Lord Stafford, then."

Amanda shook her head. "I'm still not struck by love."

Impossible. "Did Lord Stafford touch you?" Juliana asked.

"Touch me? He touched my hand, of course, during the dance when we progressed."

"But nothing else? Nothing more . . . amorous?"

"Amorous?" Amanda's eyes widened. "I should hope not! 'Tis not as though we're engaged."

They'd never *get* engaged if she didn't let him touch her. "The plan was to find someone willing to compromise you," Juliana reminded her. "And some touching, after all, will be necessary in order to convince your father that you're compromised. Perhaps a little experimentation would be wise."

Amanda appeared to quail at the very idea. "It's too soon. I've yet to decide if Lord Stafford is the man I wish to have compromise me."

"Well, your wedding is only three weeks off. You'd best make up your mind quickly, or it will be Lord Malmsey touching you instead of someone of your own choosing." The poor girl's face went white, and Juliana's heart went out to her. How a woman as reserved as Amanda would get through her wedding night was something she didn't even want to contemplate. "We'll find someone," she promised, reaching to pat her hand. "I'm just not sure it's realistic to expect to be struck by love in so little time."

Amanda bit her lip, looking more reserved than ever. "Perhaps you're right."

"If you'd allow Lord Stafford to touch you, that might help."

"He hasn't tried," Amanda said.

Surely the effect of the macaroons hadn't worn off that quickly. "Perhaps if you were a bit more receptive."

"I'll try." Amanda fiddled with her fan. "Do you enjoy it when the duke touches you?"

"Very much," Juliana assured her, wishing the duke had actually touched her so she wouldn't have to fib. "Listen. The musicians are starting a waltz. That's an excellent dance for touching."

She took Amanda's arm and marched her to where James was talking to his mother. "Lady Amanda would love to waltz," she said.

When he didn't move, Lady Stafford nudged him. "Go on, James. We can finish this discussion at home."

"Very well," he said stiffly, offering Amanda his arm. "Shall we dance again?"

As the young couple walked off, Lady Stafford gave a happy sigh and smiled at Juliana, looking as though she had something to say to her. Something nice. But just then, Lord Cavanaugh came up and smartly bowed before the older woman.

"Shall we dance again?" he asked.

Shooting Juliana an even wider smile over her shoulder, Lady Stafford went off with him.

Juliana looked around and spotted the Duke of Castleton walking out of the card room. Aiming her best, practiced smile at him, she went up and tapped him on the arm. "Shall we dance again?"

That line had worked well for everyone else, but the duke looked startled. Juliana supposed it wasn't proper for a lady to do the asking, but she was dying to see how well the macaroons had worked, so she started toward the dance floor, knowing he would follow.

And he did follow, of course. But when they started to waltz, his arms were rigid, and he held her just as far away as ever.

"Who is that dancing with Stafford?" he asked. "Do you know her?"

"Lady Amanda Wolverston, and I know her very well."

"I've never noticed her before."

Well, of course he hadn't. No one had noticed Amanda before Juliana took her in hand. "What did you think of Lord Stafford's controversial speech?"

"To which speech do you refer?"

"Yesterday's. In Parliament. Concerning smallpox vaccinations."

"How would you come to know of that?" he asked, but apparently the question was rhetorical, because he didn't wait for an answer. "I was at my club all day and night," he told her. "Playing cards."

She wondered why she found that disturbing. After all, she wanted a man who put pleasure before more serious pursuits. "Did you win?"

"Does it matter? It was an amusing way to pass the hours." He smiled down on her indulgently. "I can afford to lose, I assure you. I have plenty of money to both gamble and buy flowers for special ladies."

She was glad he thought she was special, but if he had extra funds, perhaps they'd be better spent on something more meaningful. A worthy cause. The Foundling Hospital, perhaps, or smallpox vaccinations.

Once she knew him better, she'd make the suggestion. She wished he would loosen up so she could *get* to know him better. "Did you eat any more of my macaroons?" she asked, concluding he hadn't.

"All of them," he said, surprising her. "They tasted so wonderful, and I couldn't find anywhere to put them to save them for later."

That was as she'd expected. But why weren't they working? "I'm glad you enjoyed them."

"They were very, very good."

Apparently they weren't good enough. They didn't seem to make him amorous at all. She moved a little bit closer, but he stiffened his arms until they were once more at a proper distance.

Lord Cavanaugh, she noticed, wasn't dancing nearly so properly with Lady Stafford. The two of them looked rather cozy. And Aunt Frances and Lord Malmsey were so close they were all but tromping on each other's toes. Amanda, however, was dancing at a proper distance from James.

She should have left James more macaroons, considering two had worn off too quickly and even seven hadn't affected the duke. What would make a man so resistant? Since he was a by-blow, she imagined his father might have acted distant, knowing his son was actually sired by another. But a good mother should have made up for that.

"Was your mother not affectionate?" she asked.

"Affectionate?" He looked taken aback by the mere question. "I wouldn't know. I never knew either of my parents."

Oh, how tragic. "Why was that?"

"They died when I was six months old. Drowned in a storm while crossing the Channel."

"I'm so sorry." Juliana had lost her parents as a young adult—she could hardly imagine growing up without parents altogether. Even motherless Emily and Amanda had fathers in their lives. "Who raised you, then?"

His handsome mouth compressed into a thin line. "My uncle and aunt—my father's brother and his wife. Did you know I was born in your house? The first thing they did as my guardians was sell that house to your father and then buy my current, more splendid house in Grosvenor Square. I was well satisfied to turn them out of it when I gained my majority."

She was happy to hear he had a splendid house, but she wondered at the bitterness in his tone. "Were they not nice to you?"

"Nice?" He laughed, but it was a laugh devoid of humor. "If I hadn't been born half a year before my parents died, my uncle and aunt would have been the duke and duchess. They never forgave me for robbing them of that."

He didn't offer any details, but Juliana could imagine them for herself. His uncle and aunt had been cold, cruel, and resentful. He'd received no hugs growing up, no physical affection. "I'm so sorry you had a sad childhood," she told him. No wonder he wasn't affectionate himself. No one had ever shown him how.

"You're so caring, my dear," he said, giving her a fond smile.

No one had cared for him throughout his childhood,

which was why he had a hard time getting close to others now. Like all people, he'd learned by example, and he needed a new example to learn by.

Human touch could go a long way. Once he learned to be more affectionate, he would also be more charitable. The poor man needed someone in his life to gently guide him, to help his softer side come to the fore.

He needed *her*. With her in his life, demonstrating affection and giving to others—

The dance came to an end. Before she could finish formulating her plan, he bowed formally and thanked her.

No sooner had he walked away than Lady Stafford walked up. "I must thank you for introducing me to Lord Cavanaugh."

"I thought you already knew him."

"Reintroducing me, then." She smiled, her kindly eyes reminding Juliana of her own mother. "I'm giving a little dinner party tomorrow evening at Stafford House, and Lord Cavanaugh has agreed to attend. My son will be there, too. Might I have the pleasure of your company as well?"

"I'd be delighted to attend." She liked James's mother. Lady Stafford was very motherly, and Juliana missed her mother rather a lot. Plus the dinner would give her a chance to ask James how his courtship of Amanda was proceeding and remind him to invite her to visit the Egyptian Hall. Once Amanda discovered their shared interest in Roman antiquities, she was certain to fall in love.

"I'm also going to ask the young lady with whom my son has been dancing." Lady Stafford's gaze slid to Amanda and back. "Shall I invite the Duke of Castleton to round out our party?"

"That would be lovely," Juliana said.

That would be perfect, in fact. The duke never called on Sundays, so the dinner would give her a chance to begin helping him right away. She'd be able to direct the conversation to James's cause and perhaps persuade him to contribute. She hoped the duke would like James, and vice versa. Perhaps, in the long run, she and the duke could become fast friends with James and Amanda and have more dinner parties after both couples were married. That would be an ideal situation, because she'd come to enjoy James's company in the time they'd spent together.

"Eight o'clock, then?" the older woman asked. "Lady Amanda lives on your street, does she not? On the west side of Berkeley Square? I'll have the Stafford carriage sent round for you both."

Chapter Twenty-one

APPLE AND ORANGE TART

Peel two Oranges and make into pieces, then peel some Apples into thin slices. Put in a bowle with a smidgen of Flour, a cup of Sugar, some Cinnamon and Ginger. Put into your paste with pieces of Butter all over. Cover with more paste and some Sugar and bake in your oven until browne.

Excellent to bring to a party with friends. As the apples and oranges in this tart go together, so do the people who eat it.
—Eleanor Chase, Marchioness of Cainewood, 1735

"Isn't this a stunning carriage?" Juliana asked as she and Amanda neared Stafford House.

Amanda absentmindedly ran a hand over the deep green velvet upholstery. "Lord Stafford is an earl. I'd expect him to have a nice carriage."

The well-sprung vehicle rocked, making Juliana tighten her grip on the tart she'd baked that afternoon. Was there nothing about the man that would impress her friend? "He likes chess," she reminded her, and then, even though she'd meant to let Amanda discover they had more in common at the Egyptian Hall, she added, "And you might want to ask him if he's interested in Roman antiq—"

She cut off mid-word as the carriage came to a stop and the door opened, revealing a footman dressed in crimson livery trimmed in gold. "Welcome to Stafford House," he said, offering a gloved hand to help them down.

"Gracious me," Amanda breathed, her eyes widening as she stepped out and stood before the mansion. "I've noticed this house from Green Park, but I had no idea it belonged to Lord Stafford." It was three stories tall, the facade clad in brilliant white Portland stone. "Would you look at those statues on top of that Roman Doric portico? Bacchus, Flora, and Ceres."

Juliana hadn't a clue who Bacchus, Flora, and Ceres were, but she smiled all the same. "Lord Stafford can name ancient gods and goddesses, too."

A butler ushered them inside an impressive entrance hall with curved walls, a pale marble floor, and an arched window looking out on a resplendent central courtyard garden.

"Gracious me," Amanda repeated, staring up at a strip of decorations that ran around the room below the carved oval ceiling. "That frieze looks like the one in the Temple of Jupiter." Slowly, reverently, she walked toward a large marble bust that sat on a pedestal before the window. "This is amazing." She reached a hand as though to touch it, then stopped herself. "It must be priceless."

"He doesn't look like a god," Juliana said.

"He isn't. That's Emperor Lucius Verus, the adopted brother of Marcus Aurelius who ruled with him."

Juliana examined the haughty, bearded fellow. "He's very handsome."

"He was said to be weak and indulgent. I understand that his death was rather a relief to the Empire."

"How do you know such things?" Juliana asked.

"From books, of course. My father's library has grown by leaps and bounds since he discovered the ruins on the property. Do you not read, too?"

"Most certainly." Newspapers, because she liked to keep up with what was going on in the world. Magazines by the dozen. Poetry and the latest novels discussed in polite company. And those discussed in whispers, such as the torrid Minerva Press romance currently hidden beneath her pillow. But Roman history and mythology?

She'd had no idea Amanda was so bookish.

After collecting their pelisses and umbrellas, the butler led them through a staircase hall. Or at least he *tried* to lead them through a staircase hall. Amanda stopped in her tracks, staring at a statue that was larger-than-life.

"It's a centaur," she said.

"Even I know that. My education isn't *totally* lacking." Juliana was rather fascinated by all the ridges on the creature's toned, bare chest. But Amanda had already moved on, kneeling down by a large fragment of carved stone that sat under an inlaid wooden side table.

"Part of a sarcophagus, I'd guess." She ran her fingers across the piece. "First century."

"How do you know?" Juliana wondered.

Amanda just shrugged as she rose, gesturing to two more carved stone pieces on either side of the table. "Funerary altars. Also first century. The flat surface was used for sacrificial ceremonies." She sighed expansively. "This house is just *full* of treasures."

The butler continued on, leading them down a corridor lined with gilt-framed paintings of Stafford ancestors, then turning into the most gorgeous room Juliana had ever seen. Between arched walls painted a soft pistachio green, gilded columns looked like golden palm trees, their fronds projecting high overhead. In the back of the room, a large alcove was crowned with a domed ceiling, divided into small gilt-edged squares alternately tinted green and pink.

Dressed in a burgundy gown with pink trim, Lady Stafford rose from where she faced Lord Cavanaugh across a chessboard and greeted them with a smile. "Good evening. I'm so pleased you could both come." She moved to take the dish Juliana was holding out. "What is this, my dear?"

"An apple and orange tart. The recipe was my great-grandmother's."

She lifted the lace doily that covered it. "Oh, my. It smells delicious."

"It's supposed to promote friendship," Amanda informed her, staring down at the chess set.

"Lovely!" Lady Stafford set the tart on a marble side table. "We shall serve it after dinner."

"What a beautiful chess set," Juliana said, amused by Amanda's fascination. "Roman gladiators, aren't they? Do the pieces date back to that time?"

"No, they look much newer," Amanda said. "And besides, chess isn't that old. It wasn't invented until after the Empire fell."

"My father-in-law commissioned the set to be carved." Lady Stafford lifted a crystal decanter. "Would you care for some sherry?"

"A little, please." Juliana took the first glass she poured and perched herself on a pale green satin love seat with gilt palm tree legs that had obviously been designed to match the room. "Thank you so much for inviting us to your home."

"It's my son's home," she said, handing Amanda another glass.

That son walked into the room with the duke, the two of them deep in conversation. Juliana was thrilled to see the men were becoming friends already. She smoothed the skirts of her white dress, which she'd chosen hoping the duke would think it proper and ladylike. *Very pure*, as James had said.

Sipping sherry, Amanda sat beside her. "He's so much taller," she whispered.

James *was* much taller than the duke. Which was why he and Amanda looked so good together.

"And darker," Amanda added.

Yes, James was dark. The duke looked pasty in comparison. Pasty and pale-haired. But only in comparison. And Juliana preferred pale hair.

"And *much* more handsome."

"It isn't polite to whisper," Juliana whispered back. She didn't want to think about James being much more handsome. And it wasn't true, anyway.

Was it?

"Good evening, ladies," James said, his voice low and chocolate-smooth as always. On hearing it, Juliana felt her knees weaken as always, too, even though she was sitting down.

"Good evening," the duke said in his perfectly normal voice. He smiled at Juliana. "It's lovely to see you again, my dear."

Well, why should a voice matter, anyway? The duke was a *duke*. And it was obvious he cared for her, even if he didn't touch her.

A footman appeared in the doorway and announced dinner. Lord Cavanaugh offered Lady Stafford his arm. "Shall we?"

The rest of them followed the older couple into a large formal dining room. The extra leaves had been removed from the mahogany table to make it an oval for six. While a footman drew back Juliana's chair, she took a moment to look around. The dining room featured Roman-looking marble columns, a beautiful Turkey carpet, and a carved marble fireplace. But the most impressive thing of all was the ceiling, a scalloped design with round inset panels representing classical scenes, all decorated in gold.

"It's exquisite," she said as she sank onto her forest green velvet seat.

"My late husband's pride and joy." Lady Stafford sat, too. "It was based on a ceiling in the Baths of Augustus in Rome."

Gazing up at it, Amanda sighed. "This is the most magnificent house I've ever seen. Everything in it is absolutely splendid." She turned to James beside her. "You have wonderful taste, Lord Stafford."

His mother laughed. "The taste was his grandfather's. The man hired the venerable Henry Holland as his designer. Were it up to my son, he'd probably sell the whole lot and use the money to vaccinate every last soul in England."

James frowned. "The sale of this house and its contents wouldn't begin to cover—"

"I was jesting," Lady Stafford broke in with the sort of fond smile a mother gives her exasperating-but-adored son. "I trust you not to sell off the family treasures."

Juliana saw an opportunity to segue into a matter she'd hoped to discuss. "If others would help with Lord Stafford's cause," she said as asparagus soup was served in porcelain bowls with gold Stafford crests on their crimson rims, "there would be no need to sell anything." Lifting her spoon, which was gold, too, she turned to the duke. "Eradicating smallpox is a worthy goal that all should contribute toward, don't you think?"

"All?" The duke raised his own gold spoon. "Worthy or not, I don't expect everyone can afford to donate."

"Certainly *you* can," she said sweetly.

She thought she heard choking sounds from James. Or maybe a muffled chortle.

Lord Cavanaugh took a sip of wine. "I would be pleased to contribute."

"Thank you very much," James said with an expression of startled approval. "That would be much appreciated."

Lady Stafford looked quite delighted.

Amanda turned a smile on James. "I should like to contribute, too," she said prettily, "but alas, I shall need to ask my father for the funds."

Knowing Amanda's father, Juliana was sure he wouldn't donate a penny. And she was sure Amanda knew that, too. "Time is also valuable," she said. "You could volunteer your aid in lieu of money."

Amanda blinked and pressed a hand to her pale blue muslin bodice. "Are you suggesting I give smallpox vaccinations?"

"No, of course not. Doctors give the vaccinations. But I'm sure there are other tasks you could perform that would prove helpful."

"Certainly," James put in, setting down his spoon, which Juliana had decided was actually sterling plated in gold, because, really, solid gold spoons were a little much, even for people as rich as the Staffords. "There are always new supplies arriving that need to be unpacked and arranged on the shelves behind the counter, and schedules to be made out in a hand neater than mine, and treatment rooms to be cleaned, and—"

"You're looking for people to clean rooms?" Amanda

interrupted. She pinned Juliana with a pointed gaze. "Are you going to volunteer, too, then?"

In truth, Juliana hadn't a clue why she'd suggested Amanda volunteer in the first place. She certainly didn't expect her to clean treatment rooms—she doubted the woman had cleaned anything in her life, with the possible exception of her own teeth. But something about Amanda's disingenuous offer of money had rubbed her the wrong way.

And now she'd backed herself into a corner. "I'd be happy to volunteer," Juliana found herself saying. She lifted her chin. She did like helping people, and while she was quite busy sewing baby clothes, she imagined she could spare a little time. "As I said, it's a worthy cause."

"Capital!" James exclaimed so enthusiastically she half expected him to break into applause. "How about Wednesday at one o'clock?"

"She can't," Amanda said. "She has a sewing party every Wednesday at one."

Drat. "I'll move this week's party to tomorrow."

"Sewing party?" Lady Stafford asked.

"Lady Juliana supports many worthy causes," Amanda said. "She's making baby clothes for the Foundling Hospital."

Juliana had a sudden thought. "It might be a good idea," she suggested to James, "for you to vaccinate the foundlings."

"I already do," he said, which made her admire him even more. "I visit there twice every year."

Lady Stafford turned to Juliana. "Do you need more help sewing the baby clothes, dear? I'd be pleased to attend your party tomorrow."

"That would be wonderful," Juliana said. And it was. But she spent the rest of dinner wondering how it happened that she'd ended up volunteering to help at the Institute when she'd suggested Amanda do so, and Lord Cavanaugh had ended up donating money when she'd asked that of the duke.

Maybe she was losing her touch.

Chapter Twenty-two

After dinner, when the ladies would usually have left the men alone with their port, Lady Stafford suggested they all adjourn to the Palm Room instead. While the men poured and Lady Stafford busied herself serving up the apple and orange tart, Amanda drew Juliana into the alcove at the back of the room.

"Can you *believe* this house?" she whispered, her eyes sparkling at last. "Is it not the most amazing thing you've ever seen?"

Juliana's gaze wandered the gold palm fronds, the gold and crystal chandeliers, the gold-trimmed ceiling. "There's a lot of gold."

Smiling, Amanda nodded. "Even the silverware is gold."

"It's sterling plated in gold," Juliana informed her.

"Regardless. What's truly amazing is all the antiquities. They make the terra-cotta pots and glass flasks my father's uncovered look like so much rubbish." Her whisper dropped even lower. "I want to marry Lord Stafford."

The words Juliana had been waiting to hear. But her friend's sudden change of heart was . . . well, it was very sudden. "You cannot marry for antiquities," she whispered back, fearing Amanda was making this decision for all the wrong reasons. "I would hope you would like the man more than his possessions."

"Oh, I do. I've decided you're right. My wedding is drawing ever closer, and Lord Stafford and I suit well. We're compatible. He likes chess, and he's clearly interested in all things Roman. Maybe my father was right—maybe there are more important considerations than love. Besides, you said I will learn to love Lord Stafford, and I believe you."

Amanda *sounded* sincere, Juliana thought. Perhaps she should stop worrying about the reasons and just be relieved her friend was finally consenting to marry James. They did share common interests, and Amanda didn't sicken at the sight of blood. She'd make an excellent physician's wife. It was unfortunate they hadn't the luxury to get to know each other leisurely, but the two of them had been destined to fall in love from the first. She'd said so all along, hadn't she?

She *was* relieved, she decided.

In fact, she was thrilled. How could she not be thrilled? With the possible exception of civilizing young Emily, all of her projects were progressing perfectly.

Lord Malmsey and Lady Frances were getting along swimmingly. Indeed, at the ball last night, their aging eyes had been glittering with the discovery of new love. Now that Lord Malmsey would no longer need to wed Amanda, the charmingly shy couple would live happily ever after.

The duke didn't seem to mind the company of James and Amanda, which meant that after Juliana married him, she could retain James's friendship. She and the duke would have to fall in love before marrying, of course, but maybe they were in love already. How was a woman with her lack of experience supposed to know? And in any case, love was bound to happen soon. The duke cared for her, and he needed her. On the surface, he was perfect—everything she'd been looking for in a man—but inside, he was hurt. With her help, he was going to learn to be affectionate and more charitable. She was going to be a duchess! Her grace, Juliana, the Duchess of Castleton. The name had such a lovely ring to it.

And on top of all of that good news, it looked as though she may have managed to match Lady Stafford with Lord Cavanaugh, even though she'd intended only for them to enjoy a dance.

Everything was going to work out exactly as it should.

Lady Stafford came into the alcove and handed Juliana and Amanda each a crested plate with a slice of the tart and a gold fork. "Your great-grandmother's tart is delicious," she gushed. "Thank you so much for making and bringing it."

"You're very welcome," Juliana said, following her back to the main part of the room. Plate in hand, the duke wandered into the alcove and began chatting with Amanda. The tart was promoting new friendships already.

Lady Stafford seated herself on a chair covered in pale green satin with a palm tree design worked into the fabric. Lord Cavanaugh took the chair nearest hers. James was already sitting on the love seat, digging happily into a slice of tart. There were six more palm tree–decorated chairs and four matching stools, but Juliana sat on the love seat by James, even though she knew that place should be reserved for Amanda.

It would be for but a moment. She had something very important to discuss.

James didn't seem to find anything amiss with her sitting beside him. In fact, he shifted to face her, which put him rather too close. "This tart is excellent," he said. "Did you make it?"

"Of course," she said, trying to scoot a little to the side. Apparently the love seat was too small to share with a man of his size. "Your mother is getting along very well with Lord Cavanaugh, isn't she?"

"She seems to be, yes."

"They seem perfect for each other. His title even begins with *C*."

"*C*?"

"Like her sisters, don't you see? Aurelia is Lady Avonleigh, Bedelia is Lady Balmforth, and your mother would be—"

"Cornelia, Lady Cavanaugh. Yes, I see." Looking amused, he swallowed another bite. "But I should think there are more important things for a couple to share than matching names."

"Of course there are," she said, pleased to hear he agreed that couples should have things in common. "They should share interests—for example, chess and antiquities. And in your case especially, I should think you would want a wife who isn't sickened by the sight of blood."

"I'm not a surgeon," he pointed out, "and I don't believe in bleeding patients. Nor would I expect a wife to assist me with my practice. So there is virtually no chance she would have to deal with blood."

That was a bit of a relief, although there was no reason it should be. "James . . ."

"You mentioned chess," he said. "Would you care for a game?"

"Amanda adores chess." She really had something she needed to discuss. "I prefer playing cards, especially casino."

"I enjoy whist," he said. "Perhaps someday you can teach me casino. When is our next outing?" He reached for his glass of port, rubbing up against her in the process.

She suppressed a pleasurable but rather disturbing shiver, thinking he should be touching Amanda instead. She could smell his scent again. Very male soap, with a little starch, maybe, and something else she couldn't identify. She leaned closer, in order to keep their conversation private. "You don't need any more lessons."

"Oh." He took a sip and set down the glass, looking relieved. Or maybe disappointed.

No, relieved. There was no reason for him to be disappointed, after all.

"Are you sure?" he asked.

"Quite. I've been thinking . . ."

"Yes?" Grazing her again, he forked up another bite.

Juliana lowered her voice. "We need to plan a way for you to publicly compromise Amanda."

The fork clattered back to the plate. "Compromise Amanda? Whyever would I do that?"

"In order to get her father to agree to your marrying her."

"I would never do such an underhanded thing." Juliana couldn't decide whether he looked more shocked or affronted. "And besides, why should her father not accept my suit, should I choose to marry her? I may be engaged in a profession, but after all, I'm an earl as well. It's not as though I'm a pauper."

That much was clear—a pauper didn't set his table with gold spoons. But if James refused to even entertain the thought of compromising Amanda, what would he do if he found out she was already engaged? What would he do if he realized that in order to marry her, he'd have to trick Lord Wolverston into breaking a contract with another man?

He'd refuse to marry her, that was what. He was entirely too honorable to have anything to do with something as "underhanded" as what Juliana and Amanda had planned. But their plan wasn't underhanded—it was . . . what was that word James had used to describe his own willingness to bow to Parliament's opposition to making vaccinations compulsory?

Pragmatic, that was it. Her plan was pragmatic. And justified, under the circumstances.

Lord Wolverston wasn't honorable—he was treating his daughter abominably—which meant dishonorable means were entirely justifiable if necessary to stop him.

But she knew James wouldn't see it that way. He was too good a man. Too good for his own good.

As Amanda and the duke stepped into the room from the alcove, Juliana sighed and moved to a chair so Amanda could sit beside James. But Amanda didn't, choosing another chair to sit upon instead, because, after all, she was a reserved sort of woman, and James didn't leave very much room on the cozy love seat.

Heaven forbid Amanda should sit too close to a man—even a man she was planning to marry.

Juliana shrugged and took a bite of her tart, thinking that if James and Amanda weren't going to share the love seat, she should share it herself with the duke so she could start teaching him to be more affectionate. He'd chosen the chair beside her, of course, but that wasn't close enough to show him how good being truly close could feel. Of course, before she could share the love seat with the duke, she'd have to get James to move off of it. But that shouldn't be any problem at all.

"Lord Stafford would like to pass some time playing chess," she told Amanda.

"Another time," James disagreed. "An evening is never long in good company."

"An ancient proverb," Amanda said with a small smile.

Whether it was a proverb or not, Juliana had failed to get James off the love seat. Oh, well, she sighed to herself, she'd have to sit closer to the duke next time. And so she spent the evening being good company . . . all the while pondering what she could do to help a good man like James win the happiness he deserved.

And failing utterly to come up with anything.

"What a lovely girl," Cornelia said after closing the door behind their guests.

James turned to her wearily. Spending time with Juliana—without touching her as he itched to—seemed to wear him out. "Yes, Mother," he said. "Lady Amanda is quite lovely."

"Well, yes, she is, but I was speaking of Lady Juliana." She started up the wide, cantilevered stone staircase that led to the upper floors. "Lady Juliana is lovely inside, don't you think? Not that she isn't pretty, mind you— she's a darling little thing—but I think the way she tries so hard to help is lovely in itself. She really cares about people. She brought us all a sweet she made from her great-grandmother's recipe. She makes clothing for the Foundling Hospital. And she even volunteered to help at the New Hope Institute." She paused halfway up and turned to look back at him, her hand on the trompe l'oeil–painted metal balustrade. "A lady of the *ton*, helping at your Institute!"

James was quite aware that Juliana had mistakenly manipulated herself into that position, but he wouldn't say so to his mother. Because Cornelia was right. Juliana *was* lovely inside. She wasn't nearly as frivolous as he'd once thought.

"She's a treasure," his mother declared. "I think you should marry her instead of Lady Amanda."

"I never said I was marrying anyone!" James burst out, shocked for the second time in one night. Or maybe the third. In fact, when Juliana had shocked him the first time by suggesting he compromise Amanda in order to marry her, he'd shocked himself by almost saying, *What if I want to marry you instead?*

But he wasn't ready to marry anyone. He'd have to fall in love first. And he couldn't fall in love with anyone besides Anne—not even if she was a treasure.

"Good night, Mother," he said, suddenly even wearier than he'd been earlier. But he resumed his climb, taking the steps two at a time so he could escape before Cornelia said anything more. "Sleep well," he called on the landing. Then he made his way down the corridor, ducked into his study, closed the door behind him, and dropped to the long leather sofa that sat before his father's big oak desk.

And there, without undressing, he slept.

Not in the elegant brown-and-plum bedchamber his grandfather had hired the venerable Henry Holland to decorate.

Not in the brown-and-plum-curtained tester bed he'd been born in . . . the same bed he'd later shared with Anne.

Chapter Twenty-three

"I cannot believe you didn't tell me you'd talked to Lord Stafford," Amanda said the next afternoon. "What did he say, then?"

The day had dawned bright and sunny for a change, and if it wasn't exactly warm, at least it was no longer freezing. Following Juliana's rescheduled sewing party—after which, despite everyone's help, Emily had calculated that Juliana *still* needed a hundred and seventy-eight items of baby clothes—she'd taken Amanda across the street into Berkeley Square, where they sat on a bench beneath a plane tree, eating ices from Gunter's Tea Shop.

Or at least Juliana was eating hers.

"Do you know," she said, "this is the first ice I've had all summer." She scooped the last of the frosty treat and spooned it into her mouth, savoring the heavenly flavor. "Delicious. White currant is the best."

Amanda's strawberry ice sat in her dish untouched. "What did he say?" she repeated. "When does he think we should carry out our plan?"

Juliana sighed and licked her spoon. "He doesn't think we should carry out our plan at all. He called it 'underhanded.' "

"Underhanded?"

"Yes. He wants to ask for your hand outright. He says there's no reason your father shouldn't agree."

"He doesn't know my father, then," Amanda said dejectedly. She poked her spoon at her melty pink ice, staring at the statue of King George in the middle of the square. "What did he say when you told him Father is too stubborn to break the agreement with Lord Malmsey?"

"I didn't tell him that. James—I mean, Lord Stafford—would never pursue marriage if he knew you're already engaged. He's entirely too honorable."

"Like my father, putting his honor before my happiness."

"Lord Stafford isn't selfish, just principled. It's not the same."

"Maybe not." Amanda slowly stirred what was now strawberry soup. "Why didn't you tell me this last night? On the way home in Lord Stafford's carriage?"

"I don't know," Juliana admitted. She shifted her gaze from Amanda's disappointed face to the likeness of their monarch. His Majesty was mounted on a horse, wearing some sort of drapey garment she supposed was intended to be Greek or Roman but instead made the poor man look like he was bundled against the cold. "I guess I was trying to figure out how to fix this."

"And what did you come up with?"

"Nothing."

"Nothing?" Amanda set the dish on the bench beside her. "You *always* have a plan."

"No, I don't." Juliana sighed. "I don't have a plan this time."

"Well, I do," Amanda declared.

Juliana couldn't have been more surprised if the statue of King George had suddenly come to life and galloped off. "You have a plan?"

"Yes. We shall trick Lord Stafford into compromising me."

"*We* shall do no such thing." Juliana wasn't sure which shocked her more: prissy Amanda suggesting such a plan or the thought of tricking a man who'd become her friend. "That would be reprehensible. Unethical. Completely disgraceful."

"Why? You said he wanted to marry me. If his supposed honor is standing in the way, we'd be doing him a favor, would we not?"

"No," Juliana said, and then, "Well, maybe." Amanda had a point. James *did* want to marry her. He'd said as much, hadn't he? He'd said Amanda was lovely—many times—and he'd said her father would accept his suit. He wouldn't *have* a suit if he wasn't wanting to marry her. Why else would he be courting her? He'd bought her gifts, and he'd asked her to dance. More than once. At every ball, as a matter of fact. And he'd invited Amanda to his home.

Well, technically his mother had done the inviting. But it was his home, and most certainly he'd approved. "Do you enjoy playing whist?" she suddenly asked.

"Yes, but what does that have to do with anything?"

Amanda liked whist, as did James. And chess. And she wasn't sickened by blood. No wonder James loved her and wished to marry her. And the only way to make his wish come true was to—

"I think we should do it this Saturday," Amanda declared, interrupting Juliana's line of reasoning. "At the Billingsgate ball."

Apparently Amanda had *destroyed* Juliana's line of reasoning, not just interrupted it. Because suddenly she wasn't sure everything quite made sense. "I don't know," she said. "It just seems wrong somehow to plot behind Lord Stafford's back. It makes me feel guilty."

"Guilty? I think not." Juliana couldn't remember Amanda ever sounding so sure of herself. "I told you, we'll be doing him a *favor*."

There it was, that *we* again. That guilty-making *we*. "Maybe you should do this alone, Amanda."

"Why?" Amanda shifted to face her on the bench, her eyes not sparkling but pleading. "I cannot plan this alone. I need your help, Juliana—you're the bright one of us, after all."

Well, Amanda had *that* right. The girl might be bookish, but that was not the same as bright.

"You cannot really feel guilty," Amanda added.

"Maybe just a tad."

"Well, you shouldn't."

Maybe Amanda's arguments were valid. After all, James wanted to marry her. And Lord Malmsey certainly didn't. And Aunt Frances—dear, myopic Aunt Frances—would be devastated if Amanda married Lord Malmsey. The only person who would be happy if Amanda *didn't* trick James was her dratted, conniving father. Surely that would be the greater wrong.

That all sounded well justified, didn't it?

Juliana's sisters often said that justification was one of her many talents.

"Well?" Amanda asked.

"All right. We'll make a plan."

"Gracious me." Amanda lifted her dish and happily scooped up a spoonful of strawberry soup. "I thought you'd never agree."

Wondering if she *should* have agreed, Juliana started plotting.

Chapter Twenty-four

ORANGE JUMBLES

Mix a cup of Flower with Almonds ground fine and Sugar, then add two spoones of grated rinde of Oranges and Salt. Rub in some Butter and binde with beaten whites of two Egges. When smooth, make into pieces and roll each out in the shape of an *S*. Bake on a greased tin until browne and golden.

This receipt has been in our family for a very long time. They are a homely sort of biscuit, good for taking to ailing villagers or anyone you like to make comfortable.

—Lady Diana Caldwell, 1689

James handed the hopeful young woman a pencil and slid a piece of paper across the counter. "Write your name here, please, on line fourteen."

She squinted at the page.

"There," he elaborated, indicating the number 14.

She bit her lip and wrote an awkward *X* beside it.

The eleventh *X* on the page. "Thank you," he said, suppressing a sigh, "but I don't believe you will find this position suitable."

Her shoulders slumped as she turned, and he wished

he could help. The introduction of new machinery was causing massive unemployment all over England, but his concern about that problem didn't change the fact that he required an assistant who could read and write.

As she plodded out of the New Hope Institute, Juliana danced in, gave a jaunty wave toward the Chase carriage outside, and stuck her umbrella in the stand by the door.

It was Wednesday, and—James checked his pocket watch—precisely one o'clock. Having not seen Juliana since the dinner at Stafford House on Sunday, he'd been wondering if she would actually show up. As she walked toward him, her smile seemed to brighten the entire reception room, some feat considering his current mood. It was raining outside—of course—but she was wearing a thin, sunny yellow dress that did nothing to disguise her curves. Which meant it did nothing to help contain his ever-growing lust, either. The bodice was small, as usual, which made him envision her lovely breasts popping right out of it.

Bloody hell.

"Good afternoon," he said. "No Lady Frances?"

"Oh, she'd be bored, and she doesn't care for this neighborhood. Besides, this is hardly a situation that requires a chaperone." She seemed to be staring at the area below his throat. "The carriage will return for me at four o'clock. Why are you out here?" Raising her gaze to his face—with some effort, it appeared—she placed the basket she was carrying on the counter between them. "Shouldn't you be in one of the treatment rooms, giving vaccinations?"

"I am interviewing for a new assistant." He gestured toward the HELP WANTED sign he'd once again placed in the window. "And playing the part of assistant myself until I find one."

"Did the last one you hired leave, then?"

"Yes. This morning." The pouring rain had kept a queue from forming all the way to Surrey today, but that also meant potential new employees were staying home. Juliana seemed to be waiting for an explanation, so he added, "She found herself with child unexpectedly."

"Unexpectedly? How can it be that a woman does

what it takes to get a child without expecting to find herself with one?"

He knew quite a few ways, actually—he was a physician, after all—but he wouldn't explain them to an innocent young lady. Not even one unreserved enough to raise the question while wearing a dress with a tiny bodice and staring at the little bit of skin that was exposed where he'd left his top button undone.

"She has no husband," he said, unfastening a second button to see her reaction. "The father of her child cannot afford to support a wife."

"Oh." She looked a mite scandalized, but he wasn't sure whether to attribute that to his unbuttoning or to the news that his unwed assistant had got herself with child. "She must feel perfectly dreadful."

"Less dreadful, I expect, since I gave her fifty pounds and sent her off to get married."

Her entire face lit up. "Then she won't have to give her child to the Foundling Hospital. That was wonderful, James."

He hadn't been feeling very wonderful until now, but the admiring tone of her voice made him want to kiss her. Hell, the mere sight of her made him want to kiss her. The tiny bodice didn't help, and neither did her obvious interest in his bare skin. He shifted uncomfortably, wishing they were someplace besides the Institute.

Although it was probably best that they weren't.

"I brought you orange jumbles," she said, lifting the cloth that covered the basket to reveal biscuits that smelled almost as good as she did. "They're supposed to be good for the ailing." She glanced around the crowded reception area. "Though I suppose these people aren't ailing, really, are they?"

"My goal is to *keep* them from ailing."

"Yes, of course. Well, the jumbles are supposed to help keep one comfortable as well. Try one."

As he took one of the sweets—wondering if it was so obvious that he was uncomfortable—a woman and her newly vaccinated son walked out, the youngster sucking a sugar stick. "Excuse me," James said and stepped from behind the counter. "Number forty-three!"

Another woman and her two children rose and followed him into the back. Taking the biscuit with him, he showed them to a treatment room. The orange jumble was crisp and tasted sweet and citrusy, but it was not comforting.

When he returned, Juliana was behind the counter, handing a number to a dripping family of four. "You're number fifty-seven," she said loudly and clearly. "Please be seated. Lord Stafford will call you when it's your turn."

James watched the family try and fail to find seats, then turned to Juliana. "I prefer to be called Dr. Trevor while I'm here. 'Lord Stafford' intimidates the patients."

"I'll try to remember that. There's a young woman waiting for an interview—I told her to sit until you were ready. Which of the treatment rooms shall I clean?"

"Pardon?"

"I came to clean treatment rooms, remember?" She pulled off her gloves. "I wore my oldest dress."

He eyed her oldest dress with its tiny bodice. It looked no more shabby than the one she'd worn to his house for dinner, which meant, of course, that it did not look shabby at all. "What makes you think I would expect a lady to clean anything?" he asked. "The Stafford House maids take turns coming here to clean. Three times a week."

Her pretty brow creased. "Why did you tell Lady Amanda she could clean, then?"

He shrugged, remembering Lady Amanda's attitude at dinner. Very ladylike and rather snobbish. "I just wanted to see her reaction."

"Oh." Juliana looked thoughtful, or apprehensive—he wasn't sure which. "And what did you think of how she reacted?"

"Very much like a lady," he said, leaving out the word *snobbish*.

Now she looked relieved. "Amanda is very much a lovely lady," she said. "What shall you have me do if not clean treatment rooms?"

"You seem to make an excellent assistant. Why don't you keep doing that?"

She did prove an excellent assistant, which allowed him to vaccinate patients between interviewing candidates. Two hours later, the number of people in the reception room had dwindled to something approaching normal. The orange jumbles were all gone, and they'd indeed seemed to comfort some of the patients. People waiting to be infected tended to be somewhat nervous.

He'd talked to three more women who wanted the job, but they'd all been underqualified.

"The tasks are not very difficult," Juliana said during a rare lull. Her gaze flicked toward his open shirt and back up. "Why is it that you find it so hard to hire someone acceptable?"

"My assistant must be able to read and write."

"Many women can read and write—"

"But many of those don't need employment. Educated women are likely to have fathers or husbands to support them."

"Oh. I hadn't thought of that." She handed him the box of sugar sticks he'd asked her to fetch. "I shall screen the applicants for you and let you know if I find someone acceptable. That way you can keep administering vaccinations."

He wished he could find someone as efficient as Juliana. An hour later, she announced she'd found the perfect replacement, a young woman that Miss Smith, his last morning assistant, had apparently sent and recommended. All the supplies in the treatment rooms were restocked, the storage shelves were organized, Juliana had rewritten his scribbled July schedule in a neat, legible hand, and—in part thanks to the rain—only five patients were waiting for vaccinations.

Even better, it was now four o'clock, which meant his second-shift assistant had arrived, as well as two fresh physicians. He was free, and it was Wednesday, so Parliament wasn't in session. Juliana's carriage was due to return any moment, but she had no chaperone, for once. She was still glancing where his shirt was unbuttoned whenever she thought he wasn't looking.

Maybe he could get her alone someplace where he could kiss her, he thought as he followed her toward the door. Maybe he could talk her into going somewhere besides home.

She pulled on her gloves. "Will I see you at Almack's tonight?"

Somewhere besides Almack's.

The door opened, admitting two new patients, a footman in Chase livery, and a messenger boy. "Lord Stafford?" the messenger boy inquired.

"Yes." James took the note, broke the seal, and scanned the single page. "Damn."

"Is it something dreadful?" Juliana asked, splaying a gloved hand over her breasts in their tiny yellow bodice. Which only made him notice them more. Hell. Was she trying to kill him?

"No. Aunt Bedelia fears some ailment and wishes to see me."

"I hope she will turn out to be well."

"She will, I assure you. But I'm afraid I won't make it to Almack's tonight."

"It's only four o'clock. How long can it take to examine her?"

"Very long," he fibbed. "I fear Aunt Aurelia will wish to be examined, too."

"How very unfortunate." She sighed so prettily that her breasts rose and fell beneath their little yellow bodice. Apparently she *was* trying to kill him. She pulled her umbrella out of the stand. "Shall I see you at the Billingsgate ball on Saturday, then?"

There was no way his mother would accept an excuse for not attending the Billingsgate ball. His aunts would be there, after all, so he could hardly claim they'd summoned him to deal with imaginary aches and pains. "I'll be there," he promised.

It wasn't Almack's. And Juliana would be there, too. In another tiny bodice.

Too bad he wouldn't be able to unbutton his shirt.

Chapter Twenty-five

The Billingsgate ball was in full swing, and music filtered through the open door of Lord Billingsgate's library. "This will be perfect," Juliana said, glancing around. "It's close to the ballroom, so as soon as there is a commotion, plenty of people will come running to witness your disgrace."

In a hopeless attempt to cover her bare shoulders, Amanda tugged on the tiny puffed sleeves of the pale green dress Juliana had suggested she wear. "Shall I have to kiss Lord Stafford long?"

"I shouldn't think so. As soon as he starts kissing you, I shall fetch Lady Billingsgate to assure your ruin."

"What if he doesn't wish to kiss me?"

"Of course he wishes to kiss you! He's courting you, is he not? Men are always looking to kiss ladies."

Except for the duke. Juliana was starting to wonder if she'd *ever* be kissed. He'd been too busy to pay her any calls this week—doing what, she couldn't imagine—so she had yet to find an opportunity to start showing him how to be more affectionate. She knew he liked her more than ever, though, because he'd sent roses twice. That made three times he'd sent her roses! They were all white roses, but after all, he was proper and reserved. And he'd included notes these last two times—proper notes, very kind and complimentary—so she had high hopes he was falling in love with her. After all, even Aunt Frances had received roses only once.

She turned her thoughts back to Amanda. "Take off your gloves so Lord Stafford can feel the warmth of your skin. Drape yourself elegantly on the sofa. Before you lie down, douse two of the lamps. Low lighting is more romantic."

"Douse the lamps," Amanda repeated as though trying to memorize Juliana's instructions. "And take off my gloves." She tugged up the edge of her low bodice.

"And stop playing with your dress." Juliana started back toward the ballroom. "It makes you look nervous."

"I *am* nervous." Amanda paused at the edge of the room. "Lord Stafford still isn't here. What if he doesn't come?"

"It's not even ten o'clock yet," Juliana said soothingly, scanning the glittering crush. James's mother wasn't here yet, either. Lord Cavanaugh was pacing like a caged animal waiting for food, looking as anxious to see Lady Stafford as Amanda was to see the lady's son. For different reasons, of course. "Stop worrying. Lord Stafford assured me he was attending."

"Then why isn't he here?" Amanda asked for the tenth time.

Or maybe the twentieth. Honestly, Juliana could hardly wait until midnight when James would compromise her friend, because even though tricking him still didn't sit quite right with her, it would be such a relief to have this whole business over and done with.

"Here comes the duke," Amanda said.

Juliana turned and smiled. She'd worn her most seductive dress, a pale rose confection with a neckline so wide it left her shoulders bare and enticing. But he didn't look enticed.

He did return her smile, though. "Good evening, my dear." His gaze shifted to her friend. "Good evening, Lady Amanda," he added formally.

"Good evening," Amanda replied, sounding every bit as formal.

And that was when Juliana had a sudden bright idea.

She would encourage the duke to dance with Amanda. Seeing how tiresome it was to dance with someone so reserved might help him loosen up a bit. And in the meantime, while he was dancing with Amanda in a tiresome manner, she would dance with other men in her usual vivacious way.

After all, she had no shortage of dance invitations. Perhaps a few less than normal, since she'd been dancing so often with the duke lately, but that hadn't stopped men from asking when the duke wasn't nearby to intimidate them. Dancing with other men would not only make the duke notice how much more pleasant it was to dance with a modicum of enthusiasm; it would also make him jealous and possessive. Possessive men tended to touch the ladies they were possessive of, didn't they?

"Lady Amanda would love to dance," she told him with a sweet smile. "Why don't you ask her for the next waltz?"

She didn't know who looked more startled, the duke or Amanda. But as the musicians struck up the waltz, he bowed to Amanda very properly—no surprise there—and escorted her to the dance floor.

Juliana turned, expecting to be inundated with invitations as soon as the other men noticed the duke wasn't nearby and, indeed, was dancing with another woman. Unfortunately, Corinna noticed first.

"Is your duke courting Amanda now?"

"Of course he isn't. Amanda would never consent to marry him—he's a by-blow, remember? But I thought it would be a good idea for them to get to know each other better, so I suggested they dance."

"If you wish to marry the man, you shouldn't shove him at other women. What if he kisses her? He might decide he wants her, and Amanda could change her mind—"

"He's not going to kiss her," Juliana interrupted.

Corinna measured her a moment. "How can you be so sure?"

"He isn't interested in her. He doesn't call her 'my dear.' And the man is more reserved than Amanda. He hasn't even kissed me."

"Then how on earth do you know you love him?" Corinna asked, and while Juliana was wondering yet again how an inexperienced woman was supposed to know when she was in love, her sister added, "How do you know you want to marry him?"

"What do you mean, how do I know?" He was kind. He sent her flowers. He enjoyed amusements, fine horses, balls, and entertainments. He had wealth to support himself in style. He was classically handsome, as only an aristocratic Englishman could be. And he was a duke. "Who—besides Amanda—wouldn't want to marry him?"

"You really must kiss a man before you marry him. Believe me, it makes all the difference. Since kissing several men myself, I've discovered—"

"*What?*" Corinna was a year younger than Juliana, not to mention more interested in paint than men. How was it that she'd been kissed, when Juliana had barely even been touched? "You've kissed men?"

"Yes." Corinna blinked. "Have you not?"

"No!"

"Well, what have you been doing all Season, then? Alexandra kissed Tristan before marrying him," Corinna reminded her. "And Rachael has kissed several men, too. Gentlemen don't all kiss the same," she informed her with the surety of an experienced woman. "How is a lady to know she's found her prince if she hasn't kissed a few frogs first?"

It wasn't that Juliana hadn't been trying. But at least it was with a man who'd been courting her for longer than a dance. "Really, Corinna." Corinna always *had* been a bit of a rebel, but this was quite beyond the pale. "I'd be willing to wager Aunt Frances—your chaperone, in case you forgot?—wouldn't approve of you kissing men you've barely met."

"I don't let them kiss me when I've barely met them." Corinna's chin went into the air. "I make them wait at least a week."

"A week!" Juliana had known the duke *much* longer than a week.

"At least," Corinna repeated. "And as for Aunt Frances, she's known Lord Malmsey quite a bit longer than a week. Let's ask her if she's kissed him." She signaled to their aunt as she was just coming off the dance floor.

Frances didn't notice. On Juliana's recommendation,

she still wasn't wearing her spectacles. Which was a good thing, because Juliana figured such a question might make the poor spinster faint. "You cannot ask Aunt Frances that!"

"Why not?" Corinna said, marching toward her.

Juliana followed helplessly.

"Aunt Frances!" Corinna called.

"Yes?" Frances turned and squinted. "Oh, there you are, girls. Are you having a wonderful time?"

Corinna ignored her question, which was probably rhetorical anyway. "Aunt Frances, have you kissed Lord Malmsey?"

Two bright spots appeared on Frances's cheeks. "Well . . ."

"Have you?" Corinna demanded.

Frances squared her shoulders and lowered her voice. "I'm not a green girl, you know. It's no great sin. A woman should kiss a man before she decides to marry him."

Dear heavens, Frances had kissed Lord Malmsey. And she wanted to marry him. Juliana didn't know whether she was happy her project was so successful or shocked to hear that her spinster aunt had been kissed. On second thought, she was neither happy nor shocked. She was depressed. Corinna and Frances had both kissed men. That meant she was the only grown female in all of England who remained unkissed.

Well, there was Amanda. But come midnight, when James compromised her, even straitlaced Amanda would be kissed. Which meant Juliana would stand alone as the last woman in England to feel a man's lips caress her own.

It was depressing beyond description.

"Aunt Frances!" Alexandra joined their circle with Tristan. "I've never seen you look so happy."

"I'm overjoyed, child." Frances kissed her on the cheek. "You look happy, too."

"I am, Auntie." Alexandra smiled up at Tristan. Love blazed in their eyes. "We are."

Splendid. Everyone was happy. Except Juliana.

James joined their circle next, squeezing in beside her. "Good evening."

While it was a relief that he'd finally arrived, Juliana was even more relieved he didn't look insanely happy. True, she wanted to see everyone happy, but honestly, the sight of one more blatantly happy person would likely make her gag. "Are your aunts doing well?" she asked.

"They're fine. Not that they're convinced of that—they both believe they're at death's door, more's the pity." He gestured toward the edge of the dance floor, where the two older ladies were talking to his mother. "I had to examine them this afternoon before they'd deign to dress for the ball."

"They're keeping you from getting your important work done, aren't they?"

"Yes. But they're family." He shrugged philosophically. "What can I do?"

"There has to be something." Wishing she could figure out what, she watched Lord Cavanaugh claim Lady Stafford for a dance. "Maybe they need suitors, like your mother. She's happy."

"I'm happy," Frances said with a nod of approval. "A suitor will do that for a lady."

"But I'm happy," Corinna pointed out, "and I don't have a suitor."

No, but she'd been kissed. Juliana glared at her.

Corinna glared back, then smiled sweetly. "Alexandra's happy, too."

"That's because she's with child," James said.

A little hush fell over their circle. Juliana swung to her older sister. "Is that true?"

"It is," Tristan confirmed. Beaming, he slid an arm around his wife's waist. "We're both thrilled."

Corinna and Frances shrieked, engulfing the couple in a group hug.

Juliana took a step back. Corinna had been kissed, and Alexandra and Tristan were going to have a baby. She was happy for them. And for herself, for the whole family. She was pleased. Joyous. Jubilant. And something else. Something that made her fists clench at her sides.

"You're jealous," James said.

"I am not." Dismayed, she turned to him. "I am

happy for my sister. And for me. I'll have a niece or nephew to play with. How on earth did you know she's in the family way?"

James shrugged. "I'm a physician." She didn't look very happy. "Your turn will come," he said in his best soothing doctor tone.

"Who said I wanted a turn?"

She protested too much. Of course she wanted a turn. All women wanted babies. She was jealous.

But the worst of it was, he was jealous, too.

The jealousy was a knot in his gut. It was unexpected, and sudden, but mostly it was ridiculous.

Ladies were supposed to pine for babies—men weren't. He certainly didn't want Alexandra's child, and he really couldn't say how he'd known she was breeding. It was the look of her, he supposed. And the look of her husband, the male pride evident in the man's gaze upon his wife. James had gazed at his own wife like that before he'd lost her and their child.

And then, when he'd lost them, it had all been mixed up together, his grief for Anne and for their baby. He hadn't been able to separate one from the other. They were both lost forever. He'd never have another love, which meant he'd never have another child. He hadn't thought he *wanted* another child.

But now he did.

The knot twisted tighter. Bloody hell.

"Excuse me," he said. "I think I need a drink."

Chapter Twenty-six

"You're foxed," Juliana told James later as they danced.

"Maybe." He slipped his thumb beneath the edge of her glove and teased the sensitive skin on the underside of her wrist. "Maybe not."

"You are." She laughed, suppressing an entirely too delicious shiver. "You've had three cups of punch tonight already."

"Four," he corrected. "Small cups. In two hours, which, I might point out, could hardly be considered severe overindulging. And how would you come to know how much I'm drinking? Are you watching me, Juliana?"

"Of course not," she said quickly, avoiding his eyes. Her gaze fell on his cravat, and she found herself picturing the golden skin she'd seen beneath.

"Hmm," he said, a pleased, low rumble of a *hmm* that seemed to vibrate right through her. She looked up again to find him gazing at her in that way that made her fear he could read her mind. The pad of his thumb kept caressing her wrist.

By all indications, liquor made him even more amorous than macaroons. Which was uncomfortable in a sense, but also a good thing, because it meant Amanda would find it easier to seduce him and get herself compromised.

And poor, demure Amanda needed all the help she could get.

On the other side of the dance floor, Amanda was dancing again with the duke, the both of them rigid as ever. In the two hours since Juliana suggested they dance together, she herself had danced with twelve other men. Vivaciously and enthusiastically. But the duke hadn't seemed to take note of any of those dozen dances.

It hadn't helped that he'd spent at least half of those two hours in the card room.

Between Juliana's dozen dances, the duke had emerged and danced with her twice, but despite all her efforts to draw him out, he still hadn't touched her, let alone kissed her. She tried to picture his skin in the open V of a shirt, but she imagined it would look rather pasty instead of golden. And he probably never loosened his collar, anyway. He probably went to bed fully dressed, with his shirt fastened up to his chin, a cravat knotted in layers to cover it, and a waistcoat and tailcoat besides. Both buttoned.

It was heartbreaking, really. He truly needed her in his life. She resolved to remain patient, to keep working toward his happiness, no matter how long the process took. After all, it had taken an entire childhood of cold treatment to turn him into the man he was today. She shouldn't be surprised if it took more than a few weeks of warmth to counteract that.

Thankfully, the rest of her projects were going well tonight. Aunt Frances and Lord Malmsey had kissed. Lord Cavanaugh had danced three times with Lady Stafford, and they'd probably kissed as well. And Amanda and James would be kissing soon.

Every woman in London would be kissed tonight except for Juliana.

Unless . . .

Maneuvering the last few steps of the dance to end up by Amanda and the duke, she curtsied to James and then turned to them. "Shall we exchange partners?"

The duke looked so startled at her forwardness, she almost lost her nerve. But she'd never been one to just stand by and let things happen—or in this case, not happen—so when the musicians resumed playing and the duke took her gloved hands, she steeled herself, smiled at him, and began surreptitiously inching toward a potted palm.

At least she *tried* to be surreptitious. Unfortunately, the tune wasn't a waltz but a minuet—which meant the dancers moved back and forth rather than progressing in a particular direction.

"I'm supposed to lead, my dear," the duke gently chided. "Why are you taking larger steps toward the right than the left?"

She mentally shrugged, deciding not to play coy. The duke never seemed to take a hint, so she'd best come out and say it. "I am hoping to get you alone behind that potted palm."

"Pardon?"

"I'm hoping for a kiss."

He blinked. "Before marriage?"

Now she mentally rolled her eyes. "Yes, before marriage." And though she'd never expected to quote Aunt Frances regarding intimate matters, she found herself adding, "It's no great sin, you know."

"Perhaps not, my dear, but it also wouldn't be proper."

Her heart sank. "Don't you *want* to kiss me?" she asked. "You're courting me. You've sent me flowers three times. I thought you were falling in love with me."

She shocked even herself with that admission, but when he said, "Oh, but I am," her heart soared. The depression she'd felt earlier dissipated like a moist fog in the sun's rays. The duke was falling in love with her! It was only a matter of time until she knew for sure she was in love with him, too, and then everything would be wonderful—even if she did have to wait until her wedding night to experience a kiss.

As the dance ended, the clock struck midnight. Finally. After thanking the duke rather profusely, she hurried to meet Amanda.

"It's midnight."

"I know." Amanda looked paler than normal. Paler than the duke. Paler than Juliana felt.

Juliana didn't know how a person could feel pale, but

suddenly, despite her recent elation, she did. "Are you sure you want to go through with this?"

"I cannot marry Lord Malmsey."

Of course she couldn't. That would be horrible for everyone involved. Especially dear Aunt Frances.

"You're going to have to kiss Lord Stafford," Juliana warned. The thought made her stomach turn. But only because she was about to be the only unkissed woman in London. "And you're going to have to make sure he undresses you, at least a little. A mere kiss will not be enough to guarantee a compromise."

"I know." Amanda looked quite determined. "I can do it."

"All right, then. I'll bring Lord Stafford to the library. Remember to take off your gloves. And make your voice a little breathy."

Amanda resolutely squared her shoulders as she walked off. Here she was, about to get herself engaged to a young, virile earl, and honestly, she looked about as excited as a woman going to her own funeral. If there weren't so many other people involved, Juliana would be tempted to postpone their plans. But postponement would put the compromise at risk of not happening altogether, and it wouldn't be fair to deprive James, Lord Malmsey, and Aunt Frances of their happiness just to save Amanda from a little discomfort.

Besides, Amanda would feel much better soon. There'd be a huge scandal following her compromise, of course—enough to make her father come running to London. But that was the whole idea. And once her father arrived and set everything to rights, Amanda would be happy. Happily married to James. She'd feel all tingly when he touched her and kissed her, and—

Juliana was growing all tingly just thinking about it.

She found James standing with some other men, sipping another drink while Lord Occlestone grumbled about unnecessary "reforms" that had recently been introduced in Parliament. She'd been planning to feign a troubled expression, but under the circumstances, she didn't need to. She tapped him on the shoulder.

He turned and looked down at her. "Juliana."

She pulled him away from the group. "What an un-pleasant man. His face suits his personality. His nose is square, rather like a pig's."

"I've often thought that myself," James said, a tipsy smile curving his lips.

Excellent. She wanted him tipsy and amorous. "Lady Amanda is feeling ill."

"I was just dancing with her. She looked fine."

"Well, she's feeling ill now. She went to the library to lie down. Will you come and have a look at her?"

"Of course," he said, suddenly looking sober and concerned. So sober and concerned that Juliana felt a pang of . . . guilt? She could think of nothing else the sensation could be. But it was a ridiculous pang of guilt, because this was the right thing for everyone involved.

She led him to the library, where Amanda was draped elegantly on the sofa, emitting little moans. She'd followed Juliana's instructions exactly. Her gloves were on the desk, and the room was romantically lit, not too dark and not too light.

James set his drink and his own gloves beside Amanda's, then knelt by the sofa. "Lady Amanda, where does it hurt?"

"It's my heart," Amanda said breathily, laying a graceful bare hand on the expanse of bosom exposed in her low neckline. She was a surprisingly good actress. James didn't stand a chance. Any man would fall for that sensuous voice.

Except James didn't. "You're a mite young for heart trouble," he told her.

"But it aches," she insisted, implying it ached for him. "Won't you listen to it at least?"

"If you wish." He rose to his feet.

"You cannot listen from there." Amanda patted her bosom and arched herself toward him. Dear heavens, she was practically falling off the sofa. "You need to press your ear to my heart."

"No, I don't." Seemingly oblivious to her wanton display, he walked over to the writing desk. "I can hear it better through a tube."

"Are you sure?" Amanda asked.

"I'm positive." He opened a drawer, pulled out a

piece of paper, and rolled it up. "This won't work as well as my new stethoscope, but it should be better than listening without it." He placed one end of the paper tube on Amanda's chest and lowered his ear to the other. "A little fast," he reported. No surprise, since she was likely scared out of her wits. "But strong and steady."

Apparently at a loss, Amanda looked toward Juliana.

"Maybe Lady Amanda has a rash," she said. "James, I think you should loosen her clothes and have a look."

He eyed Amanda's bare arms and low décolletage in an altogether clinical manner. "I see no evidence of a rash." He smiled at his patient, but it was a kind smile, not seductive in the least. "This ball is quite a crush. If you've no symptoms to report other than a vague ache in your chest, perhaps sitting quietly for a few minutes might help."

Juliana didn't know what to think. Amanda was doing everything right, yet James appeared unmoved. Which, oddly enough, seemed to relieve Juliana's guilt, but that was as ridiculous as feeling the guilt in the first place. And it didn't explain why.

Then she suddenly realized why. "Stay with her while she sits quietly, James. I'm going to fetch Lady Billingsgate."

She didn't, of course—there was no point in fetching Lady Billingsgate until James and Amanda got into a compromising position. Which clearly wasn't going to happen with her in the room. What a fool she'd been for not realizing James wouldn't seduce her friend with another woman watching.

She went out quietly, leaving the door slightly cracked so she could listen.

"I'm sure you'll feel better in no time," she heard James say.

"I'd feel better if you'd sit beside me."

"I cannot imagine how that could help," James said. But apparently he did sit down, because the next thing he said was, "There. Do you feel better?"

"No, not yet," Amanda said and paused. And then she added, "Why don't you kiss me to make me feel better?"

A shocked silence followed. Juliana was shocked, too. She hadn't thought Amanda had it in her to be so forward. But then the silence continued, and Juliana realized it wasn't a shocked silence. It was the silence that resulted when two people were kissing instead of talking.

Amanda's forwardness had worked.

Well, of course it had worked. James was a man, and what man alone in a room with a woman he loved would resist an invitation to kiss her? This behavior was exactly what Juliana had counted on when she'd plotted to trick him into compromising Amanda.

But now that her plot had worked, the pang returned again. The ridiculous pang of guilt at the thought of tricking a man she'd come to think of as a friend.

"I don't think that would be a good idea," James finally said.

Juliana couldn't figure out what he meant by that, exactly, but the pang subsided. She released a breath she hadn't realized she'd been holding. He hadn't kissed Amanda. Not yet, anyway. She sagged against the door in relief.

Or rather, she *thumped* against the door in relief. And then it opened, and she all but fell into the library.

James caught her by her shoulders and grinned. "I thought you were Lady Billingsgate."

Of course he had. She'd said she was going to fetch Lady Billingsgate, after all. A mistake, she now realized, because of course James wouldn't kiss Amanda while expecting Lady Billingsgate to show up at any moment.

That was what he'd meant when he'd said it wouldn't be a good idea.

But his hands felt warm on her bare shoulders, and she couldn't be sorry she'd made the mistake. She didn't want to trick James. She hadn't wanted to from the first. She was furious with herself for allowing Amanda to talk her into it.

"I'll fetch Lady Billingsgate," he said, "while *you* sit with Lady Amanda." And then he left, taking his warm hands with him.

Juliana made her way to the sofa and collapsed beside her friend.

Poor Amanda was shaking. "I did it," she said. "I forced myself to do it. And it didn't work!"

"I'm glad it didn't work. It was unethical to begin with. We mustn't try it again." It had made her feel too guilty. In fact, she *still* felt guilty. She wondered if she'd ever be able to look at James again without feeling a pang of guilt.

"But why didn't it work? I did everything you said, but he wouldn't kiss me."

That was because Juliana had led him to think Lady Billingsgate was about to walk in, but she wouldn't admit that to Amanda. Besides, Amanda was equally at fault. If she had given James any indication that she wanted him—*him*, not his antiquities—he'd have reached for her the moment he entered the darkened library. "Maybe he wouldn't kiss you because you haven't allowed him to kiss you before."

"He never *tried* before," Amanda said. "He isn't a very warm person."

Juliana felt an urge to laugh, though she wasn't quite sure whether it was from the obvious absurdity of Amanda's statement or simply from hearing Amanda, of all people, claim someone else wasn't warm.

James was the warmest man she knew. She didn't believe for a moment that he'd never tried to kiss Amanda. Amanda was plainly too reserved to respond. "You need to act more warmly toward *him*. You have to make him believe you want him."

"I *do* want him. I cannot marry Lord Malmsey! And our wedding is only two weeks away! I must tell Lord Stafford about my engagement."

"You cannot. He is too honorable to cooperate with any plan to force your father's hand."

"Then how on earth am I to get him to compromise me in time?"

"You need to let him kiss you, and I don't mean as part of a plot. A few kisses will lead to more, and eventually you'll be discovered. Society is a nosy lot, in case you haven't noticed."

"That sounds like a plot," Amanda pointed out.

"It isn't." All right, maybe it was. But it wasn't the

same sort of plot as the one they'd tried tonight. Corinna had said that a kiss made all the difference. Once James kissed Amanda, she'd fall in love with him, and they'd both want more kisses, and the rest would happen naturally.

Surely there was no reason to feel guilty about that.

"Lady Amanda!" Lady Billingsgate exclaimed, rushing in. "Are you unwell? Before Lord Stafford left, he told me you'd taken ill."

So James had left. Juliana wouldn't have to look at him again and feel a pang of guilt. But as Amanda explained to Lady Billingsgate that she was quite recovered, thank you, Juliana wondered why knowing she didn't have to face him failed to bring her a measure of relief.

Chapter Twenty-seven

RICHMOND MAIDS OF HONOUR

> Mix Curd with Butter and add 4 yolks of Eggs
> beaten with a glass of Brandy, half a cup of Sugar,
> fine white Breadcrumbs with some ground Al-
> monds and a little Nutmeg. To this put the juice
> of one Lemon and the grated yellow of 2. Press
> puff paste into your tins and fill and bake.

> *These small, rich cheesecakes are from a recipe
> said to have been in the family since Queen Eliza-
> beth's (my namesake's) time. They will melt any-
> one. Excellent for begging forgiveness.*
> —Elizabeth Chase, Countess of Greystone, 1728

The next morning dawned bright and sunny, which
should have made Juliana feel cheerful, but instead she
still felt guilty. It being Sunday, she attended St.
George's Hanover Square Church, where the sermon
was all about truth, which made her feel even more
guilty. So guilty that afterward she baked some Richmond Maids of Honour and asked Griffin to take her to
Stafford House.

"Why?" he asked.

A perfectly reasonable question, but one she didn't
want to answer. She was entirely too ashamed of her

actions to admit them to her brother. "I just want to ask Lord Stafford if he'd like me to volunteer next week at the Institute." That wasn't quite a lie, since she'd been wondering when he might need her again. "I forgot to ask him last night." With all that had gone on at the ball, she really *had* forgotten.

"You could send him a note," Griffin suggested.

"Just take me, will you?"

"Very well." Griffin shook his head in that mystified, brotherly way of his. "I cannot imagine why a note won't do, but I'll take you."

"Thank you," she said.

When he was sitting across from her in the carriage, he stretched out his legs and steepled his fingers. "How is your romance with Castleton proceeding?"

She fiddled with the platter on her lap. "He says he's falling in love with me, but he has yet to kiss me."

"He's a gentleman," Griffin said, looking not at all unpleased with that news. "He shouldn't kiss you before you are wed. Or engaged at the very least."

Trust a brother to think that. She considered telling him Corinna believed a woman should kiss some frogs so she'll know when she's met her prince, but thought better of it. For one thing, getting Corinna in trouble served no point, and for another, she was beginning to believe her sister was right. If James and Amanda had already kissed, perhaps the plot would have proved successful.

Not that she wished it had, mind you. She felt guilty enough as it was.

"The duke believes a couple should wait to kiss, too," she said instead. "You must be the only two such men in all of London."

"I'm certain he will ask for your hand soon." Griffin leaned closer and patted her knee. "I'll have a talk with him. In my stables."

"Pardon?" What did his stables have to do with anything?

"Never mind. We've arrived." The carriage pulled to a stop in St. James's Place, and Griffin started to climb out.

"Wait here," she said.

"Why?"

"Just wait, will you? I cannot stay long—I have ladies coming to sew at two o'clock." All of her projects were beginning to make her feel a bit frazzled. "It won't take me but a minute to ask one simple question."

"Very well," he said, again shaking his head in that mystified, brotherly way of his. He plopped back onto the seat.

She banged the knocker, and the door was opened by the same crimson-liveried footman who had welcomed her last week. Through the window in the back of the entrance hall, Lady Stafford waved from the courtyard garden. She hurried inside. "How are you, my dear? I didn't expect to see you until your sewing party this afternoon. What do you have there?"

Juliana handed her the platter. "Some Richmond Maids of Honour for Lord Stafford. And for you, too, of course."

"They smell divine."

"I've come to ask Lord Stafford a quick question. Is he at home?"

"He's upstairs in his study, spending this beautiful day going over the Institute's books." Shaking her head in a fond, motherly way, she started toward the staircase. "Follow me, if you will."

It was quite the most elegant staircase Juliana had ever seen. The metal balustrade was painted to look like festooned drapery. Above her head, a segmented barrel ceiling gave the impression of a classical temple interior with garlands swagged between Roman pilasters.

She assumed Lady Stafford was leading her toward the study, but instead she walked her through an impressive library and into a room so splendid it stole Juliana's breath. If she had been a fortune-hunting sort of woman, the very sight of it would have made her want to marry James. It put the gorgeous Palm Room below it to shame.

She'd never seen so much gilt in her life. It dazzled the eye. Fancy gilt columns supported a gilt ceiling. Between all the gleaming gilt, the walls were covered with painted scenes.

"We call this the Painted Room," Lady Stafford said. "Marriage is the theme."

Juliana nearly swooned over the frieze painted on the chimneypiece.

"Beautiful, isn't it?" Lady Stafford set the platter of cheesecakes on a gilt-legged marble-topped table. "It's a copy of the celebrated *Aldobrandini Wedding*, a Roman fresco excavated in the early seventeenth century and exhibited in the Vatican."

"It's exquisite," Juliana breathed. The theme of marriage continued all around the room, with some of the scenes executed directly onto the plaster and others painted on gilt-framed canvas panels. The whole mood was festive and carefree.

Above a pier glass, a circular panel displayed a painting of another Roman wedding. Other panels depicted music, drinking, and dancing. There were paintings of Cupid and Venus. Nymphs danced on the ceiling, lovers courted on the walls, and a frieze of rose wreaths and garlands of flowers went all around the cornice.

"Isn't marriage wonderful?" Lady Stafford said. "Please have a seat. I'll send in my son."

Juliana perched herself on one of four green silk sofas with gilt arms carved to look like winged lions. She folded her hands in her lap. She crossed her feet and uncrossed them. She rose and peeked at her sweets.

The winged lion sofas had six matching chairs, and she was heading for one of them when James walked in.

"Here," she said, grabbing the platter. "I brought these cheesecakes for you."

He took them, looking as mystified as Griffin. But not at all brotherly. Perhaps that had something to do with the fact that not only was he without a coat or cravat and his shirt was unbuttoned again, but he'd rolled up his cuffs, too. A good six inches of his forearms were bare—muscled forearms, lightly sprinkled with dark hair.

"What are you doing here, Juliana?"

She jerked her gaze up to his face. There was no sense putting it off. "I came to apologize. Won't you have one of the cheesecakes? The recipe is said to have been in my family since Queen Elizabeth's time."

He set down the platter. "Apologize for what?"

He wasn't going to eat any Richmond Maids of Honour. She would have to hope he'd forgive her without their magic. "For plotting with Lady Amanda to trick you into compromising her," she confessed in a rush. "In the library last night. I was hoping you would kiss her, and then I'd bring Lady Billingsgate to witness Lady Amanda's disgrace, so her father would be forced to assent to your marriage." She drew a shaky breath. "Can you forgive me?"

"That's terrible." She'd known he would disapprove, but she hadn't expected he'd look quite so dour. His fists were clenched. "Whyever would you do that? I told you, I can see no reason Lord Wolverston would reject my suit should I decide to ask for his daughter's hand."

"She doesn't believe he'd agree. He is not a very nice man."

"Surely he isn't stupid." He unclenched his fists, but only to cross his half-bare arms. "I am excellent husband material."

He had a high opinion of himself, but it wasn't unjustified. There was no doubt he would make an excellent husband for Amanda. "I'm sorry I went behind your back, but why are you so upset? However terrible the means, the outcome would have been to your benefit. You'd have found yourself married to the woman you love. Unless—"

An awful thought suddenly occurred to her.

She'd assumed that since he was still courting Amanda, he'd fallen in love with her. But what if he hadn't? What if her scheming had resulted in James being forced to marry a woman he didn't love?

"Do you not love Lady Amanda yet?" She held her breath, waiting for the answer.

"No," he said, looking quite sure. Not to mention horrified.

It was the wrong answer, so why did she feel relieved? "Maybe you're in love with her, but you don't know it," she suggested. "Maybe you don't know what love feels like." It was a reasonable question, certainly. She'd asked it of herself several times over the last few weeks.

But now he looked annoyed. "I know what love feels like, Juliana."

That surprising news made her a little uneasy. "You've been in love before?"

"Yes. With my wife."

She couldn't have been more shocked if he'd punched her in the stomach. In fact, it felt like he *had* punched her in the stomach. "You have a wife?"

"I *had* a wife," he corrected. "Her name was Anne. She died in childbirth, along with our baby. Two years ago."

"Dear heavens. I didn't know." The sharp pain in Juliana's middle shifted to an ache in her chest. "I'm sorry. I'm sorry for everything."

She watched him walk to a chair and lower himself to it wearily. He no longer looked angry or annoyed; he just looked sad. "I forgive you," he said dully. "What you did was still terrible, but I know your heart was in the right place."

"Thank you," she said softly.

"As long as you promise not to try it ever again."

"I won't. I promise. And a Chase promise is never broken. That's been our family motto for centuries." She sat in the chair beside him, grasping the two lion heads at the ends of its arms as though they could lend her their strength. She was glad to have his forgiveness, but his pain ripped her up inside. He'd loved a wife, and she'd carried their baby, and they'd both died. "I'm so sorry you lost your family."

"You've lost family, too," he said.

"But not a child. It must be hardest to lose a child."

He nodded. "We're supposed to die *before* our children."

"A child is part of you, part of your future."

"It's only recently I've realized that," he said with a sigh. "Only recently I've realized I want to have another."

Of course he wanted another baby. She wanted a baby, too. And so, she was sure, did Amanda. But he needed more time to fall in love with her.

Juliana knew grief, knew how much it hurt, knew it took a long while to resume living life fully. He'd lost a wife. It would take him time to recover, to allow himself to love another.

She hadn't realized.

He needed more time. He'd said many wonderful

things about Amanda, and he was still courting her, after all, so eventually he'd fall in love with her. But he needed more time.

A pity he had only two weeks.

Thirteen days, actually. Twelve days if he didn't see Amanda again until tomorrow. She couldn't let him wait any longer than that.

"You know," she said carefully, "you'll have to re-marry to have a child."

"Not technically," he said with a hint of his normal good humor.

"James . . ."

"Yes, I shall have to remarry to have a child. My dear mother, bless her heart, reminds me of that fact on a daily basis." He paused and looked away, his voice going lower, quieter. "Even though I'll never fall in love again, someday I'll have to remarry."

How could he say such a thing? "You cannot marry without falling in love."

"People do it all the time," he said, looking back to her. "There are many reasons people marry. Wealth, ambition, position, security, duty, honor. And to have a child. While I'd never marry an enemy, I can certainly marry a friend. One can kiss a woman and make a child without falling in love."

Though his words made her blush, she persisted. "How can you possibly know you'll never fall in love again?"

"I just do," he said flatly. "Falling in love would mean betraying Anne, and that isn't going to happen."

Wealth, ambition, position, security, duty, honor . . . to have a child. Those were sad reasons to wed, Juliana thought—and old reasons as well. Her parents had mar-ried for such reasons. Today, in these modern times, young people preferred romantic love matches.

Except . . . maybe Amanda.

Lord Stafford and I suit well, she remembered Amanda saying. *We're compatible. Maybe my father was right— maybe there are more important considerations than love. I cannot marry Lord Malmsey!*

At the time, she'd worried that Amanda had decided to marry James for all the wrong reasons. But maybe the two were even better matched than she'd thought. Marriage would give them both what they wanted. Children for James, and a young, compatible man for Amanda.

"Juliana?" James said. "What are you thinking?"

Still sad for him, she forced a smile. "I'm thinking that the two of us went out often during your lessons, but since then you've had no outings with Lady Amanda."

"You want me to take Lady Amanda riding in Hyde Park? Or to the Egyptian Hall?"

"Not exactly." If he hoped to become friends with Amanda—if he hoped to kiss and eventually marry her—he needed to take her someplace much more romantic. "I was thinking Vauxhall Gardens would be perfect."

She'd never been to Vauxhall Gardens, but judging from what she'd heard, it seemed there was nowhere more suitable for lovers, most especially at night. The gardens were described as a paradise of lush paths with many private corners, their twelve acres lit by romantic lanterns—save for a few of the walkways that were deliberately left dark.

"Vauxhall Gardens?" James repeated skeptically. From what he'd heard, the gardens mainly served as a spot for illicit trysts. "I've never been to Vauxhall Gardens."

"Haven't you?" Juliana said. "It's a lovely place."

A lovely place to steal a lady's virtue, or at the very least a few kisses. Which James had no intention of doing with Lady Amanda.

On the other hand, it could be a lovely place to visit with Juliana.

Convincing her of that, however, might be a trick to rival hers.

In truth, James had felt rather dazed upon learning that, in her determination to match him with Amanda, Juliana had been willing to resort to trickery. Dazed and a little bit panicked. Although he realized meddling was in her blood—one didn't have to know Juliana more than a few minutes to conclude that—he'd thought he'd been making progress toward attracting her.

Had his efforts to tempt her accomplished nothing?

Obviously, touching Juliana and unbuttoning his shirt were not enough. He'd have to employ stronger tactics if he wanted to kiss her and make sure she didn't ruin her life by marrying stuffy Castleton.

"I wouldn't know where to take Lady Amanda in Vauxhall Gardens," he told her, rolling his sleeves up a little more. "Perhaps you should come with me instead the first time, to show me the good places."

"I don't think—" Juliana's gaze was fastened on his arms. It wandered up to his open shirt. "The gardens are closed on Sundays. Shall we make it tomorrow night?"

"Parliament will be in session—"

"If you want a child, James," she said, finally looking him in the face, "you need to put courting ladies before the House of Lords."

Perhaps he should. Since he wasn't making any progress with his bill, perhaps it wasn't such a bad idea to make progress with Juliana his priority. For a day, at least. Or a night.

"Very well," he said.

"Good." She glanced at his arms again, which he found somewhat encouraging. "I must get home before the guests arrive for my sewing party."

He nodded and started from the room. "I'll come by for you at seven o'clock Monday."

"I'll see that Aunt Frances is ready," she said as they walked through the library.

Tempting Juliana was difficult even without an audience. The last thing he wanted was her chaperone hovering nearby. "Do you suppose Lord Malmsey would like to accompany your aunt?"

"I'm sure he would." She went lightly down the stairs, her renewed good cheer lifting James's heart. She was such a delight. A treasure. "That's a wonderful idea," she said.

Yes, it was. Lord Malmsey seemed quite enamored with Lady Frances, which meant he'd have an eye to getting her alone, which in turn would leave James alone with Juliana. The plan was sounding better and better.

"Until tomorrow, then," he said. His butler opened the front door, revealing Griffin outside pacing around the Cainewood carriage.

"Until tomorrow," Juliana echoed, starting toward her brother. "Wait," she said, turning back. "I forgot to ask if you'd like me to volunteer next week at the Institute."

She would come again without her aunt . . . If James failed to kiss her at Vauxhall, maybe he could get her alone in one of the treatment rooms. "Absolutely," he told her with a smile. "How about Friday?"

"Friday will be fine." Returning his smile, she headed toward the carriage.

The butler shut the door behind her, but not before James heard Griffin's impatient huff. "Why in blazes did it take you so long to ask the man one simple question?"

Chapter Twenty-eight

Dark was falling.

Juliana had arrived at Vauxhall Gardens with James, Aunt Frances, and Lord Malmsey at about eight o'clock Monday night, while the sun was still gracing the summer sky. It was a fine July evening, perhaps a bit chillier than usual, but without the slightest hint of rain. The pleasure gardens had proved as lovely as she'd hoped, spacious and laid out in delightful walks, bounded with high hedges and towering trees, and paved with gravel that crunched beneath their shoes.

For the first half hour they'd strolled, finding something charming around every corner. Pavilions, grottoes, temples and cascades, porticos, colonnades, and rotundas. Here was a striking pillar, there a wonderful statue, in the distance a series of large, picturesque paintings. Throngs of visitors promenaded, showing off their finest clothing, their rowdy laughter and whispered endearments filling the night air.

Now, with the sun sinking low, they were seated at a table for four by the building that housed the orchestra, a structure that struck Juliana as Moorish or perhaps Gothic—she couldn't decide which, but regardless, it was magnificent. Its second story was open in the front so the musicians were visible inside.

While they listened to a pleasing variety of popular

songs and serious compositions, they enjoyed a light supper, feasting on cold chicken and bread and cheese accompanied by French claret. Aunt Frances was astounded at the exorbitant cost of the diminutive portions.

"My word," she said disapprovingly, "this Vauxhall ham is sliced so thin one could read a newspaper through it!"

Lord Malmsey laughed and motioned to a serving girl to order more. "Would you like some cheesecake, too, my dear?"

"It cannot be as good as Juliana's," James said, shooting her a warm smile.

So he'd eaten her Richmond Maids of Honour and enjoyed them. Feeling inordinately pleased about that, Juliana smiled back.

As the musicians played the last notes of a piece composed by Handel, a piercing whistle split the night. "What is that?" she asked.

Lord Malmsey cocked his balding head. "Have you never been here before, Lady Juliana?"

She was about to tell him she hadn't, but then she remembered James didn't know that. "Not at night," she said instead. But a part of her wondered why she'd accepted James's invitation to show him around, knowing he should be escorting Amanda tonight if he was to decide to marry her before her planned wedding in twelve days' time.

"Just watch, then," Lord Malmsey said.

And she stopped musing, sucking in a breath as a thousand oil lamps came to life, lit by myriad servants touching matches to their wicks in the same instant. The effect was nothing short of sensational, bathing the gardens in a warm light that must have been visible for miles around.

"Enchanting!" Aunt Frances exclaimed.

Lord Malmsey cocked his head again. "Have *you* never been here at night, either?"

"I've never been here at all," Frances said.

Shy, retiring Aunt Frances had missed out on a lot, Juliana thought as they finished their supper, but that was about to change. She'd never been happier to see one of her projects prove a success.

"Shall we walk again?" Lord Malmsey asked, rising from the table. "The gardens feel like a different place among the lanterns."

"A lovely idea." Frances rose, too, and pulled on her gloves.

Juliana reached for her own but found her lap empty. "Where are my gloves?" She was sure she'd placed them there when she took them off for supper—it was a life-long habit, after all. She checked the ground on either side of her chair. "I cannot find them."

"How odd." Shifting his gaze to Lord Malmsey, James waved a hand toward the beckoning paths. "You two go on ahead. I'll help Lady Juliana find her gloves, and then we'll catch up to you."

As Frances and Lord Malmsey walked off, Juliana leaned to one side and peeked below the table. "I cannot imagine where they might have gone." She rose and looked under her chair. "They seem to have disappeared."

"Perhaps they are in my pocket," James said. "Right beside mine."

She looked up at him, startled. "How would they get there?"

He shrugged one shoulder, a corner of his mouth turning up in a half smile. "How indeed?"

She laughed. "Give them to me."

"I think not. I think you will need to get them for yourself."

She eyed his striped silk waistcoat, his dark tailcoat, his crisp white trousers. She didn't know which of his pockets he'd hidden her gloves in, but she wasn't about to slip her hands into his clothing to find out. She laughed again. "James . . ."

He took her bare hand in his. "Your aunt and Lord Malmsey will get too far ahead if we don't go after them. Come along."

The paths seemed gayer now that it was dark, the company enlivened with mirth and good humor. Music drifted from the orchestra through the trees. Seemingly suspended everywhere, the lamps looked like little illuminated balls glowing every color of the rainbow. Some were arranged in lines or arches, others grouped to represent the starry heavens.

Juliana thought Vauxhall Gardens the most wonderful place she'd ever been. Her heart felt light, and her hand felt warm in James's. She knew she shouldn't allow him to hold it, but just then she didn't care about proprieties. Ahead of them on the path, Aunt Frances leaned close to Lord Malmsey, oblivious to her charge.

When they caught up to the older couple, who had stopped by a tinkling fountain, Juliana pulled her hand free.

"Look!" Frances pointed overhead. "It's Madame Saqui!"

Wearing an outlandish dress decorated with tinsel, spangles, and plumes, the celebrated tightrope walker seemed to be dancing on air as she ascended a rope attached to a sixty-foot mast. Despite her glittery attire, her appearance was rather masculine. Juliana could see up her dress, and her legs were muscled like a circus strongman's. But her balance was impeccable, her steps graceful and seemingly timed to the orchestra's lilting music.

"It looks like a ballet, doesn't it?" Juliana said.

"A ballet for two," James replied as the dancer's husband mounted a second rope beside hers. "I've heard they earn a hundred guineas per week."

She slanted him a teasing smile. "A sum you'd like to see spent on smallpox vaccinations, no doubt."

He laughed. "Entertaining enchanting ladies is also a worthy cause."

A curious quiver rippled through her at the thought he might find her enchanting, although she knew quite well he was speaking of the company in general. They watched for a few minutes in breathless silence as the couple dipped and swayed, seemingly unworried they might plunge to their deaths. At the top, Madame Saqui performed an agile turn and saluted her husband as she passed him on her way down. When she reached the bottom, she dipped into a theatrical curtsy and swept up a little girl, settling her small slippered feet on the tightrope.

"She cannot be more than four years old!" Juliana gasped at the sight of the young miss climbing the rope toward the stars. She covered her face with her hands. "I cannot watch."

"She's their daughter." James slipped an arm around her waist. "Performance is in her blood," he said, drawing her against himself.

She dropped her hands, glancing to see if her aunt had noticed James's bold move.

Her chaperone was no longer beside her.

"Aunt Frances?" She looked around. "Where is Aunt Frances?"

"She went off with Lord Malmsey," James said, the suggestive tone of his voice making her picture her aunt in a very compromising position. "Shall we resume our walk?"

As he drew her down a darkened lane, still holding her close, she was struck again, as she had been at the Egyptian Hall, by how well they fit together. He smelled of starch and soap. He matched his longer gait to her shorter one, and it seemed the night was warmer, the gardens more fragrant and lush. Tall trees towered on both sides, their silhouettes dark against the lantern-hazed sky.

"When will you bring Amanda here?" she asked.

"Hmm," he said noncommittally, turning into a tiny secluded grove.

It had a stone bench and a single lantern, so it wasn't quite dark. But it was dim, with high hedges all around. She heard a couple walk by, gravel crunching beneath their feet. No one peeked in through the narrow opening.

James released her and walked over to the bench, she assumed to sit down. But he didn't. Instead, he slid off his tailcoat and draped it over the seat. "Do you think this would be a good spot to bring Lady Amanda?"

"Maybe." Amanda would surely grow closer to him in this private, hidden location. And he would grow closer to her. They'd become friends, and then they'd marry and have a child. "I mean, yes," she decided. "This would be an excellent place to bring Amanda."

"I thought so." His long fingers worked at the knot in his cravat, the sight of which seemed to make butterflies flutter in her stomach. "What do you expect I should do with Amanda when we're here?"

He should kiss her, of course, but Juliana wasn't about to say that out loud. She didn't know what to say, so she didn't say anything. She just watched him pull the cravat from around his neck, slowly and steadily, until it came off entirely and dangled from his fingers.

"Well?" His intense dark gaze was fastened on her in that way that made her wonder if he could read her mind. "Have you no suggestions?" He released the cravat, and it fluttered to the bench, a tumbled pile of white froth. "Do you think perhaps I should kiss her?"

He *had* read her mind.

She swallowed hard. "Maybe."

"I thought so." He eased open the top button of his shirt. And the second button. "I think we should practice," he said conversationally.

Her gaze was glued to the little V of golden skin where his shirt was unbuttoned. "Practice?"

"Yes, practice." He raised a wrist and unbuttoned a cuff. "You and me. Before I try it with Amanda."

"You want to kiss me?" He couldn't. He shouldn't.

"Just for practice. Come here, Juliana."

His deep, chocolatey voice made another shiver ripple through her. The butterflies fluttered faster. He wanted to kiss her. Just for practice, but still . . . *James* wanted to kiss her.

She wasn't supposed to kiss James—she was supposed to kiss the duke. But the duke had made it clear he wouldn't kiss her until they were married. He was so very, very proper. And Aunt Frances thought a kiss no great sin, and Corinna had told her she should kiss a few frogs so she'd know when she'd met her prince.

Not that James was a frog. He was . . . well, she didn't know what he was, precisely. A friend, she supposed. A friend who was rolling up his cuffs, exposing his muscled forearms to the innocent eyes of the last unkissed woman in all of England.

And unbuttoning the buttons that ran down the front of his waistcoat.

Dear heavens, if she didn't kiss him soon, he'd end up naked in the middle of Vauxhall Gardens.

"Very well," he said softly as the waistcoat fell open. "If you're not going to come to me, I will have to come to you."

And he did. He walked right up to her. She backed up, and he followed. She moved until her back was against a tall, fragrant hedge, and he followed until he was all but against her. Until there was a hairsbreadth between them, until his scent of starch and soap overwhelmed her, until her body tingled and the butterflies threatened to break free.

He was so close she could see golden flecks in his brown eyes. So close she could feel his breath upon her face. So close she found herself straining to get still closer.

"May I kiss you?" he asked, settling his hands on her shoulders.

She couldn't say yes and she couldn't say no. But she tilted her chin up, wondering, waiting, her heart pounding and her eyes drifting shut.

It was an invitation, albeit a silent one.

An invitation he accepted.

Chapter Twenty-nine

James's hands drew Juliana closer, slipped down around her, and pulled her closer still. His lips grazed hers, just a hint of a caress that left her desperate for more.

"May I?" he asked again in a husky whisper.

"Oh, yes," she whispered back, the words seemingly torn from her throat. And his mouth settled warm upon hers.

It was a divine sensation, more lovely than she'd ever imagined. She swayed against him, feeling his hard body through her thin dress. She slid her hands beneath his loosened waistcoat and all the way around to his back, his muscles rippling under her fingers.

He slanted his head, changing the angle of the kiss, deepening it. She felt as though she were melting, as though she couldn't tell where her lips ended and his started, as though she'd become a part of him.

And then he pulled back. Her heart still pounding, she opened her eyes and sighed. She wanted his mouth on hers again. It was a beautiful mouth, a sculpted mouth, the lower lip fuller than the top one. Above it, his eyes looked as dazed as she felt, warm pools of chocolate with golden flecks.

James Trevor, Earl of Stafford, was the handsomest man she'd ever seen.

She'd known he was handsome, of course. She'd told

Amanda as much, many times. But his handsomeness
had been just a fact like so many others. James was
handsome. Corinna was a good painter. Griffin had been
in the cavalry. All facts.

But now . . . She looked at James. Really looked at
him, seemingly for the first time. And what she saw
made her want him to kiss her all over again.

She rose to her toes, and he met her halfway, crushing
his mouth to hers. Not warm and caressing this time, but
hot and demanding instead. His lips coaxed hers to part,
and his tongue slipped inside, and it was shocking and
exciting. Soft, slippery, sweet, tasting of the claret they'd
drunk with supper. She was floating, whirling, she'd have
spun right off her feet if he hadn't been holding her so
tightly. One hand pressed the small of her back while
the other drifted up to cradle her head, adjusting the
angle so their lips meshed even more closely.

"Juliana!" It was Aunt Frances, her voice distant but
recognizable. "Juliana, where are you?"

"Bloody hell," James grated out, breaking the kiss.

"Dear heavens!" Juliana stared at him a moment
while her head cleared. He was standing there with half
of his clothing unbuttoned. Aunt Frances was about to
find them, and he was just standing there, unbuttoned.

"Dress yourself!" she hissed.

His fingers moved to the buttons of his waistcoat, fas-
tening them leisurely.

"Juliana!" her aunt called again.

She ran to the little grove's entrance and looked out
onto the path. Frances was nowhere to be seen, thank
heavens.

She turned back. "Hurry," she told James. "It's only
a matter of time until she finds us."

Unrolling one of his sleeves, he shrugged and saun-
tered back to the bench, where his cravat lay atop his
tailcoat in a jumbled pile. "Do I kiss better than
Castleton?"

"I haven't kissed Castleton. He's too—"

"Stuffy?" he provided, looking all too pleased at
that news.

"He's not stuffy! He's just—"

"A prig."

"He's not a prig! He's proper and reserved, which is more than I can say for you."

He grinned. "That's more than I can say for you as well. Which is a recommendation, to my mind—"

"Juliana!" Lord Malmsey's voice joined her aunt's this time. "Juliana!"

She peeked outside again. Still clear. Her heart pounding, now from panic instead of passion, she stalked over to James. He was buttoning his shirt so slowly it made her grit her teeth. "Hurry, will you?" She swept up his cravat, intending to throw it at him, but an enormous *boom* sounded overhead and she shrieked in alarm.

"Easy." The cravat drifted to the grass while James moved to wrap her in his arms. "It's just fireworks." Another *boom* exploded in the sky, accompanied by flashes of red and blue and white. "Your aunt will stop and watch," he said soothingly.

Knowing he was right, she pulled away and sat on the bench to watch the fireworks. But she wasn't soothed, and she didn't feel at ease. Not even after he'd retrieved the cravat and awkwardly knotted it and donned his tailcoat and buttoned it up. Her heart was still pounding, and her stomach felt queer. Great, fiery streaks of light burst in the heavens, and all around she heard "ooh!" and "ahh!" from all the people in Vauxhall Gardens, but all she could think was thank heavens she hadn't been caught kissing James while half of his clothing was unbuttoned.

They'd have had to marry. And she couldn't marry James. She just couldn't.

I can certainly marry a friend, she remembered him saying. *One can kiss a woman and make a child without falling in love.*

The duke was falling in love with her, and James never would. He'd only kissed her because they were friends and he wanted a child. And if he didn't marry Amanda, Amanda would have to marry Lord Malmsey—and Aunt Frances would be devastated.

She should never have let James kiss her.

James had finally kissed Juliana, and it had been better than he'd ever imagined—and God knew he'd imagined it plenty.

Countless times, he'd imagined the feel of her in his arms. Day after day, he'd imagined the taste of her on his lips. Night after night, he'd imagined the heat that would flash between them.

And it had all been better. Amazingly, exceedingly better. So much better, in fact, that it had left him rather witless.

He vaguely wondered what had driven him to unbutton so many buttons. And why he hadn't felt compelled to button them back up particularly quickly. And, most confounding of all, why he hadn't been nearly as relieved as Juliana when, after the fireworks, they'd met the older couple at the front gate of Vauxhall Gardens and her aunt didn't seem to be suspicious.

Now they were in his carriage on their way back to Berkeley Square. Seated across from him and Juliana, Lady Frances giggled like an infatuated adolescent. "Goodness gracious," she said, "when we couldn't find you, I half expected I'd be forced to tell my nephew he would have to demand the two of you marry."

Given that Lady Frances's own cheeks were much more flushed than Juliana's, James found that statement somewhat amusing.

But then Juliana smoothed her yellow dress. "We were only watching the fireworks, Auntie. Besides, you know I'm going to marry the Duke of Castleton."

And James found *that* statement supremely annoying.

And that's when everything began to slowly come clear in his mind.

It was a realization the likes of which he'd never experienced.

He'd unbuttoned so many buttons to tempt her, of course. And he hadn't felt compelled to button them back up particularly quickly because he hadn't been worried that the two of them might be caught and forced to marry.

No, that wasn't quite right. It wasn't that he hadn't been worried they might be caught and forced to marry . . . it was more like he'd been hoping they *would* be caught and forced to marry.

Because he wanted to marry her. But he hadn't been able to admit that, not even to himself, because it would be a betrayal of Anne.

Except . . . it wasn't.

He'd fallen in love with Juliana, and it wasn't a betrayal at all.

He felt like he should be appalled. Or guilty. Or disbelieving.

But he wasn't any of those things. He was in love. And he couldn't disbelieve it any more than he could disbelieve he had two hands and two feet.

He'd been telling himself all along this would never happen, but maybe some part of him had realized he could, indeed, fall in love again someday. Maybe he'd been in denial.

Maybe.

It was a possibility.

He was willing to admit to that.

But if he *had* thought such a thing—if he'd considered that someday he could fall in love with another woman without desecrating his first wife's memory—he'd thought it could happen only after Anne somehow granted him permission.

Exactly *how* he could receive permission from a dead woman wasn't something he'd really considered. Maybe he could have gone to her grave and talked to her— he'd read such scenarios in books. Or maybe she could have come to him in a dream—he'd read that in books, too. Or maybe she could have sent him a sign; maybe he could have just seen something—something seemingly insignificant—and somehow known what it meant.

But none of that had happened. Because he didn't *need* Anne's permission. Because his love for Juliana had nothing to do with Anne.

Nothing.

Loving Juliana didn't diminish the love he'd had for Anne. It didn't mean he wouldn't always cherish the memories of their time together. He didn't love Juliana more than he'd loved Anne or less than he'd loved Anne.

He loved her differently.

She was a different woman, and he loved her for different reasons. Which made sense, because he was different now, too. This new love wasn't better or worse, or deeper or shallower. It was just *different*.

And it was exactly what he needed right now. What he needed to make him feel whole again, to make his life complete.

Unfortunately, Juliana seemed bent on marrying stuffy Castleton, that ass who wanted her only because she came with a horse.

The carriage rolled to a stop in front of her brother's town house.

"Thank you," Lord Malmsey said as he stepped out.

"It was a lovely evening," Lady Frances said and stepped out, too.

Juliana didn't say anything as she stepped out to follow them. But before the footman could close the carriage door, she turned back to face James. "When are you going to take Lady Amanda to Vauxhall Gardens?"

He didn't want to take Lady Amanda to Vauxhall Gardens. He didn't want to take her anywhere. He'd *never* wanted to take her anywhere.

But he especially didn't want to take her to Vauxhall Gardens, the place where he'd discovered he was in love with Juliana.

"Never," he said. "I didn't enjoy Vauxhall Gardens much."

"Didn't you?" She narrowed her eyes as though she didn't believe him. Which was hardly surprising, since in truth he'd enjoyed himself immensely. "Well," she said, "then where shall you take her?"

He wanted to say nowhere, but he couldn't. Because then he'd have no excuse to see Juliana. She was bent on marrying the stuffy duke, which meant she wouldn't accept an invitation to accompany him anywhere unless it was for the sake of Lady Amanda.

That wasn't such a terrible thing, he consoled himself. He and Juliana were becoming fast friends, and that was good enough for now. If he continued the pretense that he was interested in Lady Amanda, he could keep touching Juliana, and kissing her, and tempting her. Juliana wouldn't try to trick him again—she'd promised not to, and he trusted her. He could afford to remain patient.

Friendship in marriage was important, and there was plenty of time to make Juliana fall in love with him.

He was just getting used to the fact that he wanted to marry her. There was no reason to rush right into it.

"I'll take Lady Amanda wherever you'd like," he said. "Except Vauxhall Gardens. As long as you come along, too."

"I cannot come along!"

"You can if you're with Castleton." It galled him to say that, but he saw no other choice. No other way to keep touching and kissing and tempting Juliana.

Well, there was Friday, when he hoped to corner her in a treatment room. But that was four days away. Entirely too long to wait.

"If we go somewhere I've never been," he told her, "I'll need you there to provide guidance."

She mulled that over for a moment, and then she said, "Very well," just as he'd expected. He'd known he could appeal to her meddling nature. She'd probably never in her life come to believe he was capable of fending for himself, but he could live with that.

In fact, he looked forward to living with that. He rather liked having her look after him. It was a never-ending source of amusement, one of her many quirks he loved best.

"I think we should go see the new Battle of Waterloo panorama in Leicester Square tomorrow," she said. "I've heard it is very romantic."

Having witnessed war himself, James didn't think it very romantic, and he had never heard the term *romantic* attached to the Leicester Square Panorama building, either. But he had heard it was rather dark, and he supposed darkness could lead to romance, and while he was well aware Juliana expected him to find romance with Lady Amanda while she found romance with that ass Castleton, he knew that wouldn't happen, so her false expectations didn't dampen his spirits in the slightest. "I believe it closes at four," he said, "so I shall return to fetch you and Lady Amanda at one o'clock."

"And Aunt Frances," she reminded him.

"And Lady Frances." Even that didn't dim his cheer.

"Invite Lord Malmsey, too, will you?" he said, reaching into his pocket. "Here are your gloves, s—" He cut off, turning the last sound into a very long *s*, as though there were more than two gloves. He'd almost called her "sweetheart." He'd best be more careful; he wanted to tempt Juliana, not scare her away.

"Thank you," she said, taking them and going into the house.

James was in an excellent mood as his carriage continued on to Stafford House. Once there, he remained in an excellent mood as he searched the morning room and the music room and the Palm Room for his mother. He took the stairs two at a time, still in an excellent mood when he finally found her in her sitting room, reading a Minerva Press novel.

He'd never seen his mother read a Minerva Press novel. They were torrid romances, and he didn't quite know how he felt about her reading such a thing, but that didn't affect his excellent mood.

"Yes, James?" she said, shutting it quickly and setting it upside down on the table beside her. "How was your evening?"

"It was rather pleasant," he said, perhaps the greatest understatement of his life. "I want to renovate my bedroom."

"You cannot change that room. It was designed by Henry Holland!"

"I don't care who designed it. Brown and plum are too somber."

Cornelia loved redecorating, but James's father had never let her touch Stafford House, so she'd had to content herself with overhauling their manor house in the countryside. James had known she wouldn't argue long. Clearly excited, she rose, belted her dressing gown more tightly, and walked over to sit at her feminine writing desk. "What colors would you like, then?" she asked, dipping her quill in the inkwell.

"Red," he decided.

"Your favorite color. Yes, I should have guessed." She scribbled. "Any other requests?"

"And yellow. Red and yellow." He'd noticed Juliana

often wore yellow, but he wouldn't explain that to his mother. The last thing he needed was her figuring out he'd finally decided to marry.

"We'll do stripes," she said, still scribbling. "Wide red and yellow stripes on the walls above the wainscoting."

"I want the wainscoting gone. It's dark wood, and I don't want anything dark in the room."

She frowned, then brightened. "We'll paint the wainscoting white, then. Bright white enamel. And use narrower stripes on the upholstery. But solid red bedclothing, I think. Perhaps with yellow pillows."

"Fine." Henry Holland's design had used floral fabrics, so stripes sounded perfect. As different as could be. "And get rid of that monstrous old-fashioned bed, will you?"

"It's been in the family since the sixteenth century."

"It looks it."

"Nine Stafford earls were born in that bed—"

"I want something modern. Without a canopy or stifling curtains."

She looked up. And then she gazed at him for a very long moment, while he wondered if she'd make the connection, if she'd realize the bed, the curtains—all of it—held too many memories.

"Very well," she finally said. "If you insist, we'll move it to a guest room."

Chapter Thirty

"It's the rheumatism, I fear," Lady Avonleigh said the next afternoon.

"It's dreadful," Lady Balmforth added. "The two of us ache every morning."

When James had fetched Juliana and the others for their outing, he'd explained that he needed to stop by his aunts' house on their way to Leicester Square. Seated in his aunts' drawing room on a peach sofa, Juliana watched him walk them toward a large picture window.

"I'm afraid some morning stiffness is to be expected at your age," he said sympathetically. He lifted Lady Balmforth's narrow hand and examined it in the window's light.

"Don't you need to use your quizzing glass?" she asked.

"Not for this. I see no evidence of swelling, and your joints don't look reddened or feel overly warm. If the achiness wears off before noon, that's a good sign." He flexed her elbow. "Does this hurt?"

"He's patient," Amanda said quietly, sitting beside Juliana.

"Yes, he is," she whispered back, lifting an embroidery hoop one of James's aunts had left on the table. It wasn't a simple sampler but an amazingly detailed scene—a cottage in the woods with animals among the trees. Oddly enough, though, it seemed to smell faintly of camphor. "Isn't this exquisite?"

"I wish he'd be a little more *im*patient. We're going to be late."

"There's no need to worry." She sniffed the embroidery hoop before she set it back down. Definitely camphor. "The rotunda doesn't close until four."

"But the duke will be waiting."

"Not for so very long." Juliana raised a half-finished crewelwork seat cover and ran her fingers over the pattern, a veritable field of flowers. "Lord Stafford's aunts are very talented."

"Lord Stafford is on his knees," Amanda said. "That cannot be good for his injury."

James was crouched on the floor, obligingly examining Lady Avonleigh's plump ankles. "There's nothing he won't do for someone he cares for," Juliana said, returning the crewelwork to the table. "You're lucky to have someone so wonderful courting you." Honestly, it was a bit annoying that Amanda didn't seem to realize how very lucky she was. "It's nice of you to be concerned for him, though. Just remember to let him kiss you."

"What if he doesn't try?"

"He'll try. Parts of the rotunda are rumored to be very dark." James would take advantage of the darkness—Juliana knew this from experience.

"What if I don't like his kisses?"

Poor Amanda seemed even more afraid of kissing than before. The failed trick must have traumatized her. "You'll love his kisses," she assured her. Another thing she knew from experience. In fact, just thinking about that particular experience made her stomach feel all queer again.

Why was that?

Her puzzlement must have shown on her face, because the next thing she knew, James was standing over her, looking concerned. "Is something wrong?"

"No, not at all," she assured him—and herself. "Are you finished?"

"I've prescribed hot, damp towels for my aunts' aches. I am certain they shall be fine."

She rose and walked over to where his aunts sat while

their maids obligingly applied the towels. "I hope you'll both be feeling better soon."

"Oh, we shall," Lady Balmforth said as her maid wrapped one of her wrists. "Our James always knows what to do. I'm sure we'll feel better by the time Cornelia comes to fetch us in an hour. We're going to Gillow's to look at some new furniture for her house."

"Your needlework is lovely. I'm having a little sewing party tomorrow afternoon, to make some baby clothes for the Foundling Hospital. Would either of you be interested in joining me?"

"Cornelia told us about your sewing parties," Lady Avonleigh exclaimed, appearing better already. The odd camphor smell was hers—along with a rather strong scent of gardenias. "They sound delightful, my dear. I should love to attend."

Lady Balmforth clasped her hands together so enthusiastically she lost a towel in the process. "I should love to attend, too."

"Thank you so much. Shall I send my brother's carriage at one o'clock?"

"Oh, no," Lady Avonleigh said. "We have our own carriage, and John Coachman has much too much time on his hands."

"He naps," Lady Balmforth added. "Even more often than we do."

Juliana noticed James and Amanda both inching toward the door. "Excellent," she said before going after them. "I live at forty-four Berkeley Square, and I very much look forward to seeing you."

"That was rather presumptuous," Amanda said as they walked out to James's carriage, where Frances and Lord Malmsey were waiting.

"I disagree," James said. "I think it was kind. My aunts were thrilled to be invited."

Juliana smiled. "They're very sweet."

"And very healthy," he said dryly. "Such a pity they don't know it."

"They just need something else to occupy their minds. That's why I invited them to my party—well, besides the fact that I do need their help. And I'm thinking I should introduce them to a few more charming gentlemen."

"I don't believe either of them is interested in gentlemen, charming or not."

"Have they never been wed?"

"Oh, yes. Aunt Bedelia was married four times."

"Four!" Amanda exclaimed.

"A baron, two viscounts, and an earl. They all died," he added as a footman opened the carriage door. "That sweet old lady must be toxic."

Juliana started to laugh, but ended up gasping instead. Inside James's opulent carriage, her aunt was *kissing* Lord Malmsey.

"Gracious me!" Amanda cried, clearly scandalized. Not because she cared that Lord Malmsey was courting Frances, Juliana thought. After all, Amanda wanted to marry James; she'd given Lord Malmsey permission to court other women; she'd told him she was going to find a way out of their marriage. Amanda would have been scandalized to see *any* two people kissing. She was scared to death of kisses.

The older couple jerked apart. A flush rushed up Frances's neck and spread to her cheeks. Not a delicate flush, either—it was more like a bright red flood.

But she kept her composure. "Are your aunts feeling better?" she asked James, folding her hands in her lap.

"Remarkably." He handed Amanda in first, then Juliana before himself. She left space for him in the middle, but it seemed there was not enough, because he ended up squished against her. "To the Leicester Square Panorama," he instructed and settled back.

They all rode in silence for a few awkward moments. James felt very warm against Juliana. Her stomach was feeling even more queer. "Lord Stafford was telling us his aunt Bedelia has been married four times," she told Frances.

"Oh, my," Frances said.

After a few more awkward moments, Juliana looked up to James. "Were there no children?"

"None that lived. And Aunt Aurelia's life has been even more tragic."

"How many husbands did *she* have?" Amanda asked in a tone that Juliana found rather disapproving.

James didn't seem to notice, however. "Only one, the

Earl of Avonleigh. But their children failed to bring her happiness. Her eldest daughter eloped with a cousin, prompting her husband to disown the girl. Aurelia never heard from her again and learned she'd died a number of years later. Her middle child, a son, drank too much and accidently drowned. And her youngest, another daughter, ended her own life soon after marrying. She jumped off the London Bridge, taking her unborn child with her."

"Oh, my," Frances said again.

"Aunt Aurelia's husband died soon thereafter. A 'visitation from God' was the coroner's official verdict, but I expect his spirit was broken."

"I don't doubt that," Lord Malmsey said.

Juliana nodded. "It's a wonder your aunt survived."

"She's a strong lady. They both are. It's a shame they have no children or grandchildren to dote upon."

"They have you," she pointed out.

"I know, and I adore them. I admire their pluck." The carriage came to a halt. "I just wish they had someone else to pluck at once in a while."

The door opened to Leicester Square and a huge round building. Over a rather nondescript entrance, a fancy marquee said PANORAMA. Before it stood the duke.

Juliana was relieved he didn't look perturbed. On the other hand, he didn't look happy, either. He looked the way he usually did.

Reserved. And rather bland. His pale blue eyes calm, his expression pleasant.

Everyone clambered out of the carriage. "Good afternoon, my dear," the duke said to her. "I was very pleased to receive your invitation."

After everyone else exchanged greetings, the men bought tickets at the box office and they all proceeded inside. A long, narrow, dimly lit corridor stretched ahead, and it got even darker when the door shut behind them.

Amanda shrieked.

"There now," a voice said, soothing her. "Take my arm."

It was the duke, not James.

James took Juliana's arm instead. Even in the dark she knew it was James, because he smelled like soap and starch instead of eau de cologne. And because her stomach felt even queerer.

"You should be escorting Lady Amanda," she whispered as they all groped their way down the hall, laughing and feeling their way along the walls.

"She'll be fine," he said.

Of course Amanda would be fine. The duke was very kind to soothe her. It was somewhat of a shock going from the busy, open square to the dim, closed-in corridor, but it wasn't really scary. In fact, it was sort of fun. However, James could hardly kiss Amanda while she was with the duke, and that wasn't a good thing.

By the time they reached the end of the corridor, Juliana's eyes had adjusted to the low light and she could see somewhat. A tall staircase spiraled up. And up. And up. The light in the stairwell grew a little brighter as they went.

"My knees hurt," Amanda complained halfway up. "Can we not stop and rest?"

"Of course we can," the duke said.

Propelled by James, Juliana passed them and kept going.

Behind her, Frances giggled. "I cannot remember the last time I turned in so many circles!"

Indeed, Juliana felt like a blindfolded child being spun around as part of a game. It was a bit disorienting. She held tighter to James, noticing he seemed to be limping a little more than usual. Maybe Amanda had been right when she said he shouldn't have been kneeling.

Suddenly the staircase ended, and they emerged to find themselves transported to another time and place. Like magic, they'd gone from Leicester Square to Belgium in a matter of minutes.

Feeling like she was still spinning, Juliana wormed her way through the crowd and gripped the platform's rail. All around her, above and below, a battlefield stretched miles into the distance. "Amazing," James breathed behind her.

It was overwhelming. She knew the panorama was only a giant painting, but everything in the rotunda was designed to trick the eyes. Indirect illumination, provided by narrow skylights beneath the edge of the domed ceiling, made it look like outdoors at dusk. Far below, a three-dimensional terrain stretched from under the platform up to the walls, filled with lifelike vegetation, objects, and figures that blended into the picture, making everything seem real.

And all around, the Battle of Waterloo raged.

Chaos reigned. Cavalrymen charged on horses with bayoneted infantry at their backs. Officers gave orders, soldiers aided the fallen, smoke rose from cannons in a stand of trees. The ground was low in places, muddy in others, fenced and open, brown and green, flat and rough and everything in between. Fields that should have been smooth were littered with the killed and wounded, the contents of their knapsacks strewn all over. As far as the eye could see, men scrambled and fought, their guns and swords flashing in the glistening haze made by spent artillery.

When Juliana finally felt steady enough to release the rail, she edged sideways around the platform, working her way through the other milling spectators. It seemed they were all standing in a pavilion on the top of a small hill in the center of the battle. The soldiers looked wet, dirty, and blue with cold. She could have sworn she saw a mounted officer raise a hat to signal an attack. A shiver ran down her spine.

"I feel seasick," Frances said from somewhere close on the platform.

"Hold on to me," Lord Malmsey said. "You have delicate nerves, my love."

His love? Blinking in the twilight, Juliana tore her gaze from the panorama and turned toward the voices.

But the couple was no longer nearby.

Chapter Thirty-one

"Where is my aunt?" Juliana cried. "And Lord Malmsey?"

James curved an arm around her, pulling her close. "We'll find them later," he said, his low voice seeming to vibrate right through her.

Though she knew she shouldn't, she leaned into him. "Where are the duke and Lady Amanda?"

"Does it matter?"

"Yes!" Amanda was supposed to be here with James in the dark. Kissing him. No matter that the thought of his kisses made Juliana's stomach feel queer.

She swayed.

"Are you feeling seasick, too?" he asked.

"No." It was just the sound of his deep chocolate voice making her dizzy. And the thought of kissing him. She couldn't kiss him. Not again. If she was going to kiss anyone, it should be the duke.

But the duke didn't want to kiss her until they were married, and in any case, he was with Amanda. In fact, Amanda had probably latched on to him knowing he wouldn't kiss her. If a woman feared being kissed, the duke was a much safer bet than James.

"Do you see them?" she asked James, trying to peer around him.

He drew her toward the staircase. "Maybe they've gone downstairs. I think we should go and see."

They walked all the way down, around and around, but the others were nowhere to be found. At the bottom, they retraced their steps down the corridor, laughingly feeling their way along the walls again. James, Juliana noticed even in the darkness, was limping even more than before. Reaching the end, they opened the door and looked out into Leicester Square.

She blinked in the bright sunshine. There was no sign of her aunt or Amanda or the other men. "They must still be upstairs," she said.

"They must." A family was approaching the door, so James drew her back inside to let them pass.

The children giggled when the door closed behind them and the corridor plunged into darkness. "Don't run!" the parents cautioned as their offspring made their way toward the staircase.

The youngsters giggled again and again, bumping each other and the walls. Still, when James took Juliana's hand and started to follow them, she could *hear* his uneven gait.

"Your leg is hurting you, isn't it?"

She felt rather than saw him shrug. "It was a tall staircase. I'm fine."

The vast number of steps hadn't occurred to her when she'd suggested today's outing. Unlike Amanda, she never really thought about James's limp at all. He never mentioned it, and it was usually so slight. "Does it hurt very often?"

"Only when it's cold and rainy."

"Dear heavens." She gripped his arm with her other hand, effectively dragging him to a stop. "It must hurt *all* the time this year."

His laughter echoed down the corridor. "It's not that painful. It's stiffer than I'd like, but the sensation is just a dull ache. Nothing to merit your concern. In a strange sort of way I actually embrace the discomfort—it reminds me how fortunate I am to still have it."

"When did it happen? And how?"

"Peninsular War," James explained. "Took a ball

right below the knee." The giggles grew fainter as, at the other end of the corridor, the family started up the staircase. "The army surgeons wanted to amputate, but one managed to save it instead."

"I'm glad," Juliana murmured, thinking he was stoic and brave.

Amanda should be so grateful to have him.

"I was lucky." The footsteps faded away, and James started walking again down the corridor. "And extremely grateful for the man's skill. Since I could no longer march with the army, I needed another profession, and—"

"*That's* why you became a doctor," she interrupted softly.

"Have you still been puzzling over that?" he wondered with a low laugh as they neared the steps. "Yes, this time you're more or less correct. Eventually, though, I chose the life of a physician over that of a surgeon. I decided I'd rather work with stethoscopes than saws."

Suppressing a sickening vision of a surgeon's saw covered in blood, Juliana took a while to notice that instead of starting up the staircase, he'd drawn her around and underneath it.

"What are you doing?" she asked.

"People will bump into us if we wait in the corridor. We'll wait here instead."

It was very dark under the steps, and James would take advantage of the dark. He'd claim he wanted to practice and try to kiss her again. She'd told Amanda as much, hadn't she, because she knew it to be true from experience. "I think we should go back upstairs."

"If we wait here," he argued, "your aunt and the others will surely come down."

"Aunt Frances won't be able to see us under here." Especially considering Frances was probably busy kissing Lord Malmsey. Bold men had a tendency to take advantage of the dark, and while Lord Malmsey might have started out rather shy, he was obviously getting bolder by the minute. Already today he'd been bold enough to kiss Frances in James's carriage and call her *my love.*

Juliana's stomach felt queer—and suddenly she knew why.

Lord Malmsey had called Aunt Frances *my love*.

Juliana wanted someone to call *her* my love.

She wanted *James* to call her my love.

Because she loved James, and she wanted him to love her back.

But that would never happen.

"I don't know what to do," she said.

She wanted to love the duke. But she loved James instead, because James was warm and affectionate and charitable and everything else the duke wasn't. It didn't matter anymore that James was too tall and had dark hair and a profession. He was brave and stoic. They fit perfectly together, and he was the most handsome man she knew, and as for his profession, well, he was trying to rid the world of the scourge of smallpox, and whatever could be wrong with that?

But she couldn't marry James, because he would never love her. Like her mother, she'd be unhappy all her days. And the duke needed her, and he was very kind, and he was sending her flowers and falling in love with her. James and Amanda belonged together. They shared interests that Juliana didn't. They filled each other's needs.

Juliana's stomach didn't just feel queer anymore—it *hurt*. And she wished she'd never said she didn't know what to do, because she couldn't possibly explain any of this to James.

Fortunately, he interpreted *I don't know what to do* in an entirely different context. "It doesn't make much sense to walk all the way up again only to turn around and come back down." Edging her even deeper under the steps, he raised a hand and traced one finger in a shivery line down her jaw. "Don't worry about whether your aunt will see us. I'll watch for her and the others. And while we're waiting, we can practice kissing."

She'd known he would say that, hadn't she? And she knew she shouldn't agree. But she also knew she shouldn't insist he walk up all those stairs again or his poor leg would pain him even more.

"You don't need to practice kissing," she told him with no small amount of conviction. James had been married, after all. She hadn't known that when she'd first suggested he might need lessons, but she knew it now. He'd *had* practice. He kissed so well a woman would have to be daft to think he needed practice.

His finger lingered at the base of her chin, tracing little circles there, threatening to break her resolve. At the far end of the corridor, the door opened, admitting more people and a little light, just enough so Juliana could see James's gaze, which was so intense she could tell he knew exactly the effect his actions were having on her.

Oh, yes, he'd had practice.

The door shut, plunging the corridor back into darkness as the people made their way to the stairwell. "It's been a long time since I've kissed a woman," he said quietly, apparently reading her mind again.

"It's been less than twenty-four hours."

"But before that, it was a long time."

His finger continued down her throat, slowly, slowly. Wishing she could see him, she swallowed hard. "You're not going to unbutton, are you?"

His laugh was quick, low, and pleased. "No, I'm not going to unbutton here." His finger zigzagged down her chest, lightly, lightly, making every nerve in her body sing. "Practice with me, Juliana," he murmured as it disappeared into the little valley between her breasts.

She couldn't breathe. No man had ever touched her there, and now his finger was tracing up and down, making her heart pound and her breasts ache.

More people were coming down the corridor, but she couldn't seem to care.

"They cannot see you," he whispered, bending his neck, angling his head, lowering his mouth toward hers. "Will you practice?" His breath whispered across her lips. "Will you?"

And she let him. She whispered, "Yes." God help her, though he clearly didn't need any practice, she allowed him to practice anyway. Just once. Or maybe twice.

She lost count.

His kisses were drugging. Little nipping ones at first, and then deeper ones, until she opened her mouth and invited him in. People went up and down the stairs overhead while his tongue tangled with hers in a dance so exciting it made heat gather low in her middle. His finger still played between her breasts, and his other hand pressed against her back, pulling her closer.

Her pulse raced, and her head swam, and she didn't want him to stop. She wanted him to kiss her forever. She wanted him to make her forget that she shouldn't be wanting him.

He shifted his finger inside her bodice and touched a nipple.

She sucked in her breath, breaking the kiss.

"I'm not unbuttoning," he murmured, rubbing the sensitive crest.

No, what he was doing was much more effective. It made the heat down lower more urgent. She rocked against him as he kept rubbing and kissed a tingling trail down her throat.

She feared her knees might fail. "James!" she breathed.

"Hmm?" He placed little damp kisses all across her low neckline, maneuvering his hand inside her bodice until he managed to free her other breast.

And his warm mouth closed over it.

"James!"

"Juliana, is that you?"

His mouth left her. "Is that you, Lady Frances?" He whirled around and started down the corridor while Juliana yanked her dress back into place.

More footsteps sounded on the stairs, growing closer. Juliana stepped into the corridor just as four dark forms made it to the bottom. "There you all are!" she said.

At the other end, James opened the door, admitting a shaft of light. "We were looking for you."

"*We* were looking for you," Frances said, blinking madly. Well, it was dim, and she wasn't wearing her spectacles. "Lady Amanda wishes to return home."

"I was dizzy up there," Amanda said.

Juliana had felt a little dizzy up there, too, but she felt much more dizzy now. Dizzy and confused. She followed the others out into Leicester Square. Her knees still felt shaky. Her breasts ached as though James were still touching them.

She wished he were still touching them.

Her stomach was hurting again.

James would never love her. He needed to kiss Amanda and marry her, or everything would be ruined.

"Where should we go now?" she asked.

"Parliament," the duke said.

James pulled out his pocket watch, opened it, and snapped it shut. "Good God, it's almost four o'clock." Indeed, people were starting to stream out of the Panorama. "The two of us should definitely go to Parliament."

How in heaven's name was James going to kiss Amanda and decide to marry her if he was always in Parliament? "I've a sewing party from one o'clock until three tomorrow, but how about if we go somewhere in the late afternoon or the evening? The House of Lords doesn't meet on Wednesdays."

"We can go to Almack's," Amanda suggested.

"No," James said at the same time Juliana said, "I think not."

She wondered why he didn't want to attend Almack's, but it didn't really signify, because Almack's was a bad idea. Aunt Frances might be rather blind these days, but the lady patronesses who ran Almack's had vision sharper than tacks. James would never be able to kiss Amanda there. "How about Vauxhall Gardens?" she suggested instead.

"I adore Vauxhall Gardens," Frances put in approvingly. "Especially at night."

"Only ladies of easy virtue attend Vauxhall Gardens at night," Amanda said, either unaware or unconcerned that she'd just insulted Frances. "I enjoy gardens, but I would prefer to visit one that is more respectable."

"How about Chelsea Physic Garden, then?" James asked.

"Chelsea Physic Garden?" Juliana had never heard of the place. "Where is it?"

"In Chelsea," the duke said dryly.

Juliana shot him a peeved glance before turning back to James. "Is it very exciting?"

"It's very peaceful. If you've not heard of it, that is because one must be a physician or apothecary to gain entrance. But I'm allowed to bring guests, and I think

Lady Amanda would like it. I shall ask my cook to prepare a picnic supper."

"It sounds perfect," the duke said. "Shall we say five o'clock? Now I think we should be off."

Chapter Thirty-two

James's aunts were even better seamstresses than Rachael and her sisters. Better and faster. As Juliana sat stitching like mad while her guests chatted, she tried to convince herself that, with Lady Avonleigh's and Lady Balmforth's help, she could successfully finish making all the baby clothes before her deadline a week from Saturday.

At the end of Monday's party, she'd had a hundred and twenty-one completed pieces and needed only a hundred and nineteen more. Well, perhaps the word *only* was a bit optimistic, especially considering a majority of the finished pieces were simple blankets and clouts. But it had been the first time the number of items accumulated exceeded the number of items still unmade, which seemed a milestone of sorts. Counting today, she had six sewing parties left. Which meant if all twelve of her guests were willing to attend every time, she'd need them to finish . . .

Her head hurt. "Emily, how much is a hundred and nineteen divided by six?"

"Miss Emily isn't here," Lady Mabel wheezed.

Oh, that was right. Emily had finished cutting, and she still refused to sew, and she'd been busy lately anyway for some reason or another. Which meant Juliana had

eleven ladies—well, twelve if she counted herself—and
needed—

"Nineteen and five-sixths," Elizabeth said, interrupting her thoughts.

"Pardon?"

"One hundred nineteen divided by six is nineteen and
five-sixths."

"You did that without paper?"

Elizabeth shrugged. "I like to exercise my brain."

"My younger daughter was like that," Lady Avonleigh
said. "She could do any calculation in her head."

"Our mother was good at arithmetic, too," Rachael
said. "I expect Elizabeth inherited that ability from her."

"Brains do tend to run in families." Lady Stafford
smiled toward Juliana. "My James was Aurelia's daughter's cousin."

"Much younger cousin," Lady Balmforth pointed out.

"Yes, had she lived she'd have been a grandmother
by now, I expect—unlike my James, who's of marriage-
able age." Lady Stafford smiled at Juliana again. "I was
noticing at my dinner party, my dear, that the Duke of
Castleton seems a mite reserved for a young lady of
your enthusiasm."

"Yes, the duke surely is reserved," Juliana said distractedly, trying to figure out if they could make nineteen and five-sixths items at each party. "But that is only
to be expected, considering his lonely childhood. Did
you know he was born in this house? His cruel uncle
and aunt sold it and made him move. The thought of it
quite breaks my heart."

Rachael nudged Juliana. "I think Lady Stafford is
hoping you'll marry her son," she whispered.

Juliana wished things were different so she could. In
fact, she wished so hard it made her grit her teeth. "Brilliant observation," she said tightly under her breath,
"but much as I like Lady Stafford, her son doesn't love
me. I'm marrying the duke. He's very nice and he
needs me."

"For God's sake," Rachael whispered, "I should think
you'd rather have a man who *wants* you."

"He does want me. He told me he's falling in love

with me. He sends me roses. He dances with me at every event."

"From about three feet away. Don't you want a man who physically wants you?"

It wasn't the duke's fault he was physically undemonstrative. He'd never known anything else. That was why he needed her.

Juliana's stomach hurt. She turned away and raised her voice. "I cannot thank you enough for coming, Lady Avonleigh and Lady Balmforth. You're both excellent seamstresses."

"Our mother taught us both to sew," Lady Balmforth said, "along with Cornelia, of course."

Lady Avonleigh nodded. "Cornelia and Bedelia didn't have daughters, but I followed tradition and taught mine to sew. My younger daughter was quite artistic and especially good with a needle."

Juliana and Rachael turned toward Lady Stafford expectantly. She didn't disappoint them. "My son is good with a needle, too. He does excellent sutures."

The cousins shared a smile, but Juliana's faded. "Do you think that together we can finish nineteen and five-sixths items this afternoon?"

"Twenty," Elizabeth said. "It's close enough to call it twenty."

"Of course. Do you think we can finish twenty? Twelve of us?"

"Of course," Corinna echoed. "We did twenty-three on Monday, remember? Without Ladies A and B."

Ladies A and B smiled, their needles flashing.

"Those were all clouts," Juliana said. "Not frocks, coats, caps, and the like, which are more complicated and take much longer."

Alexandra rubbed her belly, even though it still looked flat. "We can finish twenty pieces, even if they're more difficult," she said soothingly. "We'll just stay later, until we're done."

"We can't," Amanda said. "Juliana and your aunt and I are leaving at five to go to Chelsea Physic Garden, and we'll need time to ready ourselves first."

"Chelsea Physic Garden?" Claire looked up from the little frock she was sewing. "What is that?"

"Some garden for doctors," Juliana said. "James thinks Amanda will like it."

Rachael tied off a thread. "You call him James?"

"Lord Stafford," Juliana gritted out, "said Chelsea Physic Garden is very peaceful."

"My son knows exactly what women enjoy," Lady Stafford said. "He's taken me to the garden in Chelsea, and it is lovely."

Reaching for a spool, Rachael leaned closer to Juliana. "So tell me about *James*," she whispered.

"There's nothing to tell," Juliana said. "And we must stop whispering. It's not polite."

"You're right," Rachael said louder as she threaded her needle. "I've been wondering," she said to the company in general, "whether it's a good idea to marry a man expecting him to change."

Elizabeth's eyes widened. "Whom are you thinking of marrying?"

"No one in particular. It's just a hypothetical question."

"No," Corinna said flatly. "You cannot change people. If you marry a man expecting him to change, you will be disappointed."

"Not necessarily," Juliana disagreed. "People change all the time. Look at Amanda."

Amanda blushed.

"Amanda wanted to change," Corinna argued. "That's very different from expecting a change in someone who's happy with himself."

Claire nodded. "Just think, Juliana. How would you feel if someone married you expecting *you* to change? Or even hoping you would change? Wouldn't you prefer a man who wants you just the way you are without wishing you were different?"

"We're not talking about me," Juliana snapped. "It was Rachael asking the question."

But she knew they *were* talking about her. Or at least they could be. She was planning to marry the duke expecting him to change, and she knew the duke would probably hope she would change, too.

Whereas James liked her just the way she was. But only as a friend—he would never love her. If it seemed he wanted her in a physical sense, that was only because they were friends and he wanted a child.

And he had to marry Amanda, or else three other people's lives would be ruined.

Her stomach had never hurt so badly in her life.

Chapter Thirty-three

As James was leaving, Cornelia walked into Stafford House. "How did your day go, dear?"

"Very well." Pausing in the entrance hall, he shifted the picnic basket he was carrying. "I wasn't shorthanded today, so I was able to stop by Gillow's to see the bedroom furniture you and your sisters picked out. It looks fine."

"Good. I chose the fabrics this morning, and I have a painter coming by later this week. This is all coming together very quickly."

"Excellent," he told her. "I truly appreciate your help. Did your sisters enjoy today's sewing party?"

"Very much. They're looking forward to another one tomorrow." She reached up to smooth his hair, making him feel about six years old again. "I was surprised to learn this afternoon that you're going to the Physic Garden rather than Almack's."

He shrugged. "Lady Juliana and Lady Amanda said they'd prefer to visit the garden."

"You've been spending a lot of time with your lovely young ladies."

"They're not my ladies, Mother." He hoped Juliana was getting closer to becoming his lady—her reactions at the Panorama had been encouraging—but she wasn't his lady yet.

"Are you going to marry one of them?"

He leveled his gaze on her. "Are you going to marry Lord Cavanaugh?"

She blinked. "I'm not prepared to say. At the moment I'm just enjoying his company."

"Exactly." He bent to kiss her on the cheek. "Enjoy Almack's, will you?"

He whistled as he went out the door, whistled as his carriage made its way to Berkeley Square. Things were looking up. He might have just managed to get his mother off his back, and in any case, in mere minutes he'd be kissing Juliana.

He stopped whistling out loud when his guests joined him in the carriage, of course, but he was still whistling in his head. And toying with the deck of playing cards he'd slipped into his pocket. It was almost six o'clock by the time they reached Chelsea and alighted from the carriage on Swan Walk.

"Good evening," he said to the guard at the garden's entrance.

"Good evening, Lord Stafford." The man swung open the gate set into the old redbrick wall. "Sunset is at quarter to nine."

"The garden closes at sunset," James told his party. "Is Wheeler here?" he asked the guard.

"Not tonight. He left at four."

"Oh, that's a pity," James said, although it wasn't a pity at all. In fact, it was exactly what he was hoping to hear.

"Who is Wheeler?" Juliana asked as they walked in.

"Thomas Wheeler is the Physic Garden's Demonstrator. He's hired to explain the uses of the medicinal plants to visitors." He led them along a tree-lined path to the center of the garden. "Shall I give a tour, or would you prefer to dine first?"

"I'm famished," Castleton said. "We can look at plants later."

James suspected the man didn't want to look at plants at all, which suited his plans just fine. He chose a grassy spot by the rockery and laid out a large blanket before opening the basket his servants had prepared. The duke and Lady Amanda hung back while James opened a bottle of wine and Juliana and her aunt unpacked cold chicken, bread, and cheese.

"I don't sit on the ground," Castleton said stuffily, taking his supper to a nearby bench.

What an ass, James thought for the umpteenth time.

Lady Amanda didn't seem to agree with his assessment, however. In fact, she appeared to breathe a sigh of relief. "Neither do I," she said and joined the ass.

"You should sit by her," Juliana whispered.

"There's no more room on the bench," James whispered back. Actually, there *would* have been room on the bench if the two of them weren't sitting primly spaced apart from each other. But it was just as well, since he had no intention of sitting with Lady Amanda anyway.

"No one else seems to be here," Lady Frances observed, happily settling close by Lord Malmsey on the blanket. "This place is so peaceful and enchanting."

Juliana pulled off her gloves as she sat down by them. "Corinna would love to come here and paint."

"I can obtain a ticket for her entrance," James said. He took glasses of wine to the ass and his companion, then lowered himself to the ground by Juliana.

"What is the purpose of the garden?" Lord Malmsey asked.

James swallowed a bite of bread. "Doctors and apothecaries can visit to obtain cuttings of medicinal plants. But mostly it is used for educational and training purposes. Hundreds of medical and apothecary students visit every year as part of their studies."

Juliana waved a chicken leg toward a white alabaster statue of a man holding a scroll, dressed in a fancy robe and a full, old-fashioned wig. "Who is that?"

"Dr. Hans Sloane, a former president of the Royal College of Physicians. In the late sixteen hundreds, he visited Jamaica and brought back a cinchona tree, having learned that the bark could be used to make quinine to treat malaria. Later, when the Society of Apothecaries was at risk of losing the garden, he bought the land and leased it back to them for only five pounds a year—they still pay the same price now."

"What an unusual rock garden," Lady Frances said,

squinting toward it since she wasn't wearing her spectacles.

"The oldest in all of England, or so I've been told. It was built to provide a habitat for foreign plants that grow best in rocky soil. The white stones are from the Tower of London, the black from a volcano in Iceland, and that giant-clam shell is said to have been brought to England by Captain Cook."

"You seem to know everything," Juliana said, smiling over the rim of her wineglass. "We don't need a Demonstrator, do we, Amanda?" She turned toward the bench. "Amanda?"

Amanda was gone. As was Castleton, the ass.

"Where did they go?" Juliana asked.

"I don't know," Lady Frances mused. She turned to Lord Malmsey. "Theodore, would you help me look for them?"

"With pleasure, my dear." Belying their age, the two rose agilely to their feet, and Lord Malmsey tucked Lady Frances's hand in the crook of his arm. "Shall we, my love?"

Juliana's jaw dropped open as she watched the older couple walk off. "I cannot believe it," she muttered when they were out of earshot.

James drained the rest of his wine and started putting the remains of their dinner back in the basket. "You cannot believe what?"

She looked up at him, a little frown between her brows. "I cannot believe Aunt Frances asked Lord Malmsey to go off alone with her. She's always been so shy. And I cannot believe everyone left again."

Her eyes looked greenish, which was no surprise. After many hours of observation and analysis, James had finally puzzled out the mystery of Juliana's changeable irises: They were more blue when she was happy or aroused, more green when she was worried or angry. Right now he guessed she was rather distressed, which put their hue in the latter range.

The distress was a good sign. It wouldn't be long now before she figured out she'd be much happier with him than with Castleton. If his plans for this evening were

realized, her eyes would be blue before he was finished.
Deep, deep blue.

"Everyone will be back soon," he said. "Lady Frances
and Lord Malmsey will find the others."

"They aren't looking for them. They're off somewhere kissing."

"Really?" he said, reaching a hand to help her rise.
"I guess we should go look for Castleton and Lady
Amanda ourselves, then."

"Yes, we should," she said. "You're supposed to be
with Lady Amanda."

Having seen where her friend and the ass had gone,
James led Juliana along a path in the opposite direction,
which, happily, was the direction he wanted to take her.
Trees lined both sides of the meandering gravel walk-
way, their leaves shimmering and fluttering overhead.
The sun was dropping toward the horizon, making the
walled garden shady and romantic.

The ambience couldn't have been better.

"I don't see them," Juliana said after they wandered
a few minutes in companionable silence. "I cannot imagine where they might have disappeared to."

"Me, neither," James said, taking her hand. She'd left
her gloves on the blanket, and her fingers felt warm in
his, especially compared to the air. Juliana was wearing
a rather thin dress, and with the sun setting, it was getting a bit chilly. "Maybe they're in this greenhouse," he
suggested, leading her off the path. "They might have
gone in there to warm up."

"This greenhouse *is* warm," she said when they
stepped inside. Due to the abundance of glass, it was
almost as light inside as out. "It feels wonderful in here."

"I understand this was the first heated greenhouse in
all of England," he told her, "and maybe the first in the
whole world." He coaxed her through all the plants
toward the back wall. "Hans Sloane wrote about this
greenhouse back in 1684, marveling about the cleverness
of putting ovens under the floor." Stopping before a
door marked PRIVATE, he reached for the knob.

"What are you doing?" she asked. "I don't think
we're supposed to go in there."

"Maybe Castleton is in there with Lady Amanda."

"I think not." Still holding his hand, she pulled him away from the door. "Amanda would *never* go into a room alone with him. She's *much* too reserved for that."

"She was in a room alone with me," he reminded her. "Lord Billingsgate's library. She even tried to kiss me."

Her cheeks flushed a becoming pink. "That's because she wants to marry you."

Thinking it was too bad Lady Amanda didn't want to marry the ass instead, he reached again for the knob. "Maybe your aunt and Lord Malmsey are in there," he suggested, "kissing."

The pink deepened. Her eyes were back to blue-green. She pulled on his hand again. "I don't think—" she started, and then she gave a little shriek when he opened the door.

Smiling, he stepped in. "They're not in here. Come in and see, sw—"

Damn. He'd almost called her "sweetheart" again.

Luckily, she was so concerned about trespassing, she didn't notice. She peeked her head in, then breathed a sigh of relief. "We're not supposed to be in here, James. The door is marked private."

"It's Thomas Wheeler's office," he said with a shrug. "The Demonstrator who went home earlier. He's a friend; he wouldn't mind." He tugged on her hand. "Come in, Juliana."

Reluctantly, she came inside. "It *is* private."

It was a tiny cubby, with a small desk against the inside wall and a small round wooden table with two chairs in the center. "The table is for demonstrations," he explained. "Private demonstrations." The exterior wall was glass, of course, it being part of the greenhouse. But trees grew so closely all around that no one could possibly see in, and plenty of light filtered in through the leaves and the glass ceiling overhead.

He shut the door, shutting them off from the world.

She whirled to face him, dropping his hand. "What are you doing, James?"

He reached into his pocket and slipped out the deck of cards. "Since we can't seem to find our companions, I remembered I wanted you to teach me to play casino," he said casually. "It's cold out there and warm in here, so I thought it might be nice to sit a while and play cards."

She eyed him warily, her gaze still blue-green. "Maybe for a minute."

"Excellent." He sat and waved her toward the second chair. After she sat, he slid his chair up against hers.

Taking the cards, she frowned. "You're supposed to sit across from me."

"I will after I learn. Right now I need to see your cards."

"Very well." When she shuffled the cards, he could practically feel the vibrations. They were that close. She dealt out four cards to each of them and four more faceup on the table, then put the rest aside. "Pick up your hand," she instructed, "and see if any of your cards match the ones on the table." Then she proceeded to explain all the rules, none of which he bothered listening to, since he already knew how to play casino.

As she talked and moved the cards around, he noticed her hair shining in the waning sunlight and thought about how much he wanted to see it slip from its pins. He leaned even closer to smell it, inhaling sunshine and flowers. He rubbed his shoulder against her arm, watching her eyes turn a little bluer. He pressed his thigh up against her thin skirts.

"Are you listening, James? Did you get all of that?"

"Of course." It was a very simple game, really. At least for him. He and his brother had kept a running score for years, and he'd always stayed miles ahead. "I think I'm ready to play now."

"All right." She gathered the cards and started reshuffling them. "You can move to the other side of the table."

"I'd rather stay here for the first couple of hands. In case I need your help. By the way, what shall we wager?"

"Wager? We don't need to wager."

"I never play games without a wager. A wager makes it much more interesting and fun."

"Is that so?" She stopped shuffling and slanted him a sideways glance. "I heard about how Griffin lost thirty guineas to you last month playing chess. I have no money."

"We'll wager something else, then," he said blithely.

"Like what?" She turned to him, looking wary again. But her eyes weren't turning green. They were staying rather blue. Amused, he ran a finger down her arm and watched them get even bluer.

"How about buttons?" he suggested.

"Buttons? We didn't bring buttons."

"We have buttons on our clothes. When one of us loses, he or she can unbutton a button."

Chapter Thirty-four

Juliana was scandalized. Absolutely, positively scandalized. She'd never heard of wagering buttons. Amanda would faint dead away if he ever suggested wagering buttons with her. The mere idea seemed wicked and immoral and sinful and . . . tempting.

Dear heavens, it was tempting. It would teach James a lesson, that was for certain. After all, he was sure to lose, given that he didn't even know how to play the game and he'd been daydreaming while she'd explained it to him. Daydreaming and touching her, making her stumble over her words. If she agreed, he would lose, and then he'd know not to wager buttons with Amanda. It was very, very tempting to say yes.

She *did* enjoy seeing James with his buttons unbuttoned. And since she was certain to win, she wouldn't have to unbutton any of her own. The whole thing could turn out to be rather pleasurable and amusing. And James would learn a lesson.

"All right," she said, "we'll wager buttons."

James looked surprised, but very pleased. After that, everything started happening rather quickly. His fingers went immediately to his neckcloth, working the knot.

"What are you doing?" she asked.

"Exposing my buttons. Go ahead and deal." He all

but ripped off his tailcoat and dropped it to the floor. "Deal, Juliana."

She dealt. They picked up their cards. James spread his and smiled. "I go first—is that right?" She nodded, and he plucked a king from his hand and used it to claim the king on the table. "Aha," he said. "You have to unbutton a button."

"You haven't won yet!" she protested. "That was just a single trick." Anyone could win a trick; the real skill was winning the whole game. "Were you not listening, James? We have to play until all the cards are gone, and then we add up the points, and whoever has the most points wins. *Then* somebody unbuttons a button." She'd almost said *then you unbutton a button,* but she'd stopped herself in time. Although she was going to win, there was no reason to sound smug about it.

"Oh, no," he said. "We don't have time for that. We're playing for only a few minutes, remember? It's getting dark, and we'll have to leave. We're wagering a button for each trick."

"We are not! We're wagering a button for each game."

"We don't have time to play more than one game. A Chase promise is never broken, remember? You promised you'd wager buttons, Juliana. Unbutton a button."

"Honestly, this is ridiculous." She'd never *promised* she'd wager buttons. Not exactly. But she didn't want to argue or look petulant, so she reached behind her back and unbuttoned a button, knowing James wouldn't win many more tricks. "There. Are you happy now? It's my turn." She took an eight out of her hand and claimed a seven and an ace with it, smiling because an ace was worth an extra point. "I took a trick," she said. "Unbutton."

James didn't seem at all reluctant to unbutton the top button of his shirt. He pulled a ten from his hand and took the ten of diamonds, which was worth *two* extra points. "I think you should unbutton two buttons," he said, grinning.

"I think not," she said, amazed that he'd remembered the value of that card when from all she could tell he hadn't even listened to her instructions. "When I took the ace, you unbuttoned only one button, same as I did when you took the first trick, which had no extra points. Each trick is worth only one button, no matter how many points it contains."

"Wrong," he said, flicking open another of his buttons. "There, now I've unbuttoned two buttons for your extra-point trick. And you owe me *three* buttons for my trick with the ten of diamonds."

"I cannot reach that many of my buttons," she said petulantly, even though she hadn't wanted to sound petulant.

He smiled, a very smug smile. "You poor thing. I'll unbutton them for you." And he reached behind her back and unbuttoned three buttons.

"Really, James, this is very childish." Since there were no cards left on the table, she plucked one from her hand and set it down faceup without even looking at it. Which was a mistake, because it turned out to be the two of spades, which was also worth an extra point.

James wasted no time taking it with the two of hearts. "Two buttons," he said with a grin.

"How did you remember the two of spades was worth an extra point?" she said slowly, and that's when she realized the truth. She turned to him, outraged. "You already knew how to play casino, didn't you?"

His grin widened as he unbuttoned two more of her buttons. "I never said I didn't."

Her dress was all unbuttoned now. "You asked me to teach you!"

"Exactly. But I never said I didn't know how to play." His eyes gleaming, he watched her draw another card from her hand. "Too bad there's nothing on the table to match with that," he drawled as she tossed it down. "I don't have to unbutton any more buttons. On the other hand . . ." His last card matched that one, and he used it to claim it. "You owe me another button."

"You tricked me," she said. "After you got all mad at me for tricking you."

"Come, Juliana. This is a game. It is not at all the same as trying to trick someone into marriage."

He was right about that. Drat. Right enough to make her feel guilty. Right enough to make her drop *that* argument like a hot poker. She set down her last card, grabbed the deck, and dealt them each four more cards. "I don't have any more buttons."

"Hmm." He set down a six. "Then I think you owe me a kiss instead."

"I do not." Drat, none of her new cards matched anything on the table. She blindly chose one and tossed it down. "It's your turn."

"An ace," he mused, "imagine that." He swept both it and the six up with a seven. "Two more points," he said with another smile. "Added to the button you haven't unbuttoned yet, that makes three."

"I have no more buttons," she reminded him. "And I'm not kissing you. What are you going to do," she added dryly, "open up my dress a little more by ripping it?"

"What an interesting idea," he said slowly. "I should have thought of that myself. But no, I don't think I'll rip it. I think your aunt might notice that." And then his whole demeanor changed. His smile disappeared as he set his cards facedown on the table and then reached out and drew her loosened dress down her shoulders, leaving her breasts covered by only her filmy chemise. "You owe me three kisses, Juliana," he said softly, gazing at them in a most arousing way.

Her skin prickled, and her nipples puckered, even though it was very warm in the greenhouse. "I do not."

"I think you do." He didn't sound smug now; he sounded raspy and seductive instead. His voice was making her lose her head. He skimmed his fingers along her face and down her neck almost to her cleavage, making her shiver. "I think you do, Juliana," he said in that low, chocolatey tone. "I think you owe me three kisses."

Dear heavens, she wanted him to kiss her. She wanted to kick herself for wanting him to kiss her, but she wanted him to kiss her nonetheless. Suddenly all she could think of was yesterday's kisses under the stairs, and she wanted him to kiss her in the worst way.

And touch her breasts, like he had yesterday, too. She wanted him to touch her in the worst way. With his hands and his mouth, like he'd done yesterday, only it had happened so quickly she'd hardly had a chance to enjoy it.

And she wanted to touch *him*. She wanted to touch him in the worst way. Despite herself, despite how he'd tricked her into it, she leaned closer and raised a hand to the little V of skin where he'd opened his measly two buttons.

A faint smile curving his lips, he moved closer still. Until she could feel his breath on her mouth where she wanted his kiss. "May I kiss you now?" he asked.

Why was he asking? Why didn't he just go ahead and kiss her? He'd done the same thing at Vauxhall Gardens and in the Panorama, asking her permission, making her agree.

She wished he'd just kiss her instead of asking, because she knew she should say no, but she couldn't help herself. She wanted James, and she wanted to kiss him, and she wanted to kick herself for being too weak to say no.

"May I?" he pressed. He was so close, there hardly seemed to be space to breathe between them. "May I kiss you now? Please let me kiss you, Juliana. I want to kiss you in the worst way."

In the worst way, just like she wanted. "Yes," she breathed. God help her, she said, "Yes, please kiss me."

And he did. His mouth crossed that last little space and settled on hers, and he proceeded to kiss her senseless. Positively senseless. The cards fluttered from her hand to the floor. Her senses began swirling, whirling, as she parted her lips and invited him in. His tongue swept her mouth, and she ached, positively ached, in her throat and her heart and, most curiously, in a place between her legs.

Still kissing her, he managed to maneuver her sideways onto his lap. She sighed and leaned into him, wrapping an arm around his neck, kissing him, kissing him. "I want to kiss you here," he whispered, trailing little kisses down her throat on his way to her cleavage. "I want to kiss you here, in the worst way." Loving it, loving *him*, she tilted her head back to give him better access. And then his mouth was on a breast like she'd wanted, first kissing her through her chemise and then under it. He opened his mouth and drew in the crest, and dear heavens, it felt marvelous. Like a wanton, she arched her back, offering her breasts, offering herself, hoping he'd keep kissing them and do even more.

What she meant by *more*, she wasn't sure, but that curious ache between her legs was growing stronger. Stronger and hotter, more insistent. Dear heavens, she loved him. She knew she couldn't, knew she shouldn't, but she loved him nonetheless. And when he started caressing her, stroking her waist, her hips, her thighs, God knew she loved that, too.

And then his hand was underneath her dress, and he was stroking her thighs some more. Kissing her breasts and stroking her thighs, making her head swim. Making her heart pound and her breath come in little gasps. He abandoned her breast to recapture her lips, and her senses were spinning out of control. He was kissing her, stroking her, exploring her mouth with his tongue, and that curious ache between her legs was growing insistent to the point of being unbearable.

And then his hand skimmed the curls that guarded that ache, lightly, lightly, and he broke the kiss. "Can I touch you here, Juliana? Can I touch you here?"

Dear heavens, why was he asking? She was gasping so quickly she could barely breathe, let alone talk. The ache was becoming so exquisite it seemed to be robbing her of speech. She managed to nod, and he captured her mouth again, his tongue tangling with hers in a dance while his fingers danced below. Parting her thighs and finally, finally touching her where she ached. A gentle slide of his fingers, just once, because once was all it took. He found a spot so sweet it made the breath catch in her throat, and she tumbled over a precipice, swirling, whirling, falling into pleasure fiercer than she'd ever known.

He kissed her and kissed her while she calmed, and then he kissed her again, and her head started to clear.

Dear heavens, what had she done? What had she allowed him to do? He was supposed to marry Amanda. He *had* to marry Amanda, or Aunt Frances would be devastated. He'd touched her in a place he should touch only Amanda, and even that only after they were married. And she'd not only *let* him touch her—she'd all but asked. Or rather, he'd asked her, but she hadn't hesitated to allow it. She'd nodded and kissed him, all but begging him to touch her where no man had touched her before.

She was appalled at herself. Absolutely, positively appalled. She'd wanted him to kiss her in the worst way, and she'd wanted him to touch her in the worst way, and it really *had* been the worst way.

He shifted her on his lap. "Are you all right, Juliana?" He lifted her chin, meeting her gaze. "Your eyes are blue," he whispered, sounding pleased. "Deep, deep blue."

She didn't want him pleased with her. He needed to be pleased with Amanda. "Obviously it's getting too dark for you to see," she snapped. "My eyes are hazel."

He laughed, a low, satisfied laugh, and then he kissed her again. And she let him, which made her feel better and worse all at the same time.

"It is getting dark," he finally admitted, sounding much too regretful. "We need to go find the others before the garden's gates are locked."

She slid off his lap, and he raised her chemise and bodice with gentle fingers, and then he turned her around and buttoned her dress. And tucked in the dratted, too-straight hair that had slipped from its pins. And buttoned his two buttons and shrugged into his tailcoat and knotted his neckcloth in place, haphazardly as usual. And she reached to straighten it, unable to help herself, even though she knew she shouldn't. And she let him kiss her again, a little sweet kiss that doubtless meant nothing to him but meant much too much to her.

She had to remember he would never love her. He was only kissing and touching her because they were friends and he wanted a child. He needed to become friends with Amanda instead.

She couldn't let him kiss her again after this. Or touch her again. Ever.

He gathered the cards from the table and the floor

and slipped the deck back into his pocket, and then they left the greenhouse and went back to the middle of the garden where everyone else was waiting.

Aunt Frances had obviously been kissing Lord Malmsey; in the dim light of the setting sun, they both looked happy and flushed. Aunt Frances had finished packing up the basket, and Lord Malmsey had folded the blanket. He was holding it over his arm.

Naturally, the duke and Amanda had done nothing. They were much too aristocratic to do the work of servants. And of course they hadn't kissed. Neither of them was flushed. No doubt Amanda had gone off with the duke purposely, specifically to avoid being kissed by James.

So Juliana had been kissed instead. And touched instead. And she very much feared she was flushed. She was appalled at herself.

It wouldn't happen again, she reminded herself fiercely. She would never again play cards with James.

"Where have you been?" Amanda asked. "David and I have been looking all over for you."

For a moment, Juliana felt puzzled, but then she remembered the duke's name was David. How could she have forgotten the name of the man she expected to marry? And when had Amanda—proper, reserved Amanda—begun calling the duke by his given name? She expected to marry James, and she was still calling *him* Lord Stafford.

Nothing was right tonight. Nothing. Nothing was going well; nothing was happening as planned.

Her stomach hurt.

"We were playing cards," James explained, pulling the deck out of his pocket to prove it. "All of you went off, so we decided to go in the greenhouse and play cards."

Nobody looked suspicious. Apparently it was a reasonable explanation. Nobody, after all—most especially nobody as innocent as Frances and Amanda—would think playing cards could possibly lead to what had happened tonight.

But although that was a relief, Juliana's stomach still hurt. She had to fix everything. Somehow, some way, she had to get James together with Amanda.

"I'm going to the Pevenseys' tomorrow night," she said as they all started walking toward the Stafford carriage. "For a musical evening. I hope you'll all want to come."

What she would do when they got there, how she would get James together with Amanda, she hadn't a clue. But just getting them there would be a start.

"I would love to attend a musical evening," Aunt Frances said as she climbed in.

"I would love to attend, too," Lord Malmsey agreed, following her.

"So would I," Amanda said and climbed in next, sitting across from them.

Juliana's stomach started to ease. She climbed in herself, taking the opposite end of the seat from Amanda in order to leave space in the middle for James. She gestured to the duke, indicating the spot across from her. "I hope you'll come, too."

"Much as I would be delighted to spend the evening with you, my dear, I think I should go to Parliament," he said as he took the place by Amanda.

How annoying. How absolutely annoying. He was supposed to sit across from her and leave the space by Amanda for James. "I should think you would prefer to attend a musical evening," she said rather peevishly.

"I abhor musical evenings," he said, not peevishly in the least. And then he smiled down at her apologetically, and she realized he wasn't sitting in the space by Amanda, he was sitting in the space by *her*. Rather close, as a matter of fact, so she probably shouldn't be so annoyed. He was falling in love with her. He called her "my dear" and sent her flowers. He needed her, and this close proximity would allow her to finally start teaching him to be affectionate. She scooted a little closer, so they'd be touching.

And that was when she realized she couldn't marry him.

She wasn't going to be a duchess.

They were touching, but she didn't find it the least bit enjoyable. She couldn't even *imagine* letting him touch her the way James had in the greenhouse. Now that she knew what love felt like, she knew she would never have those feelings for the duke.

She felt terrible. The duke was so nice, and he was falling in love with her, but she couldn't love him back. He'd suffered hurt and rejection throughout his childhood, and now she was going to reject him again. How could she tell him? How could she cast him aside without destroying him completely?

And what about Griffin? Poor Griffin. He was going to be so disappointed; he was going to have to start looking for a husband for her again. She obviously wouldn't be marrying this Season—it would probably be another year at least. How was she going to tell Griffin?

James climbed in. "I abhor musical evenings, too," he said as a footman shut the door. He took the place across from her and settled back, his legs so long his knees touched hers. How annoying when she was immersed in trying to figure out a gentle way to break this distressing news to her brother and the duke.

James smiled at her as though he could tell she was annoyed. As though he enjoyed annoying her. "No man worth his salt would choose a musical evening over Parliament," he informed her.

"A Roman proverb!" Amanda exclaimed.

"It is not!" Juliana snapped.

"It is," Amanda said reasonably, sounding very bookish. "It alludes to the practice of paying Roman soldiers with rations of salt. Our English word *salary* comes from the Latin word *salarium*, which means salt money."

"She's right," the duke said. " 'A man worth his salt' has been a proverb for centuries."

Obviously he was bookish, too. How absolutely annoying.

Chapter Thirty-five

Lord Malmsey was the youngest man at the Pevensey residence.

"Where is everyone?" Amanda asked.

A rather inane question, considering the Pevenseys' drawing room was teeming with people. But all of them—save Lord Malmsey and a few doddering old men—were female. Remembering the way James and the duke had reacted to her invitation last night, Juliana sighed. "I collect most gentlemen would prefer to sit through Parliament than an evening of music."

"Except for Lord Malmsey," Amanda said.

"If it weren't for Aunt Frances, he'd probably be at Parliament, too." Indeed, Lord Malmsey had made a beeline for Frances the moment they'd walked in the door. The two of them were off in a corner, whispering, even now.

Whispering endearments, no doubt. Lord Malmsey was looking more and more in love—and more miserable that he had to marry Amanda—every day. Juliana wished more than ever that Lord Malmsey could cry off the wedding, but wishing didn't change the facts. It just wasn't possible, not if he ever wanted to show his face in society again.

Amanda clutched Juliana's arm. "I need to talk to you."

"About what?"

"My father," she said, looking even more miserable than Lord Malmsey.

If Frances knew Lord Malmsey was engaged, she'd look more miserable than both of them put together. Juliana's projects all seemed to be falling apart. She still hadn't figured out how to break the news to the duke or her brother. "What about your father?" she asked Amanda.

But before Amanda could answer, Lady Stafford waltzed up. "Good evening, Lady Juliana!" All smiles in contrast to everyone else, James's mother was accompanied by Lord Cavanaugh, who, while older than Lord Malmsey, at least wasn't in his dotage. "It's a pleasure to see you here."

"I adore music," Juliana said. "I was pleased to receive an invitation to Lady Pevensey's musical evening."

"This is your first Season, isn't it?" Lord Cavanaugh asked dryly.

"Oh, hush," Lady Stafford said. "Lady Pevensey's musical evenings are always enchanting." She turned back to Juliana. "Are you attending Lady Hartley's breakfast on Sunday?"

"I haven't decided. I'm supposed to have a sewing party."

"Oh, you must attend—it's the event of the Season. Everyone will be there."

"Including your sisters?"

"Without a doubt. I must tell you, my sisters are thoroughly enjoying your sewing parties. They haven't called on my son for an examination in two entire days."

"I have only four sewing parties left before the baby clothes are due." Three if she went to Lady Hartley's breakfast, which she might as well do if no one would be available to attend her sewing party anyway. "I told Lord Stafford his aunts would have less time to ponder their health if gentlemen were courting them, but he said they wouldn't be interested."

Lady Stafford flashed Lord Cavanaugh, who was courting her, a fond smile. "My sisters are older and set in their ways."

"I believe they're bored and need something to do.

Something to get them out of their house after my sewing project is complete."

"Perhaps you're right, dear. They've been helping me renovate one of Stafford House's bedrooms, but that will be finished soon, too. I cannot imagine what else to suggest to occupy them after that. I've tried to talk them into redecorating their own house, but they won't hear of it."

Standing on the temporary stage she'd had erected in her drawing room, Lady Pevensey clapped her hands. "If you'll all take your seats, we're ready to begin!"

"I shall think about your sisters," Juliana promised Lady Stafford before turning to find a seat. "There must be something they would find diverting."

Frances and Lord Malmsey had seated themselves in the last row, so she headed toward the front in order to give them some privacy. After this afternoon's party, she'd had a hundred and fifty-seven baby items completed, which meant she needed eighty-three more. That hadn't seemed an impossible task, with four parties remaining—slightly more than twenty items per party. Perfectly reasonable, especially if she made a few by herself in between. But with only three parties . . .

"We need to talk." As she slid onto a first-row chair, Amanda grabbed her arm. "We cannot talk in the front, right in the faces of the musicians."

Juliana didn't want to talk; she wanted to listen. Though she normally spent hours playing the harp, all her projects had left her scant time for any music of late. But her friend looked panicked. "Very well," she said, walking around to take a chair in a middle row. "What do you need to tell me about your father?"

Amanda took the chair beside her. "I've received word that he'll be arriving in three days. Early Sunday evening." She clutched her hands together in her lap, perhaps to stop them from trembling. "He's coming to see to the final details of my wedding."

Juliana patted her on the arm. "We still have time—"

"No, we don't! It's scheduled for a week from Saturday, and—"

"Ladies and gentlemen," Lady Pevensey announced, "I am honored to introduce our first guest musicians.

Miss Harriet Kent will perform Mozart's Sonata in C Major on the pianoforte, accompanied by her sister, Miss Hillary Kent, on the violin."

The room fell silent while the Kent sisters minced their way to the stage.

"A week from Saturday," Amanda said, "and—"

"Shh!" someone hissed behind them.

Juliana laid a hand over Amanda's clenched ones. "Wait," she whispered.

Her friend waited, tense as the younger Miss Kent's bowstrings. When the lively notes of the first movement filled the air, she wasted no time before resuming their conversation in a lower tone. "My wedding is a week from Saturday. My time is running out. I need James to compromise me—I must try again to trick him."

"You must not!"

"Shh!"

"You must not," Juliana repeated in a whisper. "That would be unethical and dishonest. We shouldn't have tried it the first time, and I won't try it again."

"We have no choice!"

"Shh!"

"Shh!"

"Shh!"

Juliana twisted in her chair to glance behind her. Several people were glaring. All women. A couple of the aging men were already nodding off. "Hush," she murmured, turning back to Amanda. "Of course you have a choice. You can choose to act warmly toward James. Once you become friends, he'll propose to you and agree to the compromise."

She was beginning to think it would never happen. Or maybe she was beginning to *hope* it would never happen. Because James would have to kiss Amanda before he proposed to her, and even though Juliana couldn't marry him, the thought of James kissing anyone but herself— let alone touching anyone the way he'd touched her— made her stomach hurt.

She leaned closer. "I have an idea," she whispered in desperation. She knew her friend would refuse. But she'd feel much better about abandoning the duke if she could offer a replacement, and Amanda didn't seem to want to kiss James anyway. "Would you like to marry the duke?"

"No!" Amanda looked horrified. "I told you I would never marry a by-blow!"

Whispers broke out behind them, and a few more people hissed, *"Shh!"* Juliana wished Amanda hadn't said "by-blow" quite so loud. "Whyever do you keep going off with the duke, then?" she pressed. "Why have you begun calling him David?"

"Well, he is very nice. I think we are becoming friends. There's a big difference between a friend and a husband."

Juliana was disappointed but not surprised. She'd known all along that Amanda was only going off with the duke to avoid kissing James. "Maybe you should choose another man," she suggested. Plenty of gentlemen were still asking Amanda to dance at every ball. "At the Teddington ball on Saturday—"

"I want Lord Stafford. Besides, there isn't enough time to choose another man and expect him to propose."

"We have a little more than a week—"

"No, we don't. My father will be here Sunday, and for all I know he may not let me out of the house after that."

Drat. Her friend was right. Lord Malmsey could marry Aunt Frances only if Juliana saw to it that James kissed Amanda—and not as part of a plot.

That wouldn't be easy, because Amanda feared kissing. Her reserved nature caused her to cling to people she felt safe with, allowing her to avoid intimacy. If James was to have a prayer of kissing Amanda, Juliana would have to make sure there was no one besides him for her to cling to. Not herself, not Frances, and not the duke.

Especially not the duke.

Amanda gravitated toward him, knowing instinctively he would never try to kiss her, thereby averting the closeness she feared. If James managed to kiss Amanda even once, however, all of that would change. His kisses were so wonderful, Amanda would surely want more. Then one thing would lead to another, and before Juliana knew it, James would unbutton and propose.

Her stomach hurt like the very dickens.

She would have to get Amanda alone with James. It was the only solution. Exactly how she would accomplish this, she couldn't imagine. Amanda wouldn't agree to see a man without a chaperone, but perhaps Juliana could plan another group outing and then claim Aunt Frances felt ill. And she felt ill. And the duke felt ill.

Oh, bother. That would never work. It felt like there was a dagger lodged in her stomach. She'd figure out something tomorrow. Right after she figured out how she would finish eighty-three more items of baby clothes with only three sewing parties instead of four.

"Are you all right?" Amanda asked.

"Shh!"

Amanda lowered her voice. "Why are you clutching your middle?"

Juliana unfolded her arms and tried to draw a calming breath. Another moment and she'd have found herself curled up on Lady Pevensey's exquisite Turkey carpet.

"I'm fine," she gritted out, ignoring another chorus of *Shh!* "Just fine."

But although she normally loved music and the Misses Kent were more than proficient performers, Mozart didn't prove enjoyable tonight. And neither did the Handel or Beethoven that came after. She almost envied all the men who had gone to Parliament instead of the Pevenseys'.

She should have stayed home. She needed to sew; she should have spent these hours stitching rather than listening to music. Even more important, she needed to discourage James's attentions so he'd turn to Amanda instead. And for *that*, she needed a few hours in the kitchen.

It was time to bring out her secret weapon—Miss Rebecca Chase's lemon slices.

Chapter Thirty-six

LEMON SLICES

> Take a measure of Butter and one of Sugar and mix them together with the grated rinde of two Lemons. Put in two Eggs and then Flower, a spoon of leavening, and a little Milk. Put in a loaf tin and Bake until it rises and turns golde. Make holes with a skewer and pour in the juice of two Lemons. Leave the cake until colde and then turn from the tin and cut it into slices.

> *The sour lemons will turn a man sour to your charms. I thwarted my grandmother's matchmaking scheme twice by serving these slices to the dratted suitors.*

> —Miss Rebecca Chase, 1695

For five days—ever since she'd come to his house and offered to volunteer—James had been thinking about getting Juliana alone in one of his treatment rooms. One would have expected the interludes at the Panorama and the Physic Garden to have slaked his passions, but the opposite was true. He'd spent yesterday's session in Parliament woolgathering instead of listening. Overnight, he'd dreamed impossible dreams. This morning, as he'd shaved and dressed, he'd concocted a fantasy so lurid he knew it would never happen. But he'd been looking forward to trying.

Unfortunately, life was conspiring against him.

Juliana rushed in as the clock struck one. Juggling two baskets while she folded her umbrella, she made her way through his crowded reception room. "I'm sorry, but I cannot stay long. I've instructed the driver to come back in three hours. I've too much sewing to do." She paused and blinked. "What are you doing behind the counter?"

"Playing assistant while I interview for a new one," he said, frowning at the front of her dress. For the first time ever—in his experience, anyway—she'd filled in her low neckline with some sort of froufrou scarf, which was hardly conducive to his fantasies.

"Another assistant has left?" She came around to join him and set down her baskets. "Again?"

"Unfortunately, yes. Another one found herself with child." He shook his head. "It's an epidemic."

"I suppose you gave her fifty pounds?"

"Yes. She was much relieved, but now I need to find someone new. What did you bring me?" he asked, lifting the doily that covered one of the baskets.

"Fabric." Laughing at the look on his face, she pulled out a handful of white material and waved it under his nose. "Would you care for some? Appetizing, isn't it?"

He gave her a wry smile. "I thought maybe you'd made some sweets."

"I don't have time to bake. I barely have time to breathe." She sighed and delved into the second basket. "But I baked anyway. Have a lemon slice." After he took one, she shooed him toward the back. "Go vaccinate some of these people before even more show up, or else they'll have to stand out in the rain. I'll take over here, and I'll let you know if anyone promising comes in to apply for the position."

James went, finding the lemon slice delicious but grumbling all the way nonetheless. He'd never resented having too many patients before—the more people who agreed to be immunized, after all, the sooner smallpox would become a thing of the past. But he hadn't been picturing sniffling children in his treatment rooms all week, damn it . . . Juliana was supposed to have been there.

Without a stupid scarf hiding her charms.

Between sewing baby clothes, Juliana proved a model of efficiency, but he and the other physician could vaccinate only so fast. It was almost three hours before the number of patients dwindled to the point where everyone waiting had a seat. When Dr. Payton left and two more doctors arrived for the second shift, James heaved a sigh of relief and joined Juliana behind the counter.

A frown creased the area between her brows, and though her gaze flicked to meet his for a moment, it was soon back on the task in her hands. Her shoulders looked stiff and hunched. He stepped behind her to rub them, finding her muscles tense and knotted. "Come into the back with me," he murmured. "I'll make you feel better."

"I cannot. The carriage will be here any minute, and until then I must keep sewing." Though her needle stabs seemed frantic and rather random, she was getting the job done. "Besides, we really shouldn't be alone, James. You know what will happen."

Of course he knew what would happen. He would tempt her, and it would work, which would eventually lead to better things. Though he knew it was only a matter of time before she realized that she, not Lady Amanda, belonged with him, he was beginning to get impatient. He kept massaging her, firmly but tenderly, wondering why her tense muscles weren't easing with his ministrations.

"Just for a minute," he coaxed. "Nothing will happen in just a minute."

In two or three minutes, however . . .

"Your afternoon assistant has yet to arrive," she said toward her handiwork. "We cannot leave all these people out here unsupervised."

She was right about that. He kissed the top of her head and sighed. "No luck finding a new assistant?"

"Have another lemon slice, will you?"

He didn't take one, because he didn't want to let go of her to do so. Touching her was much more appealing than sweets. And her tenseness wasn't easing, which was worrisome. "I'm not hungry," he said.

Now *she* sighed. "Your last assistant sent in a friend, but I didn't think you should hire her."

"Why not? Could the woman not read?"

She bit off the end of a thread and leaned away from him to reach into her basket for a spool, sighing again when he leaned with her. "Yes, she could read. But I feared she'd find herself with child before long."

His fingers stilled. *"What?"*

"You heard me." She pulled off a length of thread. "You've lost two assistants due to pregnancy already. Why do you think that is?"

Actually, he'd lost four assistants, not two—but he wasn't about to admit that now. "The water?" he speculated.

"Your generosity," she declared. "You're too nice, James."

"Pardon?" He relinquished her shoulders and walked around to face her. "How the devil can a person be too nice?"

"These girls are taking advantage of your generosity," she said, sticking the end of the thread in her mouth to wet it. He wanted that mouth on *him*. "They're getting pregnant on purpose. I'd lay odds that last girl sent her friend here with a promise of fifty pounds. You need to find someone older, someone more responsible."

"Older women aren't seeking work. They're busy raising children."

"I mean *much* older women." Having threaded the needle, she looked up, and he found himself lost in her greenish eyes. "Like your aunts."

He blinked. "My aunts?"

"Excuse me," she said, turning away to hand a number to a woman waiting by the counter with two children.

He hadn't even noticed they were there.

"You're number forty-two," she told the woman. "I'll call you when it's your turn." She looked back to him, meeting his gaze again, making him think she wanted to say something. But she didn't. Her eyes went even greener. She swallowed slowly and then gradually seemed to go limp, like a marionette whose strings had gone loose.

The chatter of the waiting patients grew louder in their personal silence.

He whipped out a hand and pulled the scarf from her dress.

"Hey!" She snatched it back. "Whyever did you do that?"

"You're not acting like Juliana. And you don't *look* like Juliana—not with that silly scarf or whatever it's called."

"It's a fichu," she informed him primly, stuffing it back into place.

Juliana was never prim. Or so tense and emotionally distant. Wondering what could be ailing her, he skimmed his knuckles along her chin. "What's wrong, Juliana?"

Her jaw set. "Nothing."

"You're working too hard. You're exhausted."

She reached into one of the baskets and handed him a lemon slice. "Eat this, please."

"I'm not hungry."

"Eat it," she demanded in a most un-Juliana-like way. Her gaze flicked to the door, where a footman in Chase livery had just entered. She waved to him, looking relieved. "My carriage is here. But your aunts are bored. They need something to do."

"They're both countesses, in case you've forgotten. They're not looking for employment."

"I'm not suggesting you pay them. Your mother told me they're enjoying my sewing parties, and even more significant, they've stopped calling on you to examine them. But I've only three more parties, and then they'll be bored again and back to their tricks. Unless they help you instead." She shoved the fabric, needle, and thread into the other basket. "Don't you see, James? They won't consider helping you to be employment or work; they'll see it as charity, an act of goodwill. And if they're busy helping here, they won't have time to fret about their health. They'll stop asking you to come examine them for one imagined ailment or another."

It was brilliant. In one fell swoop, Juliana might have solved both his problems, giving his aunts something to

do and providing him with assistants who wouldn't find
their bellies full of baby inside of a week. Or at all, for
that matter. He'd never considered hiring women past their
childbearing years.

Apparently Juliana's meddling really did help
sometimes.

"How do you do it?" he asked. "How do you analyze
what people need and put two and two together? Why
are you so good at what you do?"

She shrugged. "I'm just attentive to the people
around me."

It couldn't be that simple, that easy. "What if my
aunts don't want to assist here?"

"They'll be thrilled at the very suggestion," she promised with a confidence that implied she positively knew.
Which she very probably did. "Shall I ask them for
you?"

"I can ask them. I'll stop by on my way to Parliament." When he reached to touch her arm, she flinched.
A frisson of hurt took him by surprise, but then he reminded himself that she *wasn't* past her childbearing
years, and if there was one thing he'd learned in his
too short marriage, it was that younger women were
sometimes moody.

Although she'd never been moody with him.

"What is wrong, Juliana?"

"You're right. I'm exhausted. And overwhelmed. And
the dratted lemon slices aren't working."

"Pardon?" He looked down to the uneaten slice in
his hand and back up, horrified to see tears flooding her
eyes. "What do lemon slices have to do with anything?"

"Nothing," she muttered. "I'm sorry." She inched
around the counter and headed toward the door. "Eat
the lemon slices, will you? All of them. I'll see you at the
Teddington ball tomorrow. I must go home and sew."

Chapter Thirty-seven

Saturday evening, Juliana's gaze scanned the Teddingtons' ballroom. "Where is James?" she asked Griffin.

"Shouldn't you be looking for Castleton?"

"He's in the card room, gambling away his fortune."

Griffin wondered why she sounded so disapproving. "Castleton is not an inveterate gambler. He plays only to amuse himself."

She shrugged. "He only ever does anything to amuse himself."

"And you find this objectionable?" He narrowed his gaze. "Since when?" She was supposed to be in love with the man. Good God, had she changed her mind? "Do you not want to marry him anymore?"

She looked away. "He needs me."

"I should hope you'd want to marry a man because *you* need *him*."

She cocked her head at him. "Rachael says people should marry because they want each other, not need each other."

If men married all the women they *wanted*, he thought, polygamy would be the norm. "Has Castleton kissed you yet?"

"Would you want to hear about it if he did?"

He supposed he didn't; there was little more uncomfortable than thinking about one's sister in a romantic embrace. However, he knew Juliana well enough to know she wouldn't hesitate to give him the details in all their embarrassing glory, so he had to figure her answering his question with another question meant the prig hadn't kissed her yet.

He'd meant to have a talk with Castleton in his stables the next time the man paid Juliana a call, but he hadn't run into him lately. "I think I'll go play cards," he told his sister.

"Just don't lose thirty guineas."

Wherever had that caustic comment come from? he wondered as he made his way to the card room. He very rarely gambled, and never for ridiculous stakes.

Castleton was playing whist. "Yes?" he asked when Griffin walked up.

"I heard from my stableman yesterday. Velocity has been running well. You still want him, don't you?"

He shifted, tossing a card on the table without meeting Griffin's gaze. "Very much."

"Excellent. You might try kissing my sister."

Griffin turned around to see Rachael standing there, wearing a dress the same sky blue color as her eyes. It was very low-cut. She looked like she had a slight cold—her nose was a little red, her eyes a bit glassy—but that didn't make her any less alluring.

It was a good thing he didn't make a habit of marrying all the women he wanted, because he would have married her seventeen times.

"What are you doing in here?" he asked through clenched teeth.

"My sisters dragged me here tonight. And then I saw you walk into the card room." She glanced around at all the people uneasily. "I have something I'd like to ask you. In private."

"Let's find Lord Teddington's library."

"All right." She walked beside him from the room. "What does Velocity have to do with the Duke of Castleton kissing your sister?"

He hadn't realized she'd overheard that conversation. "I promised him Velocity if he married her."

"You promised him a *horse* for marrying Juliana?"

Her glassy eyes looked incredulous. "How could you do that, Griffin?"

He looked away from her, turning down a corridor he hoped would lead to the library. "She wants to marry him. I want to see her happy."

"How happy do you expect she'll be when she finds out her husband married her for a horse?"

He peeked in an open door to find a music room. "Whyever would she find that out?"

"Maybe because I told her?"

"You wouldn't." He turned to her. "Tell me you wouldn't."

"I'm not sure I shouldn't."

"Rachael, tell me you won't tell her. It would only hurt her feelings."

"You should have thought of that before you made the offer." She stared at him for a moment while he shifted uncomfortably. "All right. I won't tell her. Unless she ends up engaged to the man, at which point I think it will be in her best interests to know, whether it hurts her feelings or not."

"Thank you," he said, not sure what he was thanking her for, since in all likelihood Castleton would ask for Juliana's hand and then Rachael would go running to her. But maybe not. And at least she wasn't running to her now.

They walked to the next room, but it turned out to be a small family dining chamber. "Whatever made you think of offering a horse for your sister?" she asked, continuing down the corridor.

He shrugged. "It seemed like a good idea at the time. I think I was a little foxed."

"Well, it's a good thing you're not a heavy drinker." She stopped before another open door. "Ah, the library." Taking a deep breath, she entered and walked over to a long leather sofa. She turned and sat carefully, folding her hands in her lap. "A few weeks ago you asked if I wanted you to help me find my father. I was wondering how you'd propose to do that. Seeing as he's dead, I mean."

Although he was relieved to be on a different subject, he hated to see her so apprehensive. Leaving the door open, he joined her on the sofa. "He might not be dead," he suggested.

"In the letter I found, Mama referred to herself as a widow."

"The letter could have been deliberately misleading," Griffin pointed out, and then, seeing hope leap into her eyes, hurriedly added, "although it probably wasn't. But in either case, I may be able to help you discover his identity."

"How?" She coughed, then sniffled. "Mama left no other letters that mentioned anything about an earlier marriage. Her parents died young, and after her sister died when I was but a child, she had no family left. She never even had any close friends other than your folks—Mama always kept to herself, do you remember? I wouldn't know where to start."

"Her things? Did she keep nothing to remind her of her previous husband?"

"Nothing at all. I went through everything when I cleaned out her rooms to ready them for Noah."

Noah, Rachael's younger brother, had recently come of age and taken responsibility for the earldom—a responsibility she'd borne on her own since the tender age of fifteen. Rachael was intelligent and competent. If she'd found nothing, there was likely nothing to find.

But now that she was willing to pursue the subject, Griffin wasn't willing to give up so easily. "Perhaps you missed something. Or saw something but didn't recognize it as a clue."

She looked dubious. "There was nothing, Griffin."

"Would it hurt to look again?" If he could judge by her expression, it very well might. "I'll go through your mother's things with you," he offered. "I might notice something you missed."

She pulled a handkerchief from her sleeve and dabbed at her nose. "All of Mama's things are at Greystone," she said on a sigh, referring to her family's country estate. "Perhaps we can go through them at Christmas."

As much as Rachael clearly wished to put this off, he couldn't bear to see her unhappiness last until Christmas. It was so against her nature. "Christmas is six months away—"

"I'll think about it," she said, standing suddenly. "I'm not feeling well. I'm going home."

Aurelia and Bedelia had been thrilled when James asked them if they might help out at the Institute. They'd arrived at New Hope to be trained first thing after breakfast Saturday morning and taken to their tasks with great enthusiasm, running his reception room with a precision he hadn't witnessed since his stint in the military. As a result, James had vaccinated more patients in a day than he usually did in three.

At four o'clock, before his aunts departed to ready themselves for the Teddington ball, he'd penciled their names on his schedule, careful to make sure their assigned shifts wouldn't overlap and run him ragged. Then he'd gone home to change, decided to rest his feet and close his eyes for just a moment, and awakened four hours later.

By the time he dressed and left, it was past ten o'clock. He arrived at the ball very late and a tad grumpy. When Occlestone happened to swagger by the door as he walked in, his piggish nose high in the air, it took everything James had not to snarl. But he knew he'd feel better after sharing the day's success with Juliana, assuming she was no longer moody.

Unfortunately, Lady Amanda buttonholed him before he could find out.

He hadn't even been announced yet—he'd barely handed his things to the footman manning the cloakroom—when she approached him, wringing her hands. "Lord Stafford, where have you been? One of Lady Teddington's guests is terribly ill."

Absurdly, he noticed she wasn't wearing gloves. And she looked quite distressed. She was usually so cool and aloof, he couldn't imagine her caring enough about anyone's illness to appear so troubled. She seemed to have no friends, except for—

"Is it Juliana?" he asked, his heart suddenly beating double time.

"No. Let me show you to her." Bypassing the ballroom, she hurried him down a corridor.

"It's another lady, then? What is wrong with her?"

"I don't know." She turned into a room and swung to him so fast he all but bumped into her. "Kiss me," she said, and then, throwing her arms around him, she pressed her lips to his.

Addled, he froze for a stunned moment. When his wits began returning, he seemed only to have enough brainpower to marvel that he'd never before kissed a woman and felt nothing. Or rather, something—her stiff, closed lips were mashed against his, after all—but nothing good.

Coming to his senses, he pushed her away. "What in blazes do you think you're doing?"

"Kissing you!" Her cheeks were pink; her chest heaved. "Have you fallen in love with me yet?"

"What?"

"Juliana said that after I'd kissed you, you'd fall in love with me. Have you?"

"Hell, no." She was a very lovely girl, even more lovely now that she was a little lively for once. Her blue-gray eyes were sparkling.

But he loved a girl with hazel eyes.

"Where is Juliana?" He glanced around, his own eyes widening. "Good God, this is the ladies' retiring room." The chamber was strewn with reticules and other feminine belongings. Screens in two corners most likely hid chamber pots—but he wasn't about to make his way over and find out. "It's a miracle no one is in here. Someone could appear any minute."

"I know."

"Ladies tend to visit in bunches. Any number of guests could have seen us kissing!"

"I know."

"You know? You *know*?" He grabbed her by an arm and took a step back, and then another, and another, until they'd returned to the momentarily deserted but very public corridor. "Have you any idea what could have happened had we been caught?"

"What I was hoping would happen?"

"What you were hoping—" He broke off as the truth dawned on him. "You and Juliana planned to trick me again, didn't you?" The accusation came through clenched teeth. "I'm going to kill that meddling little chit." Was it just yesterday he'd decided her meddling was actually helpful?

"She didn't meddle," Lady Amanda said, her eyes flooding. "It was my idea this time. All my idea. She refused to help me. She said it would be unethical."

"Damn right it is!" What was it with ladies crying in his presence? Yesterday Juliana, and now Lady Amanda. Was the female race unified in their efforts to cut him to pieces?

A tear overflowed and ran down her cheek, slicing him even more. "Why can't you just agree to kiss me, then? You want to, don't you? You've been courting me for weeks."

"I most certainly have . . ."

Not. He'd meant to say *not.* But the word wouldn't pass his lips. Good God, he abruptly realized, he *had* been courting her for weeks. Or at least it must have seemed that way to her. He'd sent gifts and asked her to dance and—

Suddenly he needed to sit down. But there were no chairs in the corridor, and he seemed to have lost the strength to propel himself to another location. He leaned against the wall instead. "Well, that is . . ."

How could he explain it? Although she and Juliana had certainly been wrong to trick him, what he'd done was just as bad in its own way. His actions had implied he was interested in Lady Amanda, so he could hardly be surprised she'd come to that conclusion. He'd had no right to mislead her in order to achieve his own ends with another woman.

"I'm sorry," he said. "I—"

"My father will be home tomorrow afternoon," she interrupted in clipped tones, clearly impatient with his half-assed efforts to explain himself. "For all I know, he may not let me out of the house again before my wedding. However will I escape marrying Lord Malmsey then?"

"Escape . . . what?" He blinked. "Your wedding? I don't understand. What on earth makes you think Lord Malmsey would marry you? He's in love with Lady Frances."

"Well, he offered for my hand before he *met* Lady

Frances. And my father is going to make us marry, unless—"

"You're *engaged*?" he interrupted. "To Lord Malmsey?"

It was beyond his comprehension. All the time Juliana had been trying to match him with Lady Amanda, the woman had been engaged?

"We're to be wed a week from today. And the only way I can get out of it is if I'm caught with another man." She grabbed both his hands. Reserved Lady Amanda grabbed his hands, and she wasn't even wearing gloves. She was *that* desperate. "Can you not cooperate?"

A better man would. A better man would make amends for his actions by following through. But he couldn't.

He just couldn't.

Two women entered the corridor, heading for the ladies' retiring room. He pulled his hands from Lady Amanda's and lowered his voice. "I cannot," he said. "I'm sorry, but I cannot cooperate. I cannot marry you. I'm in love with another woman."

He turned and stalked to the cloakroom, unsure whether he was more furious with Lady Amanda for trying to trick him again, Juliana for trying to match him with an engaged woman, or himself for misleading them both. All he knew was he was in no state of mind to socialize. He wanted to go home.

"James!" he heard as he passed the ballroom.

He turned to see Juliana, a cautious smile on her face. Cautious? Juliana? Was this another one of her mercurial moods?

"How did it go with your aunts?"

"Fine," he said shortly.

Her smile disappeared. "Is something wrong?"

"Your friend tried to trick me again. Your *engaged* friend."

"Oh." Her face went white. "Dear heavens. I can explain—"

"I'm sure you can, since you always have a plan to fix everything. But I don't want to hear it tonight. I'm going home."

Still deathly pale, she hesitated a moment.

She hesitated. Juliana hesitated. Confident, self-assured Juliana.

"All right," she finally said. "Can we discuss this to-morrow at Lady Hartley's breakfast?"

"I don't think so. I have more important things to do than attend a silly breakfast." The Institute would be closed since it was Sunday, but perhaps he'd work on the account books. Or clip his nails. Anything would be better than wasting half the day smiling at people he didn't care about. He'd never enjoyed garden parties or balls—he attended them only to placate his mother, and more recently, to see Juliana.

But he didn't want to see Juliana. Or more precisely, to have her see him. To face her in a tent full of nosy spectators.

Hell, he couldn't even face himself.

Chapter Thirty-eight

After James left, Juliana returned to the ballroom, furious and intending to find Amanda. Before she had a chance, Amanda found her.

"Whom?" the older girl asked, tears spilling from her red-rimmed eyes. "Whom is Lord Stafford in love with?"

"I told you not to try to trick him again! And why on earth did you tell him you're engaged?" People were gawking at them, so Juliana hurried her to a corner of the ballroom where they could talk behind a potted palm. "Now he'll never agree—" She stopped short, suddenly registering Amanda's question. "What makes you think Lord Stafford is in love with anyone?"

"He told me! I kissed him, and then—"

"You *kissed* him?" A stab of jealousy took Juliana by surprise. Or, all right, to be honest, she wasn't surprised. But it certainly felt bad and very wrong. "What did he do then?"

"He pushed me away. You said he would fall in love with me, but he pushed me away!"

The jealousy faded as quickly as it had flared, replaced instead by elation. Unmistakable, jubilant elation. Juliana had never felt more buffeted by uncontrollable emotions, and she wondered how she could feel so exultant when Amanda was clearly so desperate. But she couldn't seem to help herself. Amanda had kissed James, and he'd reacted by pushing her away.

She must be a bad, bad person, because she wanted to scream with joy.

"I asked him if he'd just cooperate," Amanda continued with a pathetic sniffle, "and compromise me so my father would have to let me marry him. But he said he couldn't, because he's in love with another woman." She heaved another prolonged, woebegone sniff. "Who is it?"

"I don't know," Juliana said. It wasn't a lie. She had her suspicions, but she didn't *know*. James had claimed he would never fall in love with anyone. While he'd certainly never pushed her away, no declaration of love had passed his lips. He'd never called her "my love" or even "my dear." He'd never sent her flowers. And he'd seemed very angry that she'd deceived him regarding Amanda's engagement. "I don't know," she repeated, looking away.

Because although she didn't know, she couldn't help hoping . . .

Her gaze wandered the ballroom, past Lord Malmsey dancing with Aunt Frances. Had her meddling doomed them both to despair? Even if James *did* love her and eventually forgave her, how could she ever be happy with him while she knew other people she cared for were miserable? And then there was the duke . . .

Having at last emerged from the card room, he stood gazing at her, a heated look in his eyes. He'd never looked at her with that sort of expression before. Just her luck, now that she'd decided she couldn't marry him, he'd finally decided he wanted her.

Amanda shifted uneasily beside her. "Why is David looking at me like that?"

"Like what?" Juliana asked. Then she blinked. And stared.

Dear heavens, the duke wasn't looking at her at all, let alone *like that*. He was looking at Amanda. *Like that*. Could the duke love Amanda?

Amanda?

Well, why not? she suddenly realized, glancing back and forth between them and recalling all of their interactions. Honestly, it was amazing she hadn't considered the possibility much earlier. The duke and Amanda were two peas in a pod. Two perfectly round, blemishless peas, with about as much passion between them as one would expect from a pair of legumes.

The duke and Amanda were ideal for each other. Absolutely ideal. He related better to Amanda than he ever had to her. Amanda's cold upbringing had matched his own, after all. The two of them understood each other.

She turned back to face Amanda. "It's a shame you won't marry a by-blow, because that would solve everything."

Amanda bit her lip. "I would marry a by-blow if the by-blow was the duke," she said meekly.

Juliana gasped. "Are my ears deceiving me? Did you just say you would marry the duke?"

"You were right all along." Instead of looking down at her feet as she used to, Amanda met Juliana's eyes. "He's not to blame for his parents' mistakes, and he's kind and a good man."

"Then whyever did you say no last night? With such vehemence, no less?"

"You want to marry him yourself. You've been trying so hard to help me. The last thing I want to do is repay you by stealing your intended. You're such a good friend."

"You're a good friend, too." Juliana took Amanda's hands. "I don't want to marry the duke. I want you to have him instead. Wait here," she added, squeezing her fingers before she released them. "I'm going to make it happen."

As she walked toward the duke, she couldn't help noticing that his blond, pristine handsomeness matched Amanda's pale beauty precisely. If he didn't realize they belonged together yet, she would see that he soon did.

She came to a stop before him and looked up into blue eyes as bland as Amanda's. "You're not in love with me," she said. Although he had claimed he was falling in love with her, it was a statement, not a question. "You're in love with Lady Amanda."

"I wouldn't go so far as to call it *love*," he demurred. "But I hold her in some affection."

Juliana supposed it was the most Amanda could ever expect, since it was the most the woman could give herself. Neither of them possessed enough emotion for anything stronger.

"Would you like to marry her?" she asked.

He hesitated, but only a moment. "Very much. Even though she doesn't come with a horse."

"Pardon?"

"Never mind. I would definitely like to marry her. Unfortunately, I understand she's engaged to another."

"She told you that?" Juliana asked. But obviously, Amanda had. While Juliana and James were kissing, evidently Amanda and the duke had been talking. "We can fix her engagement," she said. "But first you need to ask her for her hand."

The duke nodded gravely.

"It might help to tell her how you feel," she advised as she walked him toward Amanda, thinking him the sort of man to forget that. "You may want to exaggerate a bit."

After delivering him to her friend, she backed away and watched from afar as he and Amanda conducted a conversation that looked more like a business discussion than a proposal. In the end, when Amanda nodded, he leaned forward and kissed her on the cheek.

It seemed an auspicious beginning. Maybe after a year or two they'd progress to kissing on the lips.

Perhaps within a decade they'd make a child.

The negotiations complete, they summoned Juliana. In the course of the next half hour, the three of them came up with a plan. After church tomorrow, they would all attend Lady Hartley's breakfast party, where, at precisely three o'clock, Amanda would be caught in the library with the duke, her dress unbuttoned down the back.

Amanda blanched when Juliana suggested the last bit, but they all agreed it was necessary to assure her ruin. By the time Amanda's father arrived that evening, her compromise would be a fait accompli. He would have to allow her to marry the duke.

"Will you ask Lord Stafford to help 'discover' us?" Amanda asked.

"No. He told me he won't be in attendance." Juliana thanked goodness for that, because he'd never approve of their plot. "I'm sure plenty of other people will come running when I call, so there is no need for him to be involved."

With any luck, James would never hear about what happened at all.

And after all was said and done, if she was fortunate enough to learn he loved her, she would never—never ever—meddle again.

Chapter Thirty-nine

In his study at Stafford House the next day, James pushed aside his paperwork and sighed.

Sometime during the sleepless night, the hot fury had settled into a coldness deep inside him. Cornelia had the sniffles. He'd passed the morning in a haze, hoping she would decide she was well enough to leave for Lady Hartley's breakfast. When she finally did, he'd sat down at his desk, added the same column of numbers three times, and come up with three different answers.

He couldn't concentrate. He still couldn't wrap his mind around the fact that Juliana had been hiding Amanda's engagement from him for all the time since they'd met. He'd thought he knew her.

But then again, he'd thought he knew himself, too. And when it came right down to it, his disappointment in himself was the hardest thing of all to swallow.

True, Juliana had done wrong. But she was a meddler, and he'd known that all along. Sometimes her scheming worked—with his aunts, for example—and sometimes it didn't.

Everyone made mistakes, and as bad as her actions had been, his own had been no better. He was hardly in a position to judge. They'd *both* been playing games. His games had hurt Amanda, and Juliana's games had nearly saddled him with an unwanted wife.

But he loved her nonetheless. He loved every scheming, meddling inch of her. Should he be fortunate enough to marry her, he would gladly put up with her antics for the rest of his life.

And he, for one, was finished playing games.

Decision made, he pushed back from the desk, summoned his valet, and went to his newly renovated bedroom to change. The red-and-yellow-striped bedroom he hoped to share with Juliana.

It was time to buy her roses.

Only the cream of society held "breakfasts" in the afternoon.

Beneath a tent in Lady Hartley's garden, the breakfast was well under way when James arrived just before three o'clock. As he scanned the several hundred guests seated at round tables, searching for Juliana, Lord Occlestone rose from one nearby.

"You owe some lady an apology, Stafford?"

James glanced down to the flowers he held, a dozen red roses. "Something like that." In his carriage between the florist's shop and Lady Hartley's, he'd unwrapped and nervously dethorned them. Now, rewrapped in the crumpled paper, they didn't look like much.

"I missed you in Parliament all this week. Or rather, I didn't miss you."

"I was there Thursday," James said mildly, still searching the crowd. He had more important things to do than bicker with Occlestone.

"Oh, yes, you were there Thursday. How could I forget your arguments regarding your ridiculous notion that we should return the Elgin Marbles to Greece rather than purchase them for the British Museum?"

"It's a matter of morality," James snapped. "We have no right—"

"Where the devil is my daughter?" another gentleman cut in.

Grateful for the interruption, James turned to him, then blinked at his stern demeanor. "And your daughter is . . . ?"

"Lady Amanda Wolverston," Occlestone answered for him, clapping the man on the shoulder. "Good to see you at long last, Wolverston. What has it been, two years? Three? We Tories have sorely missed your voice of reason."

While Lady Amanda's father muttered something about excavating antiquities on his property, James looked him over. He was rather short, with fair hair and beady, pale blue eyes. His mouth was compressed and turned downward, and deep lines on either side gave the distinct impression such a frown was his habitual expression.

He didn't look the least bit pleasant. Poor Lady Amanda. The thought of Wolverston as a father-in-law would make any man think twice before proposing to the unfortunate girl.

A flash of yellow caught James's eye. Juliana, leaving the tent. "Excuse me," he said quickly and moved to follow her.

He reached the garden just in time to see her enter the house. Wondering what could possibly compel her to go into a house during a garden party, he crossed the threshold just in time to see her reach the other end of what seemed an impossibly long corridor. From there, best he could tell, she turned and stole into a room.

He hurried after her, composing apologies in his head, desperate words spilling from his brain in a rhythm that matched the cadence of his rushing feet. *Juliana, I shouldn't have judged—Juliana, please listen—Juliana, I love you—*

Reaching the end of the corridor, he opened what he hoped was the right door and stepped into a library. As he quietly closed the door behind him, his mouth fell open.

It had been the right door. Between two deep red velvet curtains, Juliana stood facing a window, a dark silhouette against the light. Her dress was unbuttoned all down her back, and the bodice had slipped down her arms, revealing a slim column of tempting skin.

"Juliana," he gasped softly.

She turned and stepped forward, her hair glinting the palest blond.

It wasn't Juliana.

"Lord Stafford!" Lady Amanda's cheeks flushed

bright red. She swiftly jerked her dress up to cover herself, but not before he glimpsed an oddly shaped birthmark on her left breast. "What are you doing here?"

"What are *you* doing here?" Had he entered the wrong room? What had happened to Juliana? "Fix your clothes, will you?"

"I—I cannot!"

She was clutching her bodice for dear life, unwilling to let go in order to button her dress. Vaguely wondering how she'd managed to unbutton it in the first place, James stalked across the room to fasten it for her.

The door opened and closed again. "What are *you* doing here?" the Duke of Castleton asked in an exceedingly stuffy manner.

The ass. "Buttoning the lady's dress," James spat, stating the obvious. "What are you doing here?" The paper-wrapped roses tucked under one arm, his fingers awkwardly worked up Lady Amanda's spine as quickly as possible.

But not quickly enough. Before he was anywhere near finishing—before Castleton could even open his mouth to answer James's question—the door flew open once more, and a flood of people poured in.

Led by Lord Occlestone.

"How dare you preach morality to the House of Lords, Stafford."

James's fingers fell from Lady Amanda's buttons, and the roses fell, too. He scooped them up. "This isn't what it looks like."

Occlestone's squarish nose went into the air. He'd never looked more like a pig. "I doubt the lady's father will agree."

"My father is here?" Lady Amanda squealed.

"Lord Wolverston is looking for you. I shall fetch him forthwith."

"Please don't," she said quickly, but he was already gone.

The onlookers turned as one to watch him, then broke out in excited whispers.

"Gracious me," Lady Amanda breathed, slowly turning to face James. "What an unpleasant man."

The woman was a master of understatement. Unpleasant, indeed. James hadn't missed the smirk on the man's face. Occlestone was enjoying this tiny bit of revenge.

Unfortunately, the revenge could turn out to be far less than tiny.

Lady Amanda's gaze darted about the whispering crowd. "What are we going to do?" she asked in a low, panicked tone.

"Nothing. There is nothing we can do." His instincts said to run. But escape was impossible. Alerted by Occlestone, Lady Hartley's guests were arriving in droves, filling the doorway, cramming the room. He could only be grateful his mother and aunts weren't among them. So far, anyway. Perhaps they'd all come down with the sniffles and gone home.

A long velvet curtain swished behind him, and he turned, shocked to see Juliana step from behind it. "What the devil is going on here?" he asked.

Her gaze swept the fascinated bystanders, then settled on him as though they were the only ones there. "I'm so sorry." She *did* look sorry, not that that did any good. "We'd planned for Lady Amanda to be discovered with the duke."

James swung to Castleton in disbelief. "You were party to this? You willingly—"

"Yes," Castleton interrupted stiffly, but before he could explain anything, more people streamed into the room—Cornelia and her sisters among them, damnation—as Lord Wolverston arrived with a roar.

"Stafford, you will pay for this!"

James's stomach sank. He'd never been formally introduced to Amanda's father—in fact, he'd never even laid eyes on the man until a few minutes earlier. But he wasn't surprised to find that Wolverston knew his name. Occlestone would have supplied him with all the lurid details as the two of them made their way from the tent to the library.

He should have run.

Although he was no taller than his offspring, Lord Wolverston was commanding in his fury. "You will wed my daughter in place of Lord Malmsey. Next Saturday, as planned."

A buzz filled the room. Gasps of surprise and astonished whispers. It seemed Lady Amanda's betrothal had been a well-kept secret.

"No!" she cried. "This is all a mistake!"

Her father turned to her, his jaw clenched. "A serious mistake indeed, young lady." He swung back to James. "I'll expect you at Wolverston House at noon with a special license."

James's gaze flicked to his horrified mother before he nodded. There was nothing else he could do. Having been witnessed buttoning Lady Amanda's dress at an event attended by half of the *ton*, he had no choice but to comply or lose all honor.

"What if Baron Malmsey still wants her?" someone shouted over the babble. "Will you deprive him of his betrothed bride?"

"I would *never* go back on my word." Lord Wolverston craned his neck, searching the crowd. "Malmsey!" he bellowed. "Do you still wish to wed my disgraced daughter?"

Someone pushed Lord Malmsey forward. "I . . . I . . ." he sputtered. A meek man to begin with, he seemed to have shrunk into himself. "I—"

"The baron doesn't want her," Wolverston said.

Well, of course he didn't. He wanted Lady Frances.

"She must wed the earl," Wolverston concluded, suddenly sounding less discontented. In fact, if the man were possessed of a more pleasant demeanor, James suspected he'd have looked positively delighted.

"Please, Father!" Lady Amanda begged. "This isn't fair! Father, you must listen! You must reconsider—"

"I will not." Lord Wolverston grabbed her by the arm, making her wince. "We are leaving."

"Please, Father!" she wailed as he dragged her through the crush. "Pleeeease!"

It was a wail James feared he would hear the rest of his life.

Literally.

Chapter Forty

As Lady Hartley's guests followed the Wolverstons from the room like rats mesmerized by a piper—except in this case they were riveted by Amanda's dramatic pleadings—Juliana watched Lady Stafford push through them in the other direction.

"James!" she cried, throwing her arms around him.

He held her for a few seconds, but then extricated himself. "Please go, Mother. Take Aunt Aurelia and Aunt Bedelia back to the tent. I'll talk to you in a few minutes."

She looked to her sisters, who were standing there with their mouths open, and back to him. "But, James—"

"Go. Please. I need to talk to Juliana."

As they departed, leaving the two of them alone, he turned to her.

She felt like she hadn't breathed in the last five minutes.

And like she might never breathe again.

She thought she should cry, but she felt numb. She didn't know what to say. She didn't know what she *could* say. All the words seemed to have been sucked right out of her.

"I'm sorry," she whispered. It was all she could manage.

James only nodded.

She'd never seen him look so pale, so lifeless. Not even when he'd been deathly afraid of Emily's snake. The very sight of him in that state made anger rise in her, which finally loosened her tongue.

"Lord Occlestone should be shot."

"I may not like the man," he said wearily, "but others followed us in here as well. Lady Amanda's father would have found out one way or another. Occlestone is not to blame for this."

"I know. *I'm* to blame. But I'll fix it."

She *had* to fix it.

James's lips quirked to form something that might have been a sad smile. "You cannot fix everything, Juliana. But the fact that you never stop trying . . . well . . . it's one of the many things that made me fall in love with you."

There was no way she could live with herself if he had to marry Amanda. "I can fix this, and I will," she reiterated. "I have to." And then she froze. "One of the many things that made you . . . what?" She held her breath again, but for an entirely different reason, and then her gaze dropped to his hand. And her breath went out in a rush. "You brought roses."

He glanced down, as though he'd forgotten he was holding them. "They're a bit worse for the wear."

They *did* look a tad bedraggled. "But they're red roses."

"There aren't many of them. I couldn't easily carry more than a dozen. Not two dozen like we ordered for Lady Amanda, and compared to what Lord Malmsey sent to your aunt—"

"They're *red* roses." He wasn't handing them to her. "Are they for me?"

Abruptly, he held them out. "Who else could they possibly be for? For what other woman in all of London—nay, in all of the world—would I buy and de-thorn red roses? Bloody hell, I must've nicked myself twenty times."

"You said you would never fall in love again." She grabbed the flowers and held them tight to her chest, the paper crinkling, their sweet scent wafting to her nose. "Oh, James, I love you, too."

He held out his arms, and she bolted into them, and he held her close, the bouquet crushed between them. And then the tears that wouldn't fall finally did, because really, it was just too much.

And too late.

He'd brought her red roses. She'd been hoping he loved her, but now that she knew he did, her meddling had ruined everything.

She was going to fix it, but for now she couldn't stop weeping. Couldn't stop sobbing. Couldn't stop.

"Hush," he murmured while her tears wet his waistcoat. And, "hush," while they soaked through to his shirt. And finally, "Do you know what I hate even more than snakes?"

She shook her head, rubbing her nose in the damp warmth.

He put a finger under her chin and lifted it, until her eyes were forced to meet his. "A woman's tears," he said. "I swear to God, Juliana, they make me feel more helpless than anything."

"I'm sorry," she said, and she was. Sorry for crying, and sorry that made him uncomfortable. But mostly sorry James loved her and she loved him and everything was such a mess.

"Hush," he said one last time, and then he lowered his head and kissed her, a little soft kiss. And another one. And yet another, but it wasn't soft, it was devouring instead.

Juliana stopped crying, because she didn't want to upset James any more. Or maybe it was because his kisses were such a distraction. She wrapped her arms around his neck, and leaned into him, and threaded her fingers into the dark curls that spilled over his collar. Everything was wrong, but this—this one thing—was heartbreakingly right.

She was in love.

She couldn't remember ever being so happy and so sad all at once.

"I'll fix this," she said when he finally allowed her to draw breath. "We have five days before Saturday."

He smoothed her hair back from her face, her dratted, slippery hair. "Five short days."

"Five and a half," she whispered, inhaling his scent, starch and soap mixed with roses. She wanted to hold that scent inside her. She hugged him tighter, wishing she didn't have to let go.

But she did have to. At least for now.

"Five and a half," she repeated.

It would have to be enough.

Chapter Forty-one

The next day, Juliana paced around the drawing room while she waited for her guests to arrive for her one o'clock sewing party.

"I cannot concentrate." Seated at her easel, Corinna dabbed a bit of gray on the underside of a cloud. "I know you're going to make me sew all afternoon, so for now, will you please sit down?"

Juliana sat and stabbed her needle in and out of a little white nightshirt. For about a minute. Then she rose and began moving again, the nightshirt dangling from her clenched fingers. "There must be some way to fix this. It's disastrous for everyone involved."

"Aunt Frances doesn't think it's a disaster," Corinna pointed out.

That much was true. Although Frances had been shocked to learn Lord Malmsey was engaged, he'd managed to talk his way back into her good graces before Juliana even had a chance to help. In fact, last evening she'd returned to the tent in Lady Hartley's garden to find him proposing on bended knee—a proposal Aunt Frances had joyfully accepted.

But the fact that the two of them were thrilled hardly mitigated the disaster that had come of all her plotting.

She and James were devastated. The duke was devastated. No doubt Amanda was devastated, too, although

Juliana hadn't seen her since last night. Lord Wolverston had taken his daughter straight home—proclaiming loudly, according to several eyewitnesses, that she wouldn't be seen again in public before she was a married woman. Juliana had received an apologetic note from Amanda this morning, explaining that she wouldn't be able to attend any more of her sewing parties and her Aunt Mabel wouldn't be there, either.

Apparently, Lord Wolverston, having been less than impressed with his sister's chaperoning proficiency—or rather, her lack thereof—had given her such a lecture that she'd gone straight to bed with the asthma and expected to remain there for the week.

Out in the foyer, the knocker banged on the door. A few moments later, Adamson came into the drawing room with two letters for Juliana.

"Thank you," she said, breaking the seal on the first one and scanning the short message. "Drat!"

"What is it?" Corinna asked.

"Rachael cannot come today. She has a cold." She opened the second letter, her eyes widening as she read the words. "Double drat!"

"What now?"

"James's aunts are ill, too. And his mother. How in heaven's name am I going to make twenty-five items of baby clothes today with only you and Alexandra, Claire and Elizabeth, and Aunt Frances?"

Working feverishly in every free moment, Juliana had managed to complete seven garments on her own between her last sewing party and today, but she still needed to collect seventy-six pieces of baby clothes during just three more parties. That was more than twenty-five per party, and today she would have six fewer women contributing.

"In the scheme of things," Corinna said, "I should think those baby clothes are the least of your troubles."

"You're right." Ordering herself to stay composed and keep things in perspective, Juliana plopped down on the sofa and resumed sewing. Her gaze went to the bedraggled red roses sitting in a vase on the mantel. They looked almost as droopy as she felt. "James's forced betrothal to Amanda is much more distressing."

"Perhaps Lord Wolverston has calmed down by now," Corinna suggested. "Maybe if Amanda explains that it was all a misunderstanding, he'll reconsider."

"I don't think so. For all his bluster, it was clear he was well satisfied to see her catch an earl in place of a lowly baron." Juliana's needle dropped from her fingers. "That's it!"

"What's it?" Corinna tilted her head, perusing her work in progress.

"If the Duke of Castleton offers to marry Amanda instead of James—"

"Her father would refuse, would he not?" She dabbed at the cloud some more. "Isn't that why you plotted her compromise in the first place?"

"But everything's different now. Lord Wolverston wouldn't be breaking his word or breaching a contract. At this point, he only wants to see his ruined daughter wed and off his hands, and after all, if an earl is better than a baron, surely a duke is better still." It was so simple, Juliana wanted to kick herself for not thinking of it on the spot. All this worry could have been avoided. "Why on earth would he refuse?"

Corinna shrugged and dipped her brush. "Your logic seems sound, but Amanda thinks her father is unreasonable."

"I'll bake some wafers, then, just in case." According to the recipe in the family cookbook, wafers were reputed to have a calming effect and help make one reasonable. "But I cannot imagine why he would refuse."

"Well, then, I'm certain he won't. You always know best, after all."

Since Juliana obviously *didn't* always know best—as proven by last night's disaster—she found her sister's sarcasm somewhat annoying. But she was sure Lord Wolverston wouldn't refuse. The man would have to be an idiot to reject a duke as a son-in-law.

Five minutes later, Juliana was on Amanda's doorstep, explaining her new plan. "Why on earth would your father refuse?" she concluded.

"I cannot imagine." Amanda's eyes had been dull with despair, but now they shone with hope. "I wish he were home so we could ask him right now."

"The duke must be with us, in any case. Your father is a stickler, after all, so the duke will need to formally request your hand. And Lord Stafford should be in attendance as well, to confirm he agrees with the proposed solution. When will Lord Wolverston be home?"

"I'm not privy to his schedule. But I heard him instruct the cook to prepare roasted duck for his dinner, and he always insists on dining at precisely six o'clock."

"Perfect. I'll send a footman with notes to summon Lord Stafford and the duke, and we'll all be here at half past six."

"He won't take callers in the middle of dinner."

"Do you know for certain he'll stay home afterward?" Amanda shook her head.

"Then inform your butler beforehand that we're expected. That way he won't go to your father to ask his permission." Juliana started down the steps, then turned. "Oh, bother. I'm sure Lord Stafford is at the Institute, but I have no idea where to send a note that will reach the duke."

"He's at his club," Amanda said, "playing cards."

"Which club?"

"White's, of course."

"Of course," Juliana echoed. She wasn't surprised to learn the duke belonged to a Tory establishment—he was the embodiment of the word *conservative*. What *was* surprising, however, was that Amanda knew where the man was, while she didn't.

Despite expecting to marry him, it seemed she'd never really known him at all.

"Are you sure you're not upset that David loves me?" Amanda asked suddenly and rather warily. "I know you wanted to be the duchess."

While she wasn't sure the duke actually *loved* Amanda, Juliana shrugged. "No, I am not upset. I believe the two of you belong together." Truer words were never spoken. "Um . . . if I told you I'm the woman Lord Stafford loves, would you be upset about that?"

"Gracious me," Amanda said, "you can have him. The man's chilly as a Gunter's ice."

Chapter Forty-two

WAFERS

Rub Butter into Flour with some small amount of Salt. To this put Cream and Honey and roll out until very thin. Cut into small rounds and put them in your oven and eat them hot or cold.

A very simple treat, these have a calming effect. My grandmother used to serve them to my grandfather to make him reasonable.
—Anne Chase, Marchioness of Cainewood, 1764

Even with a flurry of activity, Juliana's afternoon had passed excruciatingly slowly. Despite the heroic efforts of her five guests, her sewing party had added only eight items to her stockpile, well short of the twenty-five she'd been hoping for. But she hadn't been able to prolong the gathering past her usual four o'clock stopping time, knowing the men would be arriving at quarter past six.

She'd shooed everyone out of the house and hurried to the kitchen to make the wafers. When the sweets came out of the oven, she donned her most modest dress—a white one—and applied just enough cosmetics to look fresh and innocent. Then she paced around the drawing room until Corinna grew irritated enough to set down her paintbrush and summon her maid to accompany her for a walk.

She hadn't *meant* to drive her sister away from the house. But all the same, she couldn't help but be a little pleased that she'd be able to explain her plan to James and the duke without enduring Corinna's usual caustic asides.

James arrived first. She hurried him into the drawing room, giving him the details as they went. "Then Amanda can marry the duke," she concluded, "which will leave you free to—" She clamped her lips shut. While James had proclaimed his love, he hadn't made an offer of marriage. "Why on earth would Amanda's father refuse?" she added instead.

"I don't know." Sounding hopeful but maybe also a bit hesitant, he glanced toward the open door, then shrugged and drew her into his arms. "But I pray he won't, because Lady Amanda is *not* the woman I wish to wed."

She laid her head against his chest, savoring his warmth, hoping she was the woman he wished to wed instead. Wishing he could be hers forever.

He *would* be hers forever. "Lord Wolverston won't refuse," she said firmly. "He'd be an idiot to reject a duke as a son-in-law."

"My confident Juliana." James tilted her chin up, and she found herself captured in his intense chocolate gaze. Something fluttered in her middle as he lowered his lips to meet hers.

He brushed her mouth with aching tenderness, then settled there, deepening the kiss. His hands skimmed down her sides and found hers, lacing their fingers together, squeezing tight. There was something different about their kisses now that they'd admitted their love, something possessive, something more meaningful.

Something she knew she'd never find with any other man.

"Ahem." They broke apart to find the duke standing in the doorway. "Your note said you have a plan?"

She blushed wildly, but kept one of James's hands in hers. "Yes," she said and quickly explained, finishing with "Why on earth would Amanda's father refuse?"

"He shouldn't," the duke said stiffly, his disapproving gaze on their clasped hands. "He won't reject me as a son-in-law. He'd have to be dumber than a box of hair to do that."

Juliana and Castleton were both sure Lord Wolverston wasn't stupid enough to reject a duke. And James had silently agreed with them—until they arrived in the man's dining room and he greeted them with all the warmth of an icicle.

"I don't recall issuing dinner invitations."

Lady Amanda set down her fork. "They're not here for dinner, Father."

"Excellent. Then I'm certain they will have the good manners to leave."

"No, they won't." In all the weeks James had spent in Lady Amanda's company, he had never seen her look so resolute. "The Duke of Castleton has something to ask you, Father."

"I do not choose to listen." He leisurely drained his wineglass before setting it down. "Hastings, see these people to the door," he said and started to rise.

"No!" Amanda jumped from her chair and pushed him back down. "You will sit here and listen."

He stared at his suddenly assertive daughter as though she had grown an extra head. "Since when—"

"Lord Wolverston," Juliana interrupted, holding forth her basket. "If you're finished with your dinner, would you care for a sweet? I baked wafers this afternoon."

He stared at *her* as though she had *three* heads. "Ladies do not stoop to the level of kitchen maids."

An awkward silence filled the room. Even stuffy Castleton seemed discomfited by the man's attitude. But he stepped forward. "My lord," he said formally, "I assure you that my wife—my *duchess*—will never step foot in a kitchen. I would like to request the honor of your daughter's hand in marriage."

"My daughter is marrying Lord Stafford," Wolverston replied stiffly. "This Saturday." He rose again. "Now I expect you all to leave before I have to see that you're thrown out."

"Father!" Tears sprang to Lady Amanda's blue-gray

eyes. "The Duke of Castleton is proposing marriage. A *duke*, Father! Surely you cannot refuse him!"

"I can, and I will." He looked to Castleton. "When next I see you at White's—this evening or another time—we shall pretend this interview never occurred," he said and turned to leave.

"No, we shall not." Castleton strode around the table and stood blocking the man's way to the door. "I wish to wed your daughter, and she wishes to wed me. If you've a valid reason to object, I want to hear it."

Wolverston hesitated a moment while his expression shifted to something resembling stone. "You don't want to hear it," he finally said mildly.

"I *demand* to hear it," the duke insisted through gritted teeth.

James had to give Castleton credit. In contrast to Wolverston's expressionless expression, the ass had never looked less reserved in his life. In fact, he looked formidable—and rather like he was preparing to strangle the older man.

Until he heard the next words from Wolverston's mouth.

"Very well, then." Calm, emotionless words. "I once had a liaison with your mother. Thirty-three years ago, to be precise. I fear you may be my son."

Juliana's basket dropped from her hand to the floor while the man pushed past Castleton as though the duke were about as substantial as a piece of paper.

"I expect you'll find that to be a valid reason for me to object to your marrying my daughter," Wolverston added as he went out the door.

For the next few moments, silence reigned.

"He didn't eat my wafers," Juliana finally whispered. "They were supposed to make him reasonable."

"They wouldn't have made a difference." James wrapped an arm around her shoulders—an arm that felt heavy as lead.

He glanced from her stunned face to the others. Castleton no longer looked formidable; instead, he looked as though he might crumple like that piece of paper. Lady Amanda *had* crumpled. In the shocked silence that had followed her father's confession, she'd folded back onto her chair and lowered her head to her lap.

"Gracious me," she breathed now, the words muffled in her skirts. "I cannot marry my brother."

"He said I *might* be his son," Castleton pointed out. But his voice sounded defeated.

"You and Amanda's father are both blond and blue-eyed," Juliana observed wanly.

There was no need for her to point out that Lady Amanda had blue-gray eyes and blond hair as well. Or that everyone had always known his natural father hadn't been the Duke of Castleton. The expression on his face made it clear he was all too aware of those facts.

He shifted uneasily. "Hair and eye color are hardly proof of paternity," he mumbled, sounding less sure of himself by the moment.

But it was more than coloring. Now that the possibility had been raised, James realized Castleton looked much more like Wolverston than the man's daughter did. It was something in the line of the jaw, something in the tilt of the head, something in the length of the nose. Something about the stiff carriage and the lack of stature.

Something twisted in his gut.

"The thought of you two marrying now . . ." Swallowing hard, Juliana put a hand to her middle. "It makes me feel slightly ill."

"It makes me feel *very* ill," Lady Amanda muttered into her lap. She slowly lifted her head, looking very ill indeed. Avoiding Castleton's eyes, she gazed unfocused at James. "We shall have to marry—"

"There's still Lord Malmsey," Juliana cut in.

She was grasping at straws, and broken ones at that. His gut now sinking as well as twisted, James moved to face her and took both her hands. "Lady Amanda can no longer wed Lord Malmsey, my love. She's been publicly disgraced. Under the circumstances, Lord Malmsey is perfectly within his rights to terminate the engagement, and furthermore, he wishes to wed Lady Frances. You wouldn't want to see him ripped from your aunt's side, would you?"

She shook her head, tears glazing her suddenly green eyes. "No," she whispered.

He gathered her close, knowing it would be for the last time. Much as he hated tears, he wanted to cry with her. He *would* cry with her if he could.

But he felt dead inside. Sinking and twisted and dead.

There was no way out. He had to marry Lady Amanda.

He had to marry Lady Amanda.

He had to marry Lady Amanda.

No matter how many times he repeated the fact to himself, it seemed impossible to believe.

Impossible to accept.

But he had to.

Slowly he released Juliana, thinking it was the hardest thing he'd ever done . . .

. . . But not as hard as it would be to say "I will" to someone else.

"I'm going home," he said. "I'll be back Saturday at noon."

Chapter Forty-three

CHOCOLATE CREAM

> Take a Quart of Cream, a Pint of white Wine, and
> a little Juice of Lemon; sweeten it very well, lay
> in a sprig of Rosemary, grate some Chocolate,
> and mix all together; stir them over the Fire till
> it is thick, and pour it into your cups.

> *Chill your cups in ice before serving. A delicious*
> *cure for melancholy.*
> —Belinda Chase, Marchioness of Cainewood, 1792

"Why are you so sad, Lady Juliana?"

"I'm not sad, Emily." *Sad* was much too mild a word
to describe how Juliana felt the next day. "You're doing
very well. Keep mixing."

The little girl looked up from the cast-iron stove in
Juliana's basement kitchen. "You *look* sad." Stirring
with one hand, she stroked the snake draped over her
shoulders with the other. "Herman, do you not think
Lady Juliana looks sad?"

Juliana half expected the reptile to answer, considering nothing else in her life was going as expected. A
talking snake would be less of a surprise than Lord
Wolverston's revelation last night.

And James's reaction to it.

He'd left. He'd held her for a moment, but then he'd left. He'd apparently come to the conclusion that he had to marry Amanda, and accepted it, and just . . . left.

By all appearances, he had no intention of discussing this tragedy. He'd said he'd be back on Saturday. He'd made up his mind, and he wasn't planning to see her again until he was a married man.

If then.

She sighed and started grating chocolate into the triple batch of cream and sugar that Emily was stirring in the pot. "I haven't seen you in quite a few days, Emily."

"A new family moved in across the square. Lord and Lady Lambourne. And they have three children. Three *girl* children."

Another surprise. Juliana usually knew everything that went on in Mayfair. Evidently she'd been a tad preoccupied of late. "What are the girls' names, then?"

"Jane, Susan, and Kate. Susan is just my age."

"That must be lovely for you." She kept grating. "And what do the Lambourne girls think of Herman?"

"Oh, they find him bang up to the mark," Emily said enthusiastically.

Usually Juliana would have smiled at the girl's use of the newest slang. But she was too dejected. Not to mention this news did not bode well for the success of her project to rid Emily of the horrid creature.

Emily stirred faster. "You're putting an awful lot of chocolate in, are you not?"

"One can never have too much chocolate," Juliana said.

So what if she'd put in twice as much as usual? She *needed* chocolate. Her mother had always said it was supposed to cure melancholy, and she'd never been more melancholy in her life.

How was she supposed to go on when the man she loved was marrying another woman? When four people's lives had been ruined? When it was *all her fault*?

Emily had stopped stirring. "You're crying," she said. "You *are* sad."

"I guess I am." Setting down the chocolate and grater, she forced a smile. "I think we're finished here."

"What is wrong, Lady Juliana?"

What *wasn't* wrong? She couldn't marry the man she loved. She'd doomed him to a dreadful future with a woman reserved beyond belief, a future full of chess and antiquities and very little else. She was exhausted and overwhelmed—she hadn't slept last night at all—and somehow, some way—God only knew how, and apparently He wasn't telling—she had to produce sixty-two items of baby clothes in the next three days even though she'd made less than three times that many in the last month and a half.

"What is wrong?" She could barely push the words through her tight throat. "Everything, it seems."

"Is it about Lord Stafford?"

She blinked. "What makes you think that?"

The girl rolled her big gray eyes. "It's obvious you like him. I've known that for ages. And he likes you."

How ironic that the truth had been obvious to an eight-year-old but not to herself. Then again, Emily always *had* been rather precocious for a girl her tender age. "Well, he doesn't seem to want to see me right now."

"Then you must go see him. You have to talk to him. You cannot just stand here and mope. You have to *do* something, Lady Juliana."

Dear heavens, Emily was right. Juliana had before just stood by and let things happen without trying to influence the outcome, and she couldn't imagine what had made her do so now. Melancholy, she supposed. But she couldn't allow melancholy to rule her.

Thank goodness she was making chocolate cream.

"Oh, you dear, dear child." She dashed the tears off her cheeks and wrapped Emily in a hug. "I'm supposed to be helping you, but you're helping me instead."

"Are you going to go see Lord Stafford now?"

"Not right now. I sent notes asking all the ladies to come sew today even though I've never held any parties on a Tuesday before. They'll be here in less than an hour, and I cannot get to the Institute and back in that short time." Dear heavens, James would be at Parliament by the time her sewing session was finished. "I shall have to go see him tomorrow. You'll stay for the sewing party, won't you?"

"Is there any more cutting to be done?"

"No. The cutting is all finished."

"Then I'm going to play with Jane, Susan, and Kate." When Juliana opened her mouth to protest, Emily held up one of her small hands—the one that wasn't stroking her snake. "You don't really want me to sew, do you? I'm sure to end up bleeding."

No, Juliana didn't want Emily to bleed. The mere thought of that made her feel sick. And the last thing she needed now was to spew a stomachful of chocolate over a stack of her hard-won baby clothes.

"Go ahead and play with the Lambourne girls. You have my blessing."

"Can I eat some chocolate cream before I leave?"

"I need to put it on ice first to make it cold. I'll bring you some tomorrow."

Emily helped her transfer the sweet pudding into three dozen cups before she departed to visit her friends across the square. After that, Juliana had just enough time to steal upstairs to her bedroom and wash her blotchy face before her guests arrived. She brushed on a little powder and went down to seat herself in the drawing room. As she picked up her sewing and Corinna kept painting without comment, she congratulated herself on how calm and composed she must seem.

Rachael was still ill, and now Claire and Elizabeth were, too. As were Lady Stafford and Lady Balmforth. Lady Avonleigh was feeling better, though, and she arrived first.

"Oh, my dear," she cried, "I am *so* sorry." And she rushed across the room to enfold Juliana in her arms.

Juliana rose from the sofa and let herself be comforted by James's aunt. Except the embrace wasn't comforting. The harder Lady Avonleigh hugged her, the harder she had to fight to keep the tears from falling again.

"I wanted you to marry my nephew," Lady A murmured, tears in her voice, too. "I wanted you to be my niece."

"I wanted you to be my aunt. I wanted Lady Stafford to be my mother." It seemed forever since she'd had a mother, and Juliana knew no one warmer or more motherly than Lady Stafford. She shuddered in Lady A's arms, inhaling camphor and gardenias. "There has to be *something* we can do."

"Our James doesn't believe there's anything to be done. But if anyone can think of something, it's you, my dear." Lady Avonleigh pulled back and wiped the moisture from Juliana's cheeks with gentle fingers. "You keep thinking, and I will, too."

"Thank you," Juliana said wanly.

She was about to say something more, but then Aunt Frances came downstairs, and Alexandra arrived, and Corinna reluctantly abandoned her painting and came over to join them all and sew. And the talk turned to Frances's pending marriage and Alexandra's burgeoning belly. Not that Alexandra's belly was actually protruding yet, but she kept rubbing the dratted thing as though she could feel the baby inside, which made Juliana insanely jealous.

Yes, jealous.

James had been wrong when he'd said she was jealous before—when she'd first learned of Alexandra's pregnancy—but she was jealous now, because God only knew when she'd have a child of her own . . . the way things were going, probably never. And now *Aunt Frances* was talking about having a child. In her midforties! While Juliana doubted that would actually happen, she had to admit it was a possibility, since Frances still complained about her monthlies on a regular basis. She wondered if *she'd* have a child before forty. Probably not. But all the talk around her was happy talk, so she gritted her teeth and forced another smile and kept sewing, because they all had been kind enough to help her make baby clothes, and there was nothing more she wanted than for everyone to be happy.

But the smile wasn't just forced, it was downright rigid.

She rang for chocolate cream, but eating it didn't seem to help. The conversation flowed around her. Lady Avonleigh got up and wandered over to Corinna's easel, admiring her latest painting. "This is impressive, my dear."

"Thank you," Corinna said.

Alexandra smiled as she plied her needle. "Did you

know Corinna plans to submit a painting to the Royal Academy next year?"

"Several," Corinna corrected. "I am hoping one will be accepted for the Summer Exhibition."

"Really?" Lady A mused. "I did tell you my younger daughter was artistic, did I not? Though it seemed unlikely, she always hoped to see one of her paintings in the Summer Exhibition, too. But her real dream was to be elected to the Royal Academy."

"That's my dream as well," Corinna said. "I know it won't be a simple matter, but I'm willing to work hard for the honor."

The older woman measured her for a moment, then returned to sit beside her. "I want to help you," she announced. "My daughter never attained her dream—I want to see you attain yours."

Aunt Frances knotted and snipped off a thread. "How can you help her?"

"I don't know, but I'll think of a way." Lady A picked up the little cap she was making and smiled at Juliana. "You're good at coming up with ideas. If you wouldn't mind helping, maybe together we can see that your sister becomes the next female member of the Academy."

That would be wonderful for Corinna. And of course Juliana wouldn't mind helping. She needed another project. It would be a lengthy project—it would likely take years—but keeping busy would make it easier to bear her and James's despair.

Well, not really. But she'd find a solution for their despair soon. She would talk to James tomorrow.

Damnation—make that *dear heavens*—she was *not* going to cry.

Chapter Forty-four

There were different ways of dealing with the blows life randomly chucked at some people. James's method—perfected during the years he mourned his brother, father, wife, and newborn child—was to bury himself in work.

Since Sunday he'd been operating in a blur—a dark, painful, all too familiar haze. The miasma had lifted momentarily on Monday, when it had seemed Juliana's plan might succeed. But since learning the truth of Castleton's birth, the dark had closed in again.

James couldn't say that what he faced now was worse than coping with death. Of course it wasn't worse. But it didn't seem better, either. Like loving Juliana compared to loving Anne, it was different.

Death was final. One mourned, one grieved, one eventually moved on. But what he faced now . . . it wasn't final—it was *forever*. It was a life sentence. It seemed so arbitrary, so accidental, so damned unfair.

And so bloody damned inescapable.

And so he'd worked. Because it seemed there was nothing else he could do.

He knew what he couldn't do. He couldn't abandon a fine young lady to a life of utter disgrace. He couldn't condemn himself to a future devoid of all honor. He couldn't make sense of anything in his irrational, haphazard world.

But he could work.

He could work at the Institute to save the world from smallpox. He could work in Parliament to better his country. He could work on his estate to improve the lives of those who depended on him.

He couldn't help himself, and he couldn't help Juliana. But there were other people he could help. Right here, right now, his work was the only thing that seemed to make sense.

One thing James knew—probably the only thing he knew for sure—was how to bury himself in his work to the exclusion of everything else. To the exclusion of everything painful. And so on Tuesday he'd risen at dawn and spent the entire day at the Institute. And the entire evening in Parliament. And then he'd gone back to the Institute and stayed there until the wee hours, finding things to do, until he could go home and fall into bed and get up and start all over again.

Today he'd risen at dawn and returned to the Institute, even though he had two physicians scheduled and really wasn't needed. There was no Parliament tonight, so he'd stay here until the wee hours, finding things to do, until he could go home and fall into bed and get up and start all over again.

He'd do the same tomorrow and Friday. Saturday would be a little different—there would be an interlude in the middle for his wedding. But then he'd come back here to the Institute and repeat the pattern again.

It wasn't an unbearable life. At least he had a purpose. And he was keeping himself so busy he didn't have time to think. Thinking threatened his mental health, and the busyness was a sort of medicine—a medicinal ointment he could smear all over everything to obscure the ills infecting his world.

The medicine, sadly, was an imperfect cure. As the Bible said—Ecclesiastes, if he remembered right— "Dead flies cause the ointment of the apothecary to send forth a stinking savor." Despite countless Sundays in church, he'd never quite understood what "stinking savor" was supposed to mean. But to put it another way, in simpler words, there was a fly in the ointment.

And the fly was women.

Women always—always, always—wanted to talk. Not the superficial talk of men—talk of news and the weather and horses—which didn't make one think. Men's talk could substitute for busyness. But women's talk was different. Because women didn't just talk.

Women wanted to *discuss* things. And discussions required him to think. Which in turn sent forth that stinking savor he was striving so hard to avoid.

If only he could avoid women.

Unfortunately, that was impossible, since approximately half the world's population was female. There was his mother, always wanting to discuss things. There were his assistants, always wanting to discuss things. The stinking savor was everywhere, threatening to make him think, bombarding him with stinking thoughts.

Since Aurelia was his only healthy relation, she was this morning's assistant and therefore his current threat.

"There must be something that can be done, James, something we haven't considered."

"There's nothing, Auntie. Would you hand me that box of sugar sticks?"

"Certainly." She reached to the shelves behind the counter. "But there must be something," she said, handing him the box. "We need to talk."

"I've got an Institute to run. I don't have time for a discussion."

"We'll have to talk later, then. I've promised to help Lady Juliana sew this afternoon, and then I was planning to stay home and nurse Bedelia this evening. But I suppose I can sneak out and meet you at Almack's."

"I won't be attending Almack's." If there was a place in London where the stinking savor was most prevalent, it had to be Almack's. And besides, the last thing he needed was a marriage mart. In three short days he'd be married.

Damnation, his pending marriage was the worst thought of all. He wasn't even really having a discussion, and yet Aurelia was making him think stinking thoughts.

Gritting his teeth, he turned from the counter. "Fifty-two! Follow me, please." A mother rose with her three little girls. Four more talking females. He led them to a treatment room as quickly as possible.

He walked another set of patients to the door and brought more patients to the room they'd just vacated. He restocked sugar sticks in all three treatment rooms. He unwrapped lancets and other supplies. He scribbled in his account books and revised next week's schedule. He returned to the reception room to fetch more patients.

"You're not needed here," Aurelia said. "You're not leaving me anything to do."

"Just keep handing out numbers. And smiling at patients. They appreciate the reassurance."

"You should go home, James. You've got circles under your eyes. Before you need a physician yourself, you should go home and rest."

Home? Where Cornelia was languishing in bed waiting to *discuss* things? "I think not." The door opened, and two people went out past another person waiting to come in. "Here comes another patient. You can give her a number." In fact, maybe he'd do that himself. Handing out numbers didn't require one to think. Turning away, he reached over the counter for one of the worn paper squares.

"You're number sixty-seven," he said as he turned back. "I'll call you when . . . Juliana."

His voice trailed off, sinking along with his heart.

"James." Walking closer, she offered him a tentative smile, a sad smile, a smile that made his heart keep sinking until it dropped clear down to his toes. "We need to talk."

Oh, no. "Have you thought of a solution?"

"Not yet. We need to think together. We need to discuss—"

"There is nothing to discuss. Nothing will come of it, Juliana. What's the point?" It would make him think. It would make him think stinking thoughts.

"Can we go somewhere private?"

"I don't want to talk."

"Please, James." Her eyes were green, deep green,

green and pleading. "Please let's just go to a treatment room."

"James," Aurelia said softly, "your patients are staring. Take her to a treatment room."

Women. If only he could avoid women. "The treatment rooms are all in use."

"Take her to your office, then," Aurelia pressed.

"Do you not think that would be improper?" he asked his aunt, and to Juliana he added, "Do you not think Lady Frances would disapprove?"

"Bosh," they said together.

"We've been together in private before," Juliana reminded him, no doubt referring to not only a treatment room here at the Institute but also a secluded grove in a lantern-lit garden, a secret hideaway under a staircase, a warm cubby inside a greenhouse. "I didn't hear you protest then."

He hadn't been trying to avoid thinking then.

"It's not as though you're likely to ravish her," Aurelia pointed out. "You're marrying another woman."

There it was. That word *marrying*. A stinking thought. And he wasn't even having a discussion.

He gave up. "Very well," he said, "but there is nothing to discuss."

He hurried Juliana into the back, determined to avoid a discussion. There was only one way he knew of to do that. One way to avoid stinking thoughts.

He tugged her into his office, shut the door, and crushed her mouth with his.

It wasn't a gentle kiss. It was a kiss borne of frustration, of disillusion, of fury and pent-up lust. It was a kiss meant to distract, a kiss meant to devour. It was a kiss full of hurt and regret and indelible, immeasurable emotion.

A kiss that consumed them both.

Juliana's arms went around him. Her lips parted under his assault, her mouth warm and sweet and tasting of passion and promise. She smelled not of a stinking savor but of sunshine and flowers and everything he desired. He didn't think, he just felt. He just felt Juliana, and she felt impossibly wonderful.

Bodies straining, they fell together to the desktop that

filled most of the tiny office. Papers flew. Buttons unbuttoned. Fingers skimmed, hearts pounded, skin prickled with delicious heat. He wanted her more than he wanted life, needed her more than he needed to breathe. "Juliana," he choked on a shuddered sigh.

She sat up. "We cannot do this."

"We cannot *not* do this." He sat up, too, brushed silky strands from her troubled eyes. "We cannot keep our hands off each other."

"You're right, but it is wrong." She slid from the desk, suddenly pale, her fingers shaking as she reached behind herself to fasten buttons. "We must talk—we must figure out—"

"We cannot change anything." Still sitting on the desk, he turned her around so he could button her dress for her. Between his spread knees, her hips felt warm through her thin dress, her back like silk beneath his fingers. "We cannot talk, not without touching, and we cannot touch, because that is wrong, and—" He swore under his breath and buttoned faster. "This is why I didn't want to see you until after Saturday."

"You were right." He heard tears in her voice, those blasted tears that seemed to rip him up inside. "I cannot see you again until after you're married, until after—"

"Don't say it." He couldn't stand that word *married*. After he was married, he'd never feel her warm body again. "I cannot bear to hear it."

"I'll go home," she said, trembling. "I have to make fifty-two more items of baby clothes, and I only have until the day after tomorrow." Her voice wobbled. "Your mother is still ill, and so are Lady Balmforth and Rachael and Claire and Elizabeth." Her tone rose in pitch. "That leaves only Alexandra and Lady Avonleigh to help me, Corinna, and Frances, and of all of us, your aunt is the only decent seamstress."

He turned her to face him. "You're going to kill yourself, Juliana." Her chin was wobbling, too. Tears trickled down her cheeks. "You cannot sew in the state you're in. The Foundling Hospital can make do with a few less clothes."

"I promised. A Chase promise is never broken—have I ever told you that before, James? It's been our family

motto for centuries. I have to make fifty-two items of
baby clothes, even though I'll never have a baby."

"Is that what you're thinking?" He didn't know which
ripped him up more, her tears or her line of thought.
"You'll have a baby, Juliana." He pulled her close, felt
the warm tears dampen his half-buttoned shirt. "You'll
have a baby with another man."

"I don't want another man's baby," she whispered.

"You say that now, but you will." Another man would
love her. Another man would make her his. Another
man would join his body with hers and give her a child.

Those were among the most stinking thoughts he'd
ever had, ever.

He'd known he shouldn't think.

Chapter Forty-five

For two days, Juliana had done little but sew baby clothes morning, noon, and night, but she *still* needed to complete thirty-three more pieces by the end of the day.

She didn't know how she was going to do it. Her sisters and Aunt Frances were sewing almost as much as she was, but none of them were very speedy or talented. Lady Avonleigh had helped them all morning, but James had needed her this afternoon at the Institute. And everyone else was still ill. Recovering—and thank heavens for that—but not yet strong enough to spend hours plying a needle.

Her fingers ached. Her vision was blurring. And she didn't have bad eyes.

"You're crying," Alexandra said sympathetically.

"I'm not. I think I must be catching everyone's sniffles."

"In your eyes?" Corinna asked with a smirk.

Alexandra nudged her. "I think Juliana needs chocolate."

"I'm not hungry." She hadn't felt much like eating the past couple of days, not even chocolate. "There are still cups of chocolate cream left, if you want some," she said, and that was when she remembered. "Oh, drat."

Aunt Frances looked up. "What's wrong, dear?"

Other than a dearth of baby clothes and the man she

loved marrying another woman tomorrow? "I promised Emily I'd bring her chocolate cream. Three days ago."

"Take her some, then," Frances said. "The fresh air will do you good."

She couldn't spare the time. Could she? "Maybe I will," she decided. It would take only a few minutes. She set down her sewing, fetched two cups from the kitchen, and walked next door to knock on the Nevilles' door.

Their gaunt butler answered. "Yes?"

"I've come to call on Miss Neville."

"I fear Miss Neville is not available."

"Is she playing with the Lambourne girls?" The fresh air *did* feel wonderful. Maybe she'd fetch three more cups and walk across the square to introduce herself. It would take only a few more minutes—a few more minutes she wouldn't be sewing in a melancholy fog.

"I'm afraid not, Lady Juliana." The old retainer looked mournful. "The poor child is in bed."

"In bed?" It was four o'clock in the afternoon, and Emily was well past the age for napping. "Is she ill?"

"Not yet, but she will be. The Lambourne girls came down with smallpox today."

"Smallpox!" Her heart suddenly beat double time. "Has she not been vaccinated?"

He shrugged his thin shoulders. "I'm only the butler, my lady."

"I'd like to visit with her, if you please."

The butler, who was pock-scarred himself, eyed her smooth, unmarked skin. "She may be contag—"

"I've been variolated, so I cannot catch smallpox. Please show me to Miss Neville."

Juliana heard Emily's sobs before she even entered the room. In her bed, the girl was buried beneath a mountain of blankets. A fire blazed on the hearth, and the windows were closed and draped, making the chamber dim and stiflingly hot. The air smelled slightly of vomit.

And a man held Emily's arm over a small bowl with her blood dripping into it.

Juliana gulped convulsively. Her mouth felt dry, her breath came short, and her stomach clenched, making her fear she might vomit next. It was silly, and it was stupid, but she couldn't help herself.

She walked closer, forcing herself to focus on Emily's tear-streaked face. "Dear heavens, what is going on here?"

"The doctor is hurting me!" Emily wailed. "I want Herman!"

Her heart pounding, Juliana set the chocolate cream on the girl's bedside table and smoothed her hair back from her brow, seeing no sign of pocks. "Surely she hasn't fallen ill already?"

"Not yet," the doctor said. "I am preparing her for the disease."

"Preparing her? I think not."

"She must be purged and bled and blistered. The procedures will help her body withstand the infection."

"They will not!" James didn't believe such things. "They will only weaken her." Juliana's gaze jerked back to the bowl of red fluid, and her head swam. She quickly looked away, but not before noticing the doctor's hands appeared none too clean. James wouldn't approve of that, either. He thought cleanliness helped prevent infection. "Please leave. Bandage Miss Neville's arm and—"

"Lord Neville sent for me—"

"Well, *I'm* sending you away!" Where was Lord Neville, anyway? Did he have any idea what this man was doing to his daughter?

"You have no authority—"

Juliana gritted her teeth and squared her shoulders. "I have every authority," she lied. "I am Lady Neville, and I order you to unhand my daughter and leave at once."

She could hardly believe those words had come out of her mouth. And even more than that, she could hardly believe the doctor believed her.

But he did.

"Pardon me, my lady. My apologies." He set down the bowl and dug in his bag, removing a cloth. "I assumed you were naught but a visitor," he explained hurriedly as he pressed it to the cut he'd made in Emily's arm.

"That will teach you to make assumptions," Juliana

said tightly, moving to hold the cloth in place. "Hush, Emily," she soothed. "You're going to be fine." At least she hoped Emily would be fine. She had no idea whether the girl might come down with smallpox, but she was certain the doctor's ministrations were of no help. "You may send a bill to Lord Neville," she instructed him, "but I'll thank you to leave now."

She kept herself busy tying the bandage while the doctor quickly gathered his things and left.

"I want Herman," Emily said as soon as he cleared the door. She struggled up to a sitting position and motioned toward a terrarium in the corner. "G-get me Herman."

Juliana walked over to the glass box, sighing as she reached in to lift the reptile. She'd never actually touched him before, and it really wasn't the thing for ladies to handle snakes. But Herman felt drier and warmer than she'd expected, and she smiled to see the little girl relax as he settled around her neck.

"Th-thank you," Emily breathed. Her sobs had diminished to shuddering sniffles. "I c-cannot believe that doctor be-believed you were my mother."

"I cannot believe it, either," Juliana said dryly. Honestly, she'd have had to have given birth at fourteen for Emily to be her daughter. Apparently the doctor thought she looked either very old or very fast, neither of which made her very happy.

But she was extremely happy he had left.

"I don't want to get smallpox, Lady Juliana."

"Of course you don't. But I don't believe what that doctor was doing would prevent it."

She had a sinking feeling there was nothing that *could* prevent it other than luck, but there was someone who would know for sure. Someone who knew more about smallpox than anyone else in London.

"I'm going to send for Lord Stafford," she said. They'd agreed not to see each other until after tomorrow, but really, she had no choice. Emily's health was at stake—maybe even Emily's life. "Wait here while I write a note and give it to one of your father's footmen." She started out the door. "No, make that one of Griffin's footmen," she amended. The Neville staff was so old, it would be tomorrow before one of them managed to shuffle to the Institute and back. And besides, she needed to send a note next door in any case, because they'd be wondering what was keeping her so long.

A few minutes later, she returned and peeled all the blankets off Emily. She banked the fire and drew back the curtains and opened the window. Gritting her teeth, she took the little bowl of blood and dumped it into the bushes outside, then rinsed it with water from Emily's washstand and dumped that out, too. When all that was finished, her heart calmed a little and her stomach felt much better. She dragged a chair to Emily's bedside, found a book, and read aloud for almost an hour until James arrived.

When the butler showed him to the room, he paused in the doorway and looked at her. Just looked at her, like he was drinking her in.

"Juliana," he said softly. He looked tired and disheveled, his hair a tousled mess and his neckcloth askew. He'd probably donned that and his tailcoat in his carriage on the way from the Institute.

Her chest ached at the sight of him. "I know we said we wouldn't—"

She cut off, noticing his gaze had shifted to Emily. And Herman. A moment ago his heart had been in his eyes, but now those eyes were glazed, and he looked very much like she'd felt when she'd seen Emily's blood. Like his pulse was thready and his stomach was clenched.

Which was very probably true.

"Emily," she said carefully, rising from her chair, "you need to give Herman back to me now. I'm going to put him in his box until Lord Stafford is finished."

"No!" Emily clutched the olive green snake. "I want to keep him."

"Emily—"

"The other doctor took him, and then he hurt me. I want to keep Herman!"

"Emily—"

"It's all right," James said, looking pale as paper. "She can keep him." He drew a deep breath and looked back to Juliana. "Your note said she was ailing?" His gaze flicked to Emily's bandage and back again. "Did she hurt her arm?"

"Not exactly. The other doctor bled her. She's been exposed to smallpox, and—"

"Where? When?" He walked closer to the bed, seemingly unafraid of the snake. Except his hand was gripping the handle of his leather bag so tightly his knuckles had turned white. "Tell me what you know."

"She's been playing all week with three girls who came down with smallpox today."

"How do you know it's smallpox? Have they spots, or only a fever?"

"Spots," Emily said. "But Susan told me she was hot the day before."

"Damn," he said under his breath. On the other side of the bed from where Juliana stood, he set his bag down on Emily's night table. "Do you feel hot?"

"No. Not now. I did before, but Lady Juliana took all the blankets off of me."

"The other doctor had her under seven of the things," Juliana explained disgustedly.

"Idiot." James leaned closer to Emily and reached toward her, flinching before he placed a hand on her forehead. "No fever," he reported, quickly pulling back from the girl and her snake. "That's a good sign. Smallpox is usually not contagious for the first week or two after exposure, but one can never be certain."

"If it's a good sign," Juliana said cautiously, "does that mean you can do something to prevent her getting it?"

"Maybe." He opened his bag and drew out items she'd seen at the Institute. "Very possibly. Vaccination within three days of exposure will usually completely prevent it. Between four and seven days, vaccination still offers a chance of protection, and at the very least should modify the severity of the disease. Has she already been vaccinated?"

"I don't know," Juliana said. "The butler doesn't know, and Lord Neville isn't here."

"The doctor sent him to the apothecary," Emily said. "To get more purg—purg—"

"Purgative," James supplied.

"Lovely," Juliana muttered. "Do you think it's been less than three days since she was exposed? Since the Lambourne girls became contagious?"

"We don't know," he said. "It would be better if Emily's friends hadn't developed spots. But then I suppose we wouldn't be certain it was smallpox, so . . ." He shrugged and lifted the quizzing glass that dangled from the chain around his neck. "Open your mouth, sweetheart," he said, bending closer to Emily.

He held his breath as he examined her, his lips clamped tight. Knowing Herman must be scaring him to death, Juliana held her breath with him. Maybe it was a bit silly to be afraid of a harmless snake, but not any sillier than to feel ill at the sight of blood. Her heart cracked at the evidence of his bravery, his determination to put the girl's health before his own fears.

How could she have ever thought his having a profession was a bad thing? Amanda had better appreciate having such a wonderful husband, she thought fiercely.

They both blew out a breath when he straightened. "What were you looking for?" she asked.

"Small red spots on her tongue and in her mouth. Pocks usually show up there first, although I wouldn't expect to see any this early, before the fever. In any case, she has none."

"That's good, right?"

He nodded and visibly steeled himself before leaning close again to unfasten the buttons that went down the front of Emily's nightgown. Herman was draped on either side of the placket, and his fingers shook a little. Regardless, Juliana had never seen anyone unbutton anything so quickly.

"I want to check the rest of her body. Spots most likely wouldn't appear there yet if she's contracted smallpox, but we can hope her friends actually have some other disease that presents differently—"

He snatched his hands back and froze, staring.

At first Juliana thought he'd gone rigid due to the snake. Then she noticed he wasn't staring at Herman, but at Emily's young, flat chest.

Or, to be more precise, at an odd, fleur-de-lis-shaped birthmark on the left side.

He frowned and murmured, "I think I've seen a birth-mark like this before."

Emily nodded. "My father has one, too. All the Nev-illes have one. In exactly the same place."

"Oh," James said. Still staring at Emily's bared skin, he frowned again. "But I've never seen your father's chest."

"Yes, you did," Juliana reminded him. "At Lady Hammersmithe's ball, remember? Lord Neville was choking, and you saved his life."

"I removed his neckcloth but not his shirt. I only loos-ened a couple of buttons. I never saw—"

He blinked. And gasped.

"What?" Juliana asked.

His gaze flew to meet hers. "It's another birthmark I remember. Because another night—the night I was caught with Lady Am—" He broke off, glancing toward Emily and back again. "With your unbuttoned friend," he revised.

Then he paused before concluding, very slowly, "I saw that birthmark on *her*."

Dear heavens, he was right. He'd seen it flashed on a half bare, hastily covered breast. Juliana suddenly re-membered seeing it herself from where she'd been peek-ing from behind the curtain.

No, she couldn't have seen it then. She'd been at en-tirely the wrong angle.

But she *had* seen a similar birthmark on Amanda.

Her brain felt fuzzy, but she knew she'd seen it. She closed her eyes and pictured it . . . in her very own bedroom, the night she'd presented the "new" Amanda to society, when she was dressing for Lady Hammer-smithe's ball.

And that meant . . .

Something hovered in the back of Juliana's mind. Some-thing significant. Across the bed from James, she followed his gaze down to Emily's chest. If all the Nevilles had that birthmark, and Amanda had that birthmark . . .

Amanda was Lord Neville's daughter, not Lord Wolverston's.

And that meant . . .

"Oh, my heavens," she breathed.

Chapter Forty-six

James's eyes met Juliana's in understanding, and it took everything they had not to voice their conclusions aloud in front of the little girl. Her father arrived, purgative in hand—muttering about hiring some servants young enough to run errands—and James asked him if his daughter had ever been vaccinated.

The answer was no, which James found rather annoying. If the educated upper class didn't make vaccination a priority, was there any hope for the common people?

To everyone's relief—except perhaps Emily's, since the last thing she wanted was to be cut again—the purgative was put aside, and James vaccinated her instead. A tiny incision, a little dip into the wound using an ivory lancet tipped with cowpox virus, and a swiftly applied bandage. It all went very quickly, even though James didn't have a sugar stick. In fact, he couldn't remember ever vaccinating anyone faster.

Herman might have had something to do with that, and it seemed the girl preferred chocolate cream, anyway.

There was nothing else to do but wait. The incubation period for smallpox generally ran seven to fourteen days, but occasionally went as long as seventeen. Emily had most likely been exposed two or three days earlier, which meant it would be at least two weeks before they knew for certain whether she was out of the woods.

But there was much reason to hope. And for now Emily was healthy, so even though she should stay at home to assure others' safety, there was no reason for her to remain in bed.

It was almost seven o'clock by the time all was said and done and James and Juliana left the Neville house. As soon as the door closed behind them, she turned to him on the doorstep. "Will Emily really be all right?"

"I cannot make any promises, but I think she will. She may not get smallpox at all, and if she does, it should be a very light case." Even a "light case" of smallpox could be arduous, but at least it wouldn't be fatal. And in any event, what would be would be. It was out of his hands at this point, and there were much more pressing matters to discuss.

Yes, he wanted a discussion.

He was ready—he needed—to think.

And after he and Juliana talked, he wanted to kiss her senseless. Or perhaps while they talked. Or before. All of the above wouldn't be a bad plan, either.

Easy, he told himself. Everything was still up in the air. Instead of kissing her, he took her hand. "Lady Amanda is not Castleton's sister."

"I know. I figured that out." She squeezed his fingers, looking more lively than he'd seen her in days. "Isn't it wonderful?"

"She may not think so," he said cautiously. "A woman who is such a stickler for propriety may be unhappy to learn she's another man's daughter."

"She'll cope with the knowledge. She'll have to. And the best part of it is, you shouldn't have to marry her when there's no good reason for her not to marry the duke." She seemed to be holding her breath. "You won't, will you?"

Much as he wanted to make her that promise, he couldn't. His honor was at stake; there was no way for a man to honorably back out of a betrothal. And while he might back out anyway were it only his own reputation on the line, his mother and aunts would also be affected. "Lord Wolverston may still insist—"

"He can take away Amanda's dowry and inheritance, but he cannot make her say 'I will.'" Sounding very sure of herself—well, she *was* Juliana—she finally released her breath. "Amanda won't need Wolverston's money if she's wed to the duke."

"The duke may not agree."

"He wants her. I think he will agree. Let's find him and ask him now." She started down the steps, then stopped and turned back to him. "Oh, drat. We can't." Her newly recovered enthusiasm disappeared, replaced by something closer to panic. "I still have to make thirty-three pieces of baby clothes before tomorrow morning."

"No, you don't." He took her face in both hands and kissed her softly on the lips. "Relax."

"I cannot. Perhaps my sisters and Aunt Frances made three or four items in the past couple of hours, but that still leaves—"

"You don't have to make any more baby clothes, Juliana." Slowly, while she stood there looking puzzled—or maybe transfixed—he skimmed his hands along her neck, across her shoulders, down her arms. Lacing his fingers with hers, he eased her down the steps and next door, stopping on the pavement in front of the large window that fronted number forty-four's drawing room. "Look," he murmured.

On the other side of the glass, Corinna leisurely painted, a dreamy smile on her face. Behind her, Lady Frances stood with her back to the window, gesturing or perhaps explaining something. On the far side of *her*, a dozen young women perched on the drawing room's chairs and sofas, hunched over the needlework in their hands.

Juliana turned to him, a bewildered frown creasing her brow. "Who are they?"

"My former assistants and a few friends they managed to scare up. Some of them may not be able to read and write, but the sort of women who live near the Institute all know how to sew."

She blinked. "How did they get here?"

"When Aunt Aurelia came to assist me today, she had such stories. Poor Lady Juliana is sewing her fingers to

the bone, dear Lady Juliana will never finish in time."
He shrugged. "So I hired them."

"You hired them?"

He nodded. "Before you summoned me to Emily's
house."

"Dear heavens." Her eyes shone with disbelief and
gratitude and something else. Something that made his
heart sing. "Have I told you I love you?" she whispered
through an obviously tight throat.

He squeezed her hand. "Yes, but I'll never tire of
hearing it."

"I hope . . ." She bit her lip. "Thank you. Thank you
from the bottom of my heart." She squeezed his hand
back. "I must go help them now, but—"

"No. Oh, no. You're much too exhausted, and we
have much more important things to do."

"James—"

"Go inside if you must, tell them Emily is all right
and you've been invited to Stafford House for dinner."

"Aunt Frances might be oblivious, but she's not stupid. She knows your mother is still too ill to be inviting guests."

"*I'm* inviting you. We'll go there as soon as we've
talked to Castleton. Your aunt is needed here to super-
vise, and this is no time to fret about proprieties, Juliana.
I'm starving, and my mother is in bed. We shan't even
wake her. Now, go. I'll wait here." He leaned to give
her a soft kiss, wanting so much more but knowing now
was not the time. Her sister was ten feet away—
thankfully absorbed in her artwork—and there was
much that still needed settling. Everything was still up
in the air.

Juliana looked like she might argue for a moment, but
then nodded and went inside. It started raining while he
waited on the doorstep, and when she came back out,
they dashed to his carriage together.

"They've made twenty-one items of baby clothes already," she reported. "With only twelve to go, they
really don't need me." Being Juliana, of course she
already had a plan. "The House of Lords is in session.
You'll have to go in alone to fetch the duke, but then

you should bring him out to the carriage so we can talk to him together.''

James sent an outrider to Stafford House to ask his cook to prepare a meal, and told his driver to head for Parliament.

Unfortunately, Castleton wasn't at Parliament.

He wasn't at his Grosvenor Square town house.

And he wasn't at White's, which was the final place Juliana could think to check.

It was rather disconcerting, really. Everything was still up in the air. They left notes at the last two locations, explaining all they'd learned, along with their conclusions, and requesting that Castleton notify them of his intentions at his earliest convenience. Then they went to Stafford House to wait, because there was nothing else they could do.

Dinner was ready when they arrived, and the table was set for two, one plate at either end of the oval table that seated six. "I'm not hungry," Juliana said.

"You have to eat," James told her, "or you'll fall ill."

He moved the dishes at the far end to the spot around the curve from his. And then they sat. Because there was nothing else to do.

James wasn't actually hungry, either. He'd lost his appetite. Everything was so up in the air. They both picked at their food, alternating between silence and spurts of forced conversation through three courses.

There was nothing else to do.

"Maybe we should go look for the duke again," Juliana suggested when they finished an hour later and James was pouring port.

He set down the bottle. "Where?" he asked, taking a rather large swallow from his glass.

"I'm not sure." She took a generous sip herself. "But there's nothing else to do."

Just then, a red-liveried footman walked in. "My lord." He set a letter on the corner of the table, gave a smart bow, and left. It was a single sheet of heavy, cream-colored paper, folded in thirds and secured with a large red seal.

James and Juliana stared at it for a moment, as though

they were both afraid to touch it. "The stationery is from White's," he finally said, pushing it toward her.

"It's from the duke." Her hand shook as she lifted it. "It has to be."

"Open it."

She turned it over, her eyes green and apprehensive. "It's addressed to you."

Obviously she felt it was his right to read it first, but James suspected she'd snatch it from his hands if he tried. "Open it," he repeated.

She nodded and broke the seal, slowly unfolding the single page. Before she even finished scanning it, she let out a little shriek and launched herself onto his lap, the letter landing on the floor as she wrapped her arms around him and held tight.

So tight he could barely breathe. "What does it say?" he asked, unsure whether her tears indicated happiness or despair. Her only answer was a heartfelt sob. Something tightening painfully in his chest, he leaned awkwardly with her attached to him, picked up the paper, and read it.

Lord Stafford,
  I wish to wed Lady Amanda Wolverston with or without her dowry. No horse will be necessary, either. I would appreciate the assistance of yourself and Lady Juliana in explaining the matter, which I expect Lady Amanda will wish to verify with Lord Neville. To that end, I shall present myself at Cainewood's home at ten o'clock tomorrow morning, unless I hear from you otherwise.
                    Yours sincerely,
                    Castleton

The pain in James's chest eased as he dragged in two lungful of the most delicious air he'd ever breathed. Apparently Castleton wasn't quite the ass he'd thought. Everything was going to work out. After the nightmare of the past week, it seemed a bloody miracle.

"No horse." Juliana sniffled into his shoulder. "He

said that once before. What on earth could he possibly mean?"

He supposed it couldn't hurt to tell her now. "Your brother promised the duke a horse as part of your dowry if he'd marry you."

She raised her head. "You've got to be jesting. A *horse*?"

"I believe Griffin was rather foxed when he made the offer. The particular horse is named Velocity, if I'm not mistaken."

"Idiot."

"Griffin? Or the horse?"

"Griffin, of course. Velocity is a very intelligent horse."

He laughed and gave her a quick kiss. "Do you expect *I* will get Velocity when I marry you?"

"It would serve Griffin right if you insist on it. Although I didn't realize you cared for racehorses."

"I don't, particularly. But the sale of such a fine animal would pay for a lot of vaccinations. I expect Castleton would bid mightily— What?" Juliana had pulled back enough to stare at him, tears streaming down her cheeks again. "What is wrong now?"

"Was that a proposal?"

He blinked. "I suppose so. But it wasn't a very good one, was it?" He rose and set her on the chair, then dropped to one knee. "Ouch."

"Try your good knee," she said with a watery laugh.

He did. Carefully. And then took both her hands in his. "My dear Juliana, my love . . . would you do me the very great honor of becoming my wife?"

"Oh, yes!" She launched herself at him again, with such force he fell back onto the floor, which, thankfully, was carpeted, since he banged his head so hard he saw stars. "I'm sorry," she said, crawling over him. "Are you hurt?"

"Not in the least." His head ached like the dickens, but he didn't care. "Are you?"

"No. I know you hate it when ladies cry, but I just can't seem to help myself."

"It's all right," he assured her, "as long as you're crying from happiness." Watching a fat drop fall from her chin to his neckcloth, he added, "You *are* happy?"

"Oh, yes," she breathed and leaned down to kiss him. *She* kissed *him*. And he wasn't even unbuttoned.

He savored that for a moment, then gathered her close and kissed her back. Her lips first, then both cheeks and her forehead and chin. And then her lips again—

"Lord Stafford? Is everything all right?"

Juliana scrambled up, and James turned his head to the side to see his housekeeper standing over him. "Very much so, Mrs. Hampton, I assure you." He pushed himself to sit and ran a hand through his hair. "We were just, um, going upstairs. Yes, that's it. We're going to drink our port in the Painted Room."

"Very well, my lord. Shall I have something brought to you?"

"Nothing. Nothing at all." He scrambled to his feet rather ungracefully and took both their glasses. "We'll just go up now."

"Should you need anything, do let me know."

"Of course," Mrs. Hampton said. And just stood there.

"We're going up now." Handing Juliana a glass, he gestured with the other in a way he hoped looked suave and above suspicion. "Lady Juliana?"

Chapter Forty-seven

At the top of the elegant staircase, James didn't walk Juliana through the library and into the gorgeous room with the lion head chairs. Instead, he took her the opposite direction.

"Um, James? Isn't the Painted Room the one with all the marriage scenes? The one where I gave you the Richmond Maids of Honour and—" She broke off, thinking this might not be the best time to remind him she'd come to apologize for tricking him. To remind him she'd thought he was in love with her friend and hadn't known he'd once had a wife.

Thankfully, he didn't seem to notice the abrupt, awkward pause. "I thought I'd show you another room. Mine, to be precise. Though it will be *ours* very soon." Stopping by an open door, he gave her a quick kiss, a kiss that left her wanting more. "Close your eyes," he said, "and wait here."

The room beyond was so dark she couldn't see anything anyway. "Why do I have to close my eyes?"

"Just do it," he said. "Humor me, please."

So she did. She closed her eyes and waited. She heard some rustling, a dull thud, and finally a rush that she guessed was a fire coming to life. And then she waited a little longer, listening to him walk around, doing who knew what, until finally he came back to her.

"All right," he said, "You can open your eyes."

So she did. He was waiting on the threshold, the sheer size of him blocking her view. "I cannot see past you," she said.

Appearing to be holding his breath, he nodded and stepped aside. "What do you think?"

Beyond him, the room now glistened with light. On the tables, atop a bureau, on the nightstands, candles flickered. At least a dozen, or maybe more.

"Dear heavens," she breathed, "it's splendid." His bedroom looked nothing like the rest of the house; there was nary a hint of gilt and nothing ancient or ornamental. The furniture was all matched, modern Hepplewhite, the height of fashionable style, carved of light satinwood in lines that were gracefully curved and distinctive. The red and yellow fabrics all looked silky and sumptuous. Even the walls were covered with silk, wide stripes above enameled white wainscoting. Arranged before a white-manteled fireplace—the fireplace he'd lit on this cold, rainy night—were a love seat and two plush chairs, upholstered with narrower stripes.

And then there was the bed. Covered in solid red damask and heaped with plump yellow pillows, it had slender, towering posts and positively dominated the room.

The very sight of it weakened her knees. Just realizing that someday—someday soon—she'd be in that bed with James, made her pulse start pounding, made her skin prickle with sudden, heated awareness.

She sipped some of the port in her glass, hoping the heady sweet wine might calm her. "It's the most beautiful bedroom I've ever seen."

Releasing a tense breath, he bent to press a warm kiss to the top of her head, a kiss so cherishing it made her insides clench. "I'm so glad you like it."

She turned and gazed up at him. "Everything looks brand-new."

"It is. I had it redecorated especially for you. For us. My favorite color is red, and you do like yellow, don't you?"

She sipped again, using her free hand to smooth her yellow skirts. "It's my favorite color." Her head swam with confusion. "But how . . . I mean . . . dear heavens, however did you redecorate it so *fast*?"

"I've known for weeks that I wanted to marry you, Juliana." His low, chocolatey voice seemed to vibrate right through her. "I'm only sorry it took me so long to tell you. We could have avoided so much heartache."

Tears sprang again to her eyes. Honestly, she was turning into a veritable waterworks. "I should have realized," she admitted, swallowing a lump in her throat. "But I was so sure you would never love me. I was so set on marrying the duke and having you marry Amanda in place of Lord Malmsey."

"We both made mistakes, love. But everything's going to be fixed now."

Yes, they had both made mistakes. She wasn't perfect; nobody was. She was human like everyone else, and the past few weeks had proved it.

It was disappointing, in a way, but in another way she knew it had always been inevitable. And she was so, so thankful that everything was turning out all right. "Oh, James, I don't think I've ever, ever been so happy." Her heart was swelling so much she feared it might burst. "I can hardly wait to climb into that bed with you."

"Oh, my love." Putting the arm that held his wineglass around her, he pulled her close and cupped her chin in his free hand. And then he kissed her, his mouth hot, his tongue plunging deep. Her senses spun, and she knew it had nothing to do with the wine.

But the caress was over all too quickly.

He drew away, a captivating smile curving his lips. "I was hoping you'd say that." He grabbed her free hand and started pulling her into the room.

"What?" He couldn't mean to climb into the bed with her here and now. "Your mother is in the house!"

"Yes, and she's ill and no doubt sleeping soundly, and her bedroom is way down the hall." When she planted her feet and stopped going with him, he reversed direction and tugged her back into the corridor. "See? That very last door. There's not a chance in hell she'll hear us, Juliana. No matter how loud I make you moan."

She blushed furiously, wondering if he'd ever made her moan before. Honestly, she couldn't remember, but she wouldn't be surprised. For all she knew, she could have been moaning thirty seconds ago. That kiss had certainly stolen her breath. If there was one thing James was proficient at, it was making her lose her head.

And it *was* a very long corridor, she conceded silently as she sipped more port. She'd noticed a door inside James's bedroom, which probably led to a sitting room or a dressing room. Or both. Doubtless his study was on the other side of those, and then his mother's dressing room before her bedroom, and maybe a sitting room for her besides. And perhaps some guest rooms in between. Stafford House was enormous.

But all of that was beside the point. "We cannot go to bed with your mother sleeping down the hall. Not before we're married. It's not the thing, James—it's highly improper."

"You've never worried about being improper before. As you pointed out to Aunt Aurelia only two days ago, we've been in private together more than once." His voice went even deeper, more seductive. "At Vauxhall, and the Panorama, and the Physic Garden . . ."

She blushed again, remembering all those times. Remembering the greenhouse in Chelsea especially. Remembering all those feelings he'd aroused in her. "But we weren't in a bed." She gulped more port.

"Do you really think a bed makes a difference, my love?" He eased her back into the room and shut the door behind them. "I've kissed you before without a bed." Edging her toward a table, he took her wineglass and set them both down. "If you'd prefer, I will kiss you right now without climbing into the bed. All right?"

And he did. He drew her against his hard, muscled form, and he kissed her, a kiss invitingly warm and deep. A kiss persuasive and divine. He tasted of lust and sweet wine and James, which made her senses begin whirling in an oh-so-familiar way. Slowly, very slowly, he inched her toward the bed, and she moved with him, her arms going up and around him, her fingers plowing into his unruly hair. His hands wandered her back and worked their way down to her bottom, still moving her, pressing her closer, so close she felt the proof of his desire straining against her. It made answering emotions rush through her, made heat pool in that place between her legs that ached whenever he touched her.

And all the while, he kept inching them toward the bed.

Before she knew it, they were *on* the bed.

"It's only a bed," he murmured. "It really doesn't make a difference." And it didn't, not really. She knew that. "It's more comfortable here," he whispered, a whisper so raspy it made her melt.

It *was* more comfortable. There had to be a feather bed under the covers, because she sank right into it. He rolled closer, rolled over her, until his body covered hers, pressing her farther into the plush, sensual mattress. It cradled her, cocooned her, and still he kept kissing her. He felt warm on top of her, and heavy, but not too heavy; he had to be supporting himself somehow, because he was just heavy enough to feel deliciously exciting. And she wanted him to kiss her forever. She knew she shouldn't allow him to do anything else, but just the feel of his mouth on hers was enough to satisfy her every desire.

But then he abandoned her mouth to kiss her throat, finding an especially sensitive hollow. She moaned . . . oh, yes, he could make her moan. Thank heavens his mother was so far down the hall, because James was so excessively proficient at making her lose her head, there was no way on earth she could help herself. She moaned again, and her breath came faster, and she wanted him to kiss her there forever.

And then he kissed the wide expanse of skin framed by her low neckline, fluttery little kisses that went everywhere, and she wanted him to kiss her there forever. And he kissed the tops of her breasts, and she wanted him to kiss her *there* forever.

And then he worked a hand beneath her body, just long enough to unfasten a few buttons. And drew her bodice and chemise down, exposing her breasts. He paused, his chocolate eyes going hazy with hunger. "Do you want me to kiss you here?" he asked in that raspy, heartrending whisper.

Her breasts tingled, and he hadn't even touched them

yet. They tingled, and he was just looking. Their tips
were puckering and making her squirm. "Oh, yes," she
breathed, and he kissed her there. One breast and then
the other. And then back to the first, and his mouth
opened, drawing her in, and the sensation was hot and
so exciting that the aching place between her legs began
to pulse. And suddenly, remembering how he'd made
her feel when he touched her there that one time, it
wasn't enough to satisfy her desire.

She wanted more.

"Oh, James," she breathed, "kiss me more."

He lifted his head, his warm breath wafting over her
bare skin. "Should I kiss you here?" he asked, indicating
her other breast.

"Oh, yes."

He did, and it felt even better, more amazing. Her
blood was rushing, and her breath was coming in little
panting bursts. Wanting to give him the same pleasure,
she touched him everywhere she could reach. His
springy, curly hair, the curve of his head underneath, the
roughness on his cheeks. His hard, sculpted shoulders.
The smooth, muscled expanse of his back.

He felt wonderful, marvelous, but she couldn't reach
any lower. Her arms simply weren't long enough.
"More," she whispered. "Kiss me more." Thinking he
would return to her mouth, thinking he would move up
so her hands could reach farther down, she breathed,
"More. Kiss me more."

But he moved down instead of up. He kissed her
through her thin yellow dress, down her middle and
across her belly. And a hand went lower still, pulling off
her slippers. And stealing beneath her skirts.

And skimming up her legs. And untying her garters
and rolling her stockings down and off, a slippery, tingly
slide of silk. And then his fingers danced up her calves,
and over her knees, and around and behind them, teasing a ticklish place on the back. And higher, between
her thighs, spreading her legs a little.

The place between them ached so badly and pulsed
so persistently, she thought she might go out of her
mind. But she knew she shouldn't let him touch her

there again, not until they were married. She couldn't ask him to touch her. "More, James," she whispered instead. "Kiss me more."

And he did. He drew up her skirts, and he kissed her knees, swirling his tongue in tantalizing strokes. And he drew her skirts higher and kissed her thighs, all over and between them, little kisses that were melting her, melting her heart, melting her resolve. And then he drew her skirts higher still, higher and higher, until they were pooled around her middle. Without lifting his head, while he was still kissing her, he bared her all the way up to her waist.

She knew she should stop him, but she was moaning, and she couldn't seem to help herself. She knew she was wanton, but she didn't care. And then he lifted his head and looked at her, used his hands to ease her legs wider and looked at her *there* . . . and she knew it was wicked.

But she'd never experienced anything better or more exciting. Ever.

"Should I kiss you here?" he rasped.

She'd never heard of such a thing. Never even imagined it. But she wanted him to kiss her there more than she'd wanted anything in her life.

That place wasn't just pulsing now, it was *throbbing*.

"Should I?" he asked, and his hot breath made it throb more. "Should I kiss you here?"

She couldn't bring herself to say yes. She couldn't bring herself to agree to something so wicked. Even though she wanted him to kiss her there so badly that tears pricked behind her eyes.

He lowered his head, but he still didn't kiss her. His hair had flopped over his forehead, those dear, unruly curls, and she couldn't see his eyes. But she knew he was looking, and that knowledge made the throbbing mount unbearably.

"Should I?" he whispered, and his breath was hotter than ever, so hot it made her hips lift right off the bed.

"Yes!" she cried. "Oh, yes!" And he kissed her there. He kissed her there over and over and over, his tongue finding that sweet spot that made her throb even more. It felt hot, slippery hot, little slippery hot strokes. She wanted to touch him more than ever, but she couldn't reach him anywhere, so her fingers curled into the damask beneath her instead. And he stroked and stroked until that slippery heat sent her flying into oblivion.

She had never, ever felt anything like it in her life. Not even in the greenhouse. She moaned. She moaned until James crawled up her body and captured the moans in his hot, talented mouth.

She thought she might calm then, like last time, but the opposite was true. His kisses were devouring her, making the ache build all over again. She tasted not only James now, not only lust and wine and James, but also the faintest hint of herself. A combination that proved the most delicious, most incredible, most arousing flavor ever.

It wasn't enough. She wanted that flavor forever, she wanted him to kiss her forever, but it wasn't enough.

And then he lifted his head and looked at her for a moment. Just looked at her. And kissed her again and lifted his head again and just looked at her again.

The expression in his eyes, the devotion and the love, was almost more than she could stand.

"Can I come inside you?" he whispered in that raspy, heartbreaking tone. "I swear, Juliana, I want you more than I want to breathe. More than I want my own life. Can I come inside you?"

She moaned again, but it was a silent moan, only a moan in her head. Why couldn't he just take her? Why did he always have to ask? Why did he make it her decision as much as his, make it so she couldn't claim he'd ever taken advantage, not even to herself?

Why, why, *why*?

But she knew why. It was because he was honorable. Because he was the best man she'd ever known. Because he was everything she'd ever wanted all along, even before she'd known herself enough to know it.

She loved him. She loved him more than she'd known it was possible to love another human being. And he was waiting. He was still waiting for her to answer. Waiting to hear she wanted him just as much as he wanted her. Patiently waiting, his heart in his chocolate brown eyes.

How could she deny him? How could she deny herself?

They'd be married soon anyway, and if anyone deserved to hear the words he was waiting for, if anyone deserved to know she wanted him with all of her heart, it was James.

She drew in a breath. And, "Yes," she whispered. "Yes, please. Please make me yours."

He froze. He didn't move; he didn't even breathe. "Are you sure, love?"

Why did he have to ask?

But she knew why. "I'm sure. I want you more than I want my life."

He didn't ask her again. He rolled off her, leaving her wanting, but only to rip off his cravat and tailcoat and waistcoat. And unbutton his shirt. And pull it off over his head. And then, while she drank in the mouthwatering sight of his firm, bare torso, his fingers went to the buttons on his falls, and she realized, somewhere in her hazy, love-drenched mind, that all this time he hadn't even unbuttoned. He'd kissed her and caressed her and sent her to oblivion without even unbuttoning.

He unbuttoned now, and before she knew it, he was naked. Dear heavens, he was magnificent. She wanted him even more, much more than she'd thought possible. He fell on her then, and took her mouth with his, and she could hardly wait to have him inside her. He kissed her, and kissed her, and—

"James? Are you home?"

It was his mother, out in the corridor.

"James, is that you?"

"Bloody hell," he gritted out and leapt off of her. Muttering obscenities the likes of which she'd never heard, he stalked to the new Hepplewhite wardrobe and slammed the door open. And yanked out a red silk dressing gown. And shrugged into it so violently she feared he might rip it.

"James?" His mother knocked on the door.

"I'm coming, Mother."

Juliana had enjoyed seeing him without the dressing gown much more than with it. Looking furious, he tied the belt and tied it again, and knotted it with a jerk, and went to the door and opened it just enough to slip through—so his mother wouldn't see her inside, thank heavens—and shut it behind him.

And then Juliana lay there on the red damask, shaking, listening to their conversation.

"Oh, James, I thought I heard you. How are you feeling, dear?"

"Tired. I was sleeping."

"Poor dear." There was a pause, during which Juliana imagined Lady Stafford ruffling James's hair, even though he was much too old to have his hair ruffled. "I'm so sorry about everything that's happened. I so wanted you to marry Juliana."

"I know." She heard James sigh. "It may still happen."

"What do you mean?" Lady Stafford sounded very excited. "What do you mean, it may still happen?"

"I'm very tired, Mother, and I don't want to explain it now. Can we talk about this in the morning? How are *you* feeling?"

"Better. Much better. I think I'll be able to attend your wedding tomorrow."

"I'm hoping there won't *be* a wedding." His voice was getting fainter. "Let me take you back to bed, Mother. We'll talk in the morning."

"I really don't want to wait until morning to hear this, James," Juliana heard very faintly.

And then she heard nothing. He must have been walking his mother back to bed. It took him a very long time to return, and at first Juliana figured that was because it was a very long corridor, but when he took even longer, she figured he was probably explaining everything to his mother. Lady Stafford was rather persistent, after all. Most mothers were. Juliana figured she'd probably be a rather persistent mother herself. If she ever got to *be* a mother.

Dear heavens, what if everything didn't work out?

James hurried back into the room and shut the door behind him. His fingers went to the knot in his belt.

She sat up on the edge of the bed, pushing her skirts down and pulling her bodice back up. "What are you doing?"

"Getting out of this damned dressing gown." He seemed to be having trouble. Apparently he'd knotted the belt too tightly when he'd jerked it. "Getting back to what we were doing."

"We cannot do it, James."

"What?" He looked up, his fingers still working the knot. Or rather, not working it. It didn't look like it was going to budge. "Whyever would you say that? I realize you've probably cooled off some while I was talking to my mother, but I'll soon have you warm again, sweetheart. I'll have you moaning in no time—"

"What if everything doesn't work out?"

"What do you mean, what if everything doesn't work out?"

"I heard you, James. I heard you tell your mother it *may* still happen. I heard you tell her you're *hoping* there won't be a wedding."

His fingers slipped on the knot, but then he bent his head and resumed fighting with it. "I was just trying to get her back to bed. I didn't want to stop and explain everything. I didn't want to have a *discussion*. I wanted to get back to you."

"We cannot go back to doing that, James. What if everything doesn't work out? We cannot make love if you're going to marry Amanda."

He stopped working the knot and looked at her. "I'm not going to marry Lady Amanda. You read Castleton's note. Everyone is in agreement."

"Her father isn't."

"He isn't even her father!"

"That doesn't signify. He's legally her guardian. He might have another objection."

James plopped to sit on the bed beside her. "What could he possibly come up with now? Who could he possibly claim slept with whom in order to make Lady Amanda and Castleton's marriage impossible?"

"I don't know. All I know is we all thought he couldn't possibly have a valid objection before, and it turned out he did. So he could have another objection. Or someone else could have an objection. We don't know, James." She rubbed his back through the red silk, thinking he felt very tense and looked very frustrated.

Well, she was frustrated, too, but that didn't change anything. "We're going to have to wait. It won't kill us. It won't be long."

"Damn right it won't be long. As soon as we straighten everything out, we'll be wed tomorrow. I was planning to get married tomorrow, anyway."

Despite her frustration, despite everything, she couldn't stop a soft laugh from escaping her throat. "Don't be ridiculous. We cannot get married tomorrow."

"Why not? It was ridiculously simple to get the special license to wed Lady Amanda—all it took was money. I can get another license with your name on it tomorrow with no trouble."

"We need more than a license, James. I need a wedding dress. And we have to deal with the whole mess regarding Amanda's parentage tomorrow, and I have to deliver the baby clothes. The Governors are expecting me at the Foundling Hospital tomorrow afternoon, with two hundred and forty items."

Thank heavens they were finished. The women James had hired had only needed to make twelve more. Everything was going to work out. She hoped.

"All right," he said dourly. "We'll get married the Saturday after that. Can I kiss you now?"

"Yes, you can kiss me. And then we need to go let Amanda know what is happening."

He kissed her and he kissed her again, and all the while, all the time she had her arms around his neck and was kissing him, she was crossing her fingers and hoping everything would work out.

Chapter Forty-eight

And so it was that James arrived at Lady Amanda's house on the day Lord Wolverston had commanded, but a full twelve hours before the man expected him. Also not according to plan, he didn't arrive by the front door.

"I think her bedroom is right there," Juliana whispered, peering up from the back garden. "That window with the pale blue drapes."

It was on the second floor. James eyed the wall, which was plain stucco with no footholds in sight. He bent down to gather some pebbles.

"What are you doing?"

"Getting Lady Amanda's attention." He tossed one, and the little *clink* sounded like it carried for miles.

She winced. "You're going to wake someone."

"Mmm-hmm. That's the whole idea." *Clink.*

"I thought you would scale the building."

Clink. "Sorry to disappoint you"—*clink*—"but you're marrying a physician, not a sportsman." *Clink, clink.* "I already have one bad knee."

"I'm marrying a physician," Juliana echoed as though she couldn't quite believe it.

James also thought it was too wonderful to quite believe. Especially since several people involved didn't even know it yet. Especially because someone might make an objection. That was the reason she'd insisted they couldn't make love, and she'd been right to insist.

But he still loved hearing those words from her mouth.

"James."

"Hmm?" *Clink.*

Before he could toss another pebble, she caught his hand. "I love you."

He turned and smiled down at her. The rain had stopped, and the sky had cleared, and the low light of the full moon gleamed off all her beautiful, straight hair that had slipped from its pins while they were in his bed. Her hair that was a million different colors of blond and brown. She reached her free hand to touch his cheek—he imagined she was feeling the slight roughness—and as he bent his head, she sucked in a breath of anticipation—

"Whatever is happening out there? Lord Stafford?" Lady Amanda had opened her window. "Whatever are you doing with Lady Juliana?" She didn't sound very approving.

James and Juliana jerked apart. "We came to wake you," he said.

They quickly explained their discovery, while Lady Amanda's eyes got wider and wider. At the end, Juliana sighed sympathetically. "I do hope you're not terribly distressed to learn you're . . . well . . . ."

"A by-blow?" Lady Amanda supplied shakily. "I shouldn't be, should I? After all, the man I love is a by-blow, too."

"Dear heavens," Juliana exclaimed with a soft laugh. "You've surely had a change of heart. Meet us at my house at ten o'clock. The duke will be waiting, and we'll all go next door to Lord Neville and verify the truth."

"My father will never let me out of the house at ten. He's expecting me to marry at noon."

"He's not your father," Juliana reminded her. "You have no obligation to obey him. I'm sure you can find a way out."

"I cannot—"

"Tell Lord Wolverston you're dressing for the wedding," she said out loud, and then softly under her breath, "Honestly, do I have to plan everything?" She sighed and raised her voice again. "I'll make sure there's a ladder from your window down to here. I'll have one of Griffin's footmen deliver it."

"I cannot climb through a window!"

"Then use the servants' exit. Either way, I'll expect you at my house at ten o'clock."

Muttering, Lady Amanda shut the window, and Juliana turned and looked at James for a moment. She raised her hands and placed them on his shoulders. "I was going to kiss you before Amanda opened the window," she said softly.

Actually, he'd been going to kiss *her*, but he didn't think it would be a good idea to argue. Especially when she was looking at him like that, with her eyes so very blue. Even with only the moonlight, he could tell they were blue.

"Can I kiss you now?" she asked.

"Yes," he said, and Juliana kissed him. After all the weeks he'd spent trying to tempt her into letting him kiss her, she kissed him. She kissed him as they walked back to the street, stumbling and kissing along the side of the house. And as they walked down the street, ignoring a carriage that rumbled by. And when they got to her doorstep, she still kept kissing him.

Finally, James pulled back with a low laugh. "You're wearing me out."

She pulled his head down and kissed him again, a joyous, quick kiss.

"I'm never going to last until next Saturday," he said. "I need macaroons for extra stamina."

"Oh," she said with a sigh, and then, "You know what, James? I don't want there to be any more secrets between us."

"I agree," he said. "No secrets, and no lies."

"I *never* lie," she said, sounding a little defensive. "Well, I did lie to that dratted doctor, but I never lie unless it's absolutely unavoidable. I don't want any lies, either, and no half-truths." She drew a deep breath. "The macaroons don't really lend a man stamina," she confessed in a rush.

"Oh, really?" He snickered.

"Did you snicker at me? Me, the woman you want to marry?"

Well, maybe he had, but only because he found her little superstitions so amusing. He wasn't superstitious at all, and he couldn't quite believe anyone would think macaroons could lend a man stamina. Or do anything else, either, other than taste delicious. But he hadn't snickered in a nasty way; he'd only snickered because he loved her, and he loved all her little quirks, especially this one. "I didn't snicker," he said, although that meant he was already telling her a half-truth.

He'd been married before, so he knew some half-truths were necessary to sustain a harmonious relationship. But he wouldn't tell her a half-truth unless it was absolutely unavoidable.

"All right," she said, and then, in a lower tone, "I actually baked them to make you amorous."

"Oh, really?" he repeated, but he didn't snicker. He was actually feeling quite amorous at the moment, even without her macaroons, which made sense because there was no way macaroons could make a man amorous, either. But he loved that she thought they did. "You're a treasure, Juliana," he told her, hoping she'd bake him macaroons many, many times in the years to come. Hoping very hard.

And then he kissed her again and left, and went home and spent all night with his fingers crossed, even though he wasn't superstitious.

Chapter Forty-nine

In the end, Amanda was the one who objected.

Shaking like a leaf, she arrived at Juliana's house at quarter past ten. "What took you so long?" Juliana asked. "You were supposed to be here at ten. You only live down the street."

"It was this dress." She brushed at huge, voluminous white skirts that were at least twenty years out of fashion. Dear heavens, they were so wide there had to be hoops under them. "Have you ever tried to climb down a ladder in a dress this big?"

"Why are you wearing it?"

Amanda looked at her like she'd lost her mind. "It's my grandmother's wedding dress. It's a tradition in my family to wear it."

Fifty years out of fashion, then. The skirts were actually somewhat yellowed, not pure white. "You're not getting married today, Amanda. That's the whole point of going to talk to Lord Neville."

"After I told my father I was getting dressed for my wedding, I couldn't very well not do that, could I?" She looked to the duke. "Besides, we're getting married today, are we not?"

"Not today," the duke said stiffly. "A ducal wedding generally requires some months of preparation."

"If you love a woman," James said disparagingly, "I should think you'd want to marry her as soon as possible."

Juliana thought she heard him mutter "what an ass" under his breath, but surely he wouldn't say that. Not about a duke. And she worried for a moment that the duke would blurt out that he didn't actually love Amanda, but only held her in some affection, which could ruin everything.

But thankfully that didn't happen. They all walked next door to Lord Neville's house, and James banged the knocker.

The gaunt butler answered. "Yes?"

"We've come to call on Lord Neville," Juliana said.

The old fellow's eyes widened when he spotted Amanda in a wedding dress that his own bride could have worn fifty years ago, assuming he'd ever married, which he probably hadn't since most people required their butlers to remain bachelors. But he was a mannerly sort of butler, so he didn't say anything. About that, anyway. "Wait in the drawing room, if you please," he said instead, "and I shall see if Lord Neville is at home."

Viscount Neville was at home, of course. He spent his evenings with various mistresses or at his club, which meant he was never out and about very early. In fact, he came downstairs looking a bit rumpled, as though perhaps his valet had needed to drag him out of bed.

Juliana could see right off that he was Amanda's father. Amanda fit in age between Emily's two brothers, the one who was married and the other one who was away at Cambridge most of the year. Lord Neville was blond and gray-eyed like both his daughters, and tall like both his daughters, too. And as he seemed to overindulge in everything, Juliana wasn't surprised to learn that he'd slept with Amanda's mother.

Or at least not as surprised as she'd have been a few weeks ago. It seemed she lived on a very promiscuous street. Besides Lord Neville sleeping with Amanda's mother, Lord Wolverston had slept with the late Duchess of Castleton when she'd lived in Juliana's house.

It was a good thing she and James would be living in

St. James's Place, not Berkeley Square. Assuming everything worked out, that was. She really couldn't wait any
longer to find out.

No one was saying anything, and, in fact, Viscount
Neville seemed a little mystified to find all these people
in his house. He seemed especially fascinated by
Amanda in her ancient wedding dress. Juliana was dying
to resolve everything, so she figured she might as well
just spit it out. "Lord Neville, are you Lady Amanda's
father? She has a fleur-de-lis birthmark in the same place
as you and Emily."

Amanda gasped and blushed wildly, and Juliana was
sorry to embarrass her, because she knew Amanda considered that private. But she figured it was better to
come out and say it than to wait and have Lord Neville
ask to see it, which would have been even more embarrassing for Amanda.

"I've been wondering about that," Lord Neville said
slowly, "for twenty-three years. Please, let me
explain."

Lord Neville had been between wives when Amanda
was conceived. He'd been very much in love with Lady
Amanda's mother, but Lord Wolverston had refused her
the divorce she wanted. Unfortunately, it was impossible
for a woman to divorce a man, although a man could
divorce his wife if she'd been unfaithful. Lord Neville
and Lady Wolverston weren't precisely sure that the
child she was carrying was the viscount's, so they'd been
planning to wait to see if the baby had the Neville birthmark, and if that proved to be true, they'd planned to
use it as leverage to pressure the earl for the divorce.
Lord Wolverston wasn't the sort of man who would have
wanted word out on the street that he'd been cuckolded,
especially if they'd had the proof to show all of society.
His honor meant everything to him. He put his reputation before everyone else's happiness.

"Well, *that's* certainly the truth," Juliana muttered.

"I'm so sorry, my dear," Lord Neville said to
Amanda. Her face had gone rather white, and she was
looking at him. Just looking at him. He started walking
toward her. "I was terribly distressed when your mother

died giving birth and Lord Wolverston refused to let me even see you. He wasn't a very nice man."

"He still isn't," Juliana said.

"I never knew for sure whether you were my daughter," Lord Neville continued, still walking toward Amanda, who was still just looking at him. "I hoped you were, but there was no way to find out. As you grew, I would see you sometimes, and I thought more than once about asking you if you had the birthmark. But you seemed a very reserved young lady, and I feared such a question would shock you clear down to your toes."

"It would have," Juliana said.

Lord Neville was standing right in front of Amanda now. "I also feared Lord Wolverston might treat you harshly, suspecting you might not actually be his daughter—"

"He did," Juliana interrupted.

Lord Neville hung his head. "I'm so sorry."

Amanda suddenly came to life. She was a very reserved woman, so she didn't jump into Lord Neville's arms like Juliana might have done, but she finally opened her mouth.

"Don't be sorry," she said. "I understand. And I'm so glad you're my father instead of Lord Wolverston."

Lord Neville did gather her into his arms, then, embracing her tightly. Amanda's arms went around him, too, but they stayed rather loose.

"I'm glad that is settled," the duke said stiffly. "Now we can start planning our wedding for next summer."

And *that's* when Amanda objected.

She released Lord Neville—heaven forbid she should stay too close to a man, even a man she'd just discovered was her father—and turned to the duke. "I object to that plan," she said, and then she added disparagingly, "If you love me, I should think you'd want to marry me as soon as possible."

Once again, Juliana feared the duke might blurt out that he didn't precisely love Amanda, which could ruin everything. But he didn't. Instead he stood there with his mouth open, just looking at her.

Amanda lifted her chin. "I'm wearing my grandmother's wedding dress. I think we should elope right now to Gretna Green."

"That wouldn't be very ducal," he finally said, "and, in fact, it would be highly improper."

Amanda raised her chin higher. "I don't care," she said, "I am tired of being proper. I want to marry you now."

And then she gave him *the look*. She glanced down, bowing her head a little to display her lashes against her cheeks. Then she swept her eyelids up, gazed at the duke full on again, and slowly—very slowly—curved her lips in a seductive smile.

The duke didn't fall at her feet. But he did sigh and say, "Very well, then."

Juliana was shocked. Positively shocked. When *she'd* tried that on the duke, he hadn't reacted at all.

Obviously she'd been right that he and Amanda were ideal for each other. The duke *needed* Amanda. With Amanda in his life, he might learn to be affectionate and manage to sire a child inside of a decade.

James's arm stole around Juliana's waist, in front of everyone. He pulled her against his side, where she fit perfectly. "Everything worked out," he said in that low, chocolatey voice that made a shiver run through her.

Everything probably had worked out, but it was too wonderful to quite believe. Especially because someone still might make an objection. "What about Lord Wolverston?" she asked Amanda, crossing her fingers. "He still might have an objection."

"He's not my father," Amanda reminded her, flashing a smile at Lord Neville. "I have no obligation to obey him. And I couldn't care a fig about my inheritance. David is all I need."

It was too bad Amanda didn't *want* the duke instead of needing him, Juliana thought. But neither of them possessed enough emotion for anything that strong. And with her help, Amanda was changing. Perhaps she wasn't quite a swan yet, but she was far from being an ugly duckling.

She uncrossed her fingers, thinking she was so, so thankful that everything had turned out all right. "Oh, James, I'm sure I've never, ever been so happy," she breathed, turning to him and throwing her arms around him. And then, her heart swelling so much she feared it might burst, she kissed him in front of everyone.

It was a divine sensation. He tasted of love and lust and James, which made her senses begin whirling in an oh-so-familiar way.

"Ahem."

The caress was over all too quickly. She broke apart from James to find the duke staring at them, looking very disapproving. Unlike Amanda, he hadn't changed much. But after all, it had taken an entire childhood of cold treatment to turn him into the man he was today. She shouldn't be surprised if it took more than a few years with Amanda to counteract that.

And Juliana *had* changed. She'd learned a lesson. And she had a declaration.

"I'm never going to meddle again," she said.

James snickered, and everyone else laughed.

"Thank you very much," one of the Foundling Hospital's Governors said in the Committee Room that afternoon. "Our next reception day is the second Saturday in August."

"The tenth?" Juliana asked.

"Yes," another Governor confirmed. "We very much appreciate you donating the baby clothes, my dear."

James held his tongue until they were outside in the Hospital's courtyard. But he couldn't contain himself any longer than that. "I cannot believe you committed to making more baby clothes! You're exhausted and overwhelmed!"

"How can I deny these poor children anything I'm able to give?" Juliana gestured to all the girls exercising in their matching uniforms. "If, due to my donation, only one more baby can be accommodated, only one more mother restored to work and a life of virtue, it will be so worth it." Apparently seeing he was not convinced, she moved closer and reached up to put her hands on his shoulders. She smelled of sunshine and flowers. "I know what I'm in for this time," she said. "I can pace myself better. Last time I started with only one party a week, but now I know—"

"You're not having any more sewing parties," he interrupted. "I will hire people to make the baby clothes."

"Much as I love you for doing that yesterday, this shouldn't be your responsibility. You have enough trouble finding people to hire for the Institute."

"You solved that problem for me, and I won't have any trouble hiring seamstresses. My former assistants all owe me favors."

"I should say so. You gave them fifty pounds each! Do you realize that's enough to cover a small family's expenses for two years? You're too nice, James. You're too generous."

He could never be too nice or too generous to her. She deserved everything he could give her and more. Quirks and all, there couldn't be a more wonderful woman in all of London—nay, in all of the world—than Juliana.

She was a treasure. She was exactly what he'd needed to make his life complete. He didn't know how he was going to wait until next Saturday.

"None of those former assistants will have to give their babies to the Foundling Hospital," he reminded her. "But they cannot really work, either; no one will allow them to bring their children to a place of employment. Yet they can sew the baby clothes at home, and I'm sure they can use the extra income even with my fifty pounds."

"But you need to save your money to pay for smallpox vaccinations."

"Oh, my precious Juliana." Was there another woman anywhere as concerned for everyone else? "I don't have enough money to rid the world of smallpox by myself, but I can do my part here in London and still afford to pay a few seamstresses. And buy you beautiful dresses and anything else you ever want. I'm not a pauper, you know."

"I know. You set your table with gold spoons."

"They're sterling plated in gold," he informed her.

"I figured that out." She sighed. "Are you sure you don't want me to make baby clothes?"

She wasn't particularly good at it, and there wasn't another lady of the *ton* who wanted to do anything more with a needle than embroider and make samplers. But then, no other aristocratic ladies he knew set foot in the kitchen, either. Juliana was different, and that was why he loved her.

He smiled down at her, loving her more than he'd ever thought possible, wanting her more than he wanted his own life. The next seven days were going to be hell.

Sheer, utter, excruciating hell.

"Of course I want you to make baby clothes," he told her. "For *our* babies."

And he watched her eyes turn blue before he kissed her.

Chapter Fifty

Saturday, August 10
Cainewood Castle

When Juliana had dreamed of walking down the aisle with the duke, she'd never pictured Amanda on the man's arm. But here in her family's ancient chapel, as a newlywed bride walking down the aisle on her way out, she glanced behind her at the two of them and realized her wedding picture was perfect.

Even with a snake accompanying the flower girl.

Everything had worked out. Emily had never come down with smallpox, and the Lambourne girls had recovered. Since Amanda and the duke had returned from Gretna Green, Juliana had sometimes seen them holding hands, and she was beginning to think they might make a child within a year. And miracle of miracles, Aunt Frances and Lord Malmsey had *already* started a child. Juliana had returned from delivering the baby clothes to find the two of them waiting in the drawing room with a minister and a special license. Two weeks later, Frances had missed her monthly.

Everyone was happy.

Except for James.

She could feel the tension in his arm, and, gazing up at him as they walked, she feared he was gritting his teeth. He'd been so frustrated when Frances, his aunts, and his mother had all insisted on having a full month to plan this wedding, and even more frustrated to find that the preparations had proved so consuming—and all the older women in his life suddenly so vigilant—that the two of them had found it impossible to steal even a moment of private time.

Well, she'd been frustrated, too, of course. But after all, she planned on marrying only once. She'd needed a wedding dress, and she'd wanted everything to be perfect. And although she knew James was so proficient at making her lose her head that she'd have been moaning and giving in had he managed to get her alone for thirty seconds, she'd suspected that waiting until they were married would make it that much more special.

Besides, it would have been highly improper. True, she wasn't reserved, but she did try her best to do what was right. She wasn't a rebel like Corinna. Kissing before marriage was one thing, making love quite another.

Still and all, waiting had been terribly difficult, and she'd found herself relieved a couple of weeks ago when Parliament adjourned, meaning the Season ended and everyone dispersed to their estates in the countryside. James had stayed in London to help his mother move to his aunts' house, and the four of them had arrived here only last night.

The hours since then had proved to be sheer, utter, excruciating hell for them both.

As they emerged from the chapel into Cainewood's quadrangle, James ran his hand down all the little covered buttons on the back of her beautiful white wedding dress. "There. We're married. Can I make love to you now?"

Despite her frustration, she laughed. "We cannot leave our guests two minutes after the ceremony, James."

There hadn't been time to plan a huge society wedding—it would have taken much longer than a month for that—but everyone she cared about was here. Her gaze skimmed the clipped green lawn that sat in the middle of the castle's towering four stories of living quarters. There, in the shadows of the crenelated walls, stood her sisters. Corinna's eyes shone with something like wonder as she laid a hand on Alexandra's blue-silk-covered middle, which was protruding a little bit now. Beside them, Tristan beamed at his wife.

People Juliana had grown up with were scattered over the grounds, a contingent from Berkeley Square by the tumbledown keep, a few countryside neighbors walking the battlements. James's friends and associates were here, too. Claire and Elizabeth were sharing a confidence, their dark heads gleaming in the setting sun. Juliana's tall, handsome cousin Noah was chatting with James's aunts.

There was Lady Stafford—finally her mother-in-law—leaning much closer to Lord Cavanaugh than was strictly proper. There were the duke and Amanda, holding hands again and talking to Lord Neville and Emily. There was Lady Mabel, who wasn't wheezing out here in the countryside. There, standing in the untamed, ankle-high vegetation way over in the old tilting yard, were Lord Malmsey and Aunt Frances—

"James? May I borrow your quizzing glass?"

Dressed formally as he was, he had it in a pocket instead of hanging from a chain around his neck. When he pulled it out and handed it to her, she raised it to her left eye.

"Aunt Frances is wearing her spectacles!"

"Lord Malmsey doesn't seem to mind," James observed as they watched the older couple steal a kiss. "They do say love is blind."

"Who says it?" she asked, handing him back the quizzing glass. "Please don't tell me it's a Roman proverb."

His low laugh vibrated right through her. "I believe I heard it at the theater. *Romeo and Juliet*, if I'm not mistaken. I'm not all that bookish, you know. I mostly prefer newspapers and novels."

So did she. And she loved the theater. They *did* have common interests. With a happy sigh, she scanned all their guests again, noticing Rachael standing off by herself, watching Griffin mount the steps to the great hall.

"It's been at least five minutes," James murmured close by her ear. "Can I make love to you now?"

"No," she said with another laugh. "I need to mingle with our guests."

With a finger on her chin, he turned her to face him. She smelled soap and starch and James, and her heart squeezed in her chest. Suddenly, she felt breathless.

"I'll give you an hour," he warned softly against her lips. "But not a minute more." Then he quickly kissed her and sent her off.

Griffin scanned the great hall one final time, pleased with what he saw. The chamber hadn't looked this good since the ball he'd thrown last year in hopes of finding Alexandra a husband.

The enormous Gobelin tapestries on either end of the hall had been cleaned and rehung, their vibrant colors defying their age. Beneath the old hammerbeam roof, the ancient planked floor gleamed with polish. Servants were busy lighting the torches mounted between each of the arched stained-glass windows, and soon the huge chamber would be ablaze with light. Up in the minstrel's gallery, the musicians were tuning their instruments. In a matter of minutes, the hall would be filled with music and dancing, laughter and glittering guests. He hoped it would be a night Juliana would remember forever. There was nothing he wanted more than to see his sisters happy.

Thank God he had only one more left to marry off.

"Griffin," he heard nearby. A low, sultry voice.

He turned to see its owner, finding her standing there in a red dress that clung to her seductive curves. Most of her hair was done up in a sophisticated style, leaving just a few loose chestnut tendrils to fall in soft waves around her face. A come-hither scent wafted from her skin, making him take an uneasy step back.

Since she'd dismissed his offer last month, he hadn't seen her. Juliana hadn't hostessed any more sewing parties, and he hadn't attended any more balls. He'd been wrapped up in the business of Parliament, followed by some mild problems here on the estate. All the damned responsibilities he'd found thrust on him along with the unwanted title had kept him too busy for any socializing.

Which had been fine by him. He hadn't clenched his teeth in five whole weeks.

"What do you want, Rachael?"

She blinked, no doubt taken aback by his unintended harshness. But she recovered her composure quickly. "If your offer is still open, then yes, I'd like your help going through my mother's things."

He smiled, his heart softening. "Before Christmas?"

She drew a deep breath and nodded. "How about next week?"

About an hour and a half later, James found himself confronted by the most daunting column of buttons he'd ever seen.

During the last month—seemingly the longest month of his life—he'd imagined this night a hundred times, if not a thousand. And up until now, it had gone more or less as he'd planned. He'd closed them both into this room—the Gold Chamber, Juliana had called it—and proceeded to kiss her senseless while faint snatches of romantic music drifted in from the great hall far down the corridor. Still kissing her as much as he could, he'd managed to rid himself of all his clothing save his trousers and his unbuttoned shirt. Still kissing her, he'd managed to remove some of hers, too—little essentials like her satin slippers and her stockings.

He'd been quite proud of himself, really, because he'd been determined to proceed slowly, because it was her first time, and if anyone deserved a first time that was slow and cherishing, a first time she'd remember forever, it was his precious Juliana. And so far, despite the fact that he'd been all but shaking with anticipation, all but trembling with need, he'd managed to keep going slowly.

But then he turned her around and saw all those buttons.

"What in heaven's name possessed you to order a dress with so many buttons?" he breathed through gritted teeth, more frustrated than he remembered ever being—ever. Good God, should he continue going as planned, should he continue going slowly, unbuttoning this damned dress was going to take *all night*. He would expire from want by the time he managed to unbutton all these buttons. He would perish of starvation. He would die from unrelenting need. "There must be at least a hundred buttons."

Juliana laughed, a low, frustrated laugh that made every nerve in his body sing. "I thought you liked buttons, James," she chided softly over her shoulder in a voice so heart-wrenchingly sensuous he feared he might go out of his mind. "For some reason, I've come to believe you like buttons. I instructed the seamstress to put so many buttons on my dress because I had the impression you'd enjoy unbuttoning all of them."

And in a sense, he did. Still clenching his jaw, he bent his head and steeled himself to the task. Slowly he swept the hair off the nape of her neck, slowly he placed a soft kiss on the sensitive, warm bit of skin above her top button. A cherishing kiss, drawing in her scent, that impossibly tempting scent of flowers and sunshine and Juliana. And then slowly he started unbuttoning the buttons, the never-ending column of buttons, kissing each precious new patch of skin as it was exposed along her sweet, slender back. And in a sense, he did enjoy it. But in another sense, the mounting pressure of anticipation seemed to be more, much more, than any man should have to bear.

It didn't take all night, but it took much, much longer than he wanted. Going slowly proved to be much, much harder than he'd hoped. Juliana sighed, and she moaned, and each of her sounds, each of her tiny, precious sounds seemed to crawl into him and lodge someplace in his heart. It seemed forever by the time he managed to unbutton all the buttons. It seemed longer than the longest month of his life.

After all the waiting, after all the torturous unbuttoning of buttons, he finally slid the loosened dress down her body, over curving hips, down silky limbs, her soft skin all burnished by the light of the flickering fire in the Gold Chamber. Finally, finally, he bore her down to the bed. And stood back, for what seemed like one everlasting moment, the last moment before he made Juliana his.

It was a moment he'd remember forever, a scene eternally imprinted in his mind. Cainewood Castle was filled with heavy, dark oak furnishings that had served her family well in the almost six hundred years they'd owned the place, but this one room had been decorated for a royal visit in some previous century, and all the furniture was gilt, all the walls and the four-poster bed draped with heavy golden fabrics.

Everything seemed to glitter. Juliana's skin seemed to glitter, beckoning him. Juliana's eyes seemed to glitter, her passion-filled, half-closed eyes a deep, deep blue glitter that taunted him. Even her hair seemed to glitter. No sooner had they entered the room than he'd released it from its pins, and now all the shining straight tresses seemed to be shimmering over her shoulders, spread across the bedclothes, glimmering in the golden light.

An answering glimmer heating his body, he shucked the last of his clothes and lowered himself slowly to meet her. He didn't ask her this time. He knew what her answer would be, and he didn't want to hear any words. He wanted only to hear her soft cries as he finally, finally slid into her, as he finally, finally came home and made her his.

Juliana had dreamed of this moment, but nothing she'd imagined matched the feeling of completion when James joined his body with hers. Nothing had ever felt so beautiful, nothing had ever felt so right. Nothing had ever felt so perfect as the two of them together. It *had* been worth waiting for, she thought fiercely just before she seemed to burst into a million glittering pieces.

But still and all, as the million pieces slowly started drifting back together, as James kissed her again, his mouth a warm promise on hers, she couldn't help being thankful that she'd never have to wait again.

Author's Note

Dear Readers,

In April 1815, Mount Tambora erupted on the Indonesian island of Sumbawa, sending more ash into the air than any volcano in the last ten thousand years. Over the next year, the dust rose into the upper atmosphere and spread slowly across the planet, obscuring the sunlight to such an extent that extreme weather conditions prevailed in places halfway around the world. The growing season was plagued by a series of devastating cold waves that destroyed crops, greatly reducing the food supply and causing widespread famine. Snow fell in June, and 1816 came to be known as "The Year Without a Summer."

The people of the time hadn't the knowledge of our modern meteorologists, so they didn't know why the weather was so cold. Countless absurd theories were proposed, including those expounded by the guests at the balls in *Tempting Juliana*. Although some people did indeed blame Benjamin Franklin's lightning rods, had Franklin still been alive, he might have guessed the real reason. During a similar cold spell in 1784 caused by the great eruption of Mount Asama in Japan, Franklin wrote of a "constant fog over all Europe and a great part of North America," speculating that the dust he observed in the sky might be due to volcanic explosions or the breakup of meteorites.

In James's time, smallpox was sometimes called the "Speckled Monster." Throughout recorded history, it killed ten percent of the population. As a youngster, before being variolated (intentionally infected with smallpox as a preventative measure), Edward Jenner was "prepared" by being starved, purged, and bled, and afterward he was locked in a stable with other ailing boys until the disease had run its course. All in all, it was an experience he would never forget—one that later inspired him to experiment and discover that immunization with cowpox prevented smallpox. In 1801, after he pioneered vaccination, Jenner issued a pamphlet that ended with these words: ". . . the annihilation of the Small Pox, the most dreadful scourge of the human species, must be the final result of this practice." Unfortunately, almost 180 years went by before his prophecy came to pass.

In *Tempting Juliana*, James was too optimistic in hoping smallpox vaccinations would soon be made compulsory. England didn't pass such a law until 1853, and the World Health Organization (WHO) didn't launch its campaign to conquer smallpox until 1967. At that time, there were fifteen million cases of smallpox each year. The WHO's plan was to vaccinate everyone everywhere. Teams of vaccinators traveled the world to the remotest of communities.

The last documented case of smallpox occurred just eight years later, in 1975. After an anxious period of watching for new cases, in 1980 the WHO formally declared, "Smallpox is Dead!" Jenner's dream had come true: The most feared disease of all time had been eradicated.

The Foundling Hospital was established in 1739 by Captain Thomas Coram, a childless shipwright concerned about the plight of unwanted babies in London. In his time, more than seventy-four percent of the poor children born in London died before they turned five, and the death rate for children put in workhouses was more than ninety percent. In contrast, the Foundling Hospital's mortality rate was under thirty percent. If that sounds high, remember that smallpox, measles, tuberculosis (consumption), and other diseases were endemic during this period. Most people did not reach old age.

In 1740, artist William Hogarth, an early Governor of the Hospital, donated the first painting to the Hospital and encouraged other artists to follow his example—and thus England's first public art gallery was born. When the wealthy came to see the art or attend concerts given by another Governor, George Frideric Handel, they were encouraged to make charitable donations. Although there is no written record of anyone donating anything besides money, I like to think that the Governors would have been open to an idea like Juliana's.

By 1954, the year the Hospital closed, it had served more than 27,000 children. Today you can visit the Foundling Museum in London, which is on the site of the original Hospital and contains artifacts as well as the art collection, displayed in fully restored interiors.

Most of the homes in my books are inspired by real places you can see. Stafford House, James's home in St. James's Place, is based on Spencer House, one of the great architectural landmarks of London. Built in the eighteenth century by John, 1st Earl Spencer (an ancestor of Diana, Princess of Wales), it was immediately recognized as a building of major importance. Should you ever find yourself in London, I highly recommend a visit. Its exquisite rooms have all been restored, and you will see many of the antiquities Amanda admired in this book. Spencer House is open to the public every Sunday except during January and August.

The Chases' town house at 44 Berkeley Square has been described as "the finest terrace house of London." It was designed in 1742 by William Kent for Lady Isabella Finch. Unfortunately, you cannot visit, because the building is currently being used as a private club. But if you go to Berkeley Square, you can see it from the outside—look for the blue door.

Cainewood Castle, where Juliana and James married, is loosely modeled on Arundel Castle in West Sussex. It has been home to the Dukes of Norfolk and their family, the Fitzalan-Howards, since 1243, save for a short period during the Civil War. Although the family still resides there, portions of their magnificent home are open to visitors Sundays through Fridays from April to October.

To see pictures and learn more about the real places featured in *Tempting Juliana*, please visit my Web site at www.LaurenRoyal.com, where you can also enter a contest, sign up for my newsletter, and find modern versions of all the recipes in this book. If you try any of the recipes, I hope you'll e-mail me at Lauren@Lauren Royal.com and tell me what you think!

If you missed Alexandra's story, you can find it in *Lost in Temptation*, the first book in my Sweet Temptations trilogy. And for a chance to revisit Juliana and James, watch for my next Signet Eclipse novel, which will arrive in stores in fall 2007. In the meantime, I'd love to hear from you! If you'd rather send a "real" letter than e-mail (I answer both!), write to P.O. Box 52932, Irvine, CA 92619, and please enclose a self-addressed, stamped envelope, especially if you'd like me to send you an autographed bookmark and/or bookplate.

'Til next time,

Lauren

Official Rules for the
Tempting Juliana Sweepstakes

NO PURCHASE NECESSARY.
A PURCHASE WILL NOT ENHANCE YOUR CHANCES OF WINNING.

Open only to U.S. residents age 18 and up.

How to Enter:

To enter the *Tempting Juliana* Sweepstakes (''Sweepstakes''), either visit www.LaurenRoyal.com and follow the entry instructions posted online or type your full name, mailing address, e-mail address (if any), along with the answer to the question listed on the back of this book and mail it to the Sponsor at the address listed at the end of these rules. (Hint: Read the prologue of *Tempting Juliana* or the online excerpt for the answer to the entry question.) The entry must contain the correct answer to the question to be eligible. Limit one entry per person. Entries must be received by 11:59 p.m. (P.S.T.) on the entry deadline date indicated in the chart below to be eligible for that month's drawing and any or all subsequent drawings. Limit one entry per person/e-mail address for the duration of the sweepstakes.

Winners:

Six winners (one per drawing) will receive a sterling silver quizzing glass—Approximate Retail Value (''ARV'') $50 per quizzing glass.

Monthly Drawing #	Drawing Date On or About	From among all eligible entries received by 11:59 p.m. (P.S.T.) on:
1	12/10/06	11/30/06
2	1/10/07	12/31/06
3	2/10/07	1/31/07
4	3/10/07	2/28/07
5	4/10/07	3/31/07
6	5/10/07	4/30/07

General:

Entries are void if they are in whole or in part illegible, incomplete, or damaged. No responsibility is assumed for late, lost,

Read on for a sneak peek at
Lauren Royal's next delicious romance

The Art of Temptation

Coming from Signet Eclipse
in October 2007

The British Museum, London
Spring 1817

"We want to see the Rosetta Stone," two feminine voices chorused.

For the third time in the past quarter hour.

"Just a few more minutes," Lady Corinna Chase promised her sisters, her gaze focused on her sketchbook.

"A few is three," Alexandra, the oldest, pointed out. "Or maybe five. But certainly not thirty. You said 'a few more minutes' half an hour ago."

"And half an hour before that," Juliana, the middle sister, added.

The squeak of wheels threatened Corinna's concentration. Alexandra was rolling a perambulator back and forth in hopes of soothing her infant son. Though it was all but unheard-of for ladies to cart their babies around town, Alexandra had insisted on buying one of the new contraptions, because she rarely let her child out of her sight.

Squeak. Squeak. Squeak. "How can you stare at statues for so long?"

"I'm not staring. I'm drawing." Corinna sketched

another line, following the curve of a muscled male thigh. "And in case you haven't noticed, the Elgin Marbles aren't all statues. This particular panel is part of a frieze from the illustrious Parthenon in Greece. Even more important, the figures are anatomically correct."

Which was why she was here, of course. Corinna wanted nothing more than to study human anatomy. Unfortunately, the anatomy classes at the Royal Academy of Arts were entirely forbidden to women.

Entirely. Forbidden.

It was infuriating. Corinna's fondest wish was to be elected to the Royal Academy, an honor unattained by any woman since 1768. Though she harbored no dreams of accomplishing this goal at her current age of twenty-two, she hoped to take her first step within a matter of months, by getting one of her paintings accepted for the Royal Academy's Summer Exhibition.

That was something women *did* accomplish on a regular basis, although not usually with portraits. Traditionally, women painted only landscapes and still lives— painting people was considered fast and unseemly. However, Corinna wanted to paint portraits. She was drawn to the human form, compelled to render personalities in oil on canvas.

But how was a woman supposed to accurately paint people if she wasn't allowed to attend anatomy classes?

"We cannot stay much longer," Juliana said. "And I want to see the Rosetta Stone," she added—for the fourth time.

"So go see it." Corinna flipped a page, refocusing on the nude form of the gorgeous Greek god before her. "I'll be right here."

Squeak. Squeak. "We cannot leave you here in the Elgin Gallery alone."

"I'm not alone. There are people everywhere." Too many people, constantly jostling her and blocking her view.

"The Rosetta Stone is in the main building."

"It is perfectly proper for two married ladies to cross the museum grounds together." Unlike Corinna, who was known as a bit of a rebel, her sisters were always concerned with being proper. "I knew I should have brought Aunt Frances along instead. She's more patient than either of you."

"She's also nine months gone with child." Alexandra sighed. "We'll be back in a few minutes."

"Make that a few hours," Corinna muttered, but they had already left. Hearing the pram squeak-squeak toward the door, she smiled and licked her lips. She and the Greek god were alone at last.

Holy Hannah, he was magnificent.

If only she could find a real man who looked like *this* . . .

Catching her lower lip in her teeth, she used her pencil to shade the fascinating muscles on the Greek god's bare, toned chest. Then looked up, suddenly spotting two men heading in her direction. As though some higher power had read her mind and sent him to fulfill her fantasy, one of them—the taller one—seemed to her a Greek god come to life.

Flipping to a new page, she started sketching the real man instead of the stone replica. Quickly, before he disappeared from view.

His angular, sculpted face was framed by crisp black curls that grew long at the back of his neck . . . long enough to make a woman's fingers itch to comb through them. His eyes were the greenest she'd ever seen. Unfortunately, he was rather more clothed than the marble gods, but having sketched quite a few of them, she fancied she could imagine what he looked like beneath his well-made but conservative trousers, waistcoat, and tailcoat. Her pencil outlined broad shoulders tapering to narrow hips—

She froze midsketch as the two men walked right up to her.

"Good afternoon," the shorter one said.

Like the taller man, he was dark-haired and green-eyed and good-looking. And much more fashionably dressed. But all in all, she decided, not nearly of the same Greek-god caliber.

Still, she swallowed hard. She wasn't accustomed to

handsome men introducing themselves—good manners dictated they ask permission of a young lady's chaperone, who would then provide the introduction.

"Good afternoon," she returned guardedly. "Mr . . . ?"

"Delaney," he said smoothly. "Sean Delaney, at your service. And this," he added, indicating the taller man, "is my good friend Mr. John Hamilton. Having noticed you sketching, he wished to be introduced to a fellow artist. You've heard of him, I presume?"

Had she heard of him? Corinna's sketchbook and pencil fell to the floor as her jaw dropped open. *Everyone* had heard of John Hamilton, the renowned, reclusive painter of landscapes. She turned to him, positively stunned. Her Greek god was John Hamilton—John Hamilton!—and he'd requested an introduction. To *her*, Corinna Chase, possibly the most *un*renowned artist in all of London.

"Mr. Hamilton," she gushed, "I cannot tell you how much I admire—"

"Please stop," he interrupted, bending to scoop up her supplies. He straightened and, with a roll of his gorgeous emerald eyes toward Mr. Delaney, handed the items to her. "I'm sorry, but I'm not John Hamilton." His lilting accent was distracting. The deep, melodious Irish voice didn't quite mesh with the Greek physique. "I'm Sean Delaney. And I'm afraid my brother-in-law here—the *real* John Hamilton—has a horrible sense of humor."

"Now, Hamilton." The other man dolefully shook his head. "There's no need to hide your identity from this charming young lady."

"It's your identity in question, and you hide it from everyone." The Greek god drew a line in the air that traced the other man from head to toe. "You'll note he's the one dressed in artistic style," he pointed out to Corinna before brushing at his own, much plainer clothes. "I am merely a common man of business."

"Please forgive Mr. Hamilton." Mr. Delaney—or Mr. Hamilton, or whoever the shorter man might be—raised a brow toward Corinna. "He's much too self-effacing."

"Blarney!" the Greek god shot back. "You're a dunce, Hamilton."

Corinna had observed a tennis match once, and she now felt like that little ball bouncing back and forth between them. She didn't know which man to believe. But since she didn't expect to see either of them ever again, she figured it didn't signify.

While the two men volleyed, she'd regained her senses enough to remember Mr. Hamilton was a member of the committee that chose artwork for the Summer Exhibition. *That* was what truly mattered.

She clutched her art supplies to her chest. "I'm an oil painter myself," she told both of them, praying one really was Hamilton. "I am here sketching the marbles to learn anatomy so I can improve my technique for portraits. It is my fondest hope that one of my canvases will be selected for the Exhibition later this year."

"I am certain Mr. Hamilton will vote for it," the shorter man assured her gravely.

"I will not. I mean"—the Greek god's fists were clenched, and his Irish lilt came through gritted teeth—"he won't. Or perhaps he will, but I am *not* Hamilton."

"Pshaw." The other man waved a smooth, graceful hand. "He's—"

"Corinna!" She looked away to see her sisters hurrying near, the pram squeaking its way toward her. "Are you finished yet?" Alexandra asked.

Corinna smiled in relief, certain Juliana would figure out which man was John Hamilton. The meddler in the family, Juliana had a skill for weaseling out secrets. "I'd be pleased for you to meet Mr. Hamilton," she started, turning back to the men.

They were gone.

Lifting her sweet baby boy from the pram, Alexandra frowned. "Mr. Hamilton?"

"The famous landscapist, John Hamilton. He was just here." Corinna scanned the gallery, to no avail. "He looks like a Greek god. Or perhaps it's his friend who looks like the Greek god, or his brother-in-law—"

"Whatever are you babbling about? John Hamilton never appears in public." Looking sympathetic, Juliana touched her arm. "I think we should go. Clearly you've been sketching too long."

"Lauren Royal knows how to make
history come alive."
—Patricia Gaffney, *New York Times*
bestselling author

Lauren Royal

Lost in Temptation

0-451-21592-3

Even the perfect lady, Alexandra Chase has always
done what was expected of her. But when Lord
Tristan Nesbitt—the man she's loved since she was
fifteen—returns from abroad, she suddenly has every
intention of shirking duty by not marrying the man
her brother has picked for her. And she's certain her
wild impulse is right, until Tristan promptly informs
her he'll never take her for his wife.

Author Website: laurenroyal.com

Available wherever books are sold
or at penguin.com

Jocelyn Kelley

A MOONLIT KNIGHT

In twelfth-century England, St. Jude's Abbey is no ordinary holy sanctuary: it trains young women in the knightly arts.

Summoned in the middle of the night, Mallory de Saint-Sebastian must leave the Abbey to protect Queen Eleanor's life as a revolt against King Henry rages. With a knight's sense of obligation, she is determined to not only shield Eleanor but to find the enemies threatening her. Arriving at St. Jude's Abbey, Saxon Fitz-Juste is amazed by the Queen's choice of a female knight as her newest warrior. A troubadour in Eleanor's royal court, Saxon is ostensibly loyal to Her Majesty, but his true mission remains to be seen.

0-451-21827-2

BARBARA METZGER
Ace of Hearts

Book One of the *House of Cards* trilogy

Never did Alexander "Ace" Endicott,
the Earl of Carde, imagine himself to be
thrice-betrothed against his will by the doings of
three desperate debutantes. So he escapes London
for his property in the country, where he follows
through with his father's last wish—to find his
long-lost step-sister.
But the search takes a detour, leading him to Nell,
and forcing him to wonder if two
mismatched lovers can make a royal pair.

0-451-21626-1

**ALSO AVAILABLE
in the *House of Cards* trilogy**

JACK OF CLUBS
0-451-21805-1

QUEEN OF DIAMONDS
0-451-21867-1

Available wherever books are sold or at
penguin.com

All your favorite romance writers are
coming together.

SIGNET ECLIPSE

COMING DECEMBER 2006:
Philippa by Bertrice Small
Without a Sound by Carla Cassidy
If Only in My Dreams by Wendy Markham

COMING JANUARY 2007:
*The Rest Falls Away: The Gardella
Vampire Chronicles* by Colleen Gleason
Salvation, Texas by Anna Jeffrey
My Lady Knight by Jocelyn Kelley